Fair Wind to Java

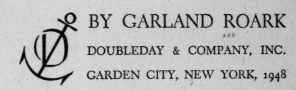

BY GARLAND ROARK

DOUBLEDAY & COMPANY, INC.

GARDEN CITY, NEW YORK, 1948

With the exception of actual historical personages identified as such, the characters are entirely the product of the author's imagination and have no relation to any person in real life.

TO CAPTAIN AND MRS. THOMAS FENLON

in gratitude for inspiration
along the salty roads of adventure

Contents

BOOK ONE ~ 1879-1885

1   THE FIGUREHEAD AFFAIR

I, TOM FLINT, DID NOT BOARD THE SHIP UNTIL EIGHTEEN HUNDRED AND eighty-five, four years after the natural opening of this story. Nor had I heard much about the great square-rigger other than praise for her lines, her speed and grace in the water, and that incident known as the "Figurehead Affair," which opened her public history and ran its length like a long baleful shadow. Since everything that followed seemed influenced to a degree by that incident, I'll tell that story first:

On a blustering evening in early December of eighteen hundred and seventy-nine, Robert Lodge Culver's Beacon Hill residence was the destination of a famous naval architect, an East Boston shipbuilder, a banker, two men of the sea, and three members of the Boston shipping firm of Culver and Adams. They arrived at number seventeen Louisburg Square singly and in groups, spoke of the unresolved weather, and moved to the cheerful hearth.

Over a glass of whisky one of the old salts said, "This is the happy-weather climax of a ship on paper. Come tomorrow, it looks as though we'll start on her, the Lord and devil willing."

"Aye." The stocky man before the fire spoke. "As always, the Lord and devil willing." He was the host, Robert Culver.

The company felt his presence. His eyes were gray and sharp. Beneath heavy black brows they seemed sharper. His nose was short and straight, and his lips were firm. Black hair and sideburns, together with a ruddy complexion and strong jaw and chin, lent his face vigor and authority. He did not look to be fifty. Seldom did he smile, and when he did there was little warmth in his expression. He was of medium height, stocky, and he stood stiffly erect. His face, bearing, and dress suggested the hardheaded Yankee. And yet he had about him the starved look of a man in search of a happiness beyond his reach.

Said the banker, "The Lord and devil willing, you say. Why the devil?"

"The Lord and devil stand watch and watch in the stream, Mr. Goodsby," Culver replied. "I should know."

A pleasant laugh from a chair near that of the banker allowed each man a moment of respite from the stern eye of the host. "Since she'll cost a pretty penny, sir, let's not build the devil into her."

"As you wish, Amos," Culver replied, softening his face into a semblance of a smile. The man called Amos was the firm's vice-president, a handsome man with blond hair and a winning smile—said by some to be the most valuable smile in Boston. Amos R. De Loach, not turned forty, had been trained by Culver to succeed the bigwig at some date far into the future. De Loach, the firm's great salesman and, oddly enough, its financial wizard, was a socialite also, an influence in Back Bay society, as well as in the shipping world.

The present company sighed: Amos effected a thaw. He brought up a whisky glass and suggested they get down to business. The blueprints were spread out and the naval architect spoke of hand winches, copper sheathing, and a dead rise of three feet. He talked on:

"Her mainmast will stand one hundred and sixty-seven feet from deck to truck; it'll measure thirty-six inches in diameter, like the foremast. Her standing rigging is to be four-stranded Russian hemp, the fore and main shrouds being twelve inches in circumference."

Culver's eyes, pensive, and as sharp as the coal of his cigar, seemed to see a rival shipowner's despairing face as the Culver-Adams ensign mounted the monkey gaff, ran up, and snapped forward in a swift passing.

Talk engendered talk; they built her that evening over whisky glasses. Only the question, "What'll ye name 'er, Cap'n Culver?" from the more shriveled of the two salts, evoked a very dead silence. Culver frowned as if offended.

Mr. Goodsby ventured an answer: "Why not call her after Miss Harriet, sir—the *Harriet Adams?*" He did not see Amos's eyebrows lift as he swept Culver with a passing glance.

"Mr. Goodsby," Amos smiled, "I'm afraid you're late with your splendid idea. I have taken the liberty of naming her myself." He turned to the shipbuilder, a paunchy, red-faced man. "Jim, you tell them."

"Aye, Amos. The *Robert Culver.*"

None of them saw the figure in the doorway. She smiled as her lips formed the words, "The *Robert Culver*." To Harriet Adams, a girl of sixteen blossoming into lovely womanhood, the honor dear Amos bestowed upon Mr. Culver seemed very proper. She thought of herself as the woman of twenty-two in the moment: when she reached that age, she would be the biggest factor in the firm by virtue of her father's shares. She sighed, saying to herself:

"But it's just as well they have honored him now."

She turned away unseen and moved slowly up the steps, thinking of Mr. Goodsby's suggestion: the *Harriet Adams*. She felt dull disappointment which she refused to admit as she passed her aunt Emily's room. She retraced her steps, opened the door to her aunt's parlor, and looked in.

"They've named the ship, Aunt Emily."

The matronly, rosy-cheeked little lady lifted her face from a book, removed her reading glasses, and snapped, "So they did." It was her way of asking the name.

"Yes, the *Robert Culver*."

"A good name," she said, fitting her glasses to her nose again. Harriet agreed.

Her aunt, her father's sister, and widow of Mr. Culver's younger brother Jim, held Robert Culver in the highest esteem.

At midnight glasses were raised. "To the *Robert Culver*," said the banker. "May she be the fastest and luckiest wind-driven vessel ever to slide down the ways."

2

In the months that followed, the ship on-paper grew out of a blueprint: she arched her ribs and made ready for the thousands of pounds of oak, pine, and copper necessary to a thoroughbred's endurance; she accepted fine weathery lines which beautifully concealed her toughness.

Robert Culver watched her fairly blossom in the molds; he patted her affectionately from cutwater to fantail. He waited impatiently for the breath of life they would breathe into her. He became so very attached to her that he flung salty imprecations at carpenters in the act of laying a warped deck plank. The great Culver was fast becoming a nuisance, one whom lesser men must tolerate and excuse since Culver the tycoon saw more than they. He, once Captain Culver of the *Barnacle Goose*, saw a ship that would work up to windward against storms of hellish force; a ship with towering masts and gigantic yards moving at a clip under taut cotton duck; a ship with air breathed into her great sails, her forefoot forward in a downhill sea until she was hull under horizon to the Orient, a roaring *Robert Culver*, the only possible twin congruous to the man whose name she would carry. There were built into her other items which became, later in her career, subjects of baffling interest: the helm and ship's bell of the old *Barnacle Goose*. These were, in a measure, symbols of the soul of Robert Culver.

During the twenty-two months between blueprint and launching, there was ample time and opportunity for De Loach and a few of Culver's friends to plan and execute the only part of the ship not ordered by him. Whenever Culver had mentioned a figurehead during the long days she lay in blueprint, there had always been a hurried change of topic. He had been quick to fathom the hushed wind, to learn that the figurehead would be their, or rather Amos's, surprise in his honor; so he said no more about it, though he heard a word here and there, enough to justify his fondest hopes.

Amos De Loach and Mr. Goodsby commissioned a carver in Portland, Maine, to do the likeness of Robert Culver for the ship's stemhead. The bearded artist, a Mr. Augustus Teale, had earned quite a reputation for his work in the past; his long hair, dreamy eyes, and breath reeking with alcohol were accepted as symbols of his artistry. He met De Loach and Goodsby while drinking, and he drank while studying the many pictures of the subject, and he was quite drunk when he accepted a liberal cash advance from Amos.

He was counting the crisp bank notes with an eye that measured his wealth in demijohns when his stout wife relieved him of the money. In the argument that followed, she struck him over the head with a wooden mallet, thereby paralyzing the professional brain to such an extent that even she was later heard to voice regret.

As time wore on, Mr. Teale eyed his work owlishly, sucked at a bottle, and frowned at the wooden image of Robert Culver, who peered out over the waves, hands on chest, long coat flying back in the breeze, his one foot forward slightly. The figure was less like Culver and more like some fourth-dimensional visitor. Mrs. Teale, her arms folded across a heavy bosom, one eye squinted shut, advised her spouse to whittle here and shave there; she even fetched him another bottle. But the carver's former passion for art was no longer a part of him; he despised the task. He drank more and cursed Culver for the spell he had cast.

Then, either crazed by drink or the awful shock of an art lost to him, or both, he shut himself off from any visitor and indulged in a spree lasting a fortnight.

But he finished the figurehead, a massive piece against a background of fluid scrolls, and he laid the paint on white and thick. Then he boxed the work and swore that no man would ever see it until the damned thing was fastened to the ship's bow at the fitting-out berth.

Robert Culver, himself, had slapped tradition in the face when he ordered the ship launched without ceremony. The big event should be the unveiling of the figurehead on a great sailing ship complete to her last spar and sail. She would gleam under fresh varnish; impressively. Then, after every admiring eye had inspected her, he, on the poop with Emily and Harriet, would wave at the crowd as she filled away for New York on her maiden voyage.

Two nights before the ceremony, Mr. Teale, with the aid of his wife's brothers and four seamen, placed the piece still wrapped under the *Robert Culver's* bowsprit; only the scroll, in gilt on the mahogany nesting piece, was visible to a curious eye. The next day he visited Culver's Atlantic Avenue offices and gained an audience with Amos De Loach.

"The image is finished, sir. And may I ask that neither you nor anyone else look at my work until it is unveiled?" When asked why, he said something about an artist's privilege for whimsies and, "Besides, it's bad luck for the ship, sir." He was paid in full, his reputation for classic perfection serving to rob Amos De Loach of any misgiving concerning the requiem. And on the following day De Loach and entourage, out of respect for Mr. Teale's reputation, decided to await the much-heralded ceremony before viewing the image of Culver at the bows.

Mr. Teale did not attend the ceremony on that pleasant day, the tenth of June of 'eighty-one; he was either drunk or else he thought the day an ideal one for picking up and moving to Montreal, and later to his first love, the sea.

A crowd of some fifteen thousand Bostonians gathered to witness the debut of the "finest ship ever built." Engraved invitations had been mailed to the Governor of the Commonwealth of Massachusetts, as well as other high dignitaries of state and city; newsmen, and Beacon Hill ladies and gentlemen in all their pomp and dignity, and a brass band on a flag-bedecked platform, all lent the occasion versatility and color. While before them stood a great ship about to be born formally.

The fashionable gathering seated in a broad semicircle about her starboard bow saw outer perfection. Her hull, a glossy reddish brown, was broken just beneath her chains by a broad stripe of bright red which ran her around; masts, yards, her every spar, including bowsprit and jib boom, were finished in natural color under deep layers of varnish; her deckhouses, from forecastle to wheelhouse, were white, and her every rope and furled sail exuded a virgin creamy tan—she was clean, fresh, and wondrously alive. Fifty men berthed before her mast. The *Robert Culver* was nothing short of a sensation.

The band struck up a lively nautical piece when Robert Culver, Harriet, and Emily alighted from an open coach. A buzz ran through the crowd and every eye turned to view the owner and his companions.

Culver carried himself erect; he wore a black silk hat and a set smile. His ruddy face, lean, sharp-eyed, irreversibly jawed, and iron-lipped, seemed to reach up for some exquisite rung in a ladder of lordship; the man then seemed to sit atop his throne and peer down his straight nose at that society which had never quite accepted him. Before seating himself, he turned that expression on the men of old families whom he had in later years influenced and driven. He had used them, aye!—as a mariner uses sail! He would continue to use them. Here was power, and here was open recognition of, and solid tribute to, that power. He made an attempt at softening his face as he turned to view the ship, a symbol of his wealth and fame. The ship which shot her bowsprit aloft, which spread her great yards from masts raised to the heavens, was worthy of his name.

And there on the bow awaiting an unveiling was a statue of a great man—himself. In the manner of a Pharisee, he thanked the Lord for this triumph.

But all attention was not his: the girl beside him claimed her share. She was Harriet Adams. Before Dean Adams's death, the firm had been simply Adams & Co. Several years after his death, her mother had requested the prefix of Culver. She, too, had passed on in 'seventy-five.

Harriet, just turned eighteen, seemed a mature woman. Her large violet-blue eyes and oval face were alive with a controlled spontaneity; she was at once queenly and democratic, and quick to inspire moments of wonder and admiration. Her gaze fell soft, clear, and direct; and her nose, slightly uptilted, seemed made to order by a precision artist who modeled with the same inspired skill that had created her eyes and lips. Her hair was a wavy brown.

She wore a white dress which barely covered her rounded bosom. Cut to emphasize her slim waist, it ran on down in a maze of ruffles, past shapely hips and projecting bustle, to lend her more height than she desired. Her five feet nine inches appeared stretched into greater proportions by the large plume on her hat. Miss Adams of Louisburg Square, Beacon Hill, like her mother before her, was accepted by the most censorious ladies, many of whom were in attendance that day only because of her.

As the band played a national air, her eyes were drawn in rising to an arresting face. It was handsome after a fashion, though bold. She swept it with a glance, then another. As the eyes of the man continued to pierce her, she admitted curiosity; she leaned to Robert Culver with a question.

Culver glanced about slowly, at last replying: "Captain Boll of the *Lydia Case*. They call him the Striker."

She wanted to ask why he was called the Striker, though she fixed her eyes on the bandstand instead.

The ceremony was getting under way. One man arose to introduce another in flowery speech; then all bowed to the Governor, who spoke briefly, who lauded the men who kept alive traditions of the sea and New England commerce. Then the mayor brought the moment around. The canvas about the figurehead was made ready for removal as he talked; his subject was Robert Lodge Culver.

"—a man as endemically salty as the sea, a man as much a part of Boston as Faneuil Hall, a man whose philanthropy and civic pride are matched only by his discerning eye and driving force. We are here to honor this man, whose dream of a ship stands before us ready to tear through the seas to foreign lands, a credit to a great man of Boston, a credit to the great city of Boston and its role in world commerce." Culver beamed justifiably; the full-rigged ship served as a monument to the mayor's subject.

"—Some ships are great, some are fortunate, others are cruel masters. We are close to great ships here, we love them, regardless of their odd personalities.

"May the good Lord bless her." The mayor was windy; he drove on, at last into a climax: "Thus we are about to view the likeness of a great Bostonian, Robert Lodge Culver, who built her; his face and soul will ever guide her over the waves. It is as it should be. Soon we shall all walk up her gangway and visit the deck and interior of the great ship."

Harriet felt the annoying eyes of Captain Boll.

"And now, before I order the unveiling of the figurehead, will the men who planned this fitting honor please stand?" The banker, Amos De Loach, two seamen, the builder, and several influential men stood.

"And the great artist, Mr. Augustus Teale—will you come forward, please?" After an interval of awkward silence, the mayor signaled the bandmaster. The rising notes of the overture sounded; a roll of the drums, and higher notes, and the cymbals crashed. The mayor ordered all to rise as he led Robert Culver, Harriet, and Emily to the center of the stage.

Then the canvas was torn loose.

Hands ready to applaud relaxed slowly, tensely; mouths ready to open for cheers and well-wishing were struck dumb. Faces pivoted on craning necks to frown and ask in silence for some verification or denial of a shocking fact.

The mayor's words echoed in every ear: "Thus we are about to view the likeness of a great Bostonian, Robert Culver——" And the likeness: it was a hideous dragon-bird with a long lumpy neck, boxy body, and stubby claws; only the wings relieved the figure of over-all grotesqueness; in another glance they stressed the hideousness of the figurehead.

The air was tense and electric; and embarrassment went without any balm of relief. The tall, handsome De Loach stood paralyzed, unable to remove his horrified eyes from the dragon-bird. The mayor chewed at a nail, and the Governor turned sour glances about him before drawing into a sullen shell.

Someone tittered. A newsman said, "It's more like Gilbert Stuart's Gerrymander." But every eye had roamed to the lone figure who stood in silence viewing his "very likeness."

Robert Culver stood with one hand across his chest, the other behind him. He did not so much as close a hand into a fist, and he stood as erect and calm as before the overture. His face was a mask: his forehead seemed no longer than usual, his eyes no sharper, his frown no deeper; there was no loss or gain of color—he peered as if in deep study of some impersonal effrontery out of a face he had long since trained into hardness.

Harriet bit at her lip, then turned to her aunt. But Aunt Emily, her face showing red splotches, as it did when she was angered, was talking in low tones to Robert Culver. Harriet heard her say: "Laugh, Robert—for God's sake laugh!"

Had Robert Culver followed her advice, he would have chosen the proper mood of the moment, a humor congruous to the situation.

Boston would have laughed with him over a huge joke, before following him on board to the waiting reception. And as for the future, his own, as well as those in the palm of his powerful hand, his merest chuckle at that moment would have saved immeasurable grief.

Robert Culver reached into his pocket for a cigar. He lit it calmly; then, as if nothing had happened to upset his schooled aplomb, he took his leave with Emily and Harriet. No one spoke to him, and only one man followed the trio to the carriage.

He was Captain Boll of the *Lydia Case.*

He stood at the carriage, his long fingers on the top of the wheel, his tall figure erect, and his slitted eyes boring deep. He did not look at Emily, nor did he look at Mr. Culver; his eyes, bold, or wicked, or both, held fast to Harriet in what seemed a disrobing stare.

Culver, either used to the vagaries of a captain of Boll's reputation, or his mind on the "image" of himself, was less observing than Harriet and Emily. Harriet blushed, and Emily made ready to speak sharply. Then Boll, as if oblivious of a sudden to the presence of women, said to Robert Culver:

"A damn dirty trick, sir."

That constituted the "Figurehead Affair," except for a puzzling anticlimax that came later in the day. It was several years later that I learned of this incident.

3

At four that afternoon, Pierce, the butler, advised Harriet of a caller, a Captain Boll, to see her. She frowned, asking if her aunt were downstairs, only to be told that Aunt Emily was having tea with several ladies in the oval salon. Thus Harriet, left alone, could only meet or refuse to meet the captain. She nodded to Pierce and, after a few minutes, she descended the stairs, suspecting some consoling remark about the shocking affair of the morning, that or a seaman's ingratiating bid designed for Mr. Culver's ear.

He bowed as she entered the parlor, then held out his hand. "Miss Adams, the quickest way to meet you was to come straight here." He did not release her hand, though the grasp of his eyes seemed the stronger. At a loss for reply in a situation entirely new to her, she was silent.

"So I'm here," he said. He did not smile; rather, he looked deep behind her eyes. She frowned and bit her lip, seeking some avenue of escape from an utterly bewildering and awkward plight. There was nothing in her schooling to aid her here; he smiled then, as if he knew this. Her anger flared, but only for a moment.

He said, "The Robert Culver is likely to give your firm trouble, Miss Adams."

"Yes?" she said, relieved. "Won't you sit down, Captain Boll?"

"Thanks, I'll stand." He released her hand and she moved to a chair. "When they put a three-foot dead rise in a ship, they rob cargo space for speed. But Mr. Culver rigged her with hemp and sparred her with wood. He's slowed her. And she'll require too many men before the mast for economical handling."

"Mr. Culver attends to such matters," she replied. Then she asked the question uppermost in her mind: "Why did you come to me?"

"Because Mr. Culver is too hardheaded for me to tell him what I've told you."

"There's little I can do, sir."

"True," he replied. "But by the time Mr. Culver admits he's built a liability, you will be able to do something about it." He grinned, his bold eyes mocking her, it seemed. "I'm in no hurry."

She sat up, truly surprised at the long bid this strange man made: she could not hope to govern her fifty-one per cent of the Culver and Adams stock for four years.

"Surely, sir, you are not serious." She laughed, rising.

He advanced until he stood close. "I was never more serious." As she raised her brows a trifle, he said, "And you'll remember that I'm serious." It sounded like a threat. It was.

He took her in his arms and kissed her fiercely. She trembled in fear even as she tried to reconcile a warm, strange surge which crept over her.

Suddenly he stood apart from her. "Now I don't think you'll forget that I'm serious, Miss Adams."

With that, he moved to the door with the stride of a king, leaving in his wake a stunned and angry girl who admitted the truth of the words: she would not soon forget!

4

In December of 'eighty-one the Robert Culver sailed from New York with a cargo of oil for Shanghai. Under a Captain Lawter, a timid master, she was almost dismasted in making her easting to St. Paul. Four men lost their lives on that voyage. She was pooped on her second voyage, and a mate lost his mind. On her third run, under a

Captain St. Charles, she leaked up to nine inches an hour for long months. The crew pumped themselves into living skeletons. The ship knew trouble, she was trouble itself: she lost time and fat cargo runs; she took lives. The *Robert Culver* seemed to invite contrary winds, adverse currents, and spells of doldrums, as well as storms. She lost underwriters' greasy slaps on the back, and she gained their curses. She was jinxed, they said.

She was a murderess, a pattern for hellships.

Culver's closest friends, old seamen who didn't seem to mind his gruff airs, told him repeatedly: "Change her name, Bob. Change her color, her personality, and put a man aboard her who'll get along with her." There was sound logic in the last remark: a thorough understanding between ship and captain was nothing short of a prerequisite to profit.

"There's Boll of the *Lydia Case*, Bob. He's a driver, and more. He'll tame a ship if he has to drive every spar and mast out of her. He made it to Frisco in a hundred days. He's a Cape Horner, he is."

Culver received other advice: "Whyn't ye remove the damned figurehead? Whyn't ye sell her?"

Culver listened, saying little or nothing. He took what he had heard home and, at dinner each evening, he repeated all to Emily. Harriet listened, thinking of Captain Boll's prediction. Then one evening she repeated what Boll had told her about the ship's faults to Emily.

"And where, Harriet, child, did you learn so much about ships?"

"Why—from Captain Boll." Aunt Emily sat erect and glared accusingly.

"He came to tell me on the day of the ceremony, Auntie."

"To tell you! You? And how did the uncouth creature gain entrance here?"

"I allowed it."

"What else did he say?"

"That by the time Mr. Culver admitted he'd built a liability, I'd be able to do something about it."

Emily laughed. "The scoundrel has a long eye."

That evening she said to Culver, "Send for this Captain Boll, Robert."

Boll came. Sensing in full Culver's predicament, he talked in bold terms: "I'll take her under these conditions—that her rigging be changed from hemp to steel wire, that she be sparred with steel." Culver balked at what seemed unnecessary expense, and Boll, smiling cynically, stood to go. It was Emily who asked him to stay and Culver to consider the advisability of Boll's demands. Culver at last agreed to meet the requirements, which evoked the captain's next words:

"Then I'll sail her—for a quarter interest in her earnings."

Culver arose, his face empurpled, his voice militant. "Young man, you're either an upstart or a rogue."

"Then let De Loach and the shipping world continue to laugh at you." Boll smiled. "Or, if you want to turn the laugh on them, do as I say—change her name to the Gerrymander and put me aboard."

Culver considered this while Captain Boll waited; he ranted, always returning to the "Figurehead Affair," and to Emily, who agreed that De Loach had embarrassed him purposely. Amos De Loach, the former favorite, had, of course, been banished from the firm long ago.

"They want me to sell her," Culver said. "They want me to remove the figurehead. I hate her too much to do either! She's going to pay, and pay, and pay, until I bleed her of every cent she'll earn—until I rob her of self-respect." He got up out of his chair, his face a study in passion, and clenched his hands into bloodless fists.

"Then I'll carry her down as a scoundrel degrades a virtuous woman! And only I know her fate in the end!"

Captain Boll smiled. His expression was penetrating and astute; he saw Culver's sensitive soul revealed to its last secret refuge; and he, Boll, the driving captain—called the Striker because of his uncanny dispatch in meeting with problem or opportunity—stored the gain of that meeting in his patient head for future use.

His chuckle was a gloating sound, it seemed, when Culver said, "I think you're just the man I want aboard that ship."

5

Along the water front in Boston, Culver's animosity toward the ship became an item of public gossip. He had never so much as set foot on the ship since that day of the ceremony. There was quite a stir along State Street and Atlantic Avenue, however, with the news that Captain Boll was her new master; and a ripple of laughter, and a wealth of superstitious predictions with the change of letters on her name plate. Robert Culver was removed. In its place there appeared: Gerrymander. There it was, fresh from a sign painter's brush on her sides and across her stern. GERRYMANDER, Boston.

It was in late December of 'eighty-four, after Boll had run the ship to her first year of profit, that I put into Boston from Liverpool on the Cape Race, a four-masted bark belonging to De Loach and Company.

I had no more than got her to her moorings than Amos De Loach came aboard. He had something to say, and we retired to my quarters to raise a glass and talk. He was quick to the point in his usual unhurried manner, and it was not long before I sat up with surprise and interest written all over my face. And for good reason.

De Loach had said: "Captain Flint, I want you to stow your captain's license for a time."

I searched my mind for any error on my part before asking if I had failed to show him profit with the bark. "No," he said. "It's not that. Nor am I thinking of demoting you. Rather, you'll do better with what I have in mind."

He launched forth into a bitter account of Culver's perfidy, as he called it. Then he said:

"Culver's big. I'm small. And since I helped keep him big, I think I'm justified in wanting a wrong righted." He leaned close, his eyes flashing a determination steeped in the memory of a wrong done him. "I want to steal his cargoes out from under him, slow his shipping, and eat at his profits from the inside."

I smiled dubiously and asked, "What's really on your mind?"

He studied me closely, then said, "What I really want is the Gerrymander, Flint. Yes, I want her for two reasons. First, she'll give me the big ship I need to open up the Orient run; but that's business, and of the head. Now here it is straight from the heart—I want the Gerrymander because she showed me the true Robert Culver who was supposedly my best friend. I want her caught in her own illegality; and this Captain Boll is a man who'll furnish that opportunity, I'm thinking. There's a partnership awaiting you, Flint, if you can do the job."

"A partnership," I dreamed aloud. "Why, I'd almost scuttle a ship for that. So you want me to sail under Captain Boll."

"As a mate," he said. "Second mate. You'll have a better opportunity to sway the crew to your side—if necessary."

I lifted my brows and said it, "Mutiny?"

"Success, Flint"—he smiled—"anyway you care to go about it."

"Very well," I said. "I'll try it. But you seem to underestimate Captain Boll."

"Quite the opposite," De Loach replied. "I've talked to him upon occasion. He's a man who worships Boll and a dollar. And it's rumored that he has a scheme afoot by which he hopes to strike it rich. Confidentially, Flint, it's more than a rumor. I don't know much about it, but it's a scheme that might embarrass Robert Culver—pray the Lord."

I frowned. "Well, shouldn't I know a little about it?"

"Naturally. But let Boll tell you. He'll need help, and if you show initiative and a stubborn head, I'm convinced he'll talk to you. That's Boll, Flint, through and through, a man who respects the strong and despises the weak."

That sounded logical, I admitted. "Well, suppose we succeed in getting the Gerrymander, what then?"

He laughed. "I'll paint her figurehead a bright red, Flint. And I'll rename her the Robert Culver. Then I'll sit back and see whom Boston laughs at last."

I didn't laugh. Perhaps I didn't understand such a far-reaching grudge as he and Culver knew and nourished. I studied him then, aware that from all one could gather he had every reason to feel as he did. I was busy sorting out wrongs and antidotes when he got up, reached into his pocket, and tossed an odd coin atop the table.

"The Gerrymander's bosun, an old seas-under salt named Wulsin, dropped it at a bar a few days back. Keep it for luck, Flint."

I studied the coin. It was about the size of a dollar, and very light. Its collar was crenated, and there was a square hole in it just off center. But what opened my eyes wide with curiosity was the replica of the Gerrymander's figurehead on one side, and the two words on the other side:

GERRYMANDER CASH.

2 ✌ RUNNING ON THE BOWLINE—1885

THE HORIZON SEEMED TO STAND OFF IN AN EFFORT TO WORK ITS WAY around us, and the center stretch of abandoned sea in which we lay was so very still it served only as a mirror to the blue dome overhead. The helm was minus any pulse on that late April afternoon of 'eighty-five. Not a rope stirred, and all sails hung limp. It was as though the small model of the big square-rigged *Gerrymander*, under glass in Robert Culver's Boston office, sat in a toy southern sea with a crew of Lilliputians aboard.

We had tacked ship in the roomy South Atlantic in an excellent run from Boston, and now we sat becalmed at thirty-six degrees south, with Tristan da Cunha a hundred miles southeast of us, the tip of Africa a good two thousand miles due east, and the fierce winds of the roaring forties below us. The doldrums held us, and at a time when new suits of sail awaited a big wind, when every halyard was coiled and ready to fly.

"A wind, Lucifer. Put a wind where it belongs," Captain Boll said over and over, throwing nickels, dimes, and quarters into the thankless sea. The coins sailed over the rail, glistening in the sun before striking the water in hollow splashes. Then he cursed sea and calm, and the devil for his obstinacy, showering the sea with more coins as he did so.

"A leading wind, Lucifer." Our raw apprentices, who had never so much as heard of a sailor whistling for a wind, let alone a captain's bid for one with money and curses, peered over the sides as if expecting a host of creatures with long arms to reach up and suck the ship under. Perhaps they would; the captain surely caused them some flurry of joy or pain down in their black world.

Captain Boll was not a man easily met. It would require a century, I thought, to fathom him to his mainspring. In the meantime he was himself, not some veiled projection of the man, as his passions scrambled behind the cold hostility of granite-gray eyes. I guessed him to be about thirty-five. His nose was sharp and straight, his lips thin and determined. A pointed chin, long jaw, and long forehead under coal-black hair completed his face except for a fact one could not but realize—there was an extravagant quality of self-reliance, inscrutability, and uncanny strength in the blend of his features. He stood the poop, tall, tanned, wide-shouldered, and heavy-biceped. A remarkable man, or force; either sufficed.

A dime struck the rail, fell to the poop, and rolled to the main deck. An apprentice with a look of delicacy on his face fell to the deck in getting out of its path, as if he expected it to burn its way into the deck planking.

Mr. Cott, the chief mate, a tall emaciated Yankee with drooping lids and over-all sensuous expression, never moved a muscle; nor did the stocky, sad-faced bosun, Mr. Wulsin. Both were veterans of some years under Boll. Mr. Cott was just what his face depicted, a man of skilled nautical talent and a flair for brutality. Old Wulsin remained a drunkard, an antiquated piece of flesh, and otherwise a mystery. But they were quite used to the contrarieties of Boll the Striker. The pressing silence, more than Boll's foolish ostentation, told of the presence of some unimagined evil. A cabin boy seemed unusually excited; and our Dutchman, van Buskin, rubbed his nose, as was his habit when excited; Jason Blue, an ex-convict, scowled; and one lad of sixteen chewed at a nail on a shaking finger, his eyes darting strangely up into the rigging. Had Captain Boll turned to them and said, "Men, we'll all step over the rail," I think the majority would have obeyed, if only for relief from that South Atlantic oppressiveness.

Boll's fist was before his face as he stared at the glittering western seam of earth and sky. "A howling wind!" It was his only departure from calm. Moments later a cloud moved out of the west, skirting north.

The moment seemed made to order for me. Tom Flint was not aboard the Gerrymander by accident; rather, I bounced in the wake of that ceremony at the fitting-out berth years before. It was my moment, one in which I could serve the crew as well as De Loach and self—I wanted Boll's measuring eye, if merely for the sake of closer acquaintance. But call it recognition.

I chuckled so he could hear me. His eye came around, sharp.

He studied me fiercely for long moments. He seemed to require time for transporting his mind from hell to deck, then time in which to place me into the knit of reality. Soon he saw the physical Tom Flint, a man of twenty-eight, five feet eleven, and one hundred ninety pounds, under short, wavy brown hair and steady washed-blue eyes.

"Mr. Flint," he said with sinister ease, "did you ever shinny up a mast?"

"Aye, sir."

"Then you'll shinny aloft and repair a bowline bridle on the main-royal."

There was little reason for any word about the coat of grease on the mast, or the mention of easier methods of reaching for that towering fifth sail, or the very fact that not a bowline bridle on any sail needed repair, or that I was a ship's officer. There was, instead, every reason for complaisance. Boll was a stickler for ship's discipline; he put a ship through; and he was an exemplar of that type of master who "held onto a halyard till hell froze over." I had long respected from a sideline his reputation as it strutted pompously by, sometimes loud, sometimes hushed.

"Sir," I replied, "I signed aboard as second, not as a Sumatra monkey," causing Mr. Wulsin to shake his old head sadly. The cook, an ex-pugilist from New Orleans, known as Little Ahab—who chewed licorice and spat its juice lustily—allowed his big knuckle-scarred jaws a fill of ebony saliva, blinked his eyes, and forgot to eject his gain over the rail. At last he spat from necessity, and Mr. Cott opened wide his left eye without affecting the set droop of the other; the steward, Lugo Giacomo, whom we called the "Boot," sighed heavily. Jason Blue, our admitted criminal, remained silent, attentive, as did Reeder, a big, hard-faced man of thirty-two.

"Mr. Flint, I'm losing my patience."

"Aye, sir," I said with veiled insolence. "But a man who hasn't any patience with God and weather can't have much with a lowly second."

A twinkle of Boll's eyes said he would reserve me for a very private plumbing.

Little Ahab spat again, and old Wulsin sighed. The lads who ran the rigging, most of them in their beardless teens, emitted glances which emphasized their youthful lack of comprehension as they eyed the greased mast, then Boll, and me. Chess, my favorite apprentice, a curly-haired boy of twelve with big soft brown eyes, seemed to gaze from the captain to me over a teething ring.

I heard Wulsin's low words: "The second'll back down—thank the

Lord." But I wasn't giving an inch. I had merely put myself up for due consideration. It was the first brush, but then a ship's sails must meet a wind for the first time, her hull the brine. Every experience has its virginity, its rape, and its memory, and I was learning the advantages or disadvantages, as well as the pain, joy, and curiosity, of rape as his eyes dug deeper into mine.

"Steward, fetch my rifle." In due time Lugo was back with it. Mr. Wulsin groaned aloud:

"May the Lord Jesus Christ and St. Ebenezer of Singapore have mercy." I chuckled, aware that no captain, even Boll, could force himself into such awkward behavior.

Captain Boll held the rifle, and my eye. Chess, his big brown eyes bulging, uttered a little cry of protest. The gun had not been raised. But now it moved up quickly. There was a sharp report, and the sail leaped up in a short quiver as its starboard edge was perforated.

"Mr. Flint, the bowline bridle needs repair. Take your time. It will give us both something to think about on this voyage."

He turned about and prayed to the devil for his wind. Minutes later I looked up and saw Chess trying his hand at repairing that bowline bridle. Boll, too, saw him, which meant trouble ahead.

Boll got his wind. It roared in at about three bells on the second watch that afternoon. The blustering anti-trades sent a mild advance breath, first from directly out of the north, and then bearing out of the west with squalls, sleet, and harder winds. Before the lights of Tristan da Cunha blinked under the blanket of fog over our starboard, he held to good driving canvas. Later in the evening, big water gushed over the sides and out the scuppers. The devil had come through with a wind.

On deck that night, she pulled ten knots under full topsails and upper topgallants. Then I heard the order from Mr. Cott's bellows, which meant we would wear steadily to the south under all the sail she could carry. "Down to the drift ice," he said with hellish pleasure to the lads with feet up in the sail stirrups. "The Striker puts a ship through. Aye, ye'll be in the sails when the green hits the yardarms. When the sail ye're trimmin' will slap you down while ye're takin' in. Aye." He laughed hatefully, adding, "Ye'll be settin' the royals next!"

I frowned at the threatened press of canvas. "Damn little sail the Old Man will keep fluted," I mused. My frown held as I drew a visible definition of a hellship: fifty men should berth before the mast; economy scored—we shipped twenty-five. Twenty-five to do the work of fifty on a big full-rigged three-sticker! Hell was in the offing.

My observation was cut short. The captain wanted me.

Soon I entered his cabin, stopped short, and raised a brow significantly: there sat Chess. He seemed to sigh as I entered, and he kept sending those big eyes my way beseechingly. He was unusually serious for a lad of twelve as he turned his cap in his hands. In the moment he caused me a surge of pride and possessiveness that wasn't mine.

Said Boll, "Sit down, Mr. Flint. I have here a man who acted against orders. He repaired the bowline bridle when the second mate failed to do it." He eyed me narrowly.

His quarters seemed designed for a king. In addition to an ornate wall desk, a round table and chairs of polished mahogany, there were three excellent oils in massive frames. The central picture was of a square-rigger in a blow; the crew took in topgallants fast as sea and wind roared up astern. On the left, a portrait of a man caught and held my eye. He was Robert Culver. Despite the artist's attempt at softening him, his face seemed to carry more storm than the seascape.

The third picture was of Harriet Adams. Her beauty caught and held me. I forgot Boll and Chess as I studied her with more admiration than I realized. Her eyes looked straight into mine, as do the eyes of any portrait, as if she wished to stare me down. I found it hard to look away.

"Come here, boy," Boll ordered. Chess gulped once or twice as he advanced bravely. "Since you acted without orders today, tell me what I should do with you."

"Sir," Chess replied, contriving a weak smile, "you've already scared the bloody hell out of me." The boy was learning to talk like a sailor, I observed; pity his tongue before we reached Java Head.

Boll asked casually enough, "Did you ever ride a bosun's chair, boy?"

"No, sir."

"I don't mean above deck, boy."

"N-no, sir."

I said, "Aren't you going a little far, sir?"

"The crew seems to think it can take liberties aboard this ship," he said, facing me. "It's too bad the new men don't know me." He studied me, then Chess, and his words seemed too painstakingly rehearsed for any quick decision. "It's about time all of us got acquainted. We will, and soon, boy. You're going to ride a bosun's chair over the side."

I was sure he jested, since few grown men could stand such a ride as he suggested in a rough sea. The *Gerrymander* sat solid with case oil, and her ten knots threw up furrows and running seas down her sides in good weather; but choppy, snarling swells at a driving ten made bosun's chair riding more than perilous.

The lad smiled in sickly fashion and turned his cap over and over as he heard the verdict; his chin quivered perceptibly, and his eyes seemed to shrink timidly from an acceptance of the fact. "I'd rather n-not, sir."

Boll sent for Mr. Cott. When the mate arrived, he asked the reading of the log line. "Eleven, sir, and the wind is hauling into the south'ard."

"Mr. Cott, I want a bosun's chair swung from a davit on the portside. Have it ready to lower away." Mr. Cott merely grinned as he glanced from the boy to me. His hanging lids twitched, and his Adam's apple bobbed in a long ugly neck.

We moved to the deck. There was a chill in the air with the brush of the southerly winds, and I could imagine cold purple noses and numbed hands before we reached forty-five degrees south.

On block and tackle from a davit was a bosun's chair, a board slung by a rope and used as a seat for work aloft and over the sides. Chess was ordered to sit in it. He obeyed, holding grimly to the line. Nor did he whimper as Boll lowered away.

It is difficult for a landsman to grasp the full gravity of such a situation. Unless one considers the force of a running sea and matches a mere lad against such a restless Goliath, the punishment fails to register deeply. But here was more than penalty inflicted on an offender; here was a gamble with death.

The water hit him, hard. At eleven knots, two more than many men will dare in an easy sea, he was forced to fight hard to sit upright. He lost here, however. I saw him, a red-lacquered marine animal in the glint of the portside riding light, smothered in sea and foam. He came out of it flattened and gasping and hanging on for dear life. Then another wave swallowed him, and the spray lifted to sting faces away up on deck.

He was up because the sea dropped from under him; he hung in mid-air, a feeble youth between his past and hereafter, but only for a moment. A smother of foam, blood-tinted from the ship's light, devoured him.

I felt Boll's eye on me. I glanced at him, careful to evince no feeling; rather, I sought out his expression as Lugo the Boot waved a greasy note and clambored for a wager—he said the lad wouldn't last out another dunking. Said Boll, "What's on your mind, Mr. Flint?"

"I could be wondering who's sitting on a bench in the Common,"

I said easily, gritting my teeth as a black wave climbed the rope supporting Chess all the way to the rail. "Or," I added, straining for a civil tongue, "I could be asking why a grown man wants to murder a boy."

"You omit the 'sir,' Mr. Flint."

I glared at him then. Boll knew my mind; he dared me with indirect cruelties. It was then I realized that he was less interested in punishing Chess and more in testing Tom Flint.

"Haul him up, Mr. Flint. I'm sure you'll enjoy telling him it was you who saved him." I hauled. I drew in a beaten boy with a belly full of brine; he was almost unconscious, and holding on so fast that it required force to pry his hands from the line. Over my shoulder: "When you've finished your womanish chores, Mr. Flint, report to my cabin."

I did not answer; instead, I lowered my eyes to a miracle, the living Chess.

I waited for my anger to cool before reporting to the Old Man.

Captain Boll sat, elbows on table, cap pushed back, drink in one hand, and pencil in the other. On the varnished round table lay a chart which his pencil point stabbed at St. Paul, a few thousand miles east. He seemed lost in meditation, and he left me standing for some time as he looked right through me.

I used his lengthened silence to study Harriet Adams of the portrait. There was a faint trace of humor about her lips, I thought. Was she a little purist or snob, or was she the true model for the portrait?

Suddenly: "Mr. Flint, we've made an extra day to this point. But I need four more. I'll get them." I stood in silence, thinking: "He'll blow the boltropes out of her." He said, "We'll probably go under Prince Edward Islands and the Crozets and swing up to St. Paul." It was nearing autumn down here, and drift ice threatened to reach up soon to fifty, then forty degrees.

He looked up at me. "We're going to drive hell out of ship and crew."

"Aye, sir."

He said, "Mr. Wulsin is getting old. I'll trust you to see that he does his job. And Mr. Cott, who is chief mate because Mr. Culver likes him, makes old-womanish excuses in storm weather. There's little pleasure in scolding an old woman."

I waited, wondering, "What next?" Soon he said, "It'll be watch and watch most of the way. I'm out to drive this ship up to four

hundred miles a day." I continued to wait as he went on: "The
Gerrymander has a reputation. They say she's a murderess. But I'm
pushing her. She's going through.

"Now, Mr. Flint," he said, leaning forward slightly, "I don't know
why you gave up a captain's berth to sail under me. But your mistakes of the past don't concern me. It's the ones you make under me.
I'll keep my eye on you. If you please me, I can make things very interesting for you. Aye, profitably so."

That was all. I went on deck with a feeling of accomplishment
surging through me; that, and a keen desire to work into whatever
scheme he had afoot, if it could serve De Loach and me.

2

Four days later our position was forty-six south, fourteen east, and
still no legendary roaring winds. Old Wulsin defined our stand in
more realistic terms: "Africa on the portside, the South Pole to
starboard, and hell ahead." I wondered more than ever why a driving
captain carried such a bosun.

But the weather came on, the big weather of the roaring forties,
gradually but surely. Cape pigeons swarmed about the ship and a few
big albatrosses kept us company. It was on the eight-to-midnight
watch of the fourth night after Boll had said that it would be hell all
the way. The waves were a dozen feet high and climbing higher. The
Gerrymander rolled a little, but she ran splendidly under fair driving
sail. As the wind freshened, I knew the helmsman was unhappy with
the pressure aft; he'd have liked to carry the helm nearly amidships
for easy steering. Why Mr. Cott didn't see fit to make the crossjack
fast in that following wind, I didn't know; nor did I care. He carried
her under Cape Horn canvas, except for the unorthodox mizzen sail.

Little Ahab spat, spraying the rail with licorice juice. "One hour
till midnight and your watch, Mr. Flint." He was leading up to something, and I waited. "I've cut open many a pig and fowl for the
galley stove. There's less entrails in a chicken. Now if you could induce me to help with the helm, and if I could induce you to tie up the
goddamn mizzen, we could travel."

At ten minutes to midnight the bell sounded the warning for the
change of watch. At eight bells sharp I took over the conn of the ship.
The starboard watch is also the captain's, and Boll stood the weather
side of the poop on the minute. The wind blew in a near gale by then.

I had all hands busy for hours. The upper main-topsail was furled, and she ran faster under three sails and one kite than under Mr. Cott's five. So I reckoned that if I had her pulling for me it was only a matter of mathematics and horse sense to lend her more power. I glanced at Boll, who watched closely.

With the fore-topmast staysail sheeted home flat, and with Little Ahab and another man at the wheel, the *Gerrymander's* forefeet drove her like a stallion. She reached out for thirteen, fourteen knots, laughing, rocking, rolling a bit, and straining at her sheets. She dipped into waves and out of them, accepting the easy tops and flying spray. She left them behind her, in a twenty-yard patch of foam from her sides, in a wake that danced white into the disappearing night. She roared on, spewing steam under her, whistling and screaming in her rigging, an express on the wet prairie of the roaring forties.

I lived her then. There was something about her that made her a twin to the portrait in the cabin; she and Harriet Adams seemed endowed with the same spirit.

"Mr. Flint," Captain Boll said, "has she another three knots in her? Same wind? Mr. Cott has seen me carry her past eighteen, and he has yet to carry her more than fifteen. Some things aren't learned by the head." He pointed to the pit of his stomach.

The night grew blacker, and it came in closer. The water on my next watch sped by us, growling and boiling. The tophamper screeched and, as an eye reached up into the converging mass, it faded into a nether world.

The *Gerrymander* reached up as if she wanted to skim off over the waves without touching them; but her one main-topsail held her down. Then her bow would sink down into troughs in a dive; and her foresail held her up. I heard Boll's voice:

"We have topgallants, Mr. Flint."

"They're out of sight," I said, adding under my breath, "And out of mind."

He took over then, and he brought every man aboard into the play. He added sail to her.

"She won't carry all that sail," I said.

"Perhaps not, Mr. Flint. It's just the maximum we're after." As I tried to correlate his words to the canvas, I heard a flapping and booming from up in the main—a topgallant had blown.

The wind grew in force, and the deck, bound tighter to the black-green sea, shipped seas with every dip of her bow. The slaves of the rigging were busy at hard labor; there was no end to their work. They sought foot- and handholds on treacherous stirrups and slick wet yards. The wind, icy and wet, chilled to the bone and drove tears out of an eye straight back to an ear. Groans and curses went unheard, and bleeding finger tips, when the nails were torn back from sail-handling, went unseen. Boll would have logged any who voiced a desire to quit.

Then an apprentice was knocked off balance by a stubborn sail; the result was a broken collarbone. The lad was none other than Chess.

But Boll had taught us a lesson: the *Gerrymander*, despite her wounds, had driven through rain and sleet squalls to do a good eighteen knots. He was satisfied.

The pace held, day after day. We slept in brief stretches, five minutes at a time, on coils, or standing; we worked, a halyard in one hand, a pannikin of coffee in the other. Beards grew, and the apprentices rubbed their fuzzy young faces at times as if suddenly discovering some sign of hairy manhood. The wind blew dry and wet, but cold; it pelleted sail and sail hand with rain, sleet, and hail. The long nights became a terror in the rigging. The wintry sun hid its warmth, until the marrow of our bones felt the chill of a slaughterhouse. A day ran into another; the Prince Edward Islands raced by on our starboard; then the Crozets slipped by; we were hitting hard for St. Paul, painfully hard. Work! Work! She would carry her starboard tacks aboard for a while, then she would feel the wind haul around with more weight; and no matter our preparation, the weather brought more work.

After long days and nights of it, sleep or mutiny seemed inevitable. Lugo staggered on deck with the usual salt beef, coffee, and talk: Mr. Cott was sick! Old Wulsin's normally sad face reminded one of a man about to put the other foot in a grave. There was little evidence of pity for the worthless bosun who shunned his work.

On the eighth day Boll ordered me to the poop. I stood before him, my sea legs wobbly. "Well, it's up to you and me, Mr. Flint."

"Aye," my tongue responded mechanically.

"You'll drive her under all she'll carry through the night."

I turned about, only to meet Chess. I paused, wondering at the strange effect the lad held over me. It was I who had set that cracked clavicle, roughly, and with no more encouragement than, "If you can swear like a young fool, you can take this." He had blanched a bit when I ground his bones together and strapped his shoulders and back with sailcloth.

"I'm dead on my feet, sir, by God and St. Ebenezer I am," he said.

"Belay, boy, belay!" I growled. "Go to my quarters and sleep!"

3

It was nearing six in the morning when I arrived at my quarters. Chess awaited me there; he slept sitting up, his head against a bunk post, a hand clutching at his collarbone. I stood in silence for a moment, then sat down. The bottle was out of my reach and I debated seriously upon the value of a draught versus the effort of reaching for it. With a heavy sigh, I got up.

As I stood there, the lad ate at my conscience, and I cursed him warmly for his meddlesome invasion. Then I drank deep. The next I knew I had eased Chess into the bunk and covered him with a blanket.

"Now, Tom Flint, do you feel better?" And Tom Flint replied, "Why should I be an ape for any lad's troubles; he came aboard of his own accord, didn't he?" Something inside me answered: "True, Tom, but you are concerned."

Then I dozed off.

Someone was shaking me, and I opened my eyes to see Chess grinning and pointing to hard bread and coffee. "And Little Ahab sent an egg, sir. It's the last one aboard." Thereupon he produced a cold fried egg in the manner of any boy showing a prize frog or grass snake. Then he frowned and said:

"Is this ship really jinxed, sir? Has she always been a hellship?"

I said absently, "There's a parent's curse on her, boy."

"Really?" His eyes leaped up with curiosity before accepting the dismal fact. "Then I wish to hell I'd never signed on."

"Yes, Chess. It goes back to her debut as the *Robert Culver*. That was four years ago. Want to hear it, or had you rather sleep?"

"Sleep here is nothing more than a wink before some fool cries, 'All hands!' "

"Very well, boy. It was in 'eighty-one——"

At that moment it came: "All hands on deck! Out, every son of a ——, on deck!" Mr. Cott's voice rang clearly.

On deck I saw men running up by the forecastlehead, and I made my way forward. It was the bobstay, the stay that held the bowsprit down. I heard Mr. Cott say with a resounding curse, "It's snapped!" It was his first appearance on deck in two days. I lifted my brows at a picture of the bowsprit bending. If it snapped, the fore-topmast would go with it. But there was time to secure it. With every dip the *Gerrymander* shuddered as if in agony. She plunged twice in a couple of ugly seas before Mr. Cott, rubbing his stubble, gave an order to take the sails off her and heave to. The order was that of a brave man, as the case proved. The ship had not a sail fast when Boll came on deck.

"What's the meaning of this, Mr. Cott?"

"The bobstay, sir. The bowsprit will go next," he managed.

"You ran the ship off for that?" Boll said. "You'll put her on her course again and secure it as we go. Pass lengths of stream chain out the hawsepipes and shackle the end to the bowsprit cap. But get under way."

I spoke up: "You want to go on before repairs?"

He turned sharply. "Now."

"Have you looked at the seas?" I said. "Every man here is weary, and you want a few of them to battle the head seas under the bows."

For long moments he stood, a sphinx in deep study of my words or his actions to follow, or both. All the while, the water beat at our weather side and leaped on deck. The ship was almost as mutinous as I in the moment. Boll seemed to be deliberating seriously as to whether I, Mr. Cott, or the elements should be the first to feel his displeasure. He soon decided.

He advanced and sent a short jab to my chin. I went down, though I was instantly up and counting slowly as I weighed the joy of striking him down against the wisdom of biding my time.

"Why don't you strike back, Mr. Flint?" he said easily.

"You know why," I said.

"Allow me to compliment you, Mr. Flint." With that he turned on his heel and strode aft.

No sooner had Mr. Cott roweled her back on her easterly course than she pitched heavily into a sea that struck hard and climbed aboard the bows like some waiting demon of the deep. Her backbone trembled to the stern post; and the wind, striking from sou'west in puffs against the wind aft, brought cross seas. A roll to port, and her rail burrowed under. Then to starboard, and that rail was seas under. The hands hugged the life lines then, ropes running each side from forecastlehead to poop, to cling to. Two men were at the helm, as usual, and they worked.

The man at the lookout strained his eyes for St. Paul late that afternoon, even as a wet sun dripped lazily and bedded down over a gray tumultuous sea before sleep was due. As if to make the deck more than untenable, the wind blew into an antagonistic whole-gale screech before the midnight-to-four watch.

Captain Boll still held to the press of canvas. With topsails ablow, his eyes seemed to contemplate topgallants. His strategy: let her run her best for a couple of hours; then, if the sea and wind came in stronger and belched up storm, he would ease her off. But, I asked, would he? Could he then, when the men could not stand the force of the wind up in the rigging, when a foot could find no stirrup?

He was master of the ship, but with a sixty-mile wind the elements would dethrone him. Boll the Striker would then find himself committed to his own overpress of sail.

Boll said, coming up from behind, "We can travel in this weather, Mr. Flint. A good wind," he said slowly, eying the murk as if he were mentally engaged in patting the devil's back.

As I stood there, Lugo fetched a bottle. Boll drank, then handed it to me, saying, "You're going to need this, Mr. Flint. Drink deep."

Boll was right—twice right.

My watch wasn't minutes old when the fury of the elements made of the earlier blow a calm by comparison. A terrific gust came in from the west, striking the ship aft. The very suddenness of the blow was something I had never experienced at sea. The *Gerrymander* lurched forward as if all force had struck her topsails to make her dive into the sea. The giant waves, fifty feet high, slapping hard up from behind, caught her stern just as she began to coast down a mountainous wave; and the gust caused her diving bow to burrow under head-high. The ship twisted and rolled even as she dived and came up, a bobbing cork with more brains and agility than the hungry seas, always a leap ahead of them.

But where the sea failed the wind scored: the upper main-topsail went. Boll bellowed: "Bend a fresh tops'l!"

As the sail was being sent aloft with a gantline, an apprentice's finger went with a halyard. Then the upper main-topsail slatted, knocking van Buskin to the deck. He could not rise; his back was broken! But that? Why, that was nothing; nothing but a human loss; and to bring the Striker's reasoning abreast of the deed, wasn't the *Gerrymander* driving on?

Aye! She was tearing through; she was running on the bowline.

I thought I had enough. I turned an eye all around me. Men dripped in salty chills even as they clung to ropes, capstans, ringbolts, and any other solid thing on deck; water gushed out of the fo'c'sle, swirling about knees and hips; a few coughed, and one weary lad vomited. I was taking a curious view of the situation—I was thinking of mutiny, and justifying the grave aspect of the word in action.

But the sorry crew—had it the essence of solidarity; did I dare approach a single one of them?

Above the hiss and roar of the elements I heard the ship's bell sound a warning of the change of watch. I waited the minutes out, then walked to the poop where he stood. My mind was made up. I would see what the other side had to offer.

"Sir," I said evenly, "sometime back you said something about making things very interesting for me. Remember?"

He eyed me slowly, calmly. "Yes," he replied.

"Well, now is the time, sir," I said.

3   THE CASH AND THE MUTINY

BOLL WAS QUICK TO OBLIGE ME. AS SOON AS HE FELT THE SHIP SAFE under Mr. Cott, he led the way to his cabin.

I left the world of deck on the hard open seas and moved into some Beacon Hill drawing room, where I sat in a bitter-green leather chair before a polished round table. Only the fact that the table was screwed to the floor seemed to alter my transport, that and the severe roll of the room. And, too, Miss Adams of the portrait remained too still. As my eyes drank in the setting, I was aware of a cozy warmth. Some faces make a man think intently, and Miss Adams's face was one of them; I wondered what was written underneath it.

Boll, seated across the table from me, cap at rakish angle, cigarette in the center of his lips, reproved me with casual indirectness when he said: "That ship in the picture—I'm having a change made in it." I did not ask what or why. "The t'gallants shouldn't be furled in such a small blow," he said.

"Of course not, sir." I chuckled. "Let the wind take them off so the crew will keep busy bending new ones."

"We think alike, Mr. Flint. Uncanny, isn't it?" He poured from a bottle. We drank.

He opened deviously: "I wonder if Mr. Cott can handle her. He'll no doubt find an excuse to cut a few sheets and reduce her speed. But," he added, his eyes boring into mine, "he's a hard man to provoke into suspension from duty."

"He should take lessons from Tom Flint," I said.

"My thoughts, exactly. He's a necessary factor while running. But" —he paused—"a poor ally for what I have in mind. Oh, he'd be willing enough, but there are other qualities I demand of a first officer in this case."

Then he said crisply, "What's on your mind?" He was worth talking to, if only for the fact that he kept a man alive and awake.

"I'm here on the behalf of the crew, sir. Nothing personal, unless——"

"Naturally," he said, smiling. He was back in his same pose, his hands as motionless and his eyes as steady as those of some pagan statue.

"Unless," I continued, "you wish to take it as personal." He used the word again—"Naturally"—and with intent to infuriate me, I realized. But I would cross him up there, I said privately.

"Go on."

"You're reaching for your eighteen to twenty knots with blood, bone, and agony."

"Is this a formal protest?"

"Purely private. The crew isn't in on it."

"Too bad," he reflected.

"Purely private," I repeated. "As for myself, I can take it. But those boys out there need sleep."

"The matter is truly serious," he mocked.

I was supposed to lose my temper; I grinned instead. "I've always heard that a captain's worst enemy is a fatigued crew."

"Sleep," he said, smiling. "Now when I think back, I am ashamed of myself." I ground my teeth for silence as he went on: "We carry a Bible here. In the book of Isaiah, the Lord gathered the outcasts of Israel and said, 'Yea, they are greedy dogs which can never have enough, and they are shepherds that cannot understand: they all look to their own way, every one for his gain, from his quarter.'"

I was as much surprised that he knew any teaching of, or any verse from, the Bible as I would have been had Harriet Adams in the portrait opened her mouth and spat a vile curse.

"'Come ye,'" he quoted, "'say they, I will fetch wine, and we will fill ourselves with strong drink; and tomorrow shall be as this day, and much more abundant.'

"Simply call me a shepherd who cannot understand, Mr. Flint. *Tomorrow shall be as this day, and much more abundant.*" Then he said, "You may recite the verse to the outcasts. Now get out!"

"Sure," I said, getting up. "But I thought more would come of this meeting than my protest and your answer."

After an interval of silence he said, "Sit down."

I was no sooner seated again than he passed the bottle. He held a glass in his hand and his eyes stretched curious seconds into minutes.

"Tom Flint," he said in preoccupied manner. "A good seaman with a good record as mate and captain—good papers, good risk." Then he sat back, exuding a thin smile. "I might overlook the bowline-bridle incident on this trip. But don't think I'll forget it.

"Now as you know, Culver owns this ship. He's not in love with her. I am. But he doesn't want to sell her. He wants to drain the last penny out of her. He looks upon her as he would a woman who'd jilted him. He sees that same woman at his mercy. I can imagine how he feels. But that's his pleasure and passion, not mine."

He turned an eye on the three oils and looked at each for some time. I caught the merest glimpse of his mystery, his life and conflict, in the moment, though it was as vague as it was evanescent. But there it was in a trio of oils.

Then he seemed to say everything in five words: "Culver's picture must come down."

I said, looking at the pictures of Harriet Adams and the ship he wanted to run under topgallants, "Just Culver's picture, or frame and all?"

"You have a long eye, Mr. Flint. Maybe you are my man."

"Maybe," I said. "But who's going to paint you in that frame?"

He leaned forward with a question as direct as his eyes: "Are you interested, Mr. Flint?"

There seemed little need of his talking in terms of money or reward; his lofty aims hurdled paltry sums, and by their very omission he offered me much. And I knew he would pay off in gold the same as I knew that one day he would exact his toll in the bowline-bridle affair. I saw the face of patient De Loach before my mind's eye; he was pleading with me to accept Boll's offer. "It's made to order," he seemed to say.

Then I looked at the face of a girl I had never met. I saw in it some gratifying glimpse of half-conceived dreams, moments of roaming pleasure; then I saw the tears of a wounded ship in her eyes as she gazed at Boll the Striker. I was making up my mind in the wrong direction—then I turned to face the other side of the table. Boll was the stronger attraction.

I was about to answer him when he said, "Ever hear of St. Ebenezer of Singapore?"

I had. St. Ebenezer was an old English trader, ex-professor and actor whom sailors under every flag sought out for a blessing: his touch and word meant good sailing in the stream. His influence was felt in the Orient since he claimed as many religions as he spoke tongues.

"It might interest you to know he's working for me—a little deal in Formosa camphor."

It did interest me. St. Ebenezer was reputed also to play a great confidence game. Just as I formed a question, Boll said:

"Think it over until your watch, Mr. Flint."

The deck wasn't the same as I had left it. The wind had backed down to a moderate-to-fresh gale, an excellent force for Boll's driving sail; but, as usual, Boll wasn't happy with traditional balance aloft. He loosed fore and main-topgallants. The *Gerrymander* cut through the sea, rocking both ways. I watched her jib boom cant its eye to the sea and the rising day out over the lonely moon-splashed waters; I used my sea legs perfunctorily as the plowing lady's top and deck leaned in slow, jerking rhythm to port, and steady, and slower still to starboard.

The day came on slowly; the moon commenced to fade from molten gold to silver, and the tiny stars eastward copied her rapid trim of hue. A washed orange impaled the bottom of the sky, hung there for long minutes, then hoisted its flame to a welcome sky and sea. The day promised fair.

Seven bells sounded; I walked straightway to Boll's cabin and rapped hard. When I entered, he raised his head and said, "We've set a record to St. Paul, Mr. Flint." When I said we had not arrived, he advised we would see land within fifty minutes. His calculation was in error by only thirty seconds.

"I want publicity on the record I'm going to set. It'll serve my purpose, not my vanity," he explained. Then he asked if I was there to accept his offer.

I nodded, and he chuckled, saying, "You spoke of unrest among the crew."

"Lack of rest, sir," I corrected.

"Let's call it unrest, smoldering mutiny which walks a thin rope. It won't ever quite reach the surface."

"It hasn't the energy," I snapped.

"Are you still championing a noble cause?" he put with mild sarcasm. "This is business, Mr. Flint."

"I'm not selling my insides, sir. Just my services. And I've got my limits even there. Incidentally, what jail do you have in mind for me when I help put your picture in Culver's frame?"

He eyed me for some time. Then he said: "I'm not running for a record to Java Head—which I'll get—for the sake of Culver and Adams. I'm doing it for my own very special reasons. But the record: I can see it in the Boston papers: 'Captain Boll of the *Gerrymander* sets new sailing time from Boston to Java Head. He ran her easting down in a record passage——'" He laughed pleasantly; it was the first time I had heard that sound.

"Culver will read all praise of his ship with angered eyes. He'll curse her, and me, for freshening a memory, for flicking at an old sore, one that won't heal. I won't let it. He'll learn something he should remember—a gerrymander has claws."

"You talk like a man I know, sir," I said. "De Loach is his name." Boll said he knew the man, that he was lacking in genius. I wasn't so sure, though I said nothing.

"But you asked about a jail. That was just to make conversation, wasn't it?" When I lifted my brows, he said, "Now there may be courts, but I don't see a jail. Let us say that I break no laws. Let us hope you don't, Mr. Flint."

"I won't." I smiled. "I'm just sitting here a party to conspiracy against a shipowner. They define such as barratry—erroneously, of course."

"Aren't you forgetting this quick run for economy, for the owner's profit? The *Gerrymander* under me is an ideal situation, one aspired to by owners, stockholders, bankers, and underwriters. I'll keep it that way. Now where's the act committed to the prejudice of the shipowner?"

"Why, it simply disappeared," I replied. "But this is all as clear as fog. Where do I come in?"

"Your opening role should be a very easy one. You seem cut out for the part of the mate who leads a crusade for the rights of the crew. You'll feel for them, you'll get them to send you to me as their spokesman. I'll give a little, but damn little. Then there is talk of mutiny, but you're a sensible man who advises that they hold their heads until we make port, suggesting that they punish me by refusing to sail out with me at the last moment. I'll help in my way, of course."

"It makes good sense up to a point. But why should you want to stir up mutiny and lose a crew?"

"I don't. You'll keep them in line. After delaying the ship in Singapore by a few weeks, in which no other crew will sign on—you'll see to that, too—the men finally come to their senses."

"Why?" I could contain myself no longer. "For what?"

"For the time I'll need to get this rolling."

Thereupon he reached into his pocket and extracted a light yellow disk, which he tossed to the table in front of me: it was a twin to the coin De Loach had given me. I picked it up, frowning, wondering just what scheme he was building around the worthless piece. On one side was a replica of our figurehead in relief; on the other were two words:

GERRYMANDER CASH.

"Consider the value of that," Boll said.

"I'm trying to do just that, sir," I replied, producing the coin De Loach had given me and placing it on the table before him. As he sat up and eyed me sharply, I said, "The man who gave this to me told me to keep it for luck."

Boll smiled. "And riches," he said.

2

It was on the following afternoon that Boll came down from the poop and ordered me to follow him. He walked directly to the sail locker and paused before a long box. He eyed it for some time before removing the black tarpaulin, upon which was printed in big white letters: EXPLOSIVES.

The big black box reminded me of a coffin. It was made of iron, a fact which caused me to lift my brows and think of a broken rule: general precautions in the stowage of explosives advised against the use of iron of any sort. Boll, a stickler for rules, carried explosives of a different kind, I realized.

He produced a key, and soon all three locks were removed. Then he raised the lid. Before me the gold of a dozen pirate treasures glittered. Gold by the peck, though it was false gold, fool's gold, in the shape of yellow coins—Gerrymander Cash pieces by the thousands.

I glanced at Boll. He eyed the box of spurious wealth with greedy, scheming eyes. Captain Boll, one of the most respected masters of the time, was not the practical, driving captain in that moment; rather, he seemed the lengthened shadow of some great pirate on the Spanish Main.

"Trade money, Mr. Flint," he said. "And enough of it to warrant my bid for time in which to get it in circulation."

"Yeah," I said absently. I was trying to reconcile the venerable captain who reached for a record run to the man who seemed to conspire against a shipowner and ship's crew as he looked far ahead into the blueprint of a baffling scheme. "It's still a puzzle to me, sir." I added, "How can you trade with this?"

"We shall get the answer to that in Singapore—from our partner, St. Ebenezer. He's using Formosa for a testing ground."

"So that's how he fits into the puzzle!"

"Yes. Now, Mr. Flint, you'll get busy with the crew and be sure I get the delay I want in Singapore."

I began work on my insidious hoax shortly after St. Paul snugged under the horizon. I felt the brush of curiosity and adventure to a distant climax. What would St. Ebenezer do with that coin? And the question threw my captious side up for exercise. Then I thought of my part in this and I could not but chuckle at a topsy-turvy situation. It was absurd for a captain to desire mutinous swelling on the one hand, and a record run on the other. But the fact remained: they walked hand in hand, and with a promise to serve Amos De Loach and Tom Flint.

Boll played the game. Swinging the *Gerrymander* into the upper westwind drift, up into the Australian and equatorial currents, he wore ship from tack to tack night and day. He crowded sail for a record run, though he seemed to court trouble in the rigging just to press the weary men. Where the variable winds and calms were due, he paid the obliging devil for a wind; he got for his trouble gales and storms.

Then, not a week after we passed St. Paul, he cut food and water rations. He offered no reason for this unwarranted act. Boll gambled with human emotions as he had gambled with sail in the tophamper. He was a consistent gambler.

Mutiny, I realized, could be a far-off state of mind in one moment, and a crime under way in the next. It was like fire when out of control. Thus I was forced to tread softly, to await the death of fluid curses and the birth of weary sullenness if I chose to string along with Boll in an effort better to involve Culver's captain; and I had made that decision. And Boll helped again when one evening after a day of storm he ordered "below watch" for an hour. His reasoning: private conversations were conducive to swelling.

I eased into the forecastle at nine that evening. Clothes hung everywhere and the smell of sweat joined with that of coffee. The door opened and sent a paper across the floor and the odors in another swirl. Bunk boards, suitcases, worn books, leather belts, oilskins, shoes, and a maze of assorted gear, from a Bible to prints of Parisian nudes, made a forecastle home. The lamp nestled in the fore-and-aft bulkhead, lighting up the scene.

The babble of voices was suddenly hushed, and I was met with frowns and scowls. "Rather icy in here." I smiled, evoking nothing more than the solid rebuke which lengthened silence can employ. "Yeah, I drove you, lads," I said at last. "But remember this, there was a thumb on my neck."

Then I laughed. "You're a sorry-looking group. Here, help yourselves to the stuff I lifted." I tossed food rolled up in sailcloth to the table; the tension eased. Then I reversed the situation completely: I sat down and cursed.

I saw the exchange of glances, and in the contained smiles, I felt the flavor of their triumph which, though justified, was nevertheless wicked. Little Ahab entered and cursed: so this was where his salt beef had gone. Did we want the steward to have the captain log him?

"We don't particularly give a damn," I said, making favor with the boys. Little Ahab rubbed at his ear and creased his black brows into a frown as he peered curiously at me. "I reckon you had a hand in cutting rations," I growled, causing him to shake his head in confounded manner. He was a comical sight, short, heavy-muscled, hairy, and small-eyed. I laughed. It was the cue for all. Amid laughter and jeers, the pugilist in him rose up, the only defense the man knew: he'd whip any two of us, he said, and "plenty damn quick"; he hadn't suggested "nothin'" to the Old Man, and he wasn't about to do so. By God and St. Ebenezer, there was plenty of food and fresh water on board!

Plenty! That sobered the lads. Simulating surprise, I said, "That doesn't make sense, Little Ahab. Are you playing both sides against the middle?"

"That settles it," he growled, advancing. Tempted to flash him a wink of an eye, I thought better of it and stood. I noticed the ever-reticent Mr. Blue ease out of his bunk.

"That doesn't settle anything as far as we're concerned," I said stoutly. "If there's plenty of food, you'll take us to it and you'll step willing." A chorus of approval sounded behind me.

"Why, sure—I'm with you." He hesitated. "But—but it's got the smell of mutiny. It's nasty, sir." It was a dazed cook who led us to the store of foodstuffs. "See? I'm not lyin', lads. Could I ask St. Ebenezer's blessin' if I was a Judas? I'm one of you, I am, a mug who loves the last damn one of you."

"Then why," piped O'Hare, "are rations cut?"

"Maybe it's because you boys are getting too fat loafing aboard ship," I put dryly before turning on them. "Lugo's against us. A hell of a steward he is." Of the entire group, only Blue, the confessed criminal, showed no interest.

"Now how many of you have got the guts to follow me to the Old Man's quarters? Wait! I'll do the talking. Now while I can't guarantee you won't be logged, I can say you'll feel yourselves men rather than the bunch of shanghaied fools you look."

"By God, I'm with you," cried Chess, provoking me into a step forward, where I caught his curly hair in a tight fist and said, "Son, your tongue is going to get you in trouble yet!" The boys were less interested in Chess's profanity and threatened punishment than in the plan afoot. Here was relief from mental doldrums, something to sharpen up the flow of weary blood—they would all go with me. They did.

I, with my stanch mutineers, laughed inwardly as I banged at the door of Boll's cabin.

Boll, glancing up after his order to enter, chuckled at what he saw: the boys stood erect, feet planted apart, arms folded across valiant chests, or stuck out akimbo; there was in them, or the pose they struck, a mixture of Captain Kidd, Nathan Hale, and Grant at Appomattox. Only Little Ahab, in the rear, had any sense of trepidation. Jason Blue had a sleepy look on his face.

"Well?" Boll smiled.

"I'll speak for them, sir," I said. "It's about the rations. Why are they cut?"

"Because I ordered it."

"But there's plenty of food and water aboard," I protested.

"And there might be ports ahead closed off by yellow fever and plague. I'm not taking any chances." There was a laugh embedded in his words, and his smile was in some way tinctured with the humor of it.

"Sir," I spoke out, "as long as you drive the hands watch and watch, I demand full rations."

"Is this a threat, Mr. Flint?" He spoke to the man whom he had engaged to frame his picture rather than to a foolish champion of dull-witted sailors. Then in hard voice he said, facing the lads one by one, "I'll increase your rations a little. But you'll work for what you get. Aye. Now get out—all but Mr. Flint."

The boys sent apprehensive and adoring glances my way. I was a man among men, one who had shown the guts to stand up for them before the Striker. I felt a little ashamed.

When the door closed behind them, Boll said, "Nice work, Mr.

Flint. St. Ebenezer would appreciate this." He added, pouring drinks, "Now the boys think they've won a victory; a small one, perhaps, but a point to lift their spirits. They need a jolt now." He meditated aloud, "I must do the unusual here. Call Mr. Cott."

When the first officer stood before him, he said, "Mr. Flint is relieved of his duties until further notice."

3

Boll made a mock hero of me. I could only grin and admire the ease with which the cat played with the mice of the crew. If the worst came to pass, open mutiny, there stood Tom Flint, hero, to turn the tide in his favor.

But I wondered at the import of this play. His only explanation had been, "For riches," and, "Trade money. St. Ebenezer and the Formosa testing ground." He had a reason for a delay in port, and he played his cards far ahead in this game, which revolved about the cash piece he had tossed to the table in front of me. It's hollow, spurious ring against the wood echoed far-reaching intrigue.

"Consider the value of that," he had said. And I, feeling the gerrymander bird in relief, the crenated edge, while peering at the words, GERRYMANDER CASH, saw only a gewgaw for stringing, or a foolish replica of the smaller Chinese cash, the common coin of China.

"Consider the value of that," he had said. I had done so. I did so long after I had first seen it. He had thrown the word GERRYMANDER on it boldly, thereby proclaiming himself, and Culver, parties to its enigmatic adventure. Did he plan that Culver should be the lawbreaker? There was every possibility that I slanted my question to a good answer, since he had leaped worded horizons when he said, "Culver's picture must come down." But again I was left hanging high and dry in a world of conjecture.

Only one fact remained: The crew was feeling the tug and pull of a mental tide, hellish and confounding, its moon a light yellow piece of metal. The Gerrymander Cash, in one sense, was already at work.

Aloud I said, "Does all this please you, Mr. De Loach?"

All the while discontent spread like some malignant growth. I was no longer second mate. The warm seas moved our way. At the bow of the ship, I faced north, seeing almost the thatched roofs of distant kampongs turned upside down in quiet moonlit lagoons and lazy rivers. We were up under Sumatra at about six degrees south, and working due east for Java Head when things began to happen.

The wind was strong out of the southeast on that late afternoon; men labored and groused as they clawed at sail, dressed spars, sweated down gear, and slaved at a maze of other chores. Mr. Wulsin was drinking heavily; he was roaming the ship, as if gloating over his position as Boll's favorite, when Little Ahab approached Boll at the poop with a message: van Buskin saw fit to die. The word ran through the ship.

A lad in the sail heard and said, "The captain murdered him." Another replied, "I heard they cut his rations too. They say the ship pitched him out of his bunk on his face one day and they let him lay there—him with a broken back."

"Well, I'll be damned! What's Mr. Flint say to that?"

"The usual, 'Bide your time, lads.' "

"Well, I've done bided mine. And Mr. Flint ain't been treated right. He'll join us. You with me, Fritz?"

"Yeah, if the crew is. Pass the word."

The word ran from rigging to deck, and on below. The group in the hold flung dunnage into the bilge, blinked hard at the gravity of the situation before leaning to the security of companionship in either victory or defeat, and moved clandestinely to deck.

"Look at old Wulsin! Roamin' around with a gut full of the cap'n's whisky. Let's fix the old buzzard now."

"Lay off the old geezer, O'Brien. He ain't the one we're after. Send for Mr. Flint and let's get organized." It was Reeder, the largest of the lot. "How do you feel about it, Jason?"

"I don't talk much," said Jason Blue.

"Are you with us?"

"Ye'll get to the poop and run," he said.

"Not us!" scoffed O'Brien.

"Then I'm with you if you stand up."

"Good. I'll start on Wulsin. Here goes."

"I said lay off the old bosun, O'Brien," Reeder snapped. "I meant it. All you'll do is upset everything." The men from below were on deck against orders, and soon they fell under Mr. Cott's stern eye. His drooping lids tightened somewhat, and he was about to leave the poop when O'Brien struck Reeder in the face. That seemed to be the spark that set off the powder.

The wind backed around to the south in the next minutes, and Mr.

Cott ordered a trim of sail. All he received was defiance as the lads in the rigging moved to deck in solid silence.

Since the announcement of van Buskin's choice of a better world, Boll had retired to his cabin. He had not been long in sending for me. "Mr. Flint," he said, "you'll attend to burial at sea. Read a verse or two and let it go at that."

4

On deck I saw the lads of both watches arming themselves with belaying pins, lengths of rope and chain, and other items that assuaged their sense of threat. Mr. Cott stood at the edge of the poop with pistol in hand; his eyes under heavy lids matched his odious leer. He was contemplating murder and steeping his mind to the joys of it.

His eyes fell upon me as I elbowed my way through the massing throng. "Stay where you are, Mr. Flint. It's your doing, and I'll take the leader first."

"Put down that gun, sir," I barked. "The situation calls for brains."

"One more step and the deck'll get yours," he replied. The manner in which he licked his lips suggested his dead seriousness. As I taxed my slow mind for some means of saving the situation, I saw the bloody face of O'Brien drawing a bead on the mate over a short pistol. I reached out and pushed the gun down, drawing for my pains a curse.

"You want to hang, O'Brien?" I said.

"Just which side you on?" he growled.

"Yeah, we thought you'd make us a good captain, Mr. Flint," growled Reeder close behind me. "Yeah, which side are you for?" a dozen voices clamored.

I raised my voice. "Listen, you pack of fools! Is this the gratitude I get for standing up for your rights? So you'd make me captain— captain of what? The first gallows, that's what! The law is against you. Why is it against you? Because Captain Boll hasn't done enough to justify mutiny."

A nasty laugh sounded nearby. I turned to see Jason Blue moving forward. So a sphinx was coming to life, and at the wrong moment! His very silence all the way from Boston threatened to give his slightest word authority. I felt the sore need of quick thinking on my part to forestall this. I acted in a hurry.

"Now here's Jason Blue," I said in conciliatory manner. "He's as apt a seaman as ever sailed, he'll tell you how far off the course you are."

"Yeah," he said in a dead-level tone of voice. "I'll tell you. You're fools who listen to words." He turned his calm, hard face my way. "His." The crowd pressed forward with that, their voices hurling threats at Mr. Cott and me. But Mr. Cott's obdurate pose slowed them.

All the while the ship tossed about in the mild south wind with only the helmsmen making futile attempts to soothe her. But they could not lower sail and haul the yards around at the same time. And there was that which I didn't know; it was enough to have made me realize that the human threat had a deadly twin. The dark somber coast of Sumatra was rising up to the north of us. Balimbing Bay and Vlakke Hoek, the Dutch name for Flat Cape, were drawing the Gerrymander in to a hungry coast. The helmsmen lashed the wheel and cut the sheets. Soon the maze of loose sails cannonaded in the south wind, a boisterous ceiling to a mutiny. Then they ran her off.

All about me hate was taking a cumulative effect. Above me stood Mr. Cott, anxious to spill blood. At my side stood an ex-convict with the same untenable joy in his face. Jason Blue's mistake was his silence at a time when I was thrown for a loss. My mistake was my company; that and my state of defeat. At Boll's suggestion, and with his help, I had stirred up something which I could no longer control. Threats rose in a babble, evaporated in a hot south wind, and in the rain which began to fall in hard drops. I moved forward until I stood on the ladder, under the eye and pistol of Mr. Cott. Then I faced them.

I yelled, "Who'll you send to the poop for a conference?"

"It's a trick! He's not on our side! Get him—get Flint!"

Reeder felt complaisance due; he possessed the temerity to lay a hand on my shoulder. I enjoyed the solid crack of my fist against his chin. He crumpled.

From above came Mr. Cott's voice: "Nice work, Flint. Come on up here."

"Only if you put that gun away."

Then I felt a hush as I faced the men, a silence in the mob born of awe or inculcated respect. Boll came to the poop.

"I suggest you humor our second, Mr. Cott." He said it with deadly calm, and when I sent him a glance, I saw his easy smile. He had reinstated me as second mate with a mere word. Not a voice lifted with jeer or threat as he moved forward and disarmed Mr. Cott, as he tossed the pistol to the crowd. Then he said contemptuously:

"I'd enjoy flogging every last one of you." The truth was lifted to its pinnacle by his lack of emphasis. "Perhaps I shall," he added, "after I've set a record to Java Head." He stood there a full minute. He seemed to have broken the back of that threat.

It is regrettable that he chose that moment to saunter off, since his presence there had the effect of oil on an angry sea. Had he remained there, that which followed shortly would not have come to pass. The effect of the crew's doing was lacking in immediate significance; rather, a climax long months hence was attained by a seemingly childish act during the course of the uprising that evening. It was thus:

At a time when Boll stood aft counting the minutes necessary to splicing cut sheets, trimming sail, and riding to the tide, I found myself faced with a crew which slowly shook off the effect of Boll's eye and words. I moved down among them, grinning out a bid for their good will, cursing them even as I did so.

"You pack of idiots! Now wouldn't he laugh to see you sitting before a judge who spits out a verdict—'I sentence you to hang for mutiny on the high seas.' Boll would enjoy seeing you squirming on the bench, toiling in some penitentiary, or swinging by your necks from a rope furnished by the law."

Under the weak deck lamps the men posed a fantastic study in facial expressions; a problem in restlessness, sadness, frustration, and anger. They seemed portraits awaiting an artist's capturing brush. There was the motion of life in them as they bobbed about on bodies in aimless wandering. Then there were sounds which snatched them back to the weary world of realities. There were then faces which belched up arguments, curses, and desires to do anything for mental relief. One man of twenty-two cried like a baby, while another youngster in his teens beat the deck with a belaying pin. It was the story of youth seeking maturity in a hurry. They hated me for my words, and at the same time they felt the truth of them. It is a part of the drama of mutiny seldom told. I talked on:

"Yeah, I'm sorry I ever tied up with you. I steal you food, and you snap at my hand like a kennel of mongrels. I stand up for your rights, and you throw me over for a fool like Jason Blue. He," I said, facing him squarely, "doesn't mind jails. He's used to them." As he braced his stalwart body, I said, "Why don't you do something about it, Mr. Blue?"

"I'd rather hear your plan." He, too, seemed amenable to only his own laws, and I, not interested in pressing him, spoke of my plan. When I had finished—I advised against any foolish uprising, suggesting that we even the score later by refusing to sail under Boll out of

Singapore—Mr. Blue was the first to chuckle. "That," he said in less antagonistic, though grating tone, "is good enough for me." He stalked off and set himself to splicing sheets without any order to do so, thereby eliminating what I thought to be the major threat.

But I was unaware of the working of adolescent minds—they were that, and bent on vandalism. The plan to desert the captain just when he was ready to sail from port appealed to their practical sense of justice, though it in no way served to appease the storm of vengeance they had brewed within themselves. I felt more secure when they scattered slowly, moving off in groups. Some asked for orders, while others slowly bunched in various spots on deck.

The Gerrymander moved into the Bay of Balimbing with the wind abeam; Boll himself stood at the wheel, and Mr. Cott and Little Ahab ran up a little sail for steerageway. Flat Cape was a dozen miles ahead, and a little island, no more than a third of a mile wide, loomed off the port bow some five miles off.

I went aft and asked about the anchorage out in that vast unknown stretch, which, dark but for northern stars and a young moon, loomed as a sequestered region in some unlit corner of a forgotten world. A peak rose up from far off, or abruptly out of the lee shore, and its height in blurred silhouette against a Dutchman's equatorial sky could have been half a thousand or ten thousand feet.

Mr. Blue had the deep-sea lead over, and he chanted out the depth. Boll, I noticed, eyed the man with a speculative eye. "We're some miles out from the five-fathom curve," Boll said. "We'll tie up at the island there and wait for the southwest wind."

He handled the wheel like a Dutch pilot, and we moved in slowly to anchorage in seven fathoms on the northeast side of the island. It was humid and hot, but it was land, and the breeze was alive with the warm, sweet scents of tropical vegetation.

It was no more than a minute after we dropped anchor when the unappeased mutineers brought their scheme into play. Boll was busy at the wheel, and every man who had volunteered for service was engaged in handling some part of the vessel. Their devilry was well timed and they, seeking some outlet for close-hauled vengeance and long-nursed acrimony, went about their work with the genius of pranksters in dead earnest. I was forward of the forecastle when I sensed something wrong.

O'Hare and eight others, including Reeder and Chess, entered the sail locker where Boll kept his big iron coffin-like box labeled: EX-PLOSIVES. They lifted it like pallbearers and moved with all the speed the weight of the box would allow to the port beam. There they hoisted it and sent it splashing overboard before any active interference could be brought into play.

It made little difference in the final outcome that Boll, in the minutes that followed, had each of the culprits lowered with ropes under their arms almost to the water, where hungry sharks espied them and moved ever closer; that he kept them there for a good hour begging for the mercy of a flogging on deck; that he paced the deck all the while, begging for the southwest monsoon's embrace with the restless sails of the *Gerrymander*—the work of the lads had been done.

Thousand upon thousands of Boll's trade coins—the balance of power in the great Gerrymander Cash scheme in months to come—had been dumped in seven fathoms near a little offshore island, the name of which was Little Fortune!

4 ✌ THE SMELL OF GAIN

WE BLEW INTO SOENDA STRAIT AT SIX BELLS ON THE GRAVE-EYE WATCH, some hours after the southwest monsoon had lowered its breath to our canvas; we tacked off the coast and spread our wings for a grapple with the current. It struck hard in an attempt to hobble the *Gerrymander's* forefeet, but with every sail flying we carried on in an uphill sea. As the strait narrowed, the current gathered force against us and our following wind slacked. We seemed to stand still under sails shaking, between Java and Sumatra, between the Indian Ocean and the Java Sea. The current won; we spent a day in gaining passage there.

Two days later we anchored in the inner roads of Singapore. Here we would meet St. Ebenezer and learn the value of the Gerrymander Cash in Formosa.

The routine of port entry was no sooner done with than Boll paid Culver's agent a visit. I went along and met Mr. Ruscomb, a slow-talking, calculating man with more polish than directness. He was tall and big, handsome of face, and crowned with a mane of graying, wavy hair. He asked of our passage and spoke of the sailing record with such marked casualness that one might think records were made daily in his world. But, as I learned, he was talking to Boll, whom he had known for years. Since Boll talked to the point, so did Ruscomb, until the business between agent and captain reached its perfunctory end. Then, in mellow tone, as if he reduced the major topic to some blithe system of probing discourse, he spoke of a huge shipment of gum camphor from Formosa.

He added, "It's odd, Captain, odd as hell. I have, of course, reported it to Mr. Culver. He should have already received my report."

There was something strange, rather ill-omened, in Boll's "Naturally."

Ruscomb continued to smile with assurance as he lifted his brows and said, "Mr. Flint is the second on board, isn't he?"

Boll replied slowly, "He's chief mate as of right now." I poled a cheek with my tongue and lifted my brows in unison with Mr. Ruscomb, who seemed not about to lapse from professional decorum. "You can talk," Boll added crisply.

"There's little to talk about." Our host smiled, eying me closely.

"Then," Boll said, "why tack off your course to the subject of camphor?"

"Because, Captain, the cargo is consigned to a Mr. Teale, Boston address. Mr. Culver will like that." He smiled, and I started. Why, I asked *sotto voce*, had Boll openly allied himself with the old figurehead carver?

"Mr. Culver won't like that," Boll corrected.

"No," Ruscomb said thoughtfully, his eyes on the seething bund of Singapore. "No, he won't, any more than he'll like another phase of the affair." He turned to face Boll once more. "The whole thing has a picaresque flavor, Captain, and St. Ebenezer's part in it makes it stink. As we both know, Mr. Culver is interested only in the *Gerrymander's* earnings, and nothing more. He will not approve your record run because of the publicity involved—or shall we say notoriety?

"Therefore, knowing our man, we must both admit it is foolish to assume that he would strike metal replicas of the figurehead which caused him embarrassment in the past.

"And by the same token, even if he chose to reverse his character role, the last man in the East to whom he would entrust the cash pieces would be our mutual acquaintance, St. Ebenezer. Right, Captain?"

Boll replied, "Don't you find unerring accuracy monotonous at times, Mr. Ruscomb? I do."

The agent paused to study the deep or shallow portent of Boll's thrust before stepping on up his precise ladder of discourse.

"Naturally the valueless coins smack of wool-pulling over the eyes of the Chinese, who own Formosa. The Government could prosecute, but——"

Boll said the rest, "The Chinese will get around to that sometime in the next century."

Ruscomb said gravely, "Mr. Culver is less dilatory, Captain."

Boll seemed to feel his wind; he made both agent and me feel it when he said, "I see a queue growing out of Culver's head also."

Mr. Ruscomb's face lost its veneered mask in the moment; surprise leaped up to widen his eyes and send his mouth into an inane pose. He gathered himself together quickly. And I, as if hired to serve as referee in a deeper-than-surface duel, laughed inwardly and created an imaginary medal for Boll.

"Captain," the agent said slowly, "Mr. Culver can relieve you of your command." He snapped his fingers, adding, "Like that."

Boll arose as if bored, and smiled. "I'll wager a thousand dollars that he won't, mister."

2

Proctor's Pub, just off the bund, hummed like a main deck, the bar the poop. The smell of the sea, the scream of the gull, blended with Eurasian girls and curtained booths, the steam of Proctor's liquors doing the work of an undulating sea. The mahogany bar under oil lamps shone like the mirror, like Proctor's hairless head; the fat nudes in frames around the walls were alternately spaced with oils of ships and schooners, as if each vessel sailed at the behest of its favorite woman. At the tables sat sailors, traders, ship chandlers, Chinese merchants, tea planters, silent Moslems in tarboosh and turban sipping at nonalcoholic drinks, Malay boatmen, and the spawn of the crossroads of the East. "A monkey for five shillings, tuan? He trim sail." "A flower for your girl, tuan?" Hawkers came and departed, as did thieves and pimps. But Proctor's Pub, layered with smoke and smelling of lamp oil, swill, disinfectant, and warm blood spilled over some chattering woman, went on day and night, quiet and deserted almost until the sunset squall from over Sumatra way ushered in a riotous, lawless evening, as sensual as it was salty.

Boll and I were to meet Mr. Wulsin and St. Ebenezer there. We arrived at about nine on our third evening at anchorage. As we stepped from a ricksha, Boll tossed the coolie a Gerrymander Cash piece and stood by for his reaction; the Chinese fingered it, bit it, smiled, and moved on. "A good omen," said Boll.

Proctor, himself, a retired British sea captain, grinned under a sweeping mustache and moved his stocky frame and double chin to meet us. Boll had set a record run, and drinks were on the house. Then we moved to a booth at the rear, Boll strutting like the Governor General himself, brushing aside the bleary-eyed hangers-on who fell all over themselves to congratulate him.

The curtain closed behind us and I made ready to meet the vaunted

St. Ebenezer. I had anticipated this meeting for some time. He was as interesting as the East; he seemed a sort of symbol of its culture, schemes, evil, and polyglot existence.

I saw a man of perhaps sixty, long-haired, short-bearded, both yellow-white; he was wide of eye: dreamy, distant, soft brown eyes in one moment, slitted, cunning eyes in the next. His eyes talked, and they caused one all sorts of wonder as to what lay behind them. Certainly he had adventured, and heavily; and equally as sure was his propensity for doing just that until he died. His mouth was small and red, and his nose was short. His face was wide and square—odd, against his huge shoulders and short stocky body. Despite his physical appearance, he had the air of some great scholar or prophet—perhaps his pale skin and ethereal eyes, the hair about his shoulders, as well as his long classically beautiful hands, had something to do with it. He wore a wrinkled but clean white suit with an open collar.

Instead of shaking my hand, he touched his forehead with relaxed fingers and leaned forward with eyes closed. A blessing in disguise, I thought, chuckling inwardly. Before I seated myself, Proctor came over.

"Two sailors departing for Hong Kong, St. Ebenezer," he said. The "saint" nodded, and soon two big Britishers stood close, their caps off, their faces sober with respect above their swaying bodies. Each handed him a handful of coins and stood with bowed heads.

St. Ebenezer stood and said in beautiful liquid voice, "May the Lord bless you with fair sailing, and luck. St. Ebenezer said it." The men bowed and moved on, and the same arresting voice said, "Dutch gin, Proctor, a quart." Then he counted the coins with a speculative eye and fell back into his normal pose.

Old Wulsin beamed; here was his hero.

"Business—down to it, gentlemen," St. Ebenezer said almost wistfully, downing an ounce of straight gin. "Let us review what I have accomplished with an eye to the future. You there, Finn, Flinn, or Flint, whatever the name, sir, tell Proctor I'm in conference. Don't wish to be disturbed." As I arose to humor him, he added importantly, "St. Ebenezer said it."

A score of seamen stood patiently on the other side of the curtain, each waiting his chance to touch the hand of a good-luck piece in human form. More arrived as I talked to Proctor. "I heard St. Ebenezer was here," each said, peering about the place. Proctor eyed them and soon prevailed upon the "saint's" graciousness: St. Ebenezer appeared with his impressive hands out before him, causing each man to bow worshipfully, a proper prelude to a forthcoming blessing. I wondered at the old man's influence, how he came by it, and how he sustained it, admiring him for an accomplishment achieved as I did so. When he sat down in the curtained booth once more, he said:

"Flint? Flint? Tom Flint! Captain Boll, you're sure of him? In the voyage of life I see him as captain, not lieutenant. I'll have your yes or no—for exonerating purposes if the need should arise." When Boll nodded, he smiled at me, saying, "A matter of form you'll excuse, Tom Flint. I'll bless any man, though I'll look deeper when I do business with him."

"Fair enough." I grinned. "But do you bless those with whom you do business?"

"With human conduct, sir, being a matter of environmental influence," he said, sweeping a hand to include the foursome, "yes." The answer was good enough for me, and I said as much.

"He's good luck to any undertaking," said Wulsin with groggy adoration. "Ask any sailor."

"Flint's in the fold," said St. Ebenezer. "Mr. Flint has a profound respect, I am sure, for pound, dollar, or guilder."

"Or cash piece," I added, causing the old boy to raise a glass in salute. Boll, I noticed, weighed me on the veriest scales of St. Ebenezer's mind.

"It is regrettable that your crew tossed the box overboard, Captain," St. Ebenezer remarked thoughtfully. "Now I can tell you why a Moslem won't eat pig or drink alcohol, or how a head-hunter in Borneo spends his wedding night, but in the co-ordination of my mental skills, I've not the slightest damned idea how one would go about striking a coin. But—since genius is pathological—I suppose that is why Mr. Wulsin, the bosun, is sitting here among us." And Mr. Wulsin, floating in a blissful state of coziness, accepted the left-handed compliment and asked for tools and material. I eyed him with a world of misgiving as I sought to reconcile a worthless bosun to a striker of coins. It was Boll's idea, however, so nothing was said about it.

"I can use ten thousand cash pieces at once," St. Ebenezer said. He spoke of Indo-China and the slow French, of the Celebes and the grasping Dutch.

"The lack of money in circulation is boon nature. The laws of economics smile on the Gerrymander Cash." He drank two ounces of gin and sat back to belch and prime both memory and tongue. Boll waited patiently.

"Now the function of money," he said at last, "is to harmonize the activities of the human being. If there is a shortage of money, the community of man is sick economically; and since such a disease strikes at stomachs and backs, the indication is that a cure is needed for the sake of human progress. Mind you—particularly you, Tom Flint—I'm an honest, benign man who seeks to correct something out of balance, a poverty caused by modern political and imperialistic contrivances. I'm a crusader, by God! Organisms of Eastern society, the native and the ruler, are positive opposites; one is lord, the other slave. I, St. Ebenezer of Singapore, stand ready to sacrifice self for mankind.

"For mankind." He downed another ounce of gin. "The Gerrymander Cash will relieve the native of his constant state of depression, if only for a time. But he'll learn to want his standard of living raised. From that point on, the primitive man will out. He'll win," he said, chuckling, "after a century or two. But I'll serve Boll the crusader. Aye! St. Ebenezer said it."

He turned a sharp eye on Boll. "Now I went to Formosa," he began, causing me to sit up with freshened interest. "As you know, Captain, you asked for camphor, not caring whether it came from hell or heaven. I engaged a leaky, smelly junk from Haiphong which had no return cargo, and persuaded the Confucianists to brave a dash across the Gulf of Siam instead of hugging the slow somber coast.

"I promised luck. I practiced Confucianism, preaching, 'Humility is the solid foundation of all virtues,' and the lumbering junk, with brown lateen sail, scull, and big baleful eyes painted on each side, sailed in the sun, by God and St. Ebenezer it did, all the way to Keelung!

"I had ten thousand of our cash pieces, the sample lot you left me, Captain. The concept of trade balance was visibly altered when I saw the pitiful lack of Chinese cash pieces in circulation. The profound negative conception of the golden rule as spoken by Confucius—'That which I do not wish others to put upon me, I also wish not to put upon others'—placed me at the crossroads of policy. Our glittering worthless cash was popular, and I was tempted to unload it and get the hell and gone with a junk heavy with camphor. It was possible, despite the British monopoly on camphor." He poured another drink and sipped at it before raising his twinkling eyes.

"By God and myself, I was tempted. However, I realized we might want more camphor.

"It was then a matter of a buzzard exercising some temporary jurisdiction over his appetite and dedicating his fast to a healthy existence.

So with the aid of a Presbyterian missionary from Indiana, with whom I discussed some nine religions over his tea and my gin, I set about to learn the desires of not only the Chinese but the head-hunters.

"He accompanied me inland, south for some sixty miles, with a Chinese escort. Beautiful country—camphor trees, bamboo thickets, and God's mountains raising their purple shoulders to the white snowy heavens, while below banana and orange groves, as wild as the land, stretched down to virgin rivers. 'The rock of ages,' I said, peering up into the cloud-fringed crags, 'since the rock is, after all, one's conception of God's whereabouts.'

"The missionary, a practical man, was eying the bush as I said it. He replied, 'Yes, St. Ebenezer, and we may attain it, literally. We're surrounded by head-hunters.'

"We were escorted to a village by the savages. They were tall men, part Indonesian, Melanesian, and Mongol. Imagine a fiercer blood. Spears, bows and arrows, long, ugly knives, together with their tattooed faces and hungry eyes, caused us to listen for the last notes from Gabriel's trumpet. That night we saw a hideous tribal dance. Poles supported trophies—skulls!—and the general idea among them was to add a few more. The moon was up and full, and stone houses and thatched roofs, as well as the banana jungle and camphor trees all around, caught the hellish pale light.

"The beauty of moonlight is, my cronies, but the reflection of circumstances, nothing more. It is the pawn of God and devil.

"I saw them sever the head from the body of one of our Chinese guards. It was very simple—an agony of fear, the stoical suppression of a scream, the spouting of blood in the moonlight, a face reacting in twitches to the shock of it, a body jerking convulsively, and stillness. It was quick. Then the head was placed on a fresh pole, and the dance around it began. Then they fed the face on the pole, and they brought it water to drink. They humored it, trying to rid it of sorrow.

"Skulls meant prosperity! Economics again. Think of the Gerrymander Cash in the same light, if you can."

I was no longer in Proctor's Pub. Mr. Wulsin's belch, Boll's flat hand on the table, his cap on the back of his head, the visor as sharp as his nose, the bottles between four connivers, all were in some moon-splashed highland village two thousand miles away. Behind the mist of a turquoise mountain lay mystery fathomed by a self-confessed saint. He talked on in beautiful voice; he lent blood-spilling a poetic vigor, did this luck charm of the Far East.

"Skulls meant prosperity," he reflected. "How very primitive is our civilization by comparison. The state of society is out of balance. Pathetic struggles of the plebeian, existing mechanisms of the rich—a skull is a skull in London, Amsterdam, or Formosa. But who am I but a saint with an eye like that on the prow of a junk—yea, dammit, who?

"So I'll drink to us, four buzzards with appetites." We drank; and the magic of the old philosopher flowed on as he told his story.

"The tribesmen danced on in a wide circle. Frenzied, one would drop out of line, reappear with his wife at the edge of a clearing, and bless her with his virility. Their social life revolved about us.

"The missionary suggested that we sing 'Rock of Ages.' We did; and I, suddenly inspired, grabbed his hand, and we joined the dancing group, shouting our song to the top of our voices. The shock was then theirs; and when all of the apes stood still, I passed out the Gerrymander Cash pieces until my pockets were empty.

"The next day they cut camphor trees, and the chips were cooked for gum camphor in huge iron kettles they'd stolen from captured Chinese over the years. Two days later we, gods of the distance who would return, left them.

"We did return a month later with every trinket my fifty pounds would buy in the port town. There I did this—listen, Captain. . . .

"I bought crude gum camphor with cash pieces, and I sold them the trinkets for the same cash pieces. It was their first experience with money. They liked it. Yes, they liked it so well that when we were ready to depart they advanced menacingly on us—gods, mind you—and robbed me of every cash piece." He laughed, then grew sober. "And the last object to meet my eye when I left was a gruesome one.

"The Chinese we'd seen beheaded was skull up on a pole, and between his teeth, which they'd pried open, was a round gleaming Gerrymander Cash."

3

Wulsin winced, and I poured a drink. The "saint" said, "Now will that rest well on your stomach or mind, Captain?"

"I smell camphor," Boll replied. "Suppose you finish your tale." I could see respect in St. Ebenezer's face. "How did you clear port, and how did Ruscomb learn about the cash?"

"As I said, I could have left Formosa flooded with Gerrymander Cash pieces. The English paid off in shillings and the Chinese cash, damn few of either. So with our money popular, camphor came in crude and refined, honestly, as well as by theft from the warehouses.

"I borrowed five hundred dollars from the missionary. I moved to Hong Kong for supplies. Chopsticks, fans, shoes, kimonos, and such, I bought sparingly. I put the money to better use with old duck eggs, bêche-de-mer, shark fins, lotus seeds for soup, idols, English parasols, and a maze of gewgaws. These I sold for the Gerrymander Cash, which I'd recently spent in buying up camphor.

"Thus the cash piece had an established value."

Boll asked, "The total cost of the venture was what?"

St. Ebenezer extended a tallied sheet and said, "Considering the camphor alone, the cost was about twenty-two cents on the dollar against the market price in Formosa!"

"Where's the profit?" I asked. "Forgetting the cash pieces, wouldn't the five hundred dollars' worth of gewgaws have turned the trick?"

"My dear Tom Flint!" St. Ebenezer said with lofty condescension. "Any trader who does business with the Chinese will tell you you'll do well to double your money."

Boll said, "Consider the value of that, Mr. Flint." Then he turned on our "saint" and said gruffly, "Now about Ruscomb. He claims reason for the Chinese Government to prosecute. What was your error, and how did he know about it?"

"He had a man up there for tea. And my error, if any was made, is that some two thousand of our cash pieces are still in circulation."

"An error can be beautiful." Boll smiled. "But you said, 'considering the camphor alone.' Now just what else did you bring?"

"Oh, that! Sometimes the activity of the tongue lends the mind a feeling of inadequacy, Captain. I often swear I'll expel gin from my diet. However, I brought opium for those who enjoy hitting the pipe."

"From camphor to opium," chuckled Wulsin. "Damn me for a poor bosun if that ain't mixin' the smells into paregoric!"

Boll's reply seemed typical of the man when he quoted the ancient writer, Juvenal: "The smell of gain is good from any source."

4

The *Gerrymander*, impervious to the doing of her master and mate, sat out days in the roads at steamy, sweaty, squally anchorage; wandering sampans, lighters, and junks floated by, their destination unknown in an equatorial lapping of the seething Strait of Singapore. The ship's horizon was haze, glare, sail and mast, a rusty steamer or two, a city on a strip of foreshore, and the distant, lonely islands of the Dutch

Riouw Archipel to the south. Without sails flying, she seemed but the husk of her mortal self.

Boll sent for me one day at sunset. St. Ebenezer lay stretched out on the silk divan, hands folded across chest. Boll eyed me, at last breaking his silence with: "Mr. Ruscomb has contracted cargo for Hong Kong." He paused for thoughtful silence, then said:

"Now about the crew, Mr. Flint. Your work is cut out for you."

The job ahead of me called for precision balancing in a play with the emotions of the crew. Boll had wanted time in which to motivate his cash pieces into action; though that was before the crew dumped them at Little Fortune Island. Now he needed time in which to strike another supply.

"It might be well for you to bend an elbow in the fo'c'sle," he added. "There's whisky in the chest 'tween decks."

As I nodded and stood to go, Boll said, "The crew is above the ordinary, Mr. Flint. I want to keep it in the end." He added a surprise when he said, "You realize the men rebelled because our ex-chief mate held a pistol on them."

I saw the light: Boll, with no excuse to relieve Mr. Cott of his duties, was creating reasons that would minimize even Culver's intervention in his behalf. The crew would serve the captain once more.

In the weeks that followed, I rose to the task assigned me with all the artistry of a misanthropic genius, despising the work with a passion. If any ship's officer had ever before toyed with a crew's mind in such manner I have yet to learn of it. In brief, they refused to sail to Hong Kong, and I advanced them pay, out of Boll's purse, for their lodging in Singapore—in order to prevent their signing aboard other ships—under the pretext of getting a better deal for all. Thus I managed to hold them intact.

In the meantime, for the benefit of the log, we ran crew after crew of sailors aboard the Gerrymander. Each remained for only a short time, always departing before the fictitious sailing date. They heard that the Gerrymander was a hellship—another part of my work.

Mr. Cott had not been informed of his discharge, though he suspected some breach in his relations with Boll. It was vague in his incredulous mind, though it was there. All the while, Boll, together with St. Ebenezer and old Wulsin, secured an old lever coining press. The dies completed, the old press spewed out a new supply of the Gerrymander Cash. Then, at Boll's signal, I turned my influence once more on the crew, blaming everything that had happened on Mr. Cott: he had a flair for brutality; it was he who had asked that rations be reduced; it was he who had wanted to empty his pistol into the angry crew during the uprising.

At last they agreed to ship under Boll—provided Tom Flint was made first officer. Jason Blue was their choice for a second. They wanted Mr. Cott dismissed.

Boll mustered them on deck one day, resorting to mild dissuasion: "Mr. Cott meant no harm." The crew was adamant, however, and Boll said, "I'll consider your demands on one condition, that you put them in writing and affix your signatures to the document."

He waited with the text of the petition ready for me, and before ten that night the last man of them had filed in to sign his name to as big a lie as any mortal ever read. Mr. Wulsin sat back, sad-eyed even as he chuckled, while the famed St. Ebenezer of Singapore blessed each man individually; and, I might add, memorably.

A half-hour later Boll sent for Mr. Cott, who had been absent, at Boll's order, that afternoon. He entered, tense, a curious twisted smile on his cavernous face; he hesitated as his drooping eyes swept the four faces which sent pitiless and expressionless eyes into him; he must have felt the breath of unhealthy judgment due in the moment, and by that rapid mental association of cause and effect, there is small doubt that he knew a flurry of guilt, deserved or not.

"Sit down, Mr. Cott," said Boll. When the mate draped himself to a chair, Boll extended the signed petition and asked, "What's the meaning of this?"

Then, "A drink, Mr. Cott?" he said nicely, extending bottle and glass. But Mr. Cott was busy with a worded sentence which he knew would call for a verdict:

We, the members of the crew of the Gerrymander, appeal to the sense of justice which the captain has always exhibited in our behalf—— Even the wording was above the level of any of the sailors; and the essence—well! Mr. Cott read on, his face twisting into anger packed with slow shock; and we eyed him like the four carrion-pickers we were. *We remained at our stations, as becomes our sublime duty while on the open sea, doing more than growling among ourselves at the cold brutalities inflicted upon us at every opportunity by the chief mate.*

Mr. Cott breathed hard, and his mouth worked over his big teeth; anger, or injury, or both, seethed into the open. *Unknown to you, we were served victuals unfit for human consumption and we suffered in silence under threat of irons or flogging in the holds.* Mr. Cott raised his face and gazed malevolently at me for some time. I noticed he did not face Boll. He poured a drink with hands shaking, ran his upper teeth with tongue, and drank. *The cook as well as the boatswain and second will attest to the above. There is also the matter of Mr. van Buskin's death, which Mr. Cott brought about by criminal negligence when he forced our deceased shipmate into the tophamper during the severest blow of our voyage.*

Mr. Cott breathed jerkily and shook all over. His nostrils flared and his upper lip twitched. Another stiff drink settled him somewhat. "I've read enough," he said.

"Read on," Boll ordered. "I'd like some word from you when you've finished."

A reply came at last, after the first officer had read a detailed account of his own crimes, after he had scanned the strong plea for his replacement: "The blackest lie that was ever written, sir."

"Surely, Mr. Cott," Boll said, as if weighing denial against charge, "such accusations are not without some foundation."

"Right." The mate laughed evilly. "They name the wrong man, and you know it; and they didn't write that, not our crew." Boll mentioned the signatures and asked if Mr. Cott denied any guilt. "Sir," came the whining answer, "you know I've served you well for years. What are you doing to me?"

"I, Mr. Cott?" Boll said, meeting his eyes squarely. "I tried to talk the crew out of this today, as any of the men will tell you. Let's put it the other way around. It seems you're trying to hand me a crewless ship. Is that the way to serve me?"

"But it's not true. You—I didn't——" As if sensing the utter futility of words, he searched each of our faces; but we met his glances with pitiless eyes. "You, Flint, you're to blame for this!" he said angrily. "You framed me." I said nothing as I continued to bore him with silent eyes. He talked on, whining, almost crying, blowing out his cheeks, and wiping his nose on his wrist, as he purged himself of growing anger and injury. But not a man of us said a word after that; we merely sat like patient hangmen, each with a cold, lazy reflection of a gallows in his eyes. Then Mr. Cott babbled out questions in defense of self; his mutterings seemed evoked more by the strain of silence rather than by the false charges of the crew. We used him up, we let him burn on his own mental kindling. The effect was worse than that of any whip.

"I'll get even!" he cried. "There's plenty Mr. Culver would like to know." He moved to the door, shaking like a man in the throes of a hard chill.

A long heavy silence hung over the room after his departure. To myself I said, "Mr. De Loach, I wonder if the partnership is worth the role I'm forced to play." Slowly the four of us eyed each other, our faces working into grins.

"The ways of the Lord are strange," St. Ebenezer said.

Boll added, "And the way of the transgressor is hard."

"We're due for weather," Mr. Wulsin said.

Some light remark was expected from me, though I was busy trying to fathom Mr. Wulsin's prediction: did he mean the elements or, worse, mighty retribution? I glanced at our audience on the wall. Mr. Culver remained impassive, and the ship seemed in no greater danger than before; but Harriet Adams!—it was there I met with a surprise an expression I had never seen before:

Her eyes were as straightforward as usual, though they seemed filled with accusation and temper; she aimed them at me! Illusions? I thought not. I jerked my head toward Boll, who at the moment said: "Good riddance is gain, and——

"The smell of gain is good from any source."

I drew the sharp eyes of St. Ebenezer and Boll when I said in a slow, tight grin, "No matter the stench."

BOOK TWO ❧ 1885

5 &cedilla; HARRIET ADAMS'S STAND

THE FIRM OF CULVER AND ADAMS LAY BEHIND AN UNIMPRESSIVE DOOR
upon which its name was done in ordinary black letters.

It was, physically, a series of small rooms stretching the length of
the building's Atlantic Avenue side. Equally unimpressive was the
scene on the other side of the door: a rail behind which were aged
desks and tables—Dean Adams's first, and no doubt set down in the
same spot forty years earlier—all symbols of a diligent thrift since; an
old cashier's cage at the back wall joined another narrow door through
which more clerks passed to other offices; tall stools for the slanting
desks of account keepers, and massive roll-top desks, dusty and messy,
above which hung maps, faded pictures, and models of barks, a rope
manufacturer's placard, or an enterprising ship chandler's greeting.
Beyond the row of small, crowded clerks' offices a narrow hallway
divided four larger rooms. The last office, overlooking the avenue
and wharves, belonged to Culver. It, too, bore the marks of unostenta-
tion; frugality, in fact.

The second-fiddle executive was a man whose title was hardly com-
mensurate with his long-term rule of Culver's domain. He was the
chief cashier, an elongated, sallow-faced, gray-haired man who seemed
more one's conception of an expressionless undertaker than plodding
genius who knew every detail of that vast business of Culver and
Adams. His name was John Boston. It was his sad, discerning eye that
penetrated ships, captains, and cargoes with an alertness to the slightest discrepancy. He had, in his earlier years, signed on board the
Quatre Bras, of which Robert Culver was captain. He, in brief, made
his wagon fast to Culver's star with a hard anchor knot. It held, and

when De Loach stumbled into disfavor, Mr. Boston gradually took over his duties, though not his title. The relationship of Culver and his executive arm was as cold and unemotional as that of two figures in wax, neither evincing a desire for any camaraderie beyond the affairs of business.

On the morning before the directors' meeting, John Boston assorted the incoming mail, wrote out checks for Culver's signature, trod the offices like some robot tyrant that never quite acted the role, talked to repairmen, wharf and warehouse managers, drank four cups of black coffee, and tidied all reports for the coming meeting before depositing them with Mr. Culver's secretary. He then took his place in the cage and eyed the money boxes, the cashiers, the office behind him, and the closed outer door. When the door opened and the bell above tinkled, he sent a sleepy gaze at the huge man who entered on fresh sea legs.

"Mr. Boston," boomed the visitor. "Glad tidings and congratulations—yer Gerrymander jest set a record to Java Head. The Boston reporters met our ship for news—we had it, by damn, we did!"

Mr. Boston spoke, working his blue lips slowly before and after his words: "Calm your voice, Captain Larcy. Mr. Culver is in."

"Lay aloft with yer fears. I ain't sailin' no Culver ship—don't ever expect to—I'm here with papers from yer agent, Ruscomb. All the way from Singypore." Mr. Boston advanced, eying the clerks, who exchanged covert glances and made a pretense of work.

"Captain Larcy, you'll favor me with the papers, which I'll properly receipt, and with a visit to a coffeehouse with your t'gallant voice."

"Aye." The captain chuckled. "The sun's over the foreyard, and ye'll talk with whisky instead o' chickory wash if ye'd learn about Cap'n Boll. But maybe the image fer as fine a piece o' carvin' as the dolphins of the stream ever swom under wouldn't like to hear how the Striker blowed so much sail——"

"Captain Larcy!" the chief cashier said impatiently.

"—that he had to borrow the shirts off the crew's back fer sail. And what's more, the Indian Ocean was streaked with canvas and blood from Africa to Australia. Blow me——"

Robert Culver stood in the doorway next to the cashier's cage, his eyes boring deep into the captain, who returned the stare with a marked loss of bravado. Mr. Boston worked his mouth around big yellow teeth, glancing from master to intruder. Culver, hat in hand, moved to the front and paused to dissect a rival firm's captain in wordless manner.

"She set a record—sir," Captain Larcy managed to say. "Good cap'n, the Striker, sir. One o' the best."

An interval of strained silence, and Culver accepted the mail sent by Mr. Ruscomb, placed hat atop his head, and passed out of the office without so much as a "Good day."

2

Harriet Adams peered at the court of Louisburg Square four floors below. The grass wore a midsummer green, though the weather, chilly and disagreeably wet, blew out of the northeast as if it had forgotten the season. The stately old square was empty of traffic, and the timed beat of horses' hoofs and the rolling of closed cabs on Mt. Vernon Street moved closer, were heard with muffled distinctness for a moment, then faded. The sound was eternal, like waves in the distance, and as soothing. Every surface below—the cobblestone of the drive, the quiet black fence, the red brick sidewalks—and every blade of grass glistened like varnished objects. A carriage turned into the square, its black top a wet mirror for a thinning sky, rolled to a stop at number seventeen. A man got out, and the horses moved slowly on around the square and turned east.

"Odd," she said. "Mr. Culver seldom comes home before noon." Then she remembered the directors' meeting scheduled for two that afternoon. She sighed heavily, realizing that today she must attend what she supposed would be a long soporific meeting which held respected reins on the destiny of Culver and Adams. Mr. Culver, by now in the house, was perhaps ordering a whisky sour in the seldom-used salon, scowling at the clock, the huge Culver table and chairs, at the vacant yet supporting faces at which he would glare and direct gruff barkings a few hours hence. He came home early always before such meetings, as if he felt it necessary to rehearse privately his various dispositions before the curtain's rise. But seldom had he arrived before noon.

She smiled; it was a tolerant, humoring little smile which any mother might show as she reviewed a spoiled child's doing: he literally gobbled up and digested the directorate, causing her to think of them as nameless dummies that nodded like trained yesmen, all rigid pawns for his ego. He stood over them, eyebrow high, a strange and terrible potentate; he sat in the big chair at the end of the table, telling them with directness and inference that he had made them, that he struck an opposite to the thinking of Sophocles, in which every man loves what he has made himself. They seemed to remind him of that despised object which he never mentioned, the great ship *Gerry-mander*.

She continued to smile even as she bit her lips and considered a fact. She had come of age since the last meeting of directors, the age stipulated in her father's will—twenty-two. The dictum, the problem then, was her right to speak with the voice of her legacy, over half of the shares in the firm of Culver and Adams. Who then should sit in the big chair at the end of the table?

She turned from the deep window seat, walked to the little French and feminine marble mantel, and looked down into the small blaze. Her room with its faded old colors of soft rose and gray, dashed with subdued blues and reds, was alive with memories antedating young womanhood. It was setting and environment, home and nest, and silent authority of the science of New England dignity. She realized with a sense of warm satisfaction that she was as much a fixture to the room as she was to the life of Beacon Hill.

Her father had died in the very house where she lived. So had her mother. She had been left in the care of her father's sister, Emily, the wife of Robert Culver's brother, Jim. The material wealth left by her parents would be hers on her twenty-second birthday. Until that time, Robert Culver, who had come to live with them before his brother's death in 'seventy-seven, would watch over her fortune.

She had been brought up in a precise and simple manner that conformed to the amenities of her station in life. She was a finished product, accomplished in a way; she enjoyed life and all that made up life in her sphere. Thus it was only natural that she should leave business affairs to men of business. Aunt Emily shaped her mind as well as her life, while Mr. Culver managed her affairs. She had faith in the judgment of both.

However, Mr. Culver's silence regarding her majority in the firm of Culver and Adams continued to annoy her. She had been twenty-two for several months, and some mention of the matter seemed proper. The very fact that it was long overdue, that she had given him several opportunities in which to at least acknowledge her voting right, fed her mind with mild anxiety. She was both curious and resentful.

As usual, whenever she paused to weigh the matter her mind went back to the evening of her birthday:

The last guest had departed, and she had turned to the living room. As she entered, Mr. Culver stood with feet apart, as if on a ship, peering straight at her. Somewhat astonished by his fixity of eye, she paused momentarily in an effort to reconcile his expression to the gaiety of minutes before.

Aunt Emily sat at the far end of the room, looking over her glasses at a pair of unframed English etchings.

"Harriet." His tone seemed to say he had suddenly discovered she was no longer a child. "A word with you." The executive was rebilling her in transit; they called it reconsignment when dealing in merchandise, and she felt the word fitted. True, he had never been noticeably unkind, or kind, to her; rather, he had always been formal. Across the table at breakfast, or on quiet Tuesday evenings at home, or in public, it was the same. He had built a wall around his inner self since the figurehead episode four years ago. And Aunt Emily, her father's own sister, had humored his silence.

She moved toward him. His lips managed a smile. After an interval in which she stole a glance at Aunt Emily before meeting his eyes directly, he said:

"You have grown up." It was as if he unwound the clock; she had been grown for years. But she suspected a compliment in his tone of discovery.

"Yes?" She smiled. Since she was woman, she felt the compliment in his eyes; but she kept a New Englander's tight rein on her small emotions.

"I am very proud," he said, as if experimenting in the art of unbending. With visible effort, he continued: "The handling of your business affairs has been an esteemed responsibility."

"Thank you." She was sure he was leading into the subject of business, and she awaited his next words anxiously.

"But now that you are of age, you form the ideal combination to draw fortune-hunters. You possess both beauty and wealth." She moved to an armchair. "Some of our very select young men are hotspurs. I saw several in a fidget this evening." He turned his eyes to the blazing fire, then up at the portrait of Harriet's mother. "I'd enjoy putting any man of your choice before the mast for a test."

She wondered at his strange approach, as well as at Aunt Emily's alert silence.

"Mettle," he said gruffly, turning upon her, "sometimes outpoints lineage in a man."

"I haven't reached the point of making a choice," she replied evenly. "However, I agree with you."

"Sometimes the choice is made by you before you realize it is happening."

"Is my conduct up for reproach, sir?"

Emily spoke up: "No, Harriet. Your mother exacted a promise from me—that the man of your choice should be of your set, or an equal in the eyes of society. Mr. Culver offered his advice at the time, and so I have asked him to broach this subject to you."

"Why not you, Auntie?"

"Simply because Robert can better explain the essential relationship of your behavior to the prestige of the firm." She sounded impatient. "And, too, he knows Captain Boll better than I."

"Captain Boll!" Harriet exclaimed.

"I'll come to that," Culver said hurriedly as Emily sighed. "But back to the subject. I told your mother that I thought the man whom society approved should be a man and not a fop." He sought support here: "Did I not, Emily?" She nodded.

"And is the combination so very impossible?" Harriet asked.

"That, my dear girl, is a question you'll direct to yourself," he replied.

"Of course. Of course," she said. "But I'm really not interested in anyone."

Her eyes leaped up to his in surprise as he said, "I am not a spy, but when a note rests on the stairs in front of me, I take the privilege of stooping for it. My position as the head of the firm is a prompter when I voice an honest objection to the man who wrote it. While your choice of friends is your prerogative, and your aunt's direct responsibility, and minus any interference from me as in the past, my interest in your welfare forces my voice."

"Note?" she said, lifting her brows.

"From Captain Boll," he said in stiff apology.

"Oh!" she said with an innocence as disarming as it was surprising.

"I didn't know you even knew him," he said with a question embedded in his tone.

"Yes. I met him on the day of the ship's ceremony. He called that afternoon—to express his regrets." She saw him swell about the neck and knit his jaw muscles to suppress the surge of anger and resentment.

"He's a good captain, Harriet." He brought up his control nicely. "And that's all."

Harriet was curious; she said, "I know little about him other than what I've heard you say about his driving a ship to a profit."

"Profit is one thing, and notes to you are another, Harriet. I'll say again that my advice here is that of the head of the firm. This Boll is an odd sort. They do not call him the Striker without reason. Ten years ago, when he was only twenty-five, he left Boston as second mate aboard the fast bark *Red Hawk*, out of Baltimore. When the ship reached San Francisco, Boll was her captain. He'd run her around in a hundred days. She'd never made it in less than four months. In the investigation, neither Boll nor the crew would talk much. The ship's log said the captain and chief mate she left with were put ashore with yellow fever. The captain turned up two years later—insane. Out of that mystery, Boll earned the title of Striker. He's a hard man to do business with. He drives a hard bargain, and always with everything shaped to his favor.

"He maneuvered the *Lydia Case* into an embarrassing position in Hamburg once. When the owners at last agreed to double his one-eighth interest in her, all difficulties disappeared miraculously. He's out to get the dollar. Fortunately, I've made things so financially interesting for him that we have little cause for worry.

"But"—he frowned—"his notes to you are cause for alarm, Harriet. Do you understand?" She did not answer. "He's a wicked man where a dollar is concerned. And I've heard—a warning, mind you—that women are drawn to wicked men."

"I really wouldn't know," she said with noticeable resentment.

She smiled mischievously and said, "In his case, mettle outranks lineage. Is that what you meant to illustrate, sir?"

Robert Culver did not answer with words; he glared. She raised her violet-blue eyes and said with feigned seriousness, "Now I must ask if the combination you seek isn't really impossible."

"Harriet!" Emily scolded.

"He's not of the Hill; he never could be!" Culver snapped.

"Nor were you," she retorted nicely. "You were a driving captain, like Boll. But you are of the Hill now."

"Which," he said, drawing himself erect and setting his thin, hard lips as if for battle, "should prove to you that the combination is not impossible. And yet, there is need for caution."

"I did not once entertain any doubt of it," she said, sure of her triumph in a moment. But she underestimated the man whom few on Atlantic Avenue chose to engage. "I think there are many eligible gentlemen on the Hill whom one might call real men."

"I know of only one," he said, moving to the doorway as if the ordeal of discourse with a mere girl bored him immensely.

"And he?" she said, smiling after him.

He turned about slowly. His reply was softly spoken, and yet it carried the tone of assurance. The one word he uttered caused her eyes to leap up instinctively; the word he spoke was:

"Myself."

Harriet turned to her aunt, who pretended more than a natural interest in the etchings. "What is this, Aunt Emily? And why, pray tell, did you permit him to meddle in my private life?"

"Now that you're of age, you can't be too careful."

"True. But why should he be the one to tell me that—to reprimand me because I received a note?"

"You owe a lot to Robert, child," her aunt said placatingly.

She moved to her dressing table and looked directly into her own eyes. "Possessiveness and authority are very much a part of him," she said. Thus she made a temporary peace with Mr. Culver, drove out any further interest in the high-back chair at the directors' table, and busied herself before the mirror.

"Captain Boll, he said, is wicked. Women are drawn to wicked men, he said. Women. So I'm not alone," she thought, her mind going back to that day in which the ship's ceremony turned into a scandal, when the bold captain they called the Striker had kissed her. He had not asked to see her again, though he continued to write to her at six-month intervals. Purely impersonal notes—about the scenery in some port—always attached to some little gift he sent along. Why? There was no answer, unless he wished to humor the biggest stockholder in the firm. She laughed lightly; she was no man's fool, let alone Captain Boll's.

She was thus engaged when timid knuckles rapped on her door. Miss Hobbes, the spinster housekeeper, said, "Mr. Culver would like to see you, Miss Harriet. He's in the oval salon."

The door to the oval salon was open and Harriet walked in.

It was a seldom-used, almost useless room. Her parents had entertained there, she recalled as she ran fond eyes over its solid mahogany doors, its richly hung walls of pale yellow silk damask, and its oval rug of tinted rose and blue-gray. A white fireplace and imported mirrors, a few old pictures and armchairs completed the furnishings except for the barbaric long table and clumsy chairs against which the room rebelled. Aunt Emily had thought it wise to accede to the wishes of her brother-in-law, Robert Culver.

On the table were papers galore. She glanced at the fireplace where Culver stood, his back to the room and arms folded across chest, perfectly motionless.

"You sent for me?" she said, moving to a sofa.

"Yes." He did not turn about. "I am not sure that I spoke to you about the necessity of your presence at all directors' meetings from now on." So he was getting around to some recognition of her inheritance. She waited expectantly, her eyes resting calmly on his back where his hands were now joined.

"Otherwise I shall exercise the usual power of vote." She said nothing. "That is all—now," he said.

So she had walked two flights of stairs for this! Tempted to voice her annoyance, she bit her lip and considered the value of silence, realizing this aspect would serve her better now. But when he turned about and seemed surprised that she had not departed, she was not so sure.

She said, frowning, "I have ample time. You requested my presence here, so you may proceed."

"I have delivered my message."

"Surely, sir, I am not to believe you would have me travel the stairs for just that." She smiled, and he stood for a moment of dispassionate examination before sending a mild glance to the table.

He said, "I'm sorry if I've inconvenienced you, Harriet."

3

She was not tardy at the meeting that afternoon; she accepted a hard chair along with the ten men present, determined to sit level with the best of them through an ordeal of talk and cigar smoke. She thought of her mother, who had once received her friends in the high-back chair, of the soft sofa nearby which had not known society's presence since the day ships invaded this room of gray, rose, gold, and Hepplewhite. But ships and men and oceans had made the room possible, and ships continued to fly under the house flag, even though the white A in a red field had been swallowed by the maw of a huge C.

She thought with amusement that she should be forced to marry a man whose name began with O if only to devour the dominant C. And with this thought came the sudden realization that a small feud was brewing between Culver and herself.

Her sensibilities were vaguely disturbed once more. The company in the room contrasted with that genteel society of her memory. Some quality of abounding life seemed to have fled, leaving behind stripped and dusty beauty like flowers pressed between the leaves of a book. In this room she had entertained the members of her class not too many years before: Claire and Lydia stood in her mind's eye before the mantel in conversation about a handsome young man, while the French teacher sipped tea with a group in the very spot where Mr. Culver's huge table sat at the moment. Her throat was suddenly tight as a mild surge of rebellion rose up in her. In the next moment the majesty of the room and its memories belittled her and a foolish problem.

Aunt Emily sat back of her, silent though dominant even as she crocheted. The faces of the men at the table were real, and she accepted them as she ran the table with appraising eyes.

Nine men and Robert Culver: with the exception of Mr. Boston, they were all short in stature, either thin or fat; a baldpate, a gray head, a leonine mane, a stringy, last-hope rim of mouse-colored hair, a nice crop of curls; and all over again with natural variations, above ruddy, sallow, and indoor faces—all minor stockholders, but voting factors nevertheless. They felt her presence, they manifested it by slow, expressionless glances her way; she smiled inwardly and decided that she would not have missed this silly meeting for a pretty penny.

The affair wore on through the reading of reports pertaining to dollars never idle; either they came into or moved out of the coffers, and reasons why were tied to ships, freight rates, real estate, cargoes, wrecks, captains, weather, and the over-all disbursement of good and poor judgment: the Governor Winthrop, unseaworthy, had been sold to a Swedish firm; the Nelly Swift had struck on a bar and was burned from necessity; the square-rigged Aladdin was still tied up in a yellow-fever port in South America; the Honolulu sugar run had earned little for two years—it was worthy of discussion—and the drop in coastwise shipping had caused two ships to be laid up at a high cost; the Shanghai Packet had earned a nice profit, as had the Atlantic Queen, though the latter's captain had cost the firm most of her profit in a suit brought by an English firm.

Harriet remembered her mother's protests at just such a meeting years before. The incongruous table and chairs had not been there; and she, ten at the time, had sat apart, quiet and somehow more afraid of subjects she did not understand than the host of men present. Her mother's arguments centered about the Atlantic Queen, her favorite of the line. There was a suit: the ship had rammed a French schooner near Brest, and Mr. Culver had spoken of the rules of the stream, declaring he would file countersuit. She remembered her mother's sigh and Mr. Culver's victory. But that had been twelve years ago. She brought her mind back to the present meeting.

The young secretary, a peculiar-looking chap with a big body and small head, peered over thick horn-rim glasses and said painfully, "And the—er—vessel under the command of Captain Boll has earned more than the combined revenue of the *Shanghai Packet* and *Atlantic Queen* for the second successive year." He named a figure and let it go at that.

Harriet asked, "What ship is that, please?"

The young man, thoroughly bewildered, replied, "The ship we number for records as G-53." A formidable silence hung over the table and it seemed loath to evaporate as every eye there took note of Miss Adams's suddenly agitated face. Then she calmly asked the name of the vessel. "The—er—Gerrymander," came the answer.

Robert Culver spoke: "We do not mention that name."

"Isn't that rather unusual, sir—having a ship we do not call by name?" Harriet asked.

"She operates officially as a number," Culver said, his eyes falling sharply on Harriet. "Now we shall continue with the business at hand. When it is completed I have something to say about the G-53."

The meeting wore on for another long half-hour. Then Robert Culver shuffled his papers, cleared his throat, and frowned at every one present. "Our agent in Singapore sent me a bit of news which I have been holding for about a month. I'll read you his first letter. It is as follows:

" 'Some months after the G-53 departed in 1884, our tea buyers returned from Formosa with news of odd and sharp trading in gum camphor. Instead of buying with the Chinese cash and the British pound, the money used was a new piece, which I enclose. It seems that the odd adventure was a success. The trader took a large supply of camphor out of Formosa. He did it in this manner: He bought camphor with this unorthodox coin, then fetched trade goods, which he sold at bargain prices for this coin. It is hardly a swindle, since he gave value received. The aftermath was a slight trade panic, and a reluctance on the part of the Chinese and natives to accept the usual return for produce.

" 'I have been slow in reporting this, due to the necessity of piecing some explanation together here. I am awaiting the return of Captain Boll to discuss the matter with him in person.' "

Culver reached for another letter. "Today Captain Larcy of the Pace Company's *Dragonfly* brought the second report. I'll read the high points of Mr. Ruscomb's letter. He says Captain Boll has a new chief mate, a Mr. Thomas Flint." He turned to Mr. Boston. "You'll check on this Flint, John."

"Sir, I've done so. Captain Larcy told me about him after you left this morning. I got busy." Culver asked him for the report. "Aye, sir. He comes from Texas. A son of an old sea captain from Galveston. Had one year at Harvard before going to sea on coastwise schooner, *City of Charleston*; captained her four years later; drove her on the rocks at Cape Cod in the seventies' storm; cited for bravery in saving most of crew; made captain of bark *Clementine* out of Cardiff a year later; demoted suddenly, then made captain of the bark *Cape Race*, owned by De Loach and Company——"

De Loach and Company! Faces sharpened and eyebrows lifted perceptibly. The chief cashier continued: "Signed on as second aboard the G-53 under Captain Boll, current voyage."

Culver's jaw tightened with the mention of De Loach; otherwise his aplomb was sustained. "You'll check further, John. Now to finish this message." He read from Ruscomb's account of the camphor deal:

" 'I have talked to Captain Boll, who did not deny that he was responsible for the coin as well as the camphor experiment. Our tea buyers have approached the Chinese Government, though the strange business looms as a puzzle, which, to quote Captain Boll, "They, the Chinese, will get around to solving it sometime in the next century!" When I said you were less dilatory, Captain Boll remarked, "I see a queue growing out of Culver's head also!" ' "

The directors sat up to view an item of interest with an expectancy that was nothing short of a pleasant balm for dullness. The smell of cleverness tinctured with profit on gum camphor seemed to awaken some long-depressed quality of adventure in each of them, with the possible exception of Culver, who whiffed at the smell of bold challenge. Where questions were due, there was silence. All awaited Culver's explanation.

He said bluntly, the seaman ruling the executive, "The man has turned into a damned rogue, it seems." Nor did he apologize for his speech.

The banker of the lot, a close friend of Robert Culver, asked, "What happened to the first officer—a Mr. Cott, I believe? Where was he?"

Said Harriet, drawing mild censoring eyes to a woman's voice in affairs of business, "When did Captain Boll find the time to execute such schemes?"

Culver replied gruffly, "There is no explanation of Mr. Cott's dismissal. He's served us diligently. And I put him aboard to keep me informed of Boll's doing. As to the last question, Captain Boll employed birds of a feather to test his unholy swindling device while he ran the ship. It's all a year old, says Mr. Ruscomb. 'A man named St. Ebenezer, a barroom saint, suspected swindler, ex-trader, linguist, at one time a professor of an Australian university, and an actor on the Sydney stage, is working with Captain Boll.'

"Another damned rogue. And to further prove the existence of premeditated fraud, Ruscomb writes: 'The shipment of camphor is booked as cargo aboard our ship G-53. The consignee is Mr. Augustus Teale of Boston.' "

The directorate sat stiff in amazement. The name Teale! Teale, the figurehead carver. Culver had spoken it! The name suggested something deeper than a scheme to be admired for sheer genius and passed off with casualness. Why Teale, if Boll was not using him for a tool, and why any association between Boll and the old figurehead carver whose duplicity had shaken Boston? Everyone there, including Harriet, asked that; silence seemed packed with the question. And even Aunt Emily, apart from them on a sofa, laid down her crocheting.

Robert Culver arose, paced the floor for some seconds, then turned to glare at everyone present, one by one. Then he said: "It seems that Boll has sold out to De Loach."

Harriet winced. She did not dare condone Boll's doing, and yet she felt that he was being tried and condemned in too much of a hurry. She said, "Sir, I would hardly go so far as to say that."

He looked at her. "And why not?"

"Why should he? You picked Captain Boll to do a job. He did it. And you paid him."

"When I make a mistake, I am quick to admit it," he said gruffly. "I still think there's a plot afoot—to swindle and disgrace us."

"But," Harriet said, "aren't you hasty in judging Amos—Mr. De Loach?"

"No!" the booming voice of Culver sounded. "They're clever, the whole lot of them. Too clever. They thought they could cover the scheme publicly by running the ship to a new record. That ship!" He grew purple about the neck and the veins on his forehead stood out like cords as he picked up the Gerrymander Cash which Ruscomb had sent along and flung it to the table.

There was a hollow, spurious sound as the coin struck. Soon the cash piece was picked up and passed around the table. When it was in Culver's hand again, he said:

"You've seen it with your own eyes. You've heard of its use in the hands of a swindler of the East, and you've heard of its connection with Augustus Teale. Boll's partners! I say again there's a plot afoot to swindle and disgrace us. But by the Lord and a purple dolphin, it's not too late to stop it!"

4

Harriet reshaped her opinion of such meetings; never had she enjoyed herself more. Her eyes shone with the spontaneity of a child, with excitement over the scheme itself, its depth of mystery and cunning. She pardoned its larcenous origin, hoping the definition hasty and in error. She considered the Gerrymander's achievement, a run to a record, and she saw sails bulging, striving forward at a captain's order. Aye, and the captain himself struck at her fancy, the man and the temerity of the man. All else was dwarfed.

She was suddenly shocked by what she was thinking. It was not like her to let her mind roam excitedly and admiringly to any questionable person or enterprise. But there was something fascinating about Boll and this cash piece. And she could not quite reprove herself, since she was sure her father's adventuresome spirit had risen up in her. She was glad, however, that her aunt could not read her mind then.

Culver spoke: "I'm going to Singapore. The *Shanghai Packet* is due in port soon, and I promise she won't tarry in the harbor." A hard, salty smile wreathed his face, whether from anticipation of a good battle, the very challenge of it, or a subdued yearning for a tussle with the sea.

"You'll announce her run, John, and get her a full hold. Captain Boll is through, and I'll spare no effort or expense to put him where he belongs.

Harriet studied the faces of the men, or vassals. They were obedient faces under the old lash they had become so accustomed to, and the sting of Robert Culver's tongue caused them sighs of pleasure, it seemed. Not one of them raised a voice in protest; not a man questioned a verdict spoken in heat. There soon appeared an exception, however, and she thanked providence for even mild strength in a man.

Mr. Boston went through all sorts of facial contortions before standing humbly. "I mention this, sir, only as a reminder. The earnings of Captain Boll's ship exceed any other two." Then he sat down to weather the storm of abuse. It came, though only in tone.

"Mr. Boston." Culver paused for icy effect. "Mr. Boston, the earnings of a Judas will never influence me. A captain's conduct is a reflection on the firm, and should Captain Boll discharge a cargo of solid gold, I think I'd continue to stand firm. Does this satisfy you, sir?"

Out of the chief cashier's silence the banker spoke. "Perhaps this whole idea lacks comprehension. The captain may be acting for the firm. Is this point worthy of consideration?"

Culver puffed. "Do you, Mr. Surrey, suggest leniency? Did we authorize him to strike this devilish coin? Would we even consider such a fantastic idea? Does any man of you wish to argue the point with me?" He ran the table with eyes that dared, that longed for battle, then spoke his authority in two words: "Boll goes." He stood for another moment before saying, "Do I hear an objection?"

"Yes." Harriet spoke up, surprised at her own voice, which jerked every face toward her. Emily dropped her hands and sat dumfounded. Harriet's eyes seemed to strike back with unwavering purpose. Even Culver retreated from a surprise attack, so said his face even as it hardened for a counterattack designed to crush her once and for all.

She smiled. "While I know little of such matters, I gather that the basic purpose of running ships is to carry freight—to make money. Am I in error?" There was no answer. "If such is true, then why rid the firm of a golden goose?"

"My dear," Robert Culver said condescendingly, "I have gone into that. Genius is valueless without integrity and loyalty."

"There is small doubt there," she replied. "I do not attempt to argue the point. But, sir, you are not sure of Captain Boll's disloyalty, and yet you are quick to condemn him."

"Am I?" He laughed. "To reverse your charge, let me say, my dear, you are quick to defend this man. I think you may rely upon the judgment of these men here in such matters. They have made few mistakes in serving your interests."

She smiled, her lips thinning somewhat. "But let us hear from these men." She sent a barb with precision aim when she asked, "Do they ever vote on issues?"

"Seldom. It is usually unnecessary."

"I can readily understand that," she said, meeting his eyes. "But I request a vote after I've finished speaking."

"You are delaying busy men," he charged.

"Policies aren't to be hurried, sir. I think I heard you say that once."

Aunt Emily arose slowly and walked to Harriet. She whispered something, then sat down, somewhat agitated, as Harriet said, "I don't agree, Auntie."

Banker Surrey sent calculating glances at the daughter of Dean Adams; he saw bales of stocks rather than beauty. Mr. Boston, working his lips, peered at her through an embalmer's eyes, it seemed, and measured her holdings. So did a few others. But all stole glances at the man who had long sat the throne. None doubted his staying power there. But here was another bid for his seat, and every man felt a personal squeeze not to his liking.

She proceeded to ignore the great Culver. "Gentlemen, I am not in favor of condoning what seems on the surface disloyalty. I merely wish to look deeper before condemning a valuable man." Culver subdued a snort, as if he had met with some deviation in business etiquette which placed him behind the pale. She went on serenely: "Captain Boll has rendered us a great service, one which we must not reward with contempt. Such would be most unseemly."

"Service!" Culver scoffed, staring at a symbol of an unstrung age in womanhood.

She did not glance at him; she spoke to Mr. Boston and the banker, it seemed. "Were I shipping goods to the Orient, I think I should be impressed by the speed of the *Gerrymander*." A few started at the spoken name. "Her record run should be a matter of pride to the firm; it should also mean full holds, and dollars."

"A worthy thought," commented Mr. Surrey.

"Why evade the issue," Culver said portentously, "when that run was a farce to further malign me? Deny that, any of you!" His fist struck the table with resounding force. He eyed Emily.

Harriet laughed lightly and managed to inject a simulation of reproof in her voice. "If I were the head of a business, I should rather enjoy being maligned with money." She saw the slow exchange of glances, a lifting of brows as these men sought to adjust to this girl who spoke with such candor and ready wit.

"I have heard my father tell of reaching for some record run, of his races against bigger and better ships to San Francisco. He never attained that record, but he told me of the agonies of a loyal crew, of days and days with no watch below, of the willingness of men who needed sleep when he cried, 'Lay aloft!' Among the unheralded great is the ship which nearly won.

" 'The sea,' my father said, 'merely serves the land, and without just reward.' I'm beginning to see it as he saw it." She paused, and silence hung as still as the pale damask of the walls. Her voice, minus fervor, had introduced foreign matter into the meeting as though it belonged there.

"I have heard my father speak of the winds of the roaring forties. They came, they went, he said, and a captain sat out a calm or hastened storm canvas. Mr. Boston, you've been to sea—you know how a man must drive to a record. Don't you?"

"Aye, miss!" He exuded a quarter-deck smile.

"Perhaps some of you have sailed ships," and she felt the glare and resentment which these words evoked in the head of the firm, whom she reproved as well as ignored. "My father spoke of his disdain at heaving to. In my memory he spoke of things to come." She added pensively, "Of Captain Boll, perhaps."

"And now"—she added a note of remonstrance as she looked directly at the iron-jawed man in the high-back chair—"that an Adams ship has hung up a record—for my father, I think—her captain is to be rewarded with dismissal!"

"We'll get back to facts now that——"

Her voice forced Culver to silence as she said in her same even tone, "I hereby make a motion that we draft a letter commending Captain Boll for his record run with our *Gerrymander*, that a nice reward be enclosed. Who will second this motion?"

"I!" Mr. Boston could not restrain his incautious tongue. "And I," said Mr. Surrey.

"Then is the next procedure a vote? Yes? Then all in favor——"

"Preposterous!" Culver shouted, even as Aunt Emily arose once more and said sharply, "Harriet!"

"—let it be known by the signs you use."

"Aye!" six of the group responded in unison.

Harriet got to her feet and moved to the door. Emily, very much upset, followed. Harriet turned about, her head lifted proudly, a smile of mingled triumph and appreciation on her face. "Thank you. I am sure my father would be very happy were he here. Now I may tell you something. If Mr. Culver goes to the Orient, I shall board the *Shanghai Packet* also—to assure Captain Boll a fair trial." She smiled full at them. "Now since I'm late to a tea on Pinckney Street, I'll bid you good day, gentlemen."

5

Night had fallen in thick misty layers over Louisburg Square. Robert Culver sat astraddle a chair in the same room before the fire, his arms folded across its back, his eyes digging beyond the weak yellow flames and locking in prodigious combat with red coals. They symbolized the directorate which he would, God help him, reduce to an ash. His supper rested cold and untouched on a tray nearby, and the gloss of table, chairs, walls, and mahogany doors caught and held for a moment the glint of a wayward flame before surrendering it to encroaching red reflections.

On the floor at his feet lay an evening paper: it had been twisted with angry hands. It had arrived by some messenger in the service of an anonymous devil who had sent it nicely wrapped and ribbon-tied. The mystery was no mystery as he read the running title: "BOSTON SHIP SETS RECORD." Barely subordinated was: "THE GERRYMANDER UNDER CAPTAIN BOLL MAKES RECORD RUN TO JAVA HEAD." He refused to read further.

He was sure it came from Amos De Loach. But that was of second importance; he was used to the dislike of his enemies. He had a gloomy air about him, though it was relieved by knotted fists and jaw muscles in sharp protest to even temporary defeat. But did he not hold a tight rein on operations? He did. And was it not in his power to correct the Waterloo of the afternoon? It was, and he would use that power with such passion that a sequel would die long before its birth. But the stigma of defeat lingered.

Emily knocked, then entered. She moved to a chair and sat down. "Your food is cold, Robert," she said at last.

He faced her then. "Emily, there are some things you have failed to teach Harriet." He scolded, it seemed. "Her behavior today was most unladylike."

"Don't try to belittle me, Robert," she replied firmly. "I've done as well with the girl as you've done with her legacy. Have I ever criticized you?"

"You have no reason."

"Neither have you. Harriet is of age. She's a mature woman, and an Adams. You'll do well to change your tactics."

"Is she serious about taking that voyage?"

"She is. It seems we'll all be going to the Orient." Emily got up and walked to the door, her last words directed to her own ears: "What a confirmed bachelor doesn't know about women!"

A dying ember popped and sent up a tiny flame as if in obedience to his mind of the moment: he saw Harriet as he had never seen her before. She moved between him and the fire, the panorama leaping out of his mind's eye exactly as his subconscious mind had captured it that afternoon. "No longer a child," he said pensively, forgetting anger in the moment. She was a mature woman, mentally and physically. She would be some man's joy of mind, soul, and body; and that man—he would control the flag of the house!

She had a mind of her own; and the courage to voice it, he reflected; the man inside him admired her spirit. He would do well to change his tactics, Emily had said. Never. He felt the crying need of policy over existing absurdities; but he was a stubborn man, he realized, very stubborn. He lived to rule, and he would not surrender an inch of ground to her. She persisted, however; she smiled as she stood in the doorway—"Now since I'm late to a tea on Pinckney Street"—her dress low at the neck, her bosom lifted as proudly as her chin, her radiant face a mirror for the warm body under a checked taffeta gown —"I'll bid you good day, gentlemen." An unholy view, said the mind of the old puritan in him; a new and interesting view, said the corporeal mind. She was very much alive, and he asked no pardon for masculine perceptions.

He had said to her on her birthday: "You possess both beauty and wealth." Peering into the crimson ashes, he sighed over two obstacles with poignant regret: the first, she would marry someday; the second, he was not young. Here were poised threats to his continued rule. A hard-muscled hand gripped his jaw as he said aloud, "But I am not an old man in any respect!"

The thought held, fixed itself in his mind, and he was not loath to dispel it. He viewed his own imperious self and saw a man quite handsome and distinguished, one of whom any woman should be very proud.

6

Robert Culver entered his offices at ten the next morning and handed the entire force a great surprise: Mr. Boston had warned each employee of the "Old Man's" probable mood; thus when Mr. Culver entered with a pleasant face atop his squared shoulders, and broke a habit of long standing by booming out a "Good morning," every face gaped with incredulity.

Robert Culver had reached a decision, one which stimulated every cell in his body. It encompassed challenge of an invigorating sort; and purpose, which to the merciless egotist was something great and ill-omened when he thought of his enemies; all his old interests, or passions, were indissolubly united to the new one. He could not rid his mind of the decision, and he did not once doubt his ultimate success upon the score. The very thought gave him moments of pleasure; it had to do with Harriet and her majority in the firm of Culver and Adams.

He, a bachelor, dared think of taking a wife—Harriet.

6 ∾ IN THE FIGUREHEAD'S SHADOW

HARRIET WAS UP EARLY. SHE ATE WHILE TELLING MISS HOBBES OF HER decision to go to Singapore aboard the *Shanghai Packet*. She talked of the necessary baggage, at last pausing to ask questions.

"Do you know of anyone who's been there, Ellen?"

"My sister's husband's sister lived there for a year. It's hot, she said." Miss Hobbes was tall and thin, perhaps thirty-five; she seemed to be older, a woman aged by some great trouble rather than by any physical cause. She seldom smiled, and the droop of her mouth together with brooding eyes advised that she would not soon recover from whatever ailed her. "They wear as little as possible," she added.

"Then I can discard my corset."

"Or keep away from public places," the spinster voiced wearily. "She said the world is sinful there, that it's second nature to want sin. But Claire was an indiscreet woman. How well I know.

"How well I know," she repeated, sighing.

Harriet eyed her curiously for a moment, then laughed. "I've never been to the Orient. I'm glad Mr. Culver decided to go."

"Mr. Culver," said Miss Hobbes, pausing with an urn of coffee, "sat in that room past midnight. He didn't touch his food, so Pierce said.

"He's a strange man," she added with finality.

"Yes," Harriet replied, her pensive eyes under a frown.

"Miss, I'd suggest you purchase summer clothes for the trip. But don't run to frills. Men there will ogle enough at even a nun—so Claire said; and you're prettier than she. My, yes. Her hipbones protruded something awful, and she had bowlegs, and her bosom was as flat as mine. But you—you're as full and straight as your mother—may the Lord watch over you. He didn't watch over Claire, or else she played truant. It got to be a habit with her."

Harriet hadn't heard. Her mind on Atlantic Avenue, she said, "Poor Mr. Boston. I'm sure he's catching the bitter end of yesterday's meeting."

The butler entered with an envelope. She accepted it, saying, "Pierce, I'll be going out in about an hour." He departed with a promise to have the carriage at the door.

"Pierce is hollow-eyed," commented Miss Hobbes. "Perhaps he sat up until Mr. Culver retired. Who knows? But the newspaper in the room was twisted like——"

"You may start packing, Ellen," Harriet said, opening the envelope. She was soon alone and reading the message.

My dear Harriet:

Please accept my sincere congratulations upon the success of the Gerrymander in setting a new sailing record. I am sure the realization of your father's great wish is most gratifying.

Rumor has it that some incident or series of incidents was discussed at the meeting of the C. A. directors yesterday, out of which my suppositive guilt of years back was seized upon and further emphasized. Therefore, may I declare once again my innocence in the figurehead affair and voice my eternal fidelity to my little friend.

Sincerely,
Amos

"Dear Amos." She smiled, her eyes watching him as he stood before the fireplace years back. "He was always so jolly, so kind and teasing." Gloom had reigned at seventeen Louisburg Square ever since the day of the ship's ceremony. She realized that Mr. Culver seemed more equivocal and bigoted at her every encounter with him. She thought of her shares in the firm, of the wrong surely done Amos De Loach. Should her next move be aimed at reconciliation—but wasn't that impossible—or some effort to clear dear Amos? She wasn't sure she wanted anything to do with business of any sort.

"I wonder," she thought, "how a man falsely accused must feel."

2

At that moment Amos De Loach sat at his desk on the third floor of a State Street building trying to answer that same question. He turned to it solely for relief—another question demanded an answer. It rose up out of a financial statement and spanned a few city blocks to a bank, where a big voice seemed to shout, "Can you meet the note today? It's your last day of grace!"

Amos knew the feeling of a man falsely accused. In his case the desire to even the score meant more than success in business, though the latter was necessary to the former. Culver's face was always before his mind's eye to drive him on and on toward his goal. He knew that if and when he ever achieved a comparable power in shipping circles he would use it to put Culver in his place.

He had worked hard; he had borrowed and begged; he had sat out hours in bankers' outer offices; he had pounded the streets in search of cargoes, smiling his best as he fought competition with a discarded bark unfit for ocean travel. After a period of success, he had obtained a huge four-master, which many maritime firms employed to combat the trend toward steam in the eighties. The Cape Race was the mainstay of De Loach and Company, the pride of the firm.

But this bread-and-butter craft had been heavily mortgaged.

So much for his gain. It was offset by loss. Before the figurehead affair, Amos De Loach had been welcomed into almost every club of the city: he had possessed an affable masculine charm, which he always had a use for, whether for his own pleasure, or some cargo which his agents had been unable to snare. Tall and distinguished, sandy-haired, with a small mustache, a contagious smile, and a magnetic voice, he had drunk his toasts neatly and managed to stand as a man among men and a debonair figure in society. Eligible and sought after, his name often suggested over a political table, he might have extended his activities to other fields. He had chosen to remain a Culver man.

But eighteen hundred and eighty-one was four years gone, and De Loach, the handsome cosmopolite and able executive of a respected firm, was, to the delight of Robert Culver, another man: his face was thin and somewhat pinched, and his eyes had lost much of their former sparkle; deep lines had etched his neck and chin with patterns of strain and weariness; his hair was the same except for a touch of gray, and his voice was slower, as if humbled. But he retained a certain charm; or, rather, he forced it to the surface upon occasion, as if he moved in his own shadow, in the wake of his former self.

The shadow lengthened and the wake ran out.

The year before had been a bad one, one which caused him to dread a sequel. Thus he had gambled ahead of his plans, as any man with an ultimate goal might do when faced with insolvency. Only he and

Tom Flint knew of his plan for evening a score with Culver, and only a man as desperate as he would have indulged in such extravagance when faced with an empty purse. But he had gambled.

He had sent Tom Flint on a mission.

The window drew his eye, and he got out of his chair and watched the traffic on a wet street. But not for long: his desk claimed him. Beside the financial statement was a letter from Flint. He turned to it again.

DEAR MR. DE LOACH:

I am now first mate aboard the *Gerrymander*. Something is afoot here; it is out of Boll's head, prodigious and ungraspable. You see it as you do the star-sprinkled canopy of the East, and, like its metaphor, when you try to pin one star down for a view, it twinkles out of the realms of understanding. It is out of Boll's head, so I'll not try to explain an unsolved mystery.

The voyage went "uneventful": a death, prayers to the devil for a wind, accompanied by coins, a subdued mutiny, planned ahead by Boll, and a record to port. You should pay Boll, not me, for as long as I serve him I am serving you. Believe me this, and lay emphasis on the statement.

The *Cape Race*, I believe, could load herself deck to water line here within a few months. This is all rather ambiguous, I'm sure, but I'm not ready to divulge more since there is no standing explanation I can give all this until later.

Sincerely,
TOM FLINT

De Loach studied the letter. " 'Something is afoot here; it is out of Boll's head . . . for as long as I am serving him I am serving you. . . . The voyage went uneventful. . . .' Hm-m," he mused. "The *Cape Race* could profit." He thought of Harriet with a surge of compunction. He thought of Culver and rubbed out all regret.

Then he slumped into his chair and sighed. "If Culver only knew it, he's got me where he wants me." But he had made Culver's coastwise ships stand idle at times, though the victory was very small. Then he faced a possibility without undue surprise:

"And I suppose Culver does know about that note I can't meet. He could take the *Cape Race* and watch me fold."

He was soon in the street where he hailed a passing carriage.

His fears increased as he urged the driver on to Mr. Surrey's bank. What assurance had he that Mr. Surrey, a director in the firm of Culver and Adams, would not allow Culver to snap up the note? None whatever. He must save the *Cape Race* somehow, or lose all. The leap was that broad.

De Loach raised his hand. "I forgot something. Drive me to Louis-burg Square—number seventeen." What he had forgotten was that he had until midnight to pay off the note. There was little use in asking Surrey for another renewal. He needed money now. Big money! Perhaps Harriet——

He read Flint's letter: *Something is afoot here; it is out of Boll's head, prodigious and ungraspable. . . . The Cape Race could load herself deck to water line here within a few months.* The coach bounced over the cobble of a narrow street on the Hill. He stared ahead, poured out his thoughts in silence until the stately walls of Louisburg Square enveloped him on three sides.

Said the butler, "Good to see you, Mr. De Loach. It is indeed. Miss Harriet? Why, she left no more than ten minutes ago, sir."

Amos De Loach smiled. He was glad to be his independent self for another few hours.

3

Mr. Boston advanced to meet Harriet, his grin uncovering big teeth. The male clerks peered up at a stranger almost, wondering if she would pause to greet them as she had done a half year back. She obliged them before turning to the old faithful of the house with a whispered word:

"Thanks for your support yesterday. You were a great help."

"You're welcome, Miss Harriet."

"I suppose you caught the full force of the storm this morning," she said, laughing. "I want you to know I felt for you."

"On the contrary, Miss Adams, he was quite gay for his usual self, if you understand what I mean."

"I do, though I can't understand his being in a good humor."

"It's quite all right. I know you're not used to going against him. None of us are. May I say that I've felt for you since that meeting?"

"Oh! Why—er——" She bit her lip, then smiled. So Mr. Culver's rare humor signified victory over her; Mr. Boston saw her cringing before the great Culver last evening. It was the only natural out-come to the chief cashier. She decided not to upset his view.

"Thank you." She smiled. "I'll wait in Mr. Culver's office."

Once inside the office, she sat and glared at Mr. Culver's chair. So Mr. Boston thought she'd won only to surrender. Perhaps they all thought so by now. Very well, and she smiled a threat, let them think so. Let Mr. Culver think so too, if it soothed his ego. She was sure by now that he did make schemes to correct his defeat of the day before.

She thought, "Captain Boll, I hope you are right. You'd better be." Mollified somewhat, she arose and moved to the outer office again and asked if the *Shanghai Packet* had docked. It had not. She returned to the office and busied herself before a small mirror on the wall.

Her eyebrows were full, like her mother's, she reflected, though her mother's eyes had been bluer. There was a mole on her neck just like her mother's. Mrs. Adams. Miss Adams. Perhaps her mother had been as vigorous as she at twenty-two. But she remembered the latter years with a clearness that fogged off her childhood memories. Her mother had been formal and perfunctory, almost diffident; a trace of sadness or weariness had enveloped her expression at times.

She sighed and turned about as if her thoughts drained her. An object atop a letter on the desk caught her eye. It was the hollow-sounding coin which Mr. Culver had flung to the table yesterday. She picked it up and studied it.

GERRYMANDER CASH! She thought of its connection with camphor and Mr. Teale. Captain Boll's doing; and suddenly she saw the captain a scoundrel.

She furrowed her brow as she gazed at the coin in puzzlement and, unable to cope with its mystery, placed it atop the letter. It was then she saw Boll's name inscribed on the sheet. She was soon reading the message penned in Robert Culver's scratchy style. It was as follows:

Dear Captain Boll:
As the head of Culver and Adams, I feel it my duty to voice the firm's heartiest praise and congratulations to you for your historical performance in setting a new sailing ship record from Boston to Java Head.
Please accept the reward attached as a token of my appreciation.

It bore the signature of Robert Culver.

She looked about the desk for a draft, which was not in evidence. Her eyes fell by chance on the wastebasket. There it was in four pieces, a draft made out to Captain Boll for one thousand dollars.

She shook her head in exasperation. "Please accept the reward attached. Why, he's sending the Gerrymander Cash!"

Culver arrived shortly, evincing no surprise at her presence there. He smiled energetically and gazed at her with a singular fixity of eye.

"I'm pleased that you've decided to take the trip, Harriet," he said.

She said nothing as her direct eyes probed him for signs of fever or mental disease. He frowned, then composed his features into a suave smile. He was doing his best with an art he had seldom practiced. "It will give us a chance to get acquainted," he said solicitously. "We have been most ungenerous toward one another, don't you think?"

She smiled quizzically and said, "Yes?"

"Life is short," he mused, sending his eyes to the desk and the cash piece atop the letter to Captain Boll. His eyes thinned for the merest instant, though he was quick to send them smiling up at her.

"I read your letter there," she said, surprising him.

"Yes?" he said slowly.

"And I've heard that great men often change their minds." She smiled. When his perplexity stood at its peak, she said, "The waste-basket proves it."

"Um-m," he grunted. She knew he cursed inwardly at her meddling, though she was determined to force the essence of his strange, fresh proposition into some acceptable pattern.

"You see," she said, simulating a sigh of pure resignation, "I annoy you. I'm afraid I'd always do that." She stood to go, her pliant limbs, vigorous body and face warming him to the core of his masculine being. He was soon smiling, surprised at himself for not glaring instead.

"Think," she said, "how Captain Boll would feel, supposing he is guilty, if he received a letter and check from you! Who would be on the defensive then, you or Captain Boll?"

"I see," he said, rubbing his chin. He was astute enough to realize that this subtlety was made to order for him; and he was so very pleased with the role he had assigned himself that he launched heartily into the campaign ahead. He beamed forth: "Bless you, Harriet, I can see our companionship blossoming into a wonderful thing! A most wonderful thing!"

She eyed him narrowly. "You know," she said, "I may have misjudged you, sir. I hope so."

"Perhaps," he returned, smiling. Then he very wisely added a warning which rose up in his favor: "Don't be too sure of anything in a hurry."

As she tried to fathom his meaning, he advanced in casual manner until he stood before her. She studied him, unaware of the rush of blood to his face or the bright gleam in his eyes. His hands reached out and caught her arms in a gesture which would appear as fatherly even as it offered him excuse to test the magic of her touch upon him.

He felt the warmth of youth. The surge of it was hot, and his desire for Harriet was greater than his desire for control of the Adams majority in the firm.

His hands tightened spasmodically. Harriet, suddenly awakened, shuddered at what she saw and felt. She was both disappointed and afraid as she faced a revolting fact.

Robert Culver realized his error: his true feelings had shown in his face just when he thought them superbly masked. To himself he said, "I must be more careful." To Harriet he said, turning to his desk:

"As I said, Harriet, don't be too sure of anything in a hurry."

Harriet, however, was unable to accept his advice; she was very sure of what she had seen in Robert Culver's face.

4

Amos De Loach stood before Mr. Surrey's bank. He stared at the impressive stone entrance and its dignified doors. The bank's name was etched deep and bold into the rock that ran its length. How warm the edifice had seemed when he was dollars deep in the vaults; and how cold, how very cold, when it was dollars deep into him. He smiled ironically and looked beyond the horizon of cold stone and into a futile defense of his plight: there was nothing solid under his feet.

It was imperative that he talk to Surrey, but about what? Nothing new had arisen to alter the grave expression on the banker's face, simulated or not; to change the steady beat of his pencil against the desk; or to suppress his own slow rise to his feet even as his mind groped for some straw of hope always just out of reach. Such a visit would serve only his physical self with entry and exit. He turned away.

It was three in the afternoon. He moved briskly to a bank on Washington Street. Timothy Haynes, whom he had befriended once, was now an officer of the bank. Mr. Haynes was glad to see him; he smiled; he asked when his bank might be favored by De Loach and Company.

"I'm here to do business now." Amos smiled. "I need money." Mr. Haynes drew his warm smile into a shell of sobriety; he lifted his brows and glanced at his desk when the amount was named. Carefully put was his inquiry, "And the bank you're doing business with?" He let his voice die there, though he spoke up minutes later, all of him in the shell, it seemed. "Our Mr. Havermann is the man you should see. Come, I'll introduce you."

Nathan Lazrus had often gambled in sailing adventures, Amos reflected. He was soon on his way to Fleet Street. Perhaps Flint's letter would interest him. Mr. Lazrus, short, thin, gray-haired, lost no time coming to the point: he admired success as much as he despised failure, and he was seldom tempted to alter a racial concept. But he had money. What did Amos have? A ship, a big four-masted ship which he was about to lose, a letter, and a big chance to profit. Mr. Lazrus listened for a long five minutes, read the letter without understanding any part of it, and turned his back in silent disdain.

It was getting late. The low sun broke through the gray overcast as if to announce a quick bedding down. Amos De Loach thought of his small office staff, realizing they would be departing soon. What unkind fate had brought them into his employ, and where would their shocked faces turn tomorrow? He shrank from the press of unpleasant thoughts and turned to embrace the anonymity of the harbor.

There she stood, proud, sleek, and long, the Cape Race, pretty in the oily lap of gray dock water. She was a large carrier, almost three hundred feet in length.

There she stood—her main deck open and quiet, no life about her from forecastle to poop, her maze of sail neatly furled and stilled to the breeze making out of the east—the Cape Race. She had a funereal air about her, even as the last shafts of a Boston sun painted her sepia-colored masts and upper yards in warm orange. She seemed sad and forgotten, sitting quiet and still, as if she did not dare turn a misty eye his way.

"A dollar separates us," he said dolefully, pinning thousands of dollars to unit and symbol. "The magnificence of a dollar!" he added. "It is as callous as it is right. It is the pattern of life." But for that symbol, she would come to life under him and ease away from that derelict pier to seek the solitudes of tropic seas, where spice islands rose up to take on color and dimension, to belch up profit.

Something is afoot here . . . The Cape Race, I believe, could load herself deck to water line . . .

The winning smile of Amos De Loach caught the last reddened glint of the afternoon sun, as did two heavy drops that rolled down his cheeks. He turned his back on the Cape Race, gave her to the encroaching shadows of a gray evening which would carve of her and stagnant dock water a somber silhouette broken only by foolish threads of dancing light.

5

On the afternoon of the following day a Boston newspaper carried on page five a line drawing of a four-masted bark. Underneath the picture six words told a story that might have served as front-page news:

LATEST ADDITION TO CULVER–ADAMS LINE

The story, very brief, was as follows: "The *Cape Race*, a four-master of twenty-seven hundred tons gross today became the property of Culver and Adams. Her recent owner was De Loach and Company of State Street."

That was all. It was enough. In downtown offices and clubs, up the water front of Atlantic Avenue and along State Street, where adventures in sail and steam were born, the news was met with I-told-you-so expressions. The Culver steam roller had scored again over opposition; it had flicked at the old sores of its memory and had taken a further toll on a less formidable enemy, who was enemy by virtue of an unlucky incident. Boston in general felt De Loach an innocent victim of a man's driving ego. But all this was of the past. The present saw him ground under the Culver heel once more.

Social Boston also scanned the newspapers, and since its interests were linked to the past as well as the demanding present, it saw more on page five that day than met the eye. It saw a favorite struck down at last by a man whose wounded ego years before had made of him a menacing stalker. His ego, said many as they paused to digest the news item on page five, had tentacles.

At five that afternoon Harriet stood in the entrance hall of a Chestnut Street house among a score of departing guests. A formal club session had just ended, and a maze of informal subjects were up for discussion, among them fashions for fall, winter resorts, the dance of that evening to honor a member of their set, and other subjects. One by one they heard some mention of Harriet's forthcoming voyage on the *Shanghai Packet*, and soon advice was rampant, particularly on the subject of clothes: Singapore was English, wasn't it? The Ellis-Hardins, who had spent a year in Australia, could tell her about the climate; she would surely visit Hong Kong and the English clubs.

While conversations mingled, the mother of the hostess entered the front door. Tall, thin, and gimlet-eyed, and known for her sharpness of speech, she stood erect and frowned over a lorgnette for a moment before declaring her whimsical presence.

"Of all the chattering I've ever heard!" The young ladies turned smiles and greetings upon her, drawing her usual bluster. "Why, when I was your age, women were demure creatures, even among themselves."

"But we were discussing a trip to the Orient—Singapore and Hong Kong and——"

"Bah! What's that to an old lady who has to spend the rest of her life listening to an unstrung age invent barbarisms? Who's going to the Orient?"

"Harriet, and on the *Shanghai Packet!*"

"Harriet?" The dear old lady scowled, drawing her lorgnette up again. "Oh, there you are. Why not go aboard the *Cape Race?* You could, you know, drape poor Amos's bankrupt body over the bow for a figurehead."

The lucid smile on Harriet's face died slowly. "I don't understand," she said.

"You should," came the retort, "since you're reputed to be a big factor in the firm. But I'm not about to enlarge my confidence, young lady. I'll just say Mr. Culver is gerrymandering in his own peculiar manner again."

The outer door of seventeen Louisburg Square admitted Robert Culver at ten that evening. He was in mellow mood, a fact made known by his inquiry about the butler's son, recuperating from illness in Salem. Pierce beamed and talked at length before saying soberly, "Miss Harriet asks an audience with you, sir. She's in the parlor."

Harriet waited, as she had done since seven, her impatience growing, and with it a slow deepening anger which she realized would not diminish under his politic shrewdness. She was dressed in white cotton, and her hair was done up in a hurried chignon. Her eyes seemed washed of all but silver shafts, thin and set to her temper, like her lips. She glanced at the clock with the sound of voices in the hall and slowed the sweep of her skirt over the rug.

She managed a sober smile as he entered. "I'll get to the point," she said evenly after his greeting. He stood as if ready to seat himself, mildly puzzled. "It's about that news item on page five, the *Cape Race.*"

"Yes?" He thinned his eyes. "Where's Emily?"

"We don't need her, sir," she replied. Without due pause she began: "I should think you'd save me the embarrassment of such news from foreign sources. I caught it in full force this afternoon."

"Embarrassment? Why should you feel that?" He stroked a black sideburn and moved to the mantel as she sat down.

"Not so much because of the deed as for what it stands for. I can scarcely be proud of the head of my father's business when he lays in wait to hurt a friend whom he supposes stole his marbles four years earlier." She smiled as he stiffened.

"Mr. Culver, you were very gracious at your office yesterday. You saw our companionship blossoming into a wonderful thing, you said. On a foundation of duplicity, I'm quite sure. But you were frank enough to warn me about changing any opinion I had of you—for which I thank you." She paused, got up and paced the floor.

"Continue."

"I shall. Beyond that aspect of the case, there is Amos De Loach."

"De Loach?"

"Yes. I asked for this audience with you, hoping you were sincere when you voiced interest in our future relationship. If you were, perhaps I can change my opinion of you again."

"Go on."

"I feel guilty, Mr. Culver. So should you—about what Culver and Adams has done to Amos De Loach. I want something done to correct this Cape Race incident."

"We are not dealing with emotions," he protested.

She turned to face him. "How odd that sounds—from you. What, then, was the incentive?"

"Business," he replied gruffly. "And business isn't interested in susceptibilities, my dear. The Cape Race is worth much more than the note De Loach couldn't meet. The ship was also the mainstay of an annoying coastal shipping outfit that contributed to our loss in that field. We profited doubly when we got her for a song."

"Let us use the word stole."

"You are not versed in business matters."

"No," she reflected. "An oversight on my part, and one which I may yet correct if the firm which carries my name on the tail end continues its sharp practices."

He waited a moment before laughing lightly. "The Lord pity the profits of tenderness."

"You have a very poor opinion of a woman's brain, haven't you?"

"In business, yes. Otherwise, no."

"You may be right. I cannot argue the point for lack of suitable illustrations. But have you ever considered the value of a woman's opposition?

"You did not once mention the fact that came into existence with my birthday months ago. You chose to ignore my voting control when I reached the age of twenty-two. Your control of my estate ended there, if you remember."

"I saw no reason to mention it," he said with surprising ease. "Your affairs were in good hands. They still are, as the returns from your shares prove. And, since you remained silent at the time when your voice was expected, I supposed you wished to leave things as they were."

She could find no answer to this; in fact, she admired his candidness, though it further vexed her. He added, "As for the handling of your business affairs, I stand ready for a probe by anyone you may choose."

"I do not criticize your efforts in my behalf, now or in the past."

"Then," he put courteously, "why all this talk?"

"We were talking about the *Cape Race* and Amos," she replied defensively. "Tell me, sir," she said as she sat once more, "wasn't the figurehead incident almost forgotten until Captain Boll's little game brought up Mr. Flint and the fact that he once worked for Amos? Didn't the cash-piece business cause you to glare at Amos again? And didn't you seek this opportunity to gloat over Amos as a means of offsetting your loss at the board meeting?"

"Harriet, answer me this—are you defending De Loach?"

"In principle, yes, since all that happened at that figurehead unveiling was unintentional. Any harm done you was in your own mind."

He laughed angrily. "Do you recall that sight? Did that damned carving at the bows look like me?"

"I'm beginning to wonder if it wasn't the image of the man inside you." She had dared to say it. She sat back almost afraid.

She waited for his answer in vain. Very wisely, he faced the mantel and busied himself with a cigar which he placed in his mouth at last. Harriet continued to watch him, hoping he would relieve the strained silence. And soon she realized he was using this silence against her. That was it, since the quiet of the room served to magnify her feeling of error and guilt at having spoken her mind in haste.

She was suddenly aware that she had defeated her purpose. She had gone too far to suggest that the firm resell the *Cape Race* to Amos on generous terms.

Slowly she arose and said, "I spoke rashly, sir." With that she left the room.

Only then did Robert Culver turn about and smile over the victory she had inadvertently handed him.

6

Harriet slept fitfully, opening her eyes at times to ask herself if the incident had been real. Only darkness answered her until she suddenly waked. She revived the picture of the man who had won a battle which had been her victory from the outset.

The wrong done Amos was less the reason for her stand of last evening, she admitted honestly. It was, rather, the emphasis which Mr. Culver had placed on his triumph by taking over the *Cape Race*; that and his singlehanded play without consulting her, the owner of more than fifty per cent of the stock in the firm. And had he consulted her, Amos would not have been embarrassed. No, Amos, old friend and favorite, would have retained his ship.

It suddenly occurred to her that she had recourse. Anxiously she glanced at the clock and the day ahead.

At ten that morning she sat in Banker Surrey's office. She had just asked a question: how could she quickly get a large sum of her own money without Mr. Culver's knowledge? The banker, anxious to serve her, came forth with the answer, adding, "Until this is done, Miss Adams, I'll advance any amount of money you may wish."

It was not quite eleven when she stepped from the carriage and smiled almost excitedly up at a building on State Street. Soon she stood inside a door and looked about anxiously, her eyes at last meeting those of a curious young man.

"I'd like to see Mr. De Loach. Oh, never mind the name. Just say an old friend calls."

Moments later Amos turned about, a look of quick surprise and incredulity on his face. It retreated hurriedly before a smile. "Harriet! Of all people. I thought another creditor was using the old ruse."

She smiled and extended a hand, appraising him as she did so. He wore a tailored suit of light gray. From his appearance one might think he owned a hundred ships.

"You look prosperous enough," she bantered, causing his grin to widen. He said something about keeping up a Harvard Club appearance. She took a chair and studied him from under a broad hat brim of white lace. "How did it happen, Amos?" she asked directly.

He said, taking his chair across the desk from her, "I learned that I could not refute the law of the minnow and the whale." He smiled blandly enough, though he could not disguise his curiousness as to the import of her visit.

"Minnow and whale," she said, her eyes lifting to the drawing of the *Cape Race* on the wall. "Why didn't you come to me before letting him do this?"

"You! The biggest voice of Culver and Adams!"

"Oh, I think I could have borne up under it. You see, I like to be right."

"You are like your mother. But east of the Hill lies State and Atlantic thoroughfares, where the old axiom, 'Might is right,' rules. Even your father was forced to rely on that force at one time for survival."

"Amos, you're being very noble. Too noble. The rightness of which I speak is two-sided. It goes back to 'eighty-one at a ceremony. You took the time and trouble to send me a note the other morning when your back was to the wall. You declared your innocence in the figurehead affair. Why?"

"Because," he said soberly, "I thought Robert might have convinced you otherwise."

"And why should you care what I thought?"

"Some things are very valuable to a man, Harriet."

"Exactly. And to a woman." She smiled seriously, then glanced from him to the ship on the wall and back again. "What Mr. Culver did went deeper than you, Amos. You know"—she leaned slightly forward—"he seems to want to prove to the world that the figurehead was created in his image after all."

He got up and walked to the window. After a run of silence, she said, "What are your plans, Amos?"

"You tack in unawares." He laughed. She put the question again. "Rather dubious," he reflected. "There is the ordeal of closing shop, which is about as pleasant as digging one's own grave, I imagine."

"And?"

"Somehow, there's a feeling of freedom attached to it." He seemed to eye distant horizons with longing eyes. "I was never meant to be a big shipper, unless employed by a better man."

"I disagree," she said slowly. "You were in a position where you worried more about the means you didn't have than the money you could make. My father used those words once."

"You're a little late with encouragement."

"That remains to be seen," she replied. He frowned. "But what, actually, had you planned to do?"

"To take the little old schooner *Euphrosyne* and see if she can hold together for a run to the Orient."

"Really?"

"Oh yes. A man of forty-five isn't too old to yearn for tropic palms, moonlight, and profit."

"Naturally, but why go to the ends of the earth to learn you're rooted to Boston?"

"Perhaps you're right." He chuckled. "Have you an alternate suggestion?"

"Yes," she replied, as if she had lain in wait for the question. "Make De Loach and Company a factor in the shipping world."

It was small wonder that he eyed her with sharp anxiety, that he turned once more to the window to debate upon her lack of acumen or loss of sanity. "With what?" he asked gruffly.

"You said you weren't meant to be a big shipper unless you worked for a better man. What about a woman?"

He turned a stupefied face to her. "You mean you?"

"I do."

He ran a hand through his hair, his smile hovering between a frown and a laugh. He sat down and eyed her seriously.

"Let's be frank," he said at last. "Are you serious in saying you would side-step a business victory which enhances the power and prestige of your company, which lends as much, by circumstance, to future profit as the *Gerrymander's* record run? If so, you are out of your mind."

"What I do is my business, Amos. This isn't charity. I demand a return, one which is in you to produce."

His eyes said she had fallen considerably in his estimation. "It won't do. I'd have to be honest with you. I'm that way."

"Think it over," she said, arising. "Ships are cheap, so I hear."

"Wait," he said, agitated, and not enjoying the feeling. Here was a problem: could he be absolutely honest with her and still claim her as a friend? He almost glared at her as he said, "Do you know why I entered business? Of course you don't."

He leaned forward, palms on desk, and said, "To fight Robert Culver, which was to fight your company, and you. That's why. And if I were to continue in business it would be the same, and nothing could change it. Not even you or your money."

He leaned back, assumed a smile, and said, "I'm sorry, Harriet, but you forced it."

Her smile held, even and direct. "I enjoy seeing a man of purpose aroused. On the rocks, you still have the courage of your convictions. But the offer stands."

"Why?"

"There's room for competition in this big world." She paused. "And a good scrap will keep both of you alive and afford me no end of pleasure."

"You're not very convincing. If you think I believe that, you're wrong. You're trying to atone a wrong. You're your mother! Sit down and listen to this."

Thereupon he told her slowly, bluntly, of his duplicity in recent months, of how he had put Tom Flint aboard the *Gerrymander* for a purpose. He left nothing unsaid except his plan to rename the ship; he even forced the letter from Flint upon her. She read: "Something is afoot here; it is out of Boll's head, prodigious and ungraspable." She saw the Gerrymander Cash. She read the letter again, pausing for reflection upon the sentences which had to do with Boll: "You should pay Boll, not me, for as long as I serve him I am serving you. Believe me this, and lay emphasis on the statement."

She was disappointed—in Boll, and in herself for championing him; and because Mr. Culver seemed eternally right. But who was this Tom Flint to influence her? Merely some independent adventurer whose name had come up for discussion at the meeting.

"Who is this Flint?" she asked.

"A man any man can trust."

"I like the way he says things."

"He's an outspoken rebel," Amos said.

"What about Boll?" she asked.

"Flint can take care of himself, if that's what you mean." It was not what she meant, though she said nothing.

There was the spark of adventure in her eyes. Her father's spirit governed her mind in that moment as it had at the directors' meeting. She peeped at an adventure she had never known; it was a beckoning freedom she could not understand, only glory in.

She walked to the window and stood there for some time, unaware that the eyes of Amos dwelled disconsolately upon her, or that there was a street below her; she saw a big ship with huge yards; and, under towers of sail, she saw a deck—the *Gerrymander's*. Boll and Flint stood there, their eyes turning incessantly toward Boston, one pair falling on Culver, and the other on De Loach. Boll seemed to sink in his own guilt, while Flint, a man she had never seen, had, with words on paper, sent her prying into coveted adventure again.

She turned about slowly. "How does this Mr. Flint serve your ultimate purpose?"

"That, Harriet, is my secret."

"Then perhaps any idea of keeping De Loach and Company alive is a mistake," she challenged.

He chuckled. "I said as much."

"But," she went on, "I believe the interests of all concerned will be better served if De Loach and Company survives." She bit her lip before facing him. "I'll be frank with you, Amos. I'm not only trying to right a wrong, as you think. I'm more interested in teaching Mr. Culver to consult me on such matters in the future."

7 &c ROBERT CULVER'S COURTSHIP

THE "SHANGHAI PACKET" LISTED INTO BOSTON HARBOR. HER BLACK HULL wore a coat of salt-gray, and a stretch of her rail above the port cathead was stove in; she had jury masts atop her fore and main.

Robert Culver stalked her decks; he scowled as he ran up the loss in rapid calculation. He cornered Captain Brown and accused him of gross negligence, and he promised a new master if the ship wasn't ready for cargo within two weeks. Captain Brown started at this; he had the temerity to ask why.

"Because," Culver thundered, "this ship is leaving for Singapore and I'll be aboard."

"But, sir, you know the value of figuring a charter so's not to get caught in the northeast monsoon."

"Who are you to talk to me about weather? Look at this ship! And damn the monsoons! Why, I've taken the old *Barnacle Goose* through a China Sea typhoon without losing a spar. I repeat, damn the monsoons!" Then he stalked out.

When he was safely ashore, the temper in Captain Brown came to life. "One fine day I'll get drunk and talk up to him." But there was small satisfaction in the lie, he reflected; it was better that he get busy and prepare for an unpleasant voyage with the owner aboard.

Near noon of her fifteenth day in port, the *Shanghai Packet* shook out her sails and filled away from Boston. Harriet, with Emily at her side, watched the city drop out of sight under the horizon, and when nothing but a smear indicated a thriving metropolis in retreat, she turned her back on the freshening wake and eyed the ship. There was a humming wind in the rigging, and the tackle creaked a bit. The quartermaster handled the wheel of the *Packet* with a skilled intimacy.

The captain walked the weather side of the poop, the chief mate the leeward side.

There was trouble in the forecastle: Captain Brown rubbed his face, and the chief mate went down to the main deck; the culprit, blood on his face, was hustled below. Had the second mate struck him? She saw Captain Brown relax into his steady pacing, his eye far out for a conn of the weather before snapping back, like a lively spring, to the maze of sail. Her father had once been a Captain Brown, and so had Mr. Culver. Both had taken their fortunes from the sea.

She sighed and smiled into the wind. What lesson had the sea in store for her? Perhaps this voyage would answer that question. She turned her mind to Amos De Loach behind her, to Captain Boll and the equally puzzling Mr. Flint ahead of her; as she turned her face to the deck, she saw the remaining factor:

Robert Culver stood beside her.

The *Shanghai Packet* pursued bad weather for several days, and when at last the fair clime of the trades met the ship, the moon, an agent which Robert Culver had intended using in his courtship of Harriet, was both tardy and dissipated. He was beginning to wonder about many things, among them his own inability to get under way; never had he dallied with the spoken word before. He promised himself that he would begin his courtship soon.

They were on the lee side of the poop one afternoon. Emily had just gone below. Both reclined in deck chairs and gazed lazily at the sharper horizons and growing blue in the approaching tropical waters. The steward hovered near, anxious to please bigwig and lady. Culver primed his mind with drinks, carefully weighing the warmth each evoked. After a time their effect seemed to announce his readiness for the pursuit of Harriet. He realized the value of simple friendliness and a slow history of his past against any anxiousness on his part. She must not suspect his intentions as he made a bid for her interest in him. He had given himself quite a task, he admitted uneasily.

He was debating on just how to open his story when a squall raced in from over the starboard quarter. They left the deck for the saloon. Culver enjoyed the pungent odors of pitch, oil, and provisions, and he sniffed with zest before settling down to scan a week-old newspaper and draw Harriet into idle conversation. He had no more than turned to the shipping news when he inadvertently said aloud what he had thought for days:

"What's holding him up?"

Harriet asked whom he meant, and he was at last drawn out.

"De Loach. With the props out from under him he should fall. But he's buying ships—two, since I got the *Cape Race*."

Harriet smiled. Her financial aid to De Loach and Company was bearing the desired return. She wanted to say, "Next time you'll consult me in such matters," though what she said was, "Perhaps it is for the best. You'd be lost without someone to fight with, sir."

He looked up as if he debated on some answer.

"Have you always been like that?" she asked.

He rose to the opening the question promised. "I was once a very mild-mannered man, Harriet. But that was before the *Barnacle Goose*, and long before the time I fell in love." As her eyes showed curiosity, he said, "I reckon it's hard to believe I was ever in love."

"Yes," she admitted. "But what happened?"

"On the *Barnacle Goose*, or were you referring to the love affair?"

"Why—both," she answered.

He frowned, pretending a lack of interest, and said he'd tell her about both someday. When she added, "Why not now?" he said almost gruffly:

"In order to know me, Harriet, I'd have to begin at the beginning—in Cardiff, Wales, where I was born, or after the death of my father. He died of scurvy."

"At sea?" Harriet asked.

"Yes. He owned a whaling ship. I was only sixteen at the time, a harpooner, and a good one at that. If he'd lived, we wouldn't have lost our ship. The Old Man knew how to handle a crew." He got up then, lit a cigar, and observed that the squall had passed.

On deck once again, Harriet asked if the crew of his whaling ship had sunk her.

"Harriet, as Emily would say, that story is a little strong for a girl."

"Of course you know best, sir. But since I'm of age, Aunt Emily must remember that I'm supposed to think for myself."

"True," he replied, wincing at a reply which, he suspected, might have been aimed at him.

"So you may tell the story if you wish," she said firmly.

"Well, I suppose your father told you that life at sea has always been hard. Sailors do strange things. They think strangely. They're the most superstitious lot you'll find anywhere. And it was superstition, with the help of rum and a woman, that cost me all my father had left. There was my mother and Jim, my little brother. They looked to me for a living, which I made until that trip to the South Pacific. I was twenty at the time."

He lapsed into pensive silence before going on. "We had two whales aboard. The rum was in casks below. It was served only when a whale was towed in and flensed. Smeared with blood and blubber, their feet sinking in flench-gut, the hands would grasp their cups and drink it down. They'd eye Reed, the chief mate, and me like dogs, their eyes talking for their greedy stomachs. It was no sight for a woman, though we had a few aboard at times—island girls. They kept below while the boats were out, a matter of whaling superstition.

"The name of this girl was Vai Manu. Her name meant Water Bird. She was an Amazon creature, shapely, with copper-shot skin, and tattooed. A veritable fish. But her passion was rum. I've seen her dance for hours—island dances, graceless and immodest. The men supplied her with rum at intervals."

"And you tolerated such behavior?" Harriet asked in surprised tone.

He experienced a sense of pleasure as he replied, "Perhaps Emily is right."

She did not answer him.

"Half the men were pressed into service. The usual procedure was to pass out rum before we embarked, get them all drunk and sick, and then teach them a thing or two about discipline as we revived them."

Harriet winced and shuddered. "How could you?"

"Your father," he remarked casually, "was once a whaler. His success might have sprung from a different practice." As she raised her brows, he went on:

"But back to Vai Manu. She was a bold creature. She'd invade the fo'c'sle or the mates' cabins in the dead of night. She'd strip cups and then hunt the key to the provision room, which I kept. Rum was an agent of the devil aboard ship, and the devil was to pay if it wasn't on board. It kept the officers busy weighing the crew's thirst against their good judgment.

"We decided to rid the ship of Vai Manu as soon as land was sighted. But we were far east of the Marquesas Islands and moving north toward the equator. I suggested placing her in a boat, and we probably would have done just that but for the business at hand.

"Early one morning the lookout at the masthead cried out, 'Thar she blows!' I had the ship put away and we moved toward a small pod of whales. Soon the boats were lowered and the ship brought to the wind with main-tops'ls hove aback. The men were out, three boats of them. In the crow's-nest, I ordered them to lay on the oars. A whale rose up close to the mate's boat and spouted. The harpooner struck, and the beast carried them a good half mile to leeward. The yards were braced and we put off in their direction. I never saw that boat or whale again, nor Mate Reed and his men.

"But before we lost sight of the boat, the old carpenter yelled out, 'Look! The pagan wench is watchin' from atop the fo'c'sle!' There was Vai Manu between the lashed boats. He'd no sooner said it than a yell from the second boat brought me around. Another whale struck with his tail just as I looked. He stove the boat in.

"Late that afternoon when the lead boat was given up for lost, the men hoisted a hogshead of rum to deck and let loose. As I went down to break up the commotion, Vai Manu came up from behind and tossed me into the sea.

"When I got aboard once more, she was running about the deck with a torch. The men cursed me for allowing the Marquesan woman to be seen by a whale. 'You know whales don't like a woman's eyes, sir. We're going to hang her as soon as we get good and drunk. And one fine day we'll see you in hell.'

"The ship was almost burned out from under them before they hoisted the girl to a yard and let her swing. The bosun, steward, and I took off in the only boat we could rouse. Several of the crew jumped. We saved ten. The rest screamed above the hiss of flames as my ship lay over on her beam."

Silence reigned for some time. "Why did you let them hang her?" Harriet asked.

"I? Why, I couldn't have done much to prevent it—even if I'd wanted to."

"Steward," he called. When the obsequious man had served him, he said:

"I lived on Fatu Hiva for nearly a year. From there I worked on board a Frenchy to Singapore. I ran opium from India to China, and sailed from Manila to Hong Kong another year. I went home with a few thousand pounds, only to find that my mother had died and my young brother had gone to America. I found Jim in Philadelphia attending school. I joined him for a few years, in an endeavor to catch up on my education. Then came the War between the States. I had a better offer from the rebels, and I ran supplies from Liverpool to Charleston until the Yankees shot the masts off the brigantine Bannockburn near Cape Romain. The next week I was pressed into the United States Navy, where I intercepted runners like the one I had been.

"A year later I was sent to Boston to outfit ships for the Navy."

"And your brother?" Harriet asked.

"Jim was wounded at Gettysburg," he said pensively. "A great lad, he was; like my mother, cut from her pattern—kind, soft eyes, and a dreamer's mind. But how I loved that boy.

"I wasn't much good for months after the war ended. Hunger put me to looking for work, and work took me to the harbor. And there I met face to bows the prettiest ship I'd ever seen. She was the *Quatre Bras!* She was later called the *Barnacle Goose.* I'll tell you about it.

"What a ship!" he beamed. "Steward!" He forgot the steward's presence. "Aye, what a ship she was," and he forgot Harriet was there. "By God, she had lines like no other ship, except——" He scowled and lapsed into silence.

"The *Gerrymander?*" she prompted.

"You persist in voicing that name in my presence!" he snapped. "I don't like it. And what's more, I'll punish her, if it's the last——" He checked his anger and turned a menacing eye on the steward. "You'll leave the bottle here. Get about your duties and show willing."

Harriet suppressed an amused chuckle and sat out the silence.

"The *Quatre Bras* had a personality felt by seamen. To some she said, 'Stay away'; to others she beckoned. As I stood watching her, an old wharfie came up and asked if I heard her talking. 'Almost,' I answered. 'Wal, she's quite a gossip, matey. Aye, so she be. To them as has the love o' the sea in 'em, she'll sing a chantey, but to them as has all gain in mind and no salt, she'll lay 'em low wi' every kind o' sailor's oath.' He walked off only to return. 'She's a Adams, she is. Aye, so she be.'

"I had heard of Adams ships. I walked up and down the wharf looking at her, going through a sail trim from kites ablow down to storm canvas. I heard my voice saying, 'She responds. By God and a purple dolphin, she does!'

"'To what!' laughed a gentleman suddenly at my side.

"'To a sailor's hand, sir. And I can tell you why. See the way she sits, and look at the mainpost there.' I went through the whole enthusiastic explanation. When I finished, I said, 'She's called me by name. Aye, she says, "Come aboard, Robert Culver."'

"The handsome stranger—he was that—mellow, but hearty and red, asked me about myself. I told him all, from whales to opium and Yankee cannon. He seemed impressed. Then he asked me one more question:

"'Young man, if she was full of gold in a storm, and the captain said run for it when the Lord had just told you to heave to, what would you do?'

" 'I, sir, would first secure all the gear, see that every hatch was battened down and securely wedged at every cleat, and—what tack are we on, sir?' I asked, as if it made any difference.

" 'Say the port,' he replied with a grin.

" 'Then I'd have the tops'ls ready for clewing, the oil bags readied, and tell the Lord, if He hadn't caught on already, that He'd better move faster because the captain had said we were going to run for it.'

"The next day I was second mate aboard her. That man, Harriet, was the A in the flag. He was your father."

Harriet was beginning to see that part of his life which he had guarded well up to this day. He had adventured, and he had been frank in his account of it. Boiled down, her over-all opinion of him needed reshaping, perhaps, and in his favor.

He smiled. He was driving the *Quatre Bras* into the episodes wherein she earned her fond nickname.

2

"There is the goose barnacle and the barnacle goose," he said. "The former is a barnacle. The latter is a goose that breeds in the far north. But I'm getting ahead of my story.

"The ship left Boston for San Francisco three days after I boarded her. We were promised increased shares if we got her there under four months. Now the trip had been made in eighty-nine days, but we didn't carry that kind of captain. Mr. Brisbane loved his tophamper, and he was not one to flick at a crew. And, too, we sat heavy with mining machinery. The chief mate was an old fogy—like Brown over there. So there was I, anxious for speed, and hamstrung. I wanted royals and studdings'ls, though the gods of the quarter-deck couldn't see above tops'ls.

"Mr. Brisbane was laid up with fever when we reached the Horn, and the chief mate couldn't stay up forever. So he split the watches. Instead of walking the weather gangway, I stood the poop; I crowded sail on her. We rounded the Horn with studdings'ls set. We blew the top out of her before we reached San Francisco. I wasn't relieved because I was needed. But when we dropped anchor I was no longer an officer.

"When Dean Adams heard about our one-hundred-ten-day run, he was pleased. And when he heard that I'd been relieved of my duties for blowing out her sticks, I was called before him and Captain Brisbane.

"'Young man,' he said, 'do you remember the question I asked you one day about the Lord and the captain?' I did. 'Well, then, what caused you to change horses?' He had a grave look on his face as I groped for some answer. Soon I had one:

"'I reckon, sir, I got confused with the voices. I couldn't figure out which was God's and which was the captain's—they sounded very much alike, sir.' He laughed deep, and Mr. Brisbane got redder the longer he glared at me. The next thing I knew, I was first officer aboard another Adams ship. And a year later, when Brisbane died, I was made captain of the *Quatre Bras*."

The ship's bell struck eight times—it was four in the afternoon. "Have you had enough of my story, Harriet?"

"I'm enjoying it." She smiled.

"Then I'll tell you about the *Barnacle Goose*.

"The *Quatre Bras* was headed for Hamburg by way of Iceland, with a cargo of cork and textiles to the latter, and heavy machinery to the former. It was that season when the ice breaks up and drifts on down into the shipping lanes. We kept two men at the masthead and dared good driving sail only by day.

"One night the chief mate walked the poop, thinking of the ice he'd seen that afternoon. He had barely enough sail on her for steerageway, and a lookout peering foolishly ahead into the black night. He had considered sending up a flare, so great was his premonition. Lanterns were swinging from the jib boom and upper yards, but they dug into the darkness just so far. I called it a half-spoke light because that's about as good a runoff as its warning would have given the helmsman.

"The mate was at that moment considering the helmsman's whine for a little more sail. She wasn't getting enough push for easy steering. He lowered a lantern to get a better view of the log line, saw that it was minus any trail. Then the ship seemed to crunch coral with her false keel forward. It was light and easy, and you wondered if you'd just imagined it. The lead was cast—and the forward keel, believe me, hadn't an inch of water under her, the stern no more than a fathom!

"The mate and helmsman looked deep into each other's eyes. Then: 'All hands on deck! Lanterns! Call the Old Man!' When I got on deck, the second was in the dory with a lantern in each hand, calling on the men to lay on the oars. Then we felt the pressure on the portside. Something was pushing us along slowly.

"There was no sleep on that ship as every man waited for the dawn. The feeling was creepy. The lead was kept over the side and dripping up. No current under us whatever. I heard prayers in the fo'c'sle, and I ordered the steward to pass a ration of whisky. The day was bound to come up soon, unless we'd drifted off the face of the earth.

" 'Could it be ice?' the first officer asked as we sat in conference in my cabin.

" 'How the hell could we get into an ice pocket?' I flung at him. I knew it was ice, though I was afraid of panic and desertion among the crew.

"The day broke thick. We put out scouting boats only to return to the horn we blew at short intervals none the wiser. We sounded the water, hoping for room to maneuver. It wasn't there. We tried to pole out, and we shifted cargo weight aft, but she wouldn't budge. We were pushed slowly southward all that day.

"Night came and no sleep. It was a hellish night: rum was served every watch; fights broke out in the fo'c'sle; some of the lads put their chests in the boats and examined the davits and lashings with eyes that looked to the future.

"The third day was the same. We made a pretense at good humor, drawing every laugh we could until the hollow ring of it wore at our ears. But the second's amusement seemed genuine when he said, 'Here we sit in the middle of the North Atlantic like a live goose weighted with barnacles.' All laughed. The ship was the *Barnacle Goose* from that day on.

"It was on the night of the third day. I had just arrived on deck and spoken to the mate about the lifting murk when a booming sound split the night. It was directly south of us. Men ran in every direction, but mostly to the boats. They seemed to wait for God or devil, asking no favor other than a chance to row away. As they stood there, feeling much the same as I, the ship was lifted up out of the water. Before it could fall on its beam ends, it went down again, leaning heavily to starboard.

" 'Ice!' I said, grabbing for a ringbolt. It was time to call it by name. 'Ice, and we're on it!' I chuckled and asked the mate how he'd done it. He didn't answer—the antics of a mad crew claimed his grave eyes in that moment. They were lowering away the boats.

"I ran down to them, the mates after me. 'Now men,' I said when they stood sullen and half subdued, 'I've got the answer to this. I know what's wrong. Obey me, and we'll get along fine. Buck me, and we'll all bleed some more.' There was no answer. 'Now make lively and heave the Hamburg cargo over the side. Then we'll make our way out!'

"Then the big decision stood before me again—the ice rose up once more and the ship with it. It settled back slowly. There was a second rush for the boats. I weighed Mr. Adams and my career against life and death, and everything against the working of nature and the time left us for escape. I felt the cheapness of life, the callousness of command. I stared at the men, seeing worthless animals herded together in terror. Any pity which I possessed up to that moment disappeared.

" 'On second thought, men, we'll not heave valuable cargo over the side. We'll sit here until morning and gamble with death.' "

Harriet sat rapt, lost in a panorama of ship and sea. Culver talked on:

"The hull grated as it leaned more, and the men drew closer together in whispered conversations. I was crazy, surely, they said in low tone; the ship was jinxed, and if the ice didn't get them, I would. They would rush me, I knew, no matter the odds. I ordered the mates to have their guns ready, to shoot if necessary. Some cursed me, and a few resorted to smatterings of a master's duty to his men.

" 'Aye,' I agreed, 'a master doesn't jeopardize the lives of his men. But it's all based on his own idea of what makes up jeopardy. From now on Captain Culver makes his own laws in dealing with men.' Inside me, I was reaching for new and lasting views; if these creatures were men, then I'd have no trouble in later years. This memory of cowards would envelop those who stood in my way. It was a wonderful discovery. It was red meat to my loneliness."

Harriet did not alter her expression. But his next words struck hard at her sense of right and wrong.

"Young Dunlap hailed from Providence. A likable sort he was, blond and blue-eyed, and good material for a future captain. He was the first to rush me. I saw the grin of a tiger on his face, and fine manhood behind the coals of his eyes. In another moment his expression underwent a change: he lay on deck with a different kind of grin on his face—it was of utter disbelief as he saw the blood running out of a hole in his body."

"No!" Harriet protested.

"Yes. I had no time to watch him. 'Men,' I said, 'I meant to wing him.' My admission of error served to further infuriate them, and I heard my sentence read:

" 'Captain, we're coming after you. Sure, you'll take some of us, but you can't get all.'

"The ice chose that moment to act up. It went down and the *Quatre Bras* seemed to fall hard into the sea. The water swished and sucked, but the ship sat down and rocked. She was free of the undersea bottom! That fact stood above all else, even though I was thrown forward and sprawled on the deck; in another moment I was unarmed and at the mercy of the crew. The mates, neither having ever shot a man, were quickly overpowered.

" 'You're a pack of fools,' I said as I measured their fear and indecision. 'Go ahead and shoot, and leave the ship. Either way, you'll hang from a scaffold stuck up in the precious land you want under your feet.'

"They blinked their eyes and exchanged glances. 'Go ahead!' I chuckled. 'But you're afraid of that, and you're afraid to cast off without me.' I eyed them for long, silent moments before saying, 'Now to your stations and make lively.'

"The weakness of man! The crew was but a single man that needed only a stronger man to shake the props from under it."

Harriet felt a chill in the air. He went on:

"The channel in that ice was a miracle of nature, not by its shape or even its very presence there, but because it lay in wait for us, a perfect trap timed to our arrival. Why? I asked myself that throughout the remainder of that voyage, through the trial in Boston in which I was charged with murder. Was it an accident?

"It was not. Fate separated the weak from the strong to reveal one man's destiny—mine."

3

"That's the story of the *Barnacle Goose*," he said, jerking them back to the deck of the *Shanghai Packet*.

"Your father," Culver said at last, "did not condone murder, neither did he overlook mutiny. I had been right, he agreed, simply because I had acted my role to the end. The court sat on a stack of cases wherein sailors had been deliberately mistreated and it was biased. I fought, and Dean Adams smiled. I won because I was strong. It's the weak who suffer in any case.

"In the next few years, I ran the seas with the *Barnacle Goose*. I ran faster with more goods; I sailed undermanned; and no sailor ever put on fat from the fare I served. Sunday belonged to the sailor and the Lord, but I stole half of it for Captain Culver. She rode on the black side of Dean Adams's ledgers. I was allowed to buy into the ship.

"Then one day I was flagged down in the stream, just as I pulled out of New York for the Orient. The Old Man wanted me in Boston. When I got there, he was in a hospital. I remember he was sitting up and sending his sternest eye my way.

" 'Bob,' he said, 'I'm afraid you've run your last cargo.' A few sharp deals of the past paraded before me, though all were in our favor. He grinned and said, 'You'll miss the *Barnacle Goose*, won't you?'

" 'Yes, sir, but what's the tack?' I asked.

" 'Just this, Bob, you're going to run the firm the way you drive a ship.'

"I did. I made many changes. No reflection on your father—one can sometimes get so close to a sail he can't feel the wind. I found in the firm a young man of unusual ability. He possessed a mathematical mind and keen insight. I pushed him up the ladder. His name was Amos De Loach. Together we moved along. I planned and he carried the budget sheet in his ready blond head. We added to the line.

"Then there came the day when I was called to Louisburg Square. You stood out in the hall, Harriet, in tears. I remember you looked up at me, a little girl about to lose something very dear to her. You and your mother walked away from the relatives gathered there and went inside with me. There your father lay propped up in bed, looking as fit as ever, except for the grave expression on his face. He hadn't long. You may remember his words:

" 'Bob, look after them.' He looked at you and your mother. 'Like you did the *Barnacle Goose*. I'm leaving you enough stock, Bob, to make you richer than you ever dreamed. You'll fight as hard to serve that biggest block as you will your own. Remember the question about the captain and the Lord?'

" 'Aye, sir.'

"He smiled. 'Then don't get the voices confused.' He said to your mother, 'Anna, trust Bob Culver in all things.' Do you remember, Harriet?"

"Yes, I remember."

Culver leaned toward her, saying in half-playful tone, "You seem to have forgotten his message of late."

"I?" she returned. "I hardly think so. You see, I'm careful, and it behooves me to think of some words along with the ones uttered after your departure that day."

"Yes?" he replied soberly, anxiously.

"He said, 'And if Bob Culver in years to come turns into a doddering old fogy, that Adams one per cent is a lever with which to oust him.' " As Culver sat up slowly in his deck chair and evoked the wrath of God into his face, Harriet laughed lightly and said, "But my father also made a fair prediction when he added, 'I don't think you'll ever need it for that purpose.' "

Robert Culver slowly relaxed. "A good prediction, don't you think?" he asked gruffly.

Harriet merely smiled and peered into the future.

4

The evening meal was served them there. Emily ate in silence, sparingly. The sea didn't agree with her, and she soon departed. It was not until they had finished that he said:

"Your mother delved into business affairs for a while." He lit a cigar and blew smoke into the breeze before continuing. "She wanted to better conditions for the common sailor. She began with the old *Nelly Swift*. She could afford it, she said, and she went to great lengths. Even De Loach, who was as socially inclined as she, tried to discourage her there. The *Nelly Swift* became the joke of the seven seas."

"You allowed her to appear ridiculous?" Harriet's tone was sharp.

"No. It's just the way it all worked out. Let us say I humored that big stock of the firm."

"You were quick to remind me of that," Harriet said amiably.

"I am, indeed," he replied bluntly. "But back to cases.

"We were thrown together by the press of business affairs. She was not only lovely in appearance, she was kind and inspiring. As the months wore into years, I found myself seeking reasons for visits to Louisburg Square. And my attention to dress underwent a change. I can hear her musical voice—so like yours, Harriet. Then one day I asked her to attend the opera with me. She refused. I turned to the harbor, and there I spent the evening in Prince Albert and silk hat playing cards with a group of captains."

Harriet sat up with renewed interest. She had never suspected that Mr. Culver had admired her mother.

"She was rather cool to me after that. I was disappointed, angry, and afraid. Then I saw the ice trough and the deck of the *Goose* and the crew. I had forged my way up with the force I found there. But there had been no woman on board. For weeks I avoided her. Then a matter of business took me to her. As I stood to go, she said:

" 'You've acted strangely of late, Robert Culver. Why?'

" 'I am a sailor at heart, madam, and you're the captain. I'm not used to giving a captain an off-course answer.'

" 'Then speak up—sailor,' she said, laughing lightly.

" 'I've acted strangely,' I said bravely, 'because I've felt that way about you.'

"She eyed me thoughtfully and served a second cup of tea. As her hand brushed mine, the cup fell to the floor, and both of us laughed. It seemed to break down a barrier. Some things aren't explainable: they strike deep into some part of you you don't know exists. Sometimes a bell at sea can take the edge off a spell of weather. The next thing I knew I had taken the short step separating us. I drew her to me. She said nothing, though there were tears in her eyes."

Harriet could not contain her surprise. She uttered a little exclamation. Culver, if he heard her, paid no attention.

" 'Anna,' I said, 'some decision must come of our meeting here to-day. I am aware of our positions. You are what you are, what is wholly appropriate to Boston. There is every reason why I should not be here today. But I am what I am, so there is every reason why I should be here.

" 'I love you, Anna,' I said. 'Will you marry me?'

"She said, 'Would you ask that if you knew I still love Dean Adams?'

" 'Aye!' I replied. 'I have never for a moment suspected that you did not.'

" 'Then you're not a wise man, Robert Culver,' she said, adding, 'I think too much of you to marry you.' "

5

He was nearing the end of his story. He wanted Harriet to view the real man rather than the prosaic man of business; he wanted her to see his every side. She must feel his strength, his suffering, and yet she must view him with curiosity. He moved toward a climax, one sure to provoke such qualities into mind.

"I resented her decision, Harriet.

"I had picked up the cup that had fallen to the rug and placed it in my pocket. Several days later I went to the wharf where the *Aladdin* was tied up and smashed the cup against her bows. I felt better.

"With that I went to the office. I took a captain to task, discharged a clerk, and raised hell in general. Amos wanted to know what was wrong with me.

" 'I don't know,' I lied. 'But I'm going to shake this firm apart until I find out.'

" 'Which part of it?' he asked, grinning.

"Amos was a great boy—then.

"I drove the firm with a whip. Business offered some relief for my defeat at the hands of the only woman I had ever loved. I took my defeat out on men by furious trading, by forcing those under me to accomplish the impossible.

"Your mother did her utmost to make things pleasant. She even changed the name of the firm to Culver and Adams. She did even more—it was she who first conceived the idea of a great ship, the greatest of all square-riggers, the *Robert Culver.*

"I met Ellen in late spring. The first time she looked into my eyes I felt her walking inside me to my empty spot. She seemed warm as a summer breeze, and as refreshing. She had the charm of a woman of thirty-five. I reckon you'd call her attractive. I don't know. All I knew was that she called me without speaking, that she offered solace without voicing it.

"I examined her as I imagine I would a slave in some foreign market. What did she mean to me; why was I attracted to her? There was no answer you could explain; you could only feel it. I arranged a first meeting, and from that a second."

He saw Harriet in the light of the ship's lanterns as she leaned forward, impressed, and curious once again. Her face merely searched, like her mother's, and held its opinions behind her eyes.

"Ellen asked nothing of any man, though she was searching for something. She was drifting, trying to forget something. We had a lot in common. And before summer's end we had memories—we disappeared over fanciful horizons together."

He saw Harriet stiffen, her hand lifting instinctively to her face. He had planted impressions, aye. She knew his strength, his weaknesses, his suffering, his hates, and loves.

"But your mother," he said in conclusion, "was stronger than Ellen and horizons I could never quite grasp.

"Aye," he sighed. "There may be captains of a *Barnacle Goose* who view men for what they are. But there is always an awareness of a strength greater than that of a captain. Next to God, it is a woman."

Harriet was confused. She could form no quick opinion of him. He was both bad and good; he was also bold and sensitive. In another moment she saw him a man both strong and weak. Opinions held even as another fact rose up for her view—he was a victim of the conflict inside him: the captain of the *Barnacle Goose* had joined with the man who had been denied the love of her mother. They fought to rob him of any happiness.

It had been so at the time of the "Figurehead Affair." It was manifesting itself again—now—as he sailed toward Captain Boll and the *Gerrymander*.

"Why did you tell me all this?" she asked.

"I told you it might be, as Emily would say, a little strong for you. Was it?"

"Well, it seems you went out of your way to let it be known that the captain of the *Barnacle Goose* has taken you over completely. And you seem to blame it all on my mother."

He sat back in his chair, silent.

"This voyage seems to prove it," she said. "You're trying to keep that man alive by renewing your foolish hate of the *Gerrymander* through Captain Boll."

"I have learned to view Captain Boll in the same light as I do the ship he sails, Harriet."

"You are at least honest," she said quickly. "But the course you are taking can only lead to the destruction of any happiness in store for you. Why not forget about scores to even with Amos and Captain Boll? Give them a chance to exonerate themselves, and you'll find yourself a greater man than the captain of the *Barnacle Goose*."

"Why, that man," he admitted, "is as much a part of me as a wife is to most men. The only thing that could ever take the place of the man born on the *Goose* is an understanding woman."

"Then I'd get myself a wife," she said bluntly.

He did not answer presently. When he did, he leaned forward and faced her. "Perhaps I should do just that. But I told you about Ellen, and all women are Ellen. There is only one Anna."

Then he got to his feet, feigning surprise at a sudden discovery, one which he had patiently nursed for just this opportunity:

"But there is another Anna!

"Harriet, you are Anna all over again!"

Harriet drew back with a stifled exclamation. Then she got to her feet and almost ran across the deck.

Robert Culver followed her with his eyes. A smile of satisfaction wreathed his face as he sent his gaze out into the tropical night through which the *Shanghai Packet* tore her way.

He had surely prepared her for his proposal in the near future.

BOOK THREE ❧ 1885-1886

8 &ᴐ THE STRIKER, THE CASH, AND CULVER

I STOOD ON THE "GERRYMANDER'S" WEATHER POOP, MR. BLUE ON THE lee side, his silence matching mine. The China Sea stretched all about us, unruffled except for our wake. We sailed close to the wind. The late December sun sent shadows of every stanchion to port. Every man was busy, and the lookout in the masthead strained his eyes for any junk or other craft that acted suspiciously. This was a pirates' sea, where they played for keeps with ships, valuables, and men.

Boll, after Mr. Cott's discharge, had sent me on to Calcutta, Hong Kong, Shanghai, and Sydney. He had feigned illness and prevailed on Mr. Ruscomb to arrange for cargoes while he recuperated. He took his rest with St. Ebenezer in French Indo-China, with his cash pieces. In the meantime, the Gerrymander ran tea, wool, jute, and general cargo. I sold sand we carried for ballast to an Indian temple at Chittagong. We had made a fair wind of it for all concerned.

"We should reach Singapore before the midwatch," I said to Mr. Blue. He spoke his "Aye" with schooled indifference and then proceeded to raise hell in general with two men who were tarring down in the main masthead. The lookout cried, "Land ho! Off the starboard bow!" The ship's bell sounded twice. All was well on deck.

"I'll be in my cabin, Mr. Blue," I said.

When I entered the captain's quarters, Chess stood, or reeled, across from me, lost in the act he was staging for his own adventure. He had not seen me.

"Sir! Sir!" he sneered, facing some invisible foe. "You dare order Chester Duval about? How very damned impertinent of you! Now fetch me the bottle, and show willing." He threw out his chest and raised a hand imperiously before hiccuping. He reached for the bottle himself, since the villain who wasn't there seemed reluctant to obey him. A wry grimace and a short oath interrupted his theatricals, but not for long. He folded his arms across his chest slowly and spread his legs. "You were once the scourge of the seas, Captain Boll, but it's my day now. Aye! Remember the time you put me in a bosun's chair and swung me over the side? Well, the same for you now, Mr. Striker. I'm in command, and your gray beard does not strike compassion in my hardened soul. I—hic—am captain, Captain Chester Duval, feared and respected in every port. Aye—hic!"

When he reached for the bottle again, I thought it time to bring down his fanciful curtain. "Look out, Captain," I warned. "He's slipping up behind you." He started, and of all the facial contortions I've ever witnessed in a race for soberness, he struck a record. I advanced, seized the bottle, and ordered him to sit before he fell. The great Captain Duval was soon the meekest of all the hard captains of the sea. I picked up a novel and eyed it.

"So this is what you're studying. It's hardly the English grammar I bought for you. And about your arithmetic. Well, what about it?"

"Little Ahab's studying it, sir." He was docile as he swayed in his chair.

"A hell of a cabin boy you are," I snapped. "I try to make something out of you and you persist in cursing and smoking. And now you've taken to drink."

"A man has his moments, sir—hic," he replied dolefully. And he fell out of his chair, drunk as a lord.

"Well!" Only then did I indulge in a grin. "When you come around, young fellow, you'll be in confinement, and on a diet of bread and water." When alone, I winked an eye at Harriet Adams in the gilt frame and proceeded to lose myself in the sea yarn Chess had left behind.

Midnight found the Gerrymander in the Singapore Road, threading the shoals and hulks and taking our bearings from a light on Malay Spit. We made quarantine anchorage and set anchor watch for the night, completely unaware of the treat, or threat, in store for our eyes the next morning.

2

The dawn warmed the eastern heavens out beyond the Dutch islands with a misty orange; the sun, not far behind, steamed the strait as it sped westward from far-off Borneo to our horizon. The day promised to break clear.

On deck, I studied the ships at anchor. Past junks, steamers, a maze of sail, and sampans and lighters, my eye fell on a strangely familiar pennant. It was the same that we flew, a huge C about to swallow an A.

"The *Shanghai Packet!*" I exclaimed. There she sat not thirty rods out from our port bow, her sails clewed up, her huge masts gleaming, and her anchors in the mud. She had arrived during the night. I raised my telescope and studied her. Her crew was busy with the usual morning chores, and the officer of the deck stood with his back to me. Then I saw another figure on the poop.

"A woman," I said aloud. So it was. With telescope up, she was trading glances with me. "No! It can't be!" I said. But there she stood. The girl of the portrait had come to life, and the vision had flown to a sister ship, where it stood alive and smiling. I grinned and lifted a hand in greeting.

"Miss Adams!" I said. "And what a gorgeous creature you are alive." At that moment Mr. Blue came up from behind, looked over the rail, and proceeded to eye me with alarm. "I was talking to a mermaid," I said, moving off.

An hour had not passed before a messenger from the *Shanghai Packet* arrived with an order for our master to appear at Mr. Ruscomb's office at ten o'clock sharp. I, acting as master, hoped Miss Adams would be there.

A mirror was a handy object that morning. At last I stood with every hair in place and busied myself with the slant of my cap. Strangely enough, it had never caused me any anxiety before. I had merely set it atop my head and forgotten its existence. I was soon armed with logbook, and other papers necessary to any ordeal ahead, and boarded a sampan.

Mr. Ruscomb greeted me with perfunctory ease and introduced Robert Culver, who grunted without rising or extending his hand. I retrieved my hand in mid-air and swore under my breath that he would never have the opportunity to repeat the act with me. Just then Harriet Adams turned from the window and enveloped me with the same eyes I knew so well in the portrait. She seemed more mature than her picture, and lovelier, I thought.

She walked toward me, surprising both Mr. Ruscomb and Culver when she held out a hand and said, "Mr. Flint, I'm very pleased to meet you, I'm Harriet Adams." Her voice was rich in timbre, and soothing. I made a mental note of that as well as other facts. I had asked what she was physically—the portrait had cut her in two—and now she stood in full view, a most pleasing answer.

"The pleasure is mine, Miss Adams," I said before standing at the back of her chair. Then I sat down between her and Mr. Culver, feeling the presence of one friend as I faced the condemning eyes before me.

"Mr. Culver would like to get at the bottom of this cash-piece mystery as soon as possible, Mr. Flint," Mr. Ruscomb said nicely. "He needs your help."

"What sort of help do you want?" I asked.

"Why, just enough to support a charge of barratry against Captain Boll."

"Barratry?" I said, lifting my brows. "Are you, Mr. Ruscomb—begging your pardon—crazy?"

"I am not." His vexation pleased me. Recovering quickly, he said, "We have heard Mr. Cott's story. It's here on paper, the full account of the voyage, including a mutiny, which he credits you with suppressing. That much is deserving of our praise." I stole a glance at Culver, and then at my right hand, which he had refused, and smiled. "You realize, of course, that since Mr. Cott was not dismissed by Mr. Culver you are chief mate only at Mr. Culver's order. Does this information prompt you to help us?"

"Not in the least," I said in level tone. "Mr. Cott's dismissal was deserved. Didn't Captain Boll show you the petition signed by the crew?" He replied that it had been forced. "And who said so, Mr. Cott?" I asked. "Now I'm afraid someone is putting personal injury up for proof, sir. Barratry is any illegal or fraudulent act committed by the officers or crew to the prejudice of the shipowner. Right?" He nodded. "Then what's the basis of the charge?"

"The ship carried case oil. The general precautions pertaining to the disposal of cargo specifically state that petroleum products should not be carried on ships which have explosives on board. Answer that one, Mr. Flint."

"Suppose you ask a question first."

"Very well. How was the big iron box labeled, the one the crew dumped off the Sumatra coast?"

"Oh, I see," I said, trapped by a technicality.

"Speak up, Mr. Flint. Mr. Culver is most anxious to hear your explanation of that."

"Yes," I laughed, "I imagine so, since somebody is reaching deep for petty charges. Well, let me tell you something—that box did not contain explosives. I'll swear to that in court."

"Then what did it contain?" Ruscomb leaned forward with that question.

"That is beside the point. The fact remains, you have nothing upon which to pin any charge against the captain."

"Did you see inside that box, Mr. Flint?" I nodded. "Then you could swear that it was falsely labeled, couldn't you? And if it contains another item, which we strongly suspect, there is further proof of illegal intent to the prejudice of the shipowner—namely this, Mr. Flint."

He tossed a Gerrymander Cash to the desk. He was a deadly sort, a man who worked hard for Culver's approval.

"Mr. Flint, Mr. Cott gave us the location of that box. Would you?"

"Aye. Little Fortune Island, seven fathoms, northeast anchorage. And I'll say this, Mr. Ruscomb: that cash piece is what you'll find in the box."

"Thanks, Flint. Mr. Culver was sure you'd help," he said with the smug air of a prosecuting attorney.

"You're off course, sir," I said, bringing his eyes up sharp. I noticed Miss Adams's surprise and Culver's frown. "You'll wait some time before you can twist a barratry charge around that box. What's more, you know it."

"What about the camphor cargo, involving the ship, and therefore the owners, with a coin upon which the ship's name is stamped without authorization? The coin was used in shady trading, and the cargo then consigned to a man whom the owner does not approve."

"You asked for the answers. You'll get them. You will have to prove there existed any shady trading, and you'll admit that an owner's dislike of a man does not constitute a legal reason for refusing cargo. Personal opinions don't pay freight rates. Now, here's another fact worth your attention. When I first saw that coin you have there, I was as curious as the next one. I dug a little into the history of the word gerrymander, and I discovered that the word was coined back in eighteen hundred and twelve and soon came into general currency. So writes John Fiske. Therefore, if Captain Boll wished to use any word of general currency, there is no law to stop him. And——

"The name Gerrymander for a ship does not exist, officially. The firm of Culver and Adams does not list such a name, although it is painted on the ship's sides. It uses, as my logbook here plainly indicates, the symbol G-53."

Culver was on his feet, glowering. I sat calm, smiling. "I hope I have saved the firm a nice sum by revealing what any court would have told you in the first place." Then I got to my feet. "I'll await your orders aboard ship," I said, bowing out. It was only then I realized that Robert Culver had not spoken a word.

The door closed behind me, only to open again. Harriet Adams called after me, and I turned about.

"Mr. Flint," she said, advancing, "there is a matter I think we should discuss." She smiled at my perplexed look. "It is very important."

"Very well. I was just trying to beat my discharge to the ship."

"Oh." She lifted her brows and pursed her lips in feigned surprise. "Are you so sure of opinions in there?"

"So you have something to discuss? Splendid."

"It is really important, Mr. Flint."

"All the better." I smiled. "Now there's a little English tearoom off the bund——"

"There's a table over there." She glanced at a corner across from the quiet old man who served as Ruscomb's secretary.

When we were seated she removed her white gloves and studied me with such directness that I felt uneasy. "Why did you leave Harvard?" she asked suddenly. She was not one to let initiative lie unclaimed, I thought, somewhat amazed. "Of course, it doesn't matter," she went on. "I mentioned it simply to produce evidence of my knowledge concerning you."

"Sure," I said, "like I knew the color of your eyes and hair before I ever saw you."

"You have a gift for apt replies, Mr. Flint. You conjured up pictures Mr. Culver didn't want to see."

I frowned at an observation: she seemed to operate under the flag ruled by Culver. Perhaps I would do well to mend matters somewhat. "I suppose I talked too much," I reflected. "So I'll keep my eyes and ears open here and my mouth closed."

"As to your last words, I don't think you can." She drew me up sharply with that, and I permitted myself a twitch of open curiosity. "I am well armed with surprising weapons," she added.

"Indeed you are." There was no mistaking my meaning as my eyes traveled her hair, face, and neck.

"I like honest men," she reproved nicely. "But, in the vernacular of your trade, let's keep the helm amidships."

"My recent conversations with you were not along this pattern. Every morning and evening aboard ship, during Captain Boll's absence, I talked to you. You were very agreeable." I experienced a rising pleasure as I saw in her face sober doubt as to my sanity. She studied me in almost disinterested silence. She did not voice her curiosity, nor did I explain. The gain, if any, was mine. I had slowed her Yankee-sure advance.

She spoke at last, and in a manner that said she had discarded any inclination for friendliness. "You were quite convincing this morning. I was almost ready to believe you, Mr. Flint, even though I held evidence to the contrary."

"What are you driving at?" I asked.

"Mr. Culver would surely sound your doom if he were as well informed as I." She paused to accuse me with her eyes. "As a beginning, I'll quote a line or two I read recently.

" 'Something is afoot here; it is out of Boll's head.' "

The words impelled me forward, frowning, and she could not suppress a smile. " 'You see it as you do the star-sprinkled canopy of the East, and . . . when you try to pin one star down for a view, it twinkles out of the realms of understanding.' Poetic, isn't it?"

"Continue."

"Thanks." She smiled. " 'The voyage went uneventful: a death, prayers . . . for a wind . . . a subdued mutiny, planned ahead by Boll, and a record to port.' There was something about a four-masted ship loading herself to the water line. But the meat of the narrative, Mr. Flint, was simply this: a certain refutation of a man's convincing argument of this morning.

"I shall qoute: 'You should pay Boll, not me, for as long as I serve him I am serving you. Believe me this, and lay emphasis on the statement.' " She smiled more accusingly.

I sat back in my chair, lit a cigarette in thoughtful seriousness, and faced her with a smile, the only weapon at my command. With chin on folded hands, she smiled right back at me.

"I'm pooped in a high sea, I reckon," I put blithely, drawing her emphatic "Yes." Then I ventured slowly, "Is Mr. De Loach back in the Culver fold?"

"Quite the opposite." She then told me sketchily of the change of ownership of the *Cape Race*.

"So De Loach is through," I sighed, "and Tom Flint loses both his jobs. Well, so much for that."

"Amos is not through, and you have lost neither job as yet."

I smiled. "What's holding us up?"

"I am," she replied.

My eyes must have leaped out of their shadows as I formed a picture of what she had just conveyed. I put bluntly, "Moments ago you were sure I was crazy."

"And I," she said, examining me closely, "am not so sure that I'm not."

"So you stepped in to save De Loach. And he told you of his lowly spy aboard a ship of your firm. And you, as adamant as your father before you, put concrete instead of wormy wood under his financial house, thus becoming the biggest voice in two shipping firms.

"While I am employed by both! But forgetting my run of luck, what a tangled mess things are in. Personalities weaving in and out, one against the other, like a bushel of eels. Boll versus all, Flint versus all, including Boll, and both of us in cahoots; De Loach versus you and Culver, and you and De Loach in cahoots. It strikes you dizzy!"

She laughed with enjoyment. I joined her, and together we wrung of the whole a sort of unspoken comradeship. But when we stopped laughing, as we did suddenly, our eyes were locked. The cord between us seemed loath to break. Perhaps this was combat, or awareness; or a far-reaching beauty of scene and sound meandering through our short memories of each other.

She freed her eyes and grew sober, as if she took pleasure in reminding me that she would never lower her reserve again in my presence. She spoke of that "something afoot," reminding me that she had openly doubted my inability to keep my mouth shut. Thereupon, I told her as much as I wanted her to know; I stepped deviously around Boll's words, "Culver's picture must come down," and St. Ebenezer's camphor expedition. I said I knew little of the Gerrymander Cash, of Boll's ultimate direction with it. She seemed satisfied after a while, and I asked why she was here.

"Among other reasons, since Mr. Culver is out to ruin Captain Boll, I'm here to see that he gets a fair trial."

I frowned, surprised once more. Then, as if she sought to put me in my place once and for all, she said, "Regarding all, Mr. Flint, I think I shall remain patient and allow each man a run to an unveiling of his true colors. This includes you, of whom I've yet to form a definite opinion. I'm not so sure you won't lean to the side that offers the greatest gain. Are you?"

"No," I replied, allowing my hand to fall over hers, "I'm not quite sure of anything right now." I added, "Except that you're beautiful."

Her eyes fell to my hand slowly, then lifted with a sudden flash of resentment. She eyed me as if she hovered in debate over a choice of mocking laughter, worded malice, or quiet dignity before combining a little of all three with her proposition that followed.

"Mr. Flint," she said, withdrawing her hand, "since you're not sure which way you'll lean, I'm prepared to make it worth your while to forget your bargain with Amos."

I studied her soberly for a long time, saying at last, "I could really come to your aid there, couldn't I? If I sold out to you, you would be free of a thorn in the side—worry over what I'll do for De Loach which might embarrass you. It seems you're in a trap of your own making."

"How much do you want, Mr. Flint?"

"And if I sold out, you'd be doing De Loach a favor by unmasking me. So it's easy for you to sit by with propositions, isn't it?"

"I'm waiting for your answer."

"Somehow, Miss Adams, I can't picture you as the type of person who would violate your agreement with Amos De Loach. So I'm not interested." She sighed and smiled, as if she were both pleased and disappointed with my answer. At any rate, I was pleased, since I would not have given her that edge over me even if I had entertained any idea of breaking with De Loach.

"What are you going to do—for Amos, I mean? And when?"

"I don't know," I said with a smile and shrug. She frowned: the suspense wasn't to her liking, since she realized that I was actually free to do what I felt was opportune; and since she knew me only slightly, whatever I might do loomed a matter of conjecture. And, too, there was nothing she could do about it. She knew this—it was written into her expression. Then she said it, and more.

"It seems I'm the loser here," she said slowly. "Of course, I could go to Mr. Culver with the truth. But I won't—just yet." I smiled knowingly, causing her a flurry of resentment.

"You're smug in your position, aren't you? Well, consider this—Mr. Culver has asked me to marry him. Would you feel so secure if I accepted, Mr. Flint?"

I could not restrain my reply: "Would you, Miss Adams?"

3

The duty of taking in or discharging cargo generally falls to the chief mate. I was greatly pleased on the following day when I was presented with our cargo manifest. With something to occupy my mind, I retired to the captain's quarters to map the vessel.

I scowled upon entering, since Harriet Adams continued to flash her superior airs from the canvas with all the freshness of my day-old memories. I advanced upon her, forgetting the business at hand. "Would you actually consider marrying that old block of frozen granite?" I asked her portrait. There was no answer, nothing but a level gaze with a faint trace of mockery in it.

I charted the stowing of cargo for some time and then proceeded to review my position in the whole affair under her direct eyes. I was concerned with every move from every side in this game, and it behooved me to view possibilities. This I did, always returning to Harriet, who had maneuvered herself into a position that seemed as untenable as that of a man atop a powder keg. She had not taken me into her confidence from choice; but despite reasons that governed her behavior, I was her sole confidant; which of course, pleased me. It served as a beginning. And I, a man who had fallen in love with her before having ever seen her in person, warmed to my opportunity.

She had my sympathy, and more. Aye, much more. And for her respect of me, not to mention my own self-respect, as well as that higher feeling I aspired to in her eyes, I was committed to my position: I would rise and fall with De Loach, no matter the gain.

I had no sooner reached that decision than Mr. Blue announced visitors. I smiled, thinking Boll and St. Ebenezer had returned, and sat back to enjoy the remainder of the afternoon.

The door was opened, and there stood Mr. Ruscomb; and behind him, with drooping lids and fleering expression, stood Mr. Cott. Both men entered and stood aside while two men walked into the cabin with an old sea chest. It belonged to Mr. Cott. The chief mate had come back—as captain!

He took pleasure in lording it over the crew the next day. The men felt themselves tricked by Captain Boll, and especially Tom Flint, who had prevailed upon them to affix their signatures to a condemning lie against Mr. Cott. He exercised his evil grin and tongue with running satisfaction, always going just so far with his threats and then holding his real intentions behind his sensual eyes and lips; they would come later, on the open sea. Aye! I could see torment stretched over long weeks and days, leaping up to reward every man's signature. The men saw it, and felt it, and, as they had made a habit of turning to me in their moments of rising apprehension, they stole every opportunity that loading cargo presented for questioning me. But Mr.

Cott stalked the men as well as me. He delighted in the pictures his anticipating mind threw before him.

It was a long road to Boston.

"I'm anxious to get under way, Mr. Flint," he said late that afternoon in his new quarters. He poured from Boll's private stock with all the glee of a man about to sample the warm blood of an archenemy. "Very anxious." He winked an eye. "And I insisted that you travel as my first officer. Yeah, Mr. Flint, since you're a man who drives a ship along."

"Sure," I said, humoring him. "That was nice of you."

"I thought so. But about that convict, Mr. Blue. He's a mean one, Flint. Not mate material, and yet——" He smacked over a glass. "And yet, he'll side with the crew if he's berthed down forward."

"Do you anticipate trouble, sir?" I smiled.

He glared at me behind his grin for a moment, then blurted out, "Aye."

I lit a cigarette and turned my eyes on the picture of Harriet Adams; she seemed to mock me in my new position. Then I smiled inwardly: the fact that Mr. Cott had taken office should please me. And since it didn't please me in the least, I said:

"Well, Mr. Cott, we might as well try to get along with one another. You don't like me any more than you do the crew. And I'm not particularly fond of you. But let me tell you right off that those lads out there aren't to be——"

The statement was never finished: the door swung in hard, and there, walking toward us with all the arrogance of a viceroy, was Captain Boll.

I grinned. Boll simply stood there a long moment before saying, "Mr. Flint, what's the meaning of this?" He jerked a thumb toward Mr. Cott, who stood defensively.

"The new captain, sir," I said, arching my brows over the grin. "Mr. Culver has arrived on the scene."

Boll chuckled then. He pulled up a chair, reaching for the bottle which Mr. Cott had opened, and sat down, ignoring the new master completely. He peered at me lazily over a glass and asked for my full report. I talked, never so much as glancing at Mr. Cott, though out of the corner of an eye I saw him standing first on one foot and then the other, as if unable to make up his mind whether to assert himself or not, whether to sit with us or not. He never quite made up his mind.

As he stood there, Boll said, "So Culver wants to press a barratry charge, does he?" He emitted a low chuckle. "Well, well. I thought

Culver was smarter than that." Then he brightened somewhat. "So she came along."

I saw Mr. Cott's face working in agitation. Boll poured another drink, then said, "I left St. Ebenezer in the Celebes." Thoughtfully he said, "So she came along. There's something about her that——"

"That what?" I asked.

He grinned and shrugged. He turned a thin eye on the three oils screwed in the bulkhead, studying first Culver, then Harriet Adams. "She's not bad-looking." He spoke abstractedly. "So Culver wants a new captain. I wonder what he'll say tomorrow when he looks at my hole card."

He studied the ship in the picture next. "I want more sail on that ship, Mr. Flint. A lot more." I felt the brush of his winds. I heard his voice in my memory as it gave off with, "A wind, Lucifer, one to blow her sticks," and I saw the coins as they sped from his hands to a hungry sea. He turned to Mr. Cott then and said: "The ship in the picture should carry more sail, don't you think, Mr. Cott?"

Mr. Cott studied the picture for only a moment before grimacing unduly. His reply, just before he turned about and stalked off, was made in his usual unctuous tone: "Aye—aye, sir."

4

Boll, by ignoring Mr. Cott, had scored over the ex-mate again, and Mr. Cott's whining plea to Culver that afternoon was nothing short of a challenge to the bigwig's authority. And the captain of the old *Barnacle Goose* knew just how to deal with such upstarts as Boll. Aye! By God and a purple dolphin, he did! He sent for Boll.

As we boarded the *Shanghai Packet* that evening, Boll said, "Mr. Flint, I've waited a year for this visit."

"Culver's?" I asked.

"Culver's," he replied, grinning. "And——" He stopped short and gazed intently at a figure seated under the deck awning aft. I followed his gaze and saw Harriet Adams.

Boll walked up to her. I stood apart from them. She extended her hand, voiced a greeting, and smiled at him.

He held her hand as he said, "I'm glad you came, Miss Adams."

"Thank you, Captain Boll."

"It has been—let me see—nearly four years." He was holding her eyes with the same ease in which he continued to hold her hand.

"Yes." Her smile seemed strained.

"So you have not forgotten my visit." I was close enough to see his eyes narrow as they roamed her face and neck, then look back to her eyes. He added, "I hope you never forget it."

"Mr. Culver is expecting you," she replied; defensively, I thought. I welcomed an opportunity to speak up then. I said:

"We're late already, sir." As Boll turned to go, I lifted my cap to her. She smiled.

I glanced back at her when Boll moved ahead. She stood watching us, a puzzled look on her face.

Culver sat alone, glaring at us as if we were wayward puppets which he would gobble up in a hurry.

His black sideburns, his sharp gray eyes under black copses, and the frown between them which seemed to run down his short nose to a mouth of iron, all warned us of his mood. Boll took a chair after an easy greeting and sat back to survey the cabin with an air of disdain. I sat at Boll's right with an expression of assumed indifference in face and pose, though I realized that this meeting was freighted with dire importance as far as my own plans were concerned: should Culver divorce Boll here, it meant that I should meet with a decided setback in serving De Loach. I would follow Boll, if he came out of this conference unscathed, to some error on his part in favor of De Loach and myself.

"Captain Boll," Culver began, "you have served me well; you have been my best money-maker. It is indeed unfortunate for both of us that you cannot stand success. I have called you here for the express purpose of advising you that you are not only through, but that you will be prosecuted to the extent of the law." He paused, fished a draft from his pocket, and said, "Here is your pay, and bonus. Good day, Captain Boll." He got to his feet and held two checks. He seemed, in a measure, disappointed that he had traveled far only to find the Striker so easily conquered. It was like wasted passion in a man who thrived on long servings of it.

Boll smiled and said, "What law?

"Mr. Culver, let us get down to cases." The head of the firm of Culver and Adams stood there wavering between the press of decision and curiosity. He glowered, true, but he spiced his expression with interest.

And Boll seized the moment: "Since it is expected of a captain to serve God, firm, and mammon, let us say I'm loyal to the last two."

Culver's hand rose slowly to his heavy watch chain, a sure sign of some mental agitation.

Boll was eying one of the checks. In a moment he passed it to me, chuckling as he said, "This is for the record run." He turned to Culver and said, "You're generous, aren't you? Maybe I should turn elsewhere with what I have in mind."

"Captain," said Culver, "I am less interested in your schemes than in your crimes and their just reward."

"Then we'll talk about my crimes. I drove your ship faster than any man ever sent a ship to this destination. I made men bleed, and I broke their bones in the effort. Call it crime, but in your day you stood up in a court and used another definition: legitimate expediency." He proceeded to flick at Culver's manly ego with, "You have grown soft. I doubt your ability to hoist a sea lead now."

"Young man," Culver blustered, "I cannot only drive a ship as good as you, I can do it better. What's more, I can wring a bigger profit out of one! By God and a purple——"

"Hold it right there, sir," Boll interrupted. "I thought you'd say that." Thereupon he shocked me as much as he did Culver when he tossed a Gerrymander Cash piece up, let it fall atop the table, and said, "Consider the value of that!"

The fool; he dared to put that dazzling symbol of his bold imagination up for his own quick finish! "So this is a crime, is it?" He grinned.

Culver stood there, rocking on his feet, his fists clenched until the veins stood out like cords. But he stared at the cash piece, and in much the same manner that he would have eyed a bold, impudent devil who suddenly sat red and leering before him. And the devil reached into his mind for possibilities heretofore overlooked; he found them, it seemed, for Culver turned his eyes upon Boll as if he had just discovered the value and joy of allowing a worthy opponent to tie his own hangman's knot. He sat down, composed his ravaged features, and said harshly:

"Talk lively, Captain Boll."

"Thanks. You claim you can wring a bigger profit out of a ship than I. I say it can't be done." There was that seldom-met emphasis in Boll's level tone. "I can prove that statement to your gain.

"You are not above fattening your purse at the expense of the native. Every cargo your ships transport from the East is some man's profit over conditions here. You're a sailor, and a businessman, and you know of what I speak. But did you ever stop to consider the value of money where there is a scarcity of it?

"The scarcity of money in this part of the world is a boon to barter. And barter rules here, as you know." The spark of interest was fanning in Culver's face; perhaps it was simple curiosity, though it seemed that the little red devil was planting other seeds. I wondered at the diverse crop he might harvest.

"That's where the cash piece comes in," Boll said, drawing from Culver a word and a question: "How?"

"I trade with it."

Culver enjoyed a snort of disdain. He then eyed Boll with pity uppermost in his face and said, "Captain, you are crazier than I imagined."

"There's profit for the taking," Boll replied.

"What kind of profit? It smells of the small-time trader. You talk strangely for a man who knows the bigger profits from cargoes in the holds. You've lost your mind."

"Yes, I've lost my mind to profit that's big. Again I tell you money is scarce here."

"And what does that prove? Nothing, unless you choose to counterfeit the pound, guilder, and franc for some damned short-lived scheme that will place you farther back in jail than I intend putting you." He added, "If that is possible."

Boll ignored the threat and said, "You asked what the scarcity of money proved. It means that the cash will serve us for money."

"Another Mississippi Bubble," said Culver deprecatingly.

"The Mississippi Bubble," Boll argued, and with effect, "was doomed because of overissue and Government opposition." He added, "It was a poor idea compared to mine."

Culver chose that moment to lift his palms in a gesture of despair. He got to his feet then, free of the tempting little devil, and said he had heard enough.

"Sit down," Boll ordered. "I'll tell you how it works—or rather, how it has already worked. Now take the cargo of camphor."

The door opened behind me. I did not turn my head at once; instead I waited until I saw the head of Robert Culver move in a slow nod. It was Harriet. Boll did not take a backward glance, though I am sure he felt her presence as she took a chair near the door and awaited some explanation of his last words.

"That camphor," Boll said, "constituted the largest shipment ever to sneak past the monopolistic British. Securing it was as important as getting it cheap—cheaper than its raw Formosa par. The cash did double work there, and here's how:

"The gum camphor was bought from head-hunter and Chinese with cash pieces. Then to establish a value, we imported trinkets and merchandise from Hong Kong, which—listen, sir—which we sold to the natives and the Chinese for the cash pieces we had distributed.

"The value of the camphor ran into thousands of dollars. The cost of the merchandise was five hundred dollars."

Culver leaned forward slowly. "Explain that again, please," he said. "Slower this time, Captain."

5

Captain Boll was ever obliging, and before long Robert Culver paced the cabin in the manner of a man assailed by doubt and temptation, both of equal strength. He fanned both, not forgetting for one moment his aversion to schemes and schemers, his hate of a ship and the man who drove her against the rocks of his own inviolate ego. He paused often to drive home argument; he said at last, "Can you repeat your success in Formosa? Answer that."

Boll replied: "The Chinese or head-hunter in Formosa will tell you of its magic value."

"Sure," Culver agreed, scoffing, "but wait until they try to spend the cash with another trader—what's it worth then, Captain?"

"I knew you'd ask that, sir. It isn't worth a damn as it stands at present. That's why I went to the trouble to interest you in the idea."

Culver considered the astonishing admission of his captain; his replies, as frank as they were impudent, predisposed a listener in his favor. Then he turned his face to Boll as if the last words had jerked him suddenly about. During the pause Harriet moved nearer, her eyes narrowed with expectancy.

Culver spoke: "Captain Boll, you're either tangled in the web of a shortsighted scheme or else you're being very captious."

"Call it the latter," Boll laughed, "since I'm talking to Robert Culver." While Culver digested the remark for its complimentary or disparaging essence, Boll grinned in the manner of a clever boxer who had learned of his opponent's weaknesses in early rounds for the gain of the moments ahead. He began his slow drive with:

"You have wondered about many things, Mr. Culver. I've wanted you to do just that. Let us consider the value of any proposition: if it pursues a man for his financial support, it is lacking in a certain conviction, no matter its value. But, if the financier pursues the proposition, where does the strength lie? Now I plan to tell you something before I unfold what's really on my mind.

"I have never been accused of jeopardizing the interests of those for whom I work. I am not called the Striker for nothing, and it was the Striker you hired to tame a stubborn ship. Where's your profit? You've made money out of that ship, and me. Aye, plenty of money. Do you deny that?"

"Continue, Captain." The answer was tantamount to a confirming nod torn out of him.

"I'm no respecter of persons in putting a ship through. Nor," Boll said, lifting a finger, "am I a respecter of persons in putting a proposition through. What you and your small-minded Mr. Ruscomb have tried to twist into a charge of barratry was not barratry, but a deliberate means on my part to fetch the financier to the proposition."

Culver started. "You mean——" He was fast blowing himself into a black gale. I stole a peep at Harriet and saw a slow smile forming on her face.

"I mean just this, sir: the record run of her easting down was made to bring you out here." I was beginning to see more than Boll had revealed, more than had met my eye up to that moment. As for Culver, curiosity stayed the flow of anger in him as one side of his mind listened to a damning confession, and the other side to the dazzling revelations of a bold adventurer.

"I'll tell you more," Boll said. "More than a year ago the cash piece was named solely for the purpose of catching your eye. That cargo of camphor was consigned to a Mr. Teale in Boston. Why?" He had asked the question I had puzzled over quite often.

"Because, sir, any shipowner confronted with the odd circumstances I've just mentioned—the record run of a despised ship, whose name made him see red, the naming of a worthless coin after that ship and engaging it in questionable trading—would begin to wonder about many things. You did. But your suspicions lacked the final ounce of proof. You were not quite sure of my intent to deliberately offend you until the camphor was consigned to Mr. Teale."

Culver stared as if he had taken a blow on the head. So did I. And Boll voiced our thoughts, mine, at least, when he said:

"That was the lure. You came."

Culver labored over a fact behind those narrow eyes he aimed at Boll, daring himself to accept the unbelievable truth: he had surely been duped! He, Robert Culver, duped, his face seemed to say as it stood silently offended out of all proportion by the insolence of a mere man. He soon rallied and said without the malice he surely felt:

"You were a problem likely to fetch any shipowner." He was thinking rapidly, drawing up plans in his astute head. Some plan seemed fashioned to his liking when he said, "Now that I'm here, what do you want?"

"One hundred thousand dollars, the Gerrymander, and a year in the Dutch Indies," Boll replied. As Culver gasped, Boll added, "To make a million dollars."

We were all sure of his insanity as he came forth to deal us another shock: "And instead of my usual twenty-five per cent of the earnings, we'll split the profits fifty-fifty."

Culver dabbed at the beads of sweat on his forehead and sat down. Harriet leaned forward, frowning. At that moment another visitor appeared; she was a little lady with more dignity than size—Harriet's aunt. She took her seat and eyed all of us over her glasses as she proceeded calmly with her crocheting.

Only Harriet among us had the presence of mind to ask a simple question: "How can you make a million dollars, Captain Boll?"

"With the Gerrymander Cash. Money is so scarce in the Indies that any symbol of money will buy up rich produce."

Culver said, "But the cash piece, Captain Boll—remember you said it wasn't worth a damn to another trader. That being true, it won't serve its purpose with the native for long."

Boll replied, "I said it wasn't worth anything at present. But I plan to make each cash piece worth one Dutch guilder in the Indies."

Culver frowned; he spread his palms as if he were the crazy one here.

We were still unable to understand how he could hope to maneuver a worthless coin into lengthened acceptance among even a race of fools, which the Dutch and subjected natives were far from being. Regardless, here was the beauty of imagination falling upon tender ears; beauty there, if only in the feeding—the pabulum was energy to minds used to the trite economy of a sane world.

"The most complex-sounding plan is often the simplest," Boll said. "Now you're wondering how I can make the cash piece worth a guilder. That should be easy. As you know, we had to carry trade goods to Formosa to back up the cash piece, to give it a buying value to the native. It had to serve the native as well as us. That's simple, isn't it?" It was. "But the value of the cash piece naturally fluctuated," he added.

"I want it to have a steady value. It will." His plan was reaching up for some blue-heaven wealth, it seemed. It was forcing the camphor deal off the main stage, as if Formosa and camphor constituted an unimportant mask rehearsal designed to hide the real show.

"Now here's how I'll get a steady value for this cash piece." He eyed the yellow disk with fond, greedy eyes. "I'll go straight to the Dutch with an offer. As you know, the dollar note is paper; it is actually as worthless as this coin in my hand. It's the góld in reserve that gives it value."

We followed him then. Even Harriet's aunt raised her head and nodded.

"So I'll post a small sum, say about ten thousand dollars, with the Dutch Javasche Bank—that will make, at the rate of exchange, around fifty thousand cash pieces worth one guilder each."

"Why a mere ten thousand dollars?" Culver asked.

Boll replied, "This plan has to be sold to the Dutch, mind you. We don't want to scare them off at the start."

"By God and a purple dolphin!" Culver beamed. "If you can do it——"

Boll said slowly, "I can do it, sir."

Culver frowned. "But it's quite a gamble."

It was then that Boll loosed his speculative bombshell:

"The Dutch bank will redeem our cash pieces, pay the bearer one guilder for each cash piece turned in. *The big profit, sir, comes from those never turned in.*"

We thought of Formosa, where twenty per cent of the ten thousand cash pieces had not shown up for what they could have purchased. The rehearsal there proved Boll's point. His Indo-China dress rehearsal further proved it.

But Culver asked a question: "What's to prevent the cash pieces from turning up at the banks?"

"That, sir," Boll said, "I won't attempt to explain, since no man can explain human nature. They simply won't all come in."

All of us, including Culver, were forced into a new and unwilling admiration of the man. The plan was bigger than big, but would it work? As I sat there, fascinated, I thought of the work cut out for me. De Loach seemed to approve the cash scheme.

Culver said, "So the firm should back the venture for a year's trial, for half the profits. What do you think of the idea, Harriet?"

"I'm not sure," she replied. "Something tells me we should not consider it." She flattered me suddenly with, "Mr. Flint, from your position, what is your opinion?"

"I've seldom dared dream beyond accepted realities," I replied.

"However, from my position," I said, with slow emphasis that put me at once in the employ of De Loach, "I see a nice gain for all concerned. Beyond that, your guess is as good as mine."

She frowned. I felt her intuitive mind searching out the future. Culver said to her, eying Boll rather circumspectly, "I'm sure Captain Boll is as anxious as we to avoid any trouble." Her frown held, as if what she saw was not to her liking. She did not like the duplicity she had been forced to accept—De Loach and I versus Culver—when she aided Amos De Loach. Her aversion shone in her eyes, as if trapped; she was now seeking some harmony with Boll's fantastic scheme, some end to schemes before it.

Emily broke the silence with: "Captain Boll, your idea sounds too good to suit me."

Harriet arose slowly and said, "I think we should remember that Culver and Adams is a shipping firm. Don't you, Captain Boll?"

"Perhaps you're right," Culver said quickly.

Something was expected of Boll in that moment when doubt and sanity scored over visions of wealth. He had won a victory almost, one which seemed to slip all too quickly into defeat. And I hardly expected Boll, who had sustained the appellation of the Striker, to step out of role at a time when big money tugged at every fiber of his brain. Nor did he. He came through with a chuckle and:

"Captain Culver of the *Barnacle Goose*." His tone was pensive, mocking. "Who, sir, could dream that you were once that man?" He looked straight at Culver. "Or the man whose image, the mayor of Boston said, 'We are about to unveil'? Or the man who said, 'She's going to pay and pay until I bleed her of every cent she'll earn'?" He glanced at Harriet and said, "I'll never forget the day of the ceremony."

As Culver stiffened angrily, Boll played for another ally. "Miss Emily," he said slowly, "you heard him speak those very words when he wanted the ship *Robert Culver* tamed, didn't you? Your judgment wasn't so bad, Miss Emily, when you insisted that he let me tame that ship."

Emily smiled. "No, it wasn't, Captain Boll, if I do say so."

"Well," Boll said, "here's his chance to bleed that ship of half a million—and get the last laugh on Boston and De Loach."

Harriet winced as Boll opened old wounds. If Culver hated Boll for his temerity, his controlled face said he hated Boston, De Loach, and the *Gerrymander* more. He smiled maliciously at Boll then, as if he saw Boll, Boston, ship, and De Loach in the same light, as if he wished to bleed Boll of all he could earn for him, as he would the Gerry-mander.

Boll stood to go, though he paused to lock eyes with Harriet. "Somehow," he said, "I thought you might wish me luck."

There was some attraction between them; it came to the surface and hung there in silence.

Boll had taken several steps to the door when Emily said, "Wait." She eyed Culver steadily, then said, "Well, Robert?"

Harriet sighed, a little pleased, I thought.

Culver spoke, his eyes on Harriet. "You wanted Captain Boll to get a fair trial. Which of us shall be the judge?" He seemed to put up policy, in a bid for an answer to his proposal of marriage, for her consideration. As Harriet wavered, unable to hand down any decision, he said with unction:

"I am in favor of going along with Captain Boll."

9 ☖ TOM FLINT AND A GIRL

ONE MORNING SEVERAL DAYS LATER, CAPTAIN BOLL SAID, "WE'LL shake out her sails with high water tomorrow." When I asked our course, he said, "Java." The news took me to deck; there I studied the *Shanghai Packet* where Harriet made her home. I was determined to spend some time with her, and I began my search for some ruse that should bring us together that evening.

Mr. Wulsin came aboard that morning, weaving under the load of alcohol he carried. He rubbed his red nose and stroked his beard in a dazed manner. Behind the old bosun, a young Malay walked with a red silk umbrella, his eyes sparkling like the batik and brocade of his blouse and coat. He wore a turban of blue-and-white-striped silk at a rakish angle and carried a Malay creese, a serpentine dagger, in his belt, its ornate hilt at his belly.

I chuckled. "The Gaekwar of Bombay and Boston."

"Allah! Allah! Allah!" laughed Mr. Wulsin. "I'm too blankety-blank sober to know which direction to bow, Mr. Flint."

"It's a great world, eh, Mr. Wulsin?" I laughed.

"Aye. Round and round she goes, sir."

Several big boxes moved up in the slings after Mr. Wulsin got on deck, each labeled: EXPLOSIVES. An apt metaphor, I thought, since each box contained more than a quarter of a million cash pieces. Next the old lever coining press arrived in a lighter and was soon hoisted aboard. I was eying the press, thinking of the Gerrymander Cash pieces it would spew out in the future, when I heard a commotion on deck.

I turned about to see Chess strutting forward on the main deck.

The crew burst into laughter, and for good reason: Chess wore the garb of the Malay boy who had escorted old Wulsin aboard. He was a comical sight in brocade and batik.

"Allah! Allah!" He laughed.

"How did you come by that?" I asked.

"A roll of the dice, sir," Chess replied. "I think I'll send this costume home."

At about that time, Mr. Wulsin ran out on deck, cursing Chess and chasing after him. Chess raced to the ratlines and climbed. Mr. Wulsin then fell flat on his face, too drunk to arise. The climax came when the Malay boy, naked, ran out on deck and leaped overboard. The last we saw of him, he was swimming toward the bund.

There was plenty of shipboard activity that morning. Fresh water arrived before noon, as did sides of beef, live chickens, and pigs. The crew licked its chops and expatiated upon Little Ahab's culinary art, naming each pig and fowl Sir Ahab the first, the second, and so on. Trade goods arrived all during the morning—tobacco, pipes, bolts of silk, cotton, and woolen fabrics, fans, umbrellas, boxes of trinkets and perfumes, combs, pandan hats, beads, and no end of other wonderful products of civilization. Above combined sounds of men slushing the masts with grease, checking the running rigging, scraping the chain cables, grunting at the windlass, and hoisting the cargo slings, there was the clatter of boxes and crates, the eternal beat of the carpenter's hammer, and the hum of Malay and Chinese jargon on deck and on board the boats at both our sides. The grunt of a steamer's horn and the pounding of her engines were close in one long minute, then fading, and gone.

The counter and stern post of the *Shanghai Packet* blazed in the late tropical sun. The water lapped sluggishly and reddened in retreat to the islands of the Riouw Archipel. The evening promised a big moon, causing me to send long, fond glances toward the city, where the mysterious bund came to life with the sunset squall. Singapore and the moon seemed to invite my visit; though not alone.

I looked at the *Packet* again. Under her awnings I saw two people. The telescope brought them up close—Boll and Harriet. I thought aloud, "So this is his game." We were not in accord on that subject.

"Mr. Blue," I cried, "you'll take over." Before it was dark, I was aboard a sampan and moving toward the *Packet*. I approached her portside as Boll departed from her starboard.

Harriet was on deck. She wore a dress of white cotton, and its maze of ruffles with lace edges picked up the red glint of the sky over

Malacca Strait like a white rose reaching for the dawn. She smiled graciously and invited me to a deck chair.

"No," I said, thinking of the prying eyes of Culver, her aunt, and Mr. Cott. "A little matter of business brought me. I'm wondering if we could talk it over tonight—say, while we visit the city."

She smiled rather dubiously before sweeping the water front in a slow gaze. The lights were twinkling on along the bund. "What sort of business?" she asked.

"Well, it could pertain to some De Loach ship loading herself deck to water line."

"As vague as that, sir?" She lifted her brows.

"And," I replied, "there's a big moon due, Harriet." She studied me closely, as if she sought to reconcile her first name to my unauthorized use of it, or the moon to business.

"I'm sure the big moon would please Aunt Emily, Mr. Flint."

"So she must come too? Does she know about you and De Loach?" When she said "No," I spoke gravely about the urgency of the business ahead, adding, "We're putting out for Java tomorrow."

"Mr. Flint, just what is the nature of this important business?" She eyed me with open doubt behind a pleased expression.

."Frankly, it's showing you Singapore at night." She laughed lightly and frowned in debate while measuring me against some pattern she had cut in her own mind for the man who was Tom Flint, or so it seemed to me. Whatever the result of her scrutiny, she kept it to herself as she said blithely:

"Then Aunt Emily can come along."

I spoke of the hard trip in rickshas, the long tireless pantomime of Chinese actors, reminding her of the exhausting effect of these on an older person. "Poor Aunt Emily couldn't stand it," I said in conclusion.

"You're not very convincing." She laughed.

"But persistent," I replied quickly. As I saw Mr. Cott eying me, I said, "Soon Mr. Culver and Aunt Emily will wonder what I've got to talk to you about."

"Mr. Flint, it isn't proper for me to go without a chaperon."

"Of course not," I teased. "But it's fun. Imagine sedate Aunt Emily feeding the monkeys or betting at a cockfight; or eating chutney and Bombay duck at the bazaars."

"I can hardly imagine myself doing——" Aunt Emily's call— "Harri-et"—at that moment failed to slow the rising interest in her face, however. She answered her aunt, then said to me, "Let's just say it isn't prudent, Mr. Flint."

"We've said that!" I seized her hand as if I hoped to wring agreement out of her, which was entirely true. I held it, expecting her aunt at any moment, and said: "Listen! Forget Beacon Hill for one evening. It'll keep a few hours without you. Now how about it?"

Aunt Emily was moving across the deck in the twilight. I dropped Harriet's hand and awaited an answer. It came: "I'll manage it somehow."

"Portside—nine o'clock," I said, moving off. As I passed her aunt, I spoke with zest: "It's a nice evening, Miss Emily."

2

She was punctual, and we were soon moving toward the lights of nocturnal Singapore under as bright a moon as ever painted the mysterious East. It sailed in and out of thin clouds as if bent on inoculating every mortal with some beguiling drug.

"Pretty, isn't it?" I said. She sat close to me, warm and fragrant.

"You're afraid of it, aren't you? It's a holiday the Boston in you doesn't want to miss, or sanction, isn't it?"

"You could be right, Mr. Flint."

"Ever try saying Tom? It isn't such a hard word. Try it."

"Tom," she said.

"Now, let's keep it that way for one evening."

"Very well—Tom," she sighed, "since you're the only one who has so much as offered to show me the city."

"Good. Then you're deep in debt to me. I'll try to keep you that way."

In the hours ahead of us, she forgot that she was a shipowner, and Tom Flint forgot that he was a deck officer; we were on equal footing. That evening rushed headlong toward another morning, and I was unable to check its speed. From sampan to ricksha, from temple to temple, from a Chinese open-air theater to a European restaurant— smiles, banter, and sober exchanges of opinions over bubbling champagne and French cuisine—then the bund once more, a waiting sampan, and a new awareness of fleeting moments.

She seemed excited and thrilled with the strange show. I had bought her a maze of trinkets and a Chinese doll, which she promptly named Blossom, and a heart-shaped pin set with small rubies. They weren't gifts, I had argued, merely little reminders of a memorable evening. As we boarded a sampan, she laughed and said she was loaded like a Christmas shopper.

"A sandalwood-and-spice evening," I said. "And this time tomorrow——"

Her eyes seemed to sober in the moonlight as they flashed a look up at me. She smiled out over the water and spoke softly: "Sandalwood and spice."

"It's been a wonderful night, Harriet."

"Yes." She did not lift her eyes from the water.

The little wooden-shoe boat moved into fields of sparkling, gentle wave tops, threading its way out of her kind and toward the big ships anchored out in the roads. When clear, the boatman hauled up his one lugsail with its battens running across and beat into the wind. A river junk moved toward us, its deck alive with household goods, produce, and the Chinese family who made its home aboard her. It eased on past us with only a lapping of water and a baby's squeal to rob the scene of a dreamy moon-bathed silence. Farther out, the moon etched the yards, bowsprits, and deck lines of sleeping square-riggers in silver on an indigo canvas. I sighed and turned my eyes from the scene to Harriet, only to discover that she was looking at me.

She said suddenly, "I suppose you've wondered why I helped Amos."

The leap from bazaar and moonlight to trite business was too quick. "Why blot out the moon," I asked, "just when it's shining so brightly?"

"Perhaps compensation is due the moon. But I might as well admit that my reason for slipping away with you tonight was to arrive at a better understanding of our business arrangement."

"Stow the sandalwood and spice 'tween decks, lads." I laughed, disappointed. "The lady seeks a profit on this run." Then I asked harshly, "What's on your mind?"

"Haven't you wondered why I helped Amos after he told me about your mission?"

"Not in the least," I lied glibly. "I've been too busy wondering about your answer to Mr. Culver when he proposed."

She chose to ignore the question. Her tone was level and her eyes direct as she said, "Mr. Flint, I'm sure I wouldn't have gone to Amos's rescue with a complete heedlessness to consequences had it not been for Mr. Culver's motive and method in getting the *Cape*

Race. I was angry at him for running roughshod over me and the stockholders in order to achieve a public triumph."

"You don't owe me any explanation, Harriet."

She stiffened with that. "Mr. Flint," she said with an upsurge of resentment, "please realize my reason for telling you what I did was simply this—you're the only one except Amos who knows of my dual role."

"Sorry, Harriet. I was a bit rough. Suppose you tell me all you want me to know."

"Very well. I'll start at the beginning, back at the ceremony in 'eighty-one." She told me of Boll's visit on the day of the Figurehead Affair, of her part in putting Boll aboard the Gerrymander several years later, ending her story with the events that brought Culver to Singapore. "I wanted Captain Boll to get a fair trial."

"What does Boll mean to you?" I asked, thinking of what she had said about his kissing her after the figurehead incident.

"Why—nothing. I admire him, yes. He's a fascinating man."

"Fascinating?" I chuckled. "By the way, I saw him with you today. I suppose you had a nice visit."

"Yes, we did. For a driving captain he's quite a dreamer."

"Sure. Sure. I suppose he made a million dollars and retired with an heiress to a farm in New England." I added, "Holding your hand as he did so."

"Only it wasn't New England," she replied, smiling. "French Tahiti."

"So he's fascinating. Well, aren't you about to marry Mr. Culver?"

"Did I say that?"

"No. You intimated as much, however. Now let's see—you've got yourself in a trap. And I'm the handy man who might be able to get you out of it—so you can marry Culver. Right?"

"Mr. Flint, you presume a lot, don't you?" she said icily.

"Sure. I've taken advantage of a few hours in your company to meddle into matters that really don't concern me."

"Matters that don't concern you?" she said. When I said I could step out of the picture without any qualm or loss, she said, "Now can you?"

"No," I replied in milder tone. "But tell me why you should even consider marrying Robert Culver. Are you trying to make him over in order to get him to forgive Amos De Loach, or so he'll forget his threat to the Gerrymander?" As she slowly turned her back on me, I went further: "Or do you have in mind a union of shares?"

"I'm sorry I brought up the subject."

In the next moment I spun her around and held her shoulders in my grip. She was startled for an instant, and then her eyes met mine with level challenge. "Then why did you bring up the subject?" I asked, adding, "I didn't want to talk business."

Her gaze fell under my level out upon the water. "I—I don't think anyone, especially a woman, would want to leave the wrong impression about a secret interest in a rival firm." She looked up at me then and laughed. "The right impression is bad enough."

"You're letting that worry you."

"It wouldn't look good in the papers. And I'm so involved now that, whatever I do, I'm working against myself."

"And," I said what I was thinking, "you aren't quite sure of what I'll do, are you?"

"Frankly, Mr. Flint, no."

"Very well. Listen—you are the Miss Adams who practically owns both the firms I serve. You're the cream of Boston and you're an heiress. But these facts don't interest Tom Flint. The fact that does is this—you're a beautiful woman, one whom I've been in love with for a long time."

Her eyes were wide as I continued. "Now there's little I wouldn't do for you, Harriet Adams. I'll tell De Loach I'm through if you want it that way."

"No," she said slowly. "I've made a bargain with De Loach."

"Then why did you try to buy me off—just to see what I was made of?"

"Perhaps." She smiled up at me.

"You're a brave little thing," I said with true admiration. "What do you want me to do?"

She replied after a time, sighing heavily into a smile, "Whatever is best for all concerned—I'll leave that to you."

The moonlight did wonders to her lovely face as she continued to smile up at me. The confidence she placed in me was also flooded with moonlight, it seemed. I remembered St. Ebenezer's words about the moon being a pawn for circumstances, or vice versa. I drew her to me then, evoking a flash of trepidation from her eyes.

"Well, we're back to sandalwood and spice again," I said.

"It's been a wonderful evening—Mr. Flint—up to now." She drew away from me, a little bewildered by it all. "Let's keep it that way."

I caught her hand and drew her gently toward me. "Yes, Harriet, let's keep it that way." She flashed me a quick glance: it was pregnant with questions, appraisal, doubt, and interest. Only a fool would have hesitated with those eyes full upon him.

"I said I'd been in love with you for a long time, didn't I?". There was no answer; she frowned, though there was no attempt on her part to break away from my arms.

"And a man can't help falling in love, can he? No, Harriet, he can't." She seemed content to listen. Her eyes were close to mine, and alive with a sort of dreamy helplessness. I wanted to ask her for a kiss, though there seemed little reason to spoil a sweet moment with unnecessary words.

I closed the distance between us and, despite her momentary stiffening, kissed her full upon her warm lips. She relaxed, and there was some sweet response in her. She was, as I had said, a woman; and that woman I had fallen in love with did not consider in that short space of seconds her wealth or the power of her shares of stock. When I raised my face and peered deep into hers, she did not drop her eyes; she seemed to feel the brush of something new, some understanding that baffled explanation.

"Tom," she murmured, as if dazed. Then suddenly recovering, she stood apart from me, a trembling hand rising instinctively to her open mouth. "Tom!"

I drew her close to me again and asked, "Now what did you tell Mr. Culver when he proposed?"

Just then someone hailed us from the deck of the *Shanghai Packet*. We were at its side, the sampan motionless, its Malay owner smiling. And up on the gangway almost above us, there stood Mr. Cott—and Aunt Emily.

Harriet turned away from me without any answer to my question, leaving me with the puzzle to rack my brain over in the long days ahead.

But there was a sweet side to it, at least: she left me also a memory of a kiss and that one word she had uttered—"Tom."

3

Late in the next afternoon, Boll sounded the familiar call: "All hands at stations!" Then—the anchor came in dripping, and with sails set and yards braced, the long *Gerrymander* slipped gently forward, creaking in her timbers and tophamper, and inched into the stream of Singapore Road for Durian Strait and the road to Batavia.

The *Shanghai Packet* moved away from us and into another world —Boston and the world of Louisburg Square; a cloud came over the sun, dimming her glistening mizzen truck. A symbol, almost, I thought, as I saw a living white dot on her stern deck disappear—Harriet Adams.

10 THE INDIES AND THE DUTCH BANK

HARRIET WAS FAR BEHIND ME; THE GREAT ADVENTURE LAY AHEAD.

The *Gerrymander* had put Singapore beyond her wake. She ran on, tack and tack, with beam wind, head wind, and following wind, sometimes moving north for a wind to give her southing. The four-knot current in the temperamental stream, flanked by the maze of islands down the north Sumatra coast, caught the ship and sent her tearing on along the road to Java.

Boll's prayers to raise a wind where the winds came in strong took on a new meaning. Instead of saying, "A wind, Lucifer!" he might have better expressed his desires had he simply said: "Big business, Lucifer!"

But he talked to the right party, it seemed, for the devil owns the winds of those strange tropical monsoons which feed upon their own energy as they blow hot across the Greater and Lesser Sunda Islands. It was the world of the East. . . .

A world that had been divided into two classifications, geography and commerce. If there was a third definition for it in any Boston, New York, or Liverpool shipping house, I had never heard of it. The human element involved was in short a slave to commerce after its development in a geographical sphere. What the English and Dutch didn't want, the French grabbed. The Dutch hoisted their red, white, and blue bars over the stretching monster islands of the Indies, while the English went them one better with India and Singapore on the west, and Australia to the south. The tricolor flew over Indo-China; and up above Borneo, the flag of Spain cast its shadow from the Philippines. So much for a setting and the maze of tongues under the prevailing colors of the East.

The main attraction was gain, and the flags and ensigns of all nations crowded the ports, from Melbourne to Shanghai, and from Bombay to Darwin in the other directions. The smell of gain, as Boll had said, was good from any source. And every source of gain made up the East. Every sin and virtue, every hell or heaven, everything civilization had been able to contribute to all of these, could be found in the East; and more: wealth bubbled up in a seething caldron of trade, out of sea and jungle, temple, paddy, and kampong. Blood ran, and yellow, brown, and black man still smiled on under the burden of a white man's riches.

A map of the Indies was a guide to the products the Western world desired: mother-of-pearl, tea, cinnamon, sandalwood, teak, ebony, dyes, cocoa, wax, batik, trepang, rattan, Makassar oils, and more. Traders and captains of big sailing ships sat over their drinks and adventured into the islands as far east as Portuguese Timor, or Tanimbar, slanting their eyes up to the ancient spice routes to Amboina and Ternate in the Moluccas, and westward to the Celebes and Borneo. They talked of gain, routes, and anchorages—and trade goods.

Money was as scarce as native independence. Barter ruled the outposts. A squatting native with pearl in hand grinned fatuously up at a trader armed with bottle and gewgaw. The bottle was blessed with fire that made "belly warm and head hot in swim"; it evoked sweet pain in the loin and joys of decapitating a brother. The gewgaw could be any worthless article that appealed to the fancy of a savage. Aye! I've seen them fight over pearl buttons, when there lay out in their lagoons tons of mother-of-pearl. Gain? It stood up for the taking.

A trader discussed the customs of the natives, the pattern of which was drawn by both a primitive economy and the outward manifestations of a dozen religions. The blending of religions was brought about by the intermarriage of races, Hindu, Arab, Chinese, Buginese, Malay, and Polynesian, not to mention the races of the Occident. And many a trader smelled out gain from the most aboriginal religious rites.

There was, too, the rule of Dutch fiefs and stadtholders, the overlapping rule of sultans and rajas (they spelled the word "radja"), which caused strife and wars. Polygamy, concubinage, smuggling, slave trading, and piracy thrived. The latter was costly to ships of all nations. Piracy was an organized business, and Dutch gunboats were kept busy on the seas up about the Celebes and on east; as busy as Dutch troops in the Lesser Sunda Islands who tried to enforce Dutch law as well as keep peace among the sultans and radjas.

And this was the world into which the *Gerrymander* had sailed. It was therefore difficult to view Captain Boll through any moral screen. He followed the precepts of Yankee and British shipowners and captains whose houses were big and impressive, whose church pews were elaborate and respected in their own Bostons and Liverpools. The laws of the sea, the laws of the jungle, and the laws of commerce were one and the same, no matter the phraseology—the law of tooth and fang; the survival of the fittest.

Boll, hard-case captain, was consistent in his observation of this law. Aye, he, a man after any shipowner's heart, might have written the law himself. But since he could not claim any credit for laws of man and Nature before his time, he followed in their long living wake, a student-philosopher and opportunist, a man whose aim was to apply the screws of the tooth and fang to the setting.

2

Boll walked into the Javasche Bank of Batavia with all the pomposity of the Governor General of the Indies; he moved straight to a big door as if he owned the place and paused to announce our presence.

"Inform Mijnheer van Vollenhoven that Captain Boll and Mijnheer Flint are here." The man behind the barred cage leaped from his stool with, "Ja, ja," and in another moment disappeared.

The heads of the bank, composed of Dutch financiers and Government officials, were expecting us. They sat at a long desk eying us as if we were curiosities or harbingers of some new economy designed to cheat the Dutch, if the latter were possible. We were no sooner seated than Boll asked if they had reached any decision.

"Not quite, Kapitein," van Vollenhoven replied in English. "We have more questions." He rubbed his stubby hands and worked his tiny lips. He was very fat, short, and bald. "His Majesty's Government of the Indië would learn more than you told us yesterday. We have questions."

"Out with them," Boll snapped.

"Ja." The Dutchman cocked his head and peered at Boll. "Now your trade token here." He paused to pick up a Gerrymander Cash. "You desire to use it in trade, to represent the value of one guilder? Ja?" Boll nodded. "Pardon, Kapitein, but we can supply you with the guilders in quantity at the exchange rate of your American dollar."

"Did I ask for that?" Boll said brusquely.

"Neen. Neen. But, Kapitein, you sail to stuurboord when the

course is to *bakboord*. We feel that you present a scheme rather than a proposition."

"There are all kinds of Dutchmen, I've heard," Boll said deprecatingly. "I'm beginning to believe it, though I've never before met one who scoffed at a profit."

"We are careful."

"Yes, too careful to allow me to spill a few thousand guilders in your lap."

"Perhaps that is why we're wary. Why should not any man keep his money for himself?"

"I've sailed a ship too long to scoff at insurance, mijnheer, which is one of the advantages I'm actually seeking."

"Insurance? Just what do you wish to insure?"

"Profits, mijnheer!"

Out of exchanged glances and shrugs of resignation, the head of the Javasche Bank said: "I'm afraid we do not quite understand your motive. Mijnheer Kroom here, who is of the Military, will tell you that the Dutch are the protectors of the native with whom we suppose you plan to trade."

"Let's not be pious," said Boll. "If you wish to pose as protectors, do so, but remember you're talking to a man who knows a little about the Indies. Just what do you protect them from? Certainly not the English trader or the pirate. I could give you a few lessons in Dutch economy, mijnheer."

"*Ja*," van Vollenhoven said, reaching for specious words. "We do not doubt that. In fact, the lesson value of your venerable proposition is what we're seeking."

"And you'll never have a better chance to learn it profitably," Boll said. "I want my Gerrymander Cash honestly to represent your guilder, for trade purposes only. And I have agreed to post a guarantee of ten thousand American dollars"—he showed Culver's check—"in order that the Dutch Indies Bank will pay any bearer of my cash piece one guilder when it is presented at any bank in the provinces."

They could understand that: the American dollar was worth several times more than the silver Dutch guilder; and he proposed to underwrite the Gerrymander Cash for circulation with American dollars which he would post with the Bank of the Indies. It was as simple as any Government backing up its paper money with gold in reserve. And no money of paper or worthless metal was worth anything for long unless it was backed by gold or silver. They could understand that. But what baffled them was Boll's motive.

"Furthermore, I have agreed to pay the bank a premium of five per cent for every guilder redeemed," Boll said.

Five per cent? The smell of gain put Dutch pencils to work in eight Dutchmen's hands; the exchange rate of ten thousand American soon threw the guilder up for a rapid paper profit. Five per cent! Not much. Yet here were more than two thousand guilders earned without risk. Captain Boll was surely a fool, and the Dutch smacked their lips at a chance to mulct a fool. They were no different from any other race in this respect, though they seemed more astute in looking ahead for repercussions. But five per cent; the figure did much to obscure the future.

Mijnheer Kroom, a gaunt man with a sallow, aggressive face, spoke up. "Why, when you could save that premium by carrying guilders of established value instead of your worthless money?"

Boll threw up a superb lie under a cover of sarcasm: "Because I do not wish to risk a fortune in real money in the pirate-infested waters of your Indies."

I chuckled inwardly when this Kroom's face assumed a beaten yet satisfied expression. Boll had scored a point, a fact made manifest by van Vollenhoven's idle remark: "Many a guilder and cargo has been taken by the pirates of the Sundas. When I think of the ships robbed, stolen, and scuttled by the pirate, Pulo Besar, I can understand why you desire insurance. But this kind of insurance—it is most unusual. And yet, how clever."

But the point gained soon suffered under further hedging and indecision: the stolid van Vollenhoven suspected more than met the eye—no man would go to that trouble for mere protection—and he seemed loath to bestow his blessing upon an enigma; with a clearer view, yes. Boll did not seem inclined to sweep away the fog just yet.

"And what security have we that you will not flood our trade with a million of these worthless pieces? Of course we would refuse to honor them, but our people would be robbed. And trade would suffer."

"Your security?" Boll chuckled. "I've never heard of a Dutchman who failed to attend to that detail."

They considered his reply in silence, then talked among themselves. Mijnheer Kroom said that one cash piece in circulation over the fifty thousand guilders, which ten thousand American dollars guaranteed, could constitute fraud.

Boll did not rise to that mention of fraud; perhaps he thought it was too early for that. "Mijnheers, what I offer you is a trade stimulant. Your trade is sluggish; your subjects resort to barter. You men here, who regulate the economy of the Indies, encourage the robbery of Dutch subjects. What does it get you in return?

"Dissatisfaction, misrule among your fiefs, wars, and open piracy. All these things are costly. You, Mijnheer Kroom will verify this."

"Ja!"

"You are men of high finance who are here to see that your countrymen grow rich on exports. Now if you could stimulate export trade and minimize costly internal wars, piracy, and general discontent, the Colonial Government would be blessed by Amsterdam."

They asked Boll how he could hope to aid them in bringing such a dream down to earth. "Through prosperity," he said. "Discontent springs from one source, mijnheers—economic slavery."

"You are a crusader." Van Vollenhoven laughed.

"Aye," Boll agreed, "a crusader for profit."

"And your trade money could bring about a change of conditions in the Indië? How?"

Boll had his answers: "With more trade money in circulation, a native could purchase more necessities, and a few luxuries—all Dutch products, of course. If a native lived better, he would not be so quick to sanction piracy, slavery, and wars."

The men nodded in silence. "That would be too good to be true," smiled van Vollenhoven. "And a prosperity which we could not sustain would cause His Majesty William the Third to frown upon us."

"You are better financiers than I," Boll said. "Once you achieved it, you'd sustain it. Aye! I'm merely telling you how to do it."

I grinned: Boll was merely telling one of the world's smartest set of financiers *how to do it!* He was driving a cash piece to a guilder wedding as he drove a ship. Or was he?

"There are two kinds of prosperity, Kapitein," van Vollenhoven said. "True and false. Perhaps if you explained your motive, we could quickly define your plan as one or the other of these."

"Very well," Boll said, feigning a last-resort reluctance, "I'm seeking what is known as a trade monopoly. If I popularize the cash piece, I'll get the most out of it in trade goods. And you'll make money out of it. I'm enhancing the value of your guilder to you by five per cent without borrowing a single guilder from you. Consider the value of that."

"True. True, Kapitein Boll. Your motive is just what we thought it was. But there is one small question I would ask. Why should you go to the trouble of striking this coin of yours for trade on so small a scale?"

"What do you mean?" Boll asked.

"You speak of a trade monopoly, and all you propose is small money —ten thousand American dollars to back a mere fifty thousand guilders. Is this consistent with big trade?"

I could see that Boll had lain in wait for that question. Culver had asked, "Why a mere ten thousand dollars?" and Boll had replied, "This plan has to be sold to the Dutch, mind you. We don't want to scare them off at the start." But what would he do with the Dutch-man's question?

He said: "No, it is not consistent with big trade. And were I desirous of trading a bar of soap for a peck of rice, I'd be splitting tacks on a small schooner instead of the big ship *Gerrymander*.

"But—mijnheers, I do not take you for fools who would sanction at the outset the proposition I have in mind—in which I would post one hundred thousand dollars or more to back up my *Gerrymander* Cash trade."

The Dutchmen sat up then; they exchanged significant nods, nods of approval. Boll said, "Let's feel our way along in this, so that neither of us can make any big error."

That did it. Boll, by putting their own wisdom up for view, had complimented Dutch sagacity. Through policy he wrung from them a very important letter which carried the bank's hand and seal, the effect of which, in the months to come, was destined to tumble fortunes and aspirations in the islands. But that lay ahead, another story, another adventure in human nature versus accepted rules of behavior. The gain of that day was simply this:

Fifty thousand pieces of the *Gerrymander* Cash had been stabilized by no less a body than the dominant financiers of the Indies.

11   THE KIM KIM EPISODE

SELDOM DID CAPTAIN BOLL REJOICE OUTWARDLY, THOUGH HE DID so after his own pattern that day on leaving the bank. He allowed a thin smile a play on his face when he stood at a harbor bar.

"Read, Mr. Flint," he said, touching his glass to mine as he proffered the letter. "The Dutch Indies. Lay one end in San Francisco and the other end will reach to Bermuda. They're ours to work. Free for the cash." He ordered drinks again and paid for them with Dutch money. Then he flung a Gerrymander Cash to the bar, saying to the puzzled barkeeper a moment later, "It's worth one guilder at the bank, mijnheer."

I read the letter, and I raised my brows at one paragraph which the Dutchmen had written into the letter—it stated that one cash piece above the fifty thousand authorized for trial purposes would constitute fraud. When I spoke to Boll about this, he chuckled, saying:

"They'll be quick to change that when they smell the gain."

A dozen schooners were anchored in old Batavia's harbor, some with their goods and Malay crews on deck, others minus any life whatever. The harbor presented a lazy scene despite its activity; it seemed to revere its lapping shadows standing out from the sides of the boats in oily grays and occasional clear blues and greens. Terns dipped and rose, their white breasts reflecting the color over which they flew. Farther on, a schooner shook out her sails for a run to some island. The lazy, cruel tropics spoke with a far-reaching, beautiful voice. The mask was beauty.

But schooners were the attraction that drew Boll and me and we were soon engaged in conversation with the captain of a forty-ton craft. She bore the name *Gouden Paarl,* or *Golden Pearl;* a misnomer, I reflected, as I scanned her weatherworn hull, deck, and sails. But what the schooner lacked in paint and repair she made up in the convalescent languor she exuded. She smelled tropical.

"Where to?" Boll asked the young captain.

"Makassar, as soon as I move cargo. My cargo? Rattan. The market!" He cursed. He was Australian and Dutch, and named Charlie Blink. "The dandies must have quit swingin' Malacca sticks," he said.

Boll smiled. "A smart trader would have fetched ebony or sandalwood. I'm buying."

"What else?" the young man sneered openly.

"Tortoise shell, mother-of-pearl, pepper—you name it. Too bad you don't own the schooner."

"That's the trouble. *Verdomd,* I do! That's why I set out time waitin' for a buyer. Then I'm off again, hopin' to make enough to put paint and new sail on her. Then the pirates strike. Ever hear of Pulo Besar? But who are you?"

"A man who'll set you right, who'll pay your first price for rattan."

"Then I am crazy," grinned Charlie Blink. We were soon on deck counting bundles of rattan. He named a price and stood by for Boll's refusal. But Boll nodded, and the lad blinked his eyes and grimaced. The next step was the payment, which forced us to the *Gerrymander.*

Charlie Blink had never seen such a captain's cabin as he saw there. His cunning little eyes bulged with awe and admiration while Boll counted out a cash piece for every guilder involved. "Here, Mr. Blink, you may verify the count," Boll said at last. The lad lowered his eyes, then lifted them, his perplexity standing out on his face like the eyes of a lobster.

"So I wasn't crazy," he said, flashing anger.

"Your cargo is still on your schooner, isn't it?" Boll said gently. "Very well, keep it there until you visit the Javasche Bank and verify the value of my money."

This he did, and the Dutch bank paid him guilder for cash piece. And Charlie Blink, who held the unique distinction of being the first man who sold his cargo for the Dutch-validated cash, served us well after that day.

2

On the following afternoon a huge three-masted junk listed into the harbor of Batavia. The big eyes painted on the sides of her bow, "to see with," seemed cocked as her slanted deck drew closer. The maneuver to anchorage required a wealth of seamanship, which the Chinese aboard seemed to possess. The sails—stripped with horizontal battens, which lend the junk an oriental distinction as quaint and stirring in the open roads of the sea as some towering pagoda in Chinese silhouette—were trimmed to offset her list rather than to propel her.

She was out of Makassar, the property of a rich Chinese merchant, I learned, as I watched the harbor police board her. Suspected of carrying contraband, as were all Chinese, I was told that she might be feigning difficulty. I studied her closely as she moved in, concentrating more on the huge Mongolian who stood the high poop and argued with the Dutch. He was Captain K'ung K'ung, and he was here to trade for his illustrious master, Hoppo Two, who, my informer added, was considered a power in the rich Celebes. Captain Boll arrived, advising of his success in renting a warehouse. He was not long in engaging a translator and speeding up the usual routine delay in gaining an audience with this Captain K'ung K'ung.

To those who have never boarded a Chinese junk, such an experience is better unrealized, since it is both shocking and revolting. On the disorderly deck, human beings bedded down next to crates of fowls and open cages of goats and pigs, all of which tramped in the excrement of a full voyage. The smell of the deck struck a nose long before a foot was placed on the unscrubbed planks, where lay rotting fish and refuse from the galley. We were almost forced to fight our way among darting carnivorous birds to the poop. But the Chinese sailors seemed perfectly contented: they squatted on deck, their backs against anything solid, and smoked as they eyed us with sleepy malevolence and unconcern.

K'ung K'ung awaited us in the space under the high Portuguese-like after-deck. On the portside stood a huge temple table, a fine piece carved by Chinese artisans centuries before. A large image of Buddha, fantastic eidolons, and other religious paraphernalia cluttered the top of the piece. The space accommodated sailcloth, spars, carpenter's tools, provisions, and items necessary to a ship's voyage, all strewn in disorderly fashion. The only attraction other than the temple table was K'ung K'ung himself.

He was a veritable giant with an evil face, to which he lent, by the look in his eyes, the expression of a jolly butcher about to swing a blade. He wore a black sea cap and white trousers. Otherwise, he was bare, which heightened his grotesque spraddle-legged pose atop a short stool. He smoked a long pipe, the bowl of which rested on the low Chinese table which served him for desk. He emitted a grunt and swept a hand to indicate that we seat ourselves. There being no chairs, we stood.

Boll tossed a cash piece to the floor, a sign of his business as well as of his independence. K'ung K'ung reached for it, and after an interval of silence he flipped it into the air, then bit it, and tossed it to the floor at Boll's feet. "Neen," he said. Thereupon Boll tossed him a guilder, drawing a greedy smile and a "Ja" from him. Boll advanced, snatched the guilder free, and laid it alongside the cash piece. To the translator, he said, "Tell him they're the same."

K'ung K'ung laughed so loud the ship seemed to shake. He soon sobered and crawled on his hands and knees to peer at the coins at Boll's feet. Back at his place, he busied himself with a sore toe before saying in English, "What's on the head?"

"Cargo. Is it for sale?"

"Pretty much." When asked what he shipped, he sing-songed his wares: gum dammar, coconut oil, Makassar hair oil, silver and gold filigree, nutmeg, and a few rare pearls. When asked if he wished to sell, he replied, "No to hurry. Rather to slow. But you like trade?" At Boll's nod he stuck his thumbs up in the oriental fashion that means, "Fine," and led us on deck. There he showed us game roosters and goats.

"Show me big money goods," ordered Boll.

K'ung K'ung bowed low; he searched the sides of the junk as if for any persistent Dutch police, then led us down a hatch. Boll examined his nutmeg, the bottom sacks only, asked how much he expected to get for it, and scoffed at the reply. "Make price," said the Chinese. "Make price. Is sold—but only if take this I show." Boll made a low bid, which the Chinese considered before lifting his thumbs in acceptance. "But agree take this I show for long money," he warned. Boll nodded, expecting a catch, but not the one that followed.

Past bales and bundles in the after hatch, K'ung K'ung moved toward a wooden partition. He put other goods up for sale, and Boll bought them at ridiculously low prices.

"But only if take this I show for long money. No say all."

I said to Boll, "He's got something up his sleeve, and we're stuck with it, whether it's monkey, crocodile, or python." Boll replied, "Yes," eying the Chinese circumspectly.

At last K'ung K'ung stood before a partition with ham hands on hips, his yellow midriff oozing sweat. "You take this." He leered

odiously, jerking his head toward the partition. "Ja, for long money."
Soon he threw his weight against an upright beam, and, after an
interval in which he strained his huge muscles, the entire partition
opened a few inches.

"Come," he said. "See."

Boll pressed his face close, only to jerk it back quickly. Blood ran
from a long scratch on his forehead. "So it's a tiger," he said menacingly.

"No tiger," the giant said, laughing. "I show this." Thereupon he
reached for a chain at the top of the opening and pulled hard. The
upper boards of the port half raised like a bamboo blind. It was then
I got a view of the contraband he carried.

What leaped into my eye was hard to believe, and harder to reconcile to the trading instincts of man. But the smell of gain hovered
over the maze of traffic of the East, and while the sails and steam of
civilization carried the blood of sacrifice without the slightest compunction, the less subtle junk, schooner, and sampan transported the
mortal wrappings. The item of trade was a woman!

"This for long money to hurry."

I turned to eye Boll, who showed no surprise or any emotion whatever at the unexampled trick the heathen had turned. And then I
studied the female in the close quarters before me. Only her eyes were
visible since she wore the veil of Moslem modesty, that and a cheap
striped sarong which covered even her feet. There was a large ring
of plain gold on her finger.

"Long money. Much," grunted the giant.

Said Boll. "Ugly. Short money."

"Neen!" shouted K'ung K'ung. "Merrycan fool!" Thereupon he
leaped the barrier and, braving the sharp claws of the item of cargo,
he soon pinned her hands to her back and removed the veil. A face
beautiful even in anger met my shocked eyes; in it one could see the
unmistakable blend of races: the somnolent, royal almond eyes of the
East, the modified, hybrid nose of a possible Shanghai-Paris union,
the exotic lips of two worlds, wherein the beauty of neither was resistance to the passions of the tropics. Her beauty was then more a
confused melody rising out of a fusion of vigor, and one could only
wonder at her humors and graces, at the sharp flavor of her true
beauty.

"Now! Long money!" shouted the junk master with a show of
triumph. "How much?"

"Short money," Boll replied. "Fifty guilders."

I caught Boll by the arm and packed protest into my voice. "That's a human being!"

"Fifty guilders," he repeated.

K'ung K'ung cursed in fluent Dutch and slapped the girl when she spat in his face. When I tensed to spring over the barrier, Boll restrained me. Then the Chinese jerked the sarong from her shoulders and let it hang from her small naked waist. Her pointed breasts, firm, full, and round, seemed to proclaim her virginity; and they seemed to express in golden metaphor prolific green gardens and flowering vine crowned with tropic distances. But the show was too extravagant for the imagination, and hence it served to dispel aesthetic impressions. It drew a mind into rigid awareness of the classical evil of her captor, who at that moment grinned insinuatingly and said:

"One thousand guilder, Merrycan?"

"One hundred," Boll replied.

"You buy short money for that when I say long money for this!"

"Two hundred guilders," Boll said, as if to humor him.

And K'ung K'ung, behind his trader's mien, was awake and watching, as he gazed at Boll with a singular fixity of eye even as he held the coffee-colored body of the girl up for appraisal and gain. "Master Hoppo Two keep. I sell for long money."

Boll grinned: he leaned on his elbows, exacting the greatest enjoyment from the combined sight of a Chinese giant in a rage and the rose-shot flesh of an Eastern female nude to the waist.

"Three hundred guilders," said Boll, causing the enraged K'ung K'ung to tear the sarong from her waist and hips in a single, vicious jerk.

There she stood, completely naked, her mouth a line of scarlet hate, her eyes lolling in shame and fury as her breasts heaved in and out of their shadows, as her small sloping abdomen moved under the sweat of exertion. K'ung K'ung placed his knee in the small of her back and jerked her arms up behind her until she uttered a low animal moan. She trembled in the passionate writhing of rebellion. She was animal, woman, temptation, and hate, all naked before the three defilers who viewed her.

"This firm flesh," smiled K'ung K'ung. "Make good slave. No man touch."

"Four hundred."

The Chinese threw the girl against the ship's timbers and cursed Boll for his miserliness in Chinese, Dutch, and Malay; he shook his fists and engaged himself in various pantomime. The girl lay still for some moments, then opened her eyes and searched the enclosure for a weapon. Finding none, she arose slowly in a crouch, shaped her long tapering fingers into claws, and moved toward the giant. K'ung K'ung turned sharply, just as she leaped for his throat with the spring of a jungle cat. A fist struck her down, but a small success was hers. Her claws had drawn blood.

Boll said, "Four hundred and twenty-five guilders."

The slave girl, bruised and trembling, got to her feet slowly and roved about the small enclosure like an animal in search of some means of escape. Her eyes drove pleadingly into mine, then left my face when she saw no hope there. She measured the barrier and the proximity of the devil-giant K'ung K'ung, and turned about frantically, her breasts and stomach heaving to her quick breathing. Her long wavy hair, more brown than black, was now disarranged and hanging down to her buttocks as she forgot nakedness in her search for a freedom she could not find.

"Five. Hoppo Two say keep if no get. You pay long money?" When Boll answered negatively, the Chinese pulled a short dagger from his belt and advanced on the girl. She did not cringe; she threw her head up proudly and stood against the wall, her hands clutching at the sarong which covered her breasts and torso again. She knew shame, though she rose above fear in that moment. Then K'ung K'ung tore the garment from her and placed the point of his knife against her lower throat. He pressed gently yet firmly as he eyed Boll, who said:

"Four hundred and twenty-five."

The knife pierced her skin; a drop of blood, and another, and still she did not move or cry out. "Five?" K'ung K'ung glowered. "Great pirate, Pulo Besar, pay more."

"Then take her to Pulo Besar," Boll replied. "Four hundred and twenty-five. Not a stuiver more."

There was the quality of greatness in the girl's defiance; she stood bravely expecting death. I added this to her rare beauty of face and body and captured a fleeting glimpse of her fierceness and loyalty to the man who chanced to own her love.

Then I said to Boll, "Can't you stretch a point to save her?"

There was no answer as he nursed the same unconcerned smile. K'ung K'ung, not to be outdone, raked the point of the knife a fraction of an inch down, drawing more drops of blood. "Pretty soon," he growled.

"Go ahead," Boll challenged. "Slit her throat."

K'ung K'ung stared at Boll with speculative eyes for some time before slowly turning his face to the knife. He was tempted in either direction, it seemed, since he wavered. Then slowly he withdrew the knife, and slower still he placed it in his belt and faced Boll.

His thumbs came up. Boll chuckled, even as the Chinese paid him tribute with, "K'ung K'ung honor for meet great trader. Hoppo Two honor. Come Makassar some mebby day. So?"

"Someday," Boll said. There was promise in his tone.

The transaction was duly completed with the Gerrymander Cash standing up for the respected guilder, but only after K'ung K'ung had visited the bank.

The item of contraband was clandestinely rowed to the Gerrymander in the dead of a tropic night—the slave, paid for with worthless cash pieces, whose name was Kim Kim.

3

In the two weeks that followed, Boll worked diligently to effect a course for the Gerrymander Cash: instead of steering the piece to the Javasche Bank, he endeavored to send it in the other direction. The big profit on the venture lay in those cash pieces that would never reach the bank. In the meantime he traded as closely as though his full profit came out of each haggling encounter.

We frequented water-front saloons, where Boll, with a big bag of cash pieces, bought drinks for schooner and junk captains who worked the Lesser Sunda Islands, the Moluccas, and Celebes. He enlisted the aid of traders, ship chandlers, pearl and wood buyers in helping him sell the roving captains on the idea of spreading the cash into remote spots. And he sold these captains cash pieces, after the doubters saw him pay for whisky with them, and after they had read the letter from the Dutch bank.

There was a Captain van Dee. He was known for his miserliness and sharp trading. He owned his schooner, the *Roode Hind*, which worked the Lesser Sunda and Molucca trade. Barter ruled the islands, money being as scarce as missionaries. Boll smiled, poured liquor into the visitor's glass, and sniffed along the old spice roads when he said, "I can use pepper, nutmeg, and mace." The fat proprietor of the saloon hovered near.

"Naturally," the captain replied. "But the price is always up when a boat leaves here, and it's down when she returns. There are other items. Right now I've made a deal with the Radja of Mataram, who's at odds with the Dutch."

"At odds, did you say?" Boll said with interest.

"Ja. He's stadtholder of Lombok and Bali, and a tyrant. But he wants wild birds from the Moluccas for his palace grounds." He leaned forward to share a confidence: "And some of the birds don't have wings. Women! But he's never satisfied. He wants Salome and Cleopatra."

"I might find him one," said Boll. I thought of Kim Kim, whose presence aboard ship had provoked all sorts of conjecture. Boll and the captain talked on. The subject wore around to money again, and soon Boll dug into the valise and produced five rolls of cash pieces.

"Advance money, Captain van Dee—a sign of good faith. Fetch me pepper, mace, and nutmeg." The proprietor guffawed loudly when van Dee's eye fell on the strangest money he had ever seen.

"Kapitein," the proprietor said, "I'll trade you a guilder for every piece there. So will the Javasche Bank."

"Yeah," Boll averred. He then caught the astonished captain's arm and said, "I have learned from experience that these *gold* coins of mine will buy more from the native. Why not make a specific test at, say—Ende, on the island of Flores?"

The captain's frown soon turned into a smile.

During the two weeks in Batavia, several sailors appeared from the Celebes wearing a familiar coin on a string about the neck—the Gerrymander Cash. Our inquiries evoked answers similar to this one from a Dutch mate:

"*Ja! Lieve hemel,* it's a good-luck token! Where did I get it? From an old man in Makassar who is a saint. St. Ebenezer, he calls himself. He sells them for a guilder apiece."

I grinned. "So the old saint has made a good-luck piece out of the cash." I was forced to admit that Boll had a long eye. But I felt the breath of a certain irony in the situation when several sailors aboard the *Gerrymander* asked where they might secure one of the good-luck charms.

4

Kim Kim was less sullen when we dropped breast anchors in Cheribon Road. Mr. Blue and I had every reason to adopt her former ill-humor, since our quarters had been assigned her.

We met Cheribon at sunrise, our hooks in about four fathoms as we stood our two-mile distance from the small town. The sun lifted over the misty Java Sea from Semarang, breaking the horizon like some glowing brazier of a Hindu god racing to us at sea level and lifting above our grasp with a clearing away of the pink-and-pearl fog; it shot the obedient clouds of the northwest monsoon with copper, gold, and red, and satellite hues of lavender and orange-rose. To the south, the town seemed to sleep in steamy languor under a canopy of coconut palms which stretched to velvety blue horizons in either direction; and with the sun's pleasant yawn upward, the thin white breakers rolling in the distance formed a sparkling line to divide sea and land. Beyond, over the coastal rise and silent inland forests, the far-off top of a peak shed its azure haze slowly and accepted the majestic tints of morning. Only her base seemed lost in the clouds. Near the ship a flock of red-footed boobies went into long graceful dives for fish, and a larger group of red-tailed tropic birds flew toward Cheribon Bank. As the day broke clear I saw several schooners where an hour before there had loomed only lights, and a steamer of the Koninklijke line.

Cheribon, asleep, offered teakwood and indigo. Awake, it offered its lighters to transport such riches to our deck. But Captain Boll seemed less enthusiastic at breakfast that morning. His mental diet of the Gerrymander Cash for every course seemed to sap at him. He called Lugo and said:

"Serve Kim Kim now."

Serve Kim Kim now! I eyed my plate. Less than a fortnight back he had run up a bid in the manner of a buyer at an animal show, saying, "Go ahead. Slit her throat." And now it was, "Serve Kim Kim now." I wondered how Harriet Adams or Culver would react to the auction of a girl. And suddenly I started inwardly. Perhaps the situation offered possibilities of my serving De Loach. Slowly I raised my head and stole a glance at Boll. He was studying me. Suddenly he got to his feet and said he was going after cargo.

I sat there thinking of the Eurasian girl, or rather the crime Boll had committed under Dutch, international, and humane laws, and loathed of fellow creatures. But the law; did it involve a ship? I felt cheap in the moment. No, when I played the cards I was waiting for, I would play them straight. I arose and moved to deck and sunshine.

Boll and boat formed a tiny speck on the sapphire waters of Cheribon Road. Teakwood and indigo, Kim Kim and a Gerrymander Cash piece, the quick blazing-white impact of a dry sun over northern Java, and a welter of stretching waves.

The picture on the wall of Boll's cabin seemed to call me. I talked to the picture of Harriet for some time, and then I gave it up. There was no answer forthcoming; only the violet-blue pigment which formed her eyes returned my glance and word. Her face was nothing but one incongruous and monotonous expression rising out of tubes of dead colors, which can, by some virtue or curse, almost attain life; but never quite. There is a limit to man's ingenuity; he can only supply images which fall short of their goal when one views the living pattern. How, I asked, could I hope to recapture the warm touch of my lips to hers from the face of an image or from the fields of my memory? I could not, though I longed for her with all the fierceness of my being. I, Tom Flint, on the north Java coast, felt a tug at my heart from a girl somewhere behind me.

"So that's what ails me, or is it the tropics getting under my skin?" I sighed, and moved off to make the rounds of the ship.

Mr. Wulsin, Lugo, and Little Ahab were playing cards under the awning. "Drones in the shade," I said in passing. On deck I felt the blast of the sun. The mountains, hills, and coconut palms danced frenziedly in the distance, and the forward part of our ship copied their antics. "Ye c'n cook meat on the deck, sir," a lad said. "Me old man died o' sunstroke, sir," he added with a whine. Up forward, a few hands were broiling as they painted the port rail. "Even the paint is bubblin', sir," young O'Hare complained. "Then I'd stand so my body would shade it," I replied. Suddenly I missed Chess, remembering I had assigned him to the paint crew earlier in the day.

I came upon him at last, at the entrance to Kim Kim's quarters. The door was ajar and he lay flat on his belly with elbows spread, his palms a prop for his head. He seemed to be enjoying himself. I advanced noiselessly until I gained a view of the interior of my former quarters. Kim Kim, unaware of prying eyes, seemed contented also.

She stood before a small mirror, pinning her hair atop her head. Soon she turned, smiling, her eyes on a bolt of brilliant red silk splashed with white tropical flowers. I remembered that Boll had tossed her that bit of wealth on the night he had fetched her aboard in much the same manner a man humors a dog with a gory bone. But in the interim he had given her three long dresses and as many veils in order that she might cover her body and face in the Moslem manner. Strangely enough, these did not appeal to her, though the red silk struck her fancy. As I watched her, she brought the cloth to her face and rubbed it against a cheek with a feeling of complete lassitude. She draped the cloth into a semblance of a veil with a slit for her eyes, and emitted a tinkling little laugh at the picture in the mirror. In another moment she drew herself up majestically, draped a hand about the back of her head, and drew it slowly across her hair and neck, smiling as if she had just discovered her own beauty or the joys of reveling in it. Reared a Moslem, she had perhaps never seen a mirror before. Slowly she undressed, her languorous smile enveloping her face, like some ecstasy sustained beyond its normal influence, until she stood minus all but a loincloth.

She ran her finger tips over the splendid arch of her ribs and down her sides to her hips, as if she delighted in the touch of her tawny, satiny skin; her smile held as she planted her legs apart and bent her head back to the floor in the manner of a boneless and flexible work of art stretching itself out of some carving in a Hindu temple. She exercised muscles of legs, body, arms, and hands, and even her long fingers, like a woman rising from heavy slumber; her antics, slow and sensuous, were reminiscent of a picture I had seen of the Dance of the Apsarases. Then she struck poses and held them, all of which emphasized the resilience of her spine; the deformations seemed dances in which the body could never recover its original shape. A melody, pagan, and as hypnotic as her transport to the realm of dreams, escaped her lips; it was slow, soft, and variant.

She ran the gamut of thought-kindling exercises. She possessed a grace in that long, slim waist which many dancers seek in vain. Somehow I felt that her coverings on the day of her purchase were surely a lie—she was a daughter of Brahma rather than Mohammed, a symbol of the "great-goddess" consort of Siva.

Tiring of her waist dance, she returned to the yards of silk, which she unwound from the cylinder. One end of the piece was thrown over her shoulders and spread out across her breasts and hips. After eying the effect, she draped herself in a sarong and turned to view the train behind her. Suddenly she flashed a smile and balanced herself on one foot, raised her hands above her head, and lifted a knee at right angle from her hip in slow motion, in prelude or salute to the dance that followed. It was slow, the hands and arms playing as much a part as the pivot of her waist and long shapely legs.

The finale: she whirled on one foot until the last yard of red-and-white-flowered silk was wound about her. And then she fell to the floor, swathed in the gift of her new captor, where she giggled like a child.

She was just Kim Kim, though she kindled fires in a man. She provoked one's thoughts into vivid transport: she seemed to represent the music, the languor, and the very soul of the tropical East. But she was problem also. I shook my head despairingly.

I had forgotten Chess until he emitted an enraptured murmur, followed by, "Lordy, she's beautiful!" I eyed him under a slow frown and smile. "Yeah," he sighed, "I could pack any show in Boston with her at fifty cents a head."

I was about to rip his adolescent dreams apart with a remark about an unpainted fife rail when a foot behind me was planted solidly at his rump. I turned about quickly to see Boll with hands on hips. He eyed me narrowly as he said:

"Not a bad investment, is she, Mr. Flint?"

"Now that depends on what you bought her for, sir," I replied.

5

The Gerrymander pointed her jib boom east-northeast late that afternoon. Boll, on the weather poop, asked for twelve knots out of her all the way to Soerabaja; he wanted to enter the West Gat before sundown on the morrow and moor in the harbor before dark. It was quite an order, though the northwest monsoon was blowing down lively. I tacked steadily east-northeast until we were well into the stream. The coast of Java dropped under the horizon before sundown, and only the head of old Keromong caught the shafts of the dying sun. As we added more light canvas, the sun shot its last rays at the land behind us and sent its inflected red farewell high up into the western heavens. The reflection masked the waters beyond our wake with a crimson-wine color until the heavy bosom of rain clouds raced toward us from over the Java Sea to dispel it. Soon the squall pelleted sail and deck and hissed on obliquely inland. Sails and cordage dripped, and the Gerrymander leaned forward under the press of kind wind and clear evening.

The sea ran strong before the change of the watch, and the wind held, eddying into the huge curves of bellying sail with driving force. The ship skimmed the surface, it seemed, though she tossed somewhat under the great spread of her canvas. But she roared on under the stars of the Southern Hemisphere.

The heavens seemed smeared with candlelight that night; it poured like molten tallow from the top of the black velvet dome as if some phosphorescent fairy clan warned the ships up there of deep pits in an immense void. One almost heard the songs of nymphs, though a practical ear traced the sounds to the wind humming in the rigging. The lookout saw other lights: not a mile off, the green riding light of a big square-rigger slowly fell behind us.

"She's lacking twelve, Mr. Flint," Boll said. We relieved her mizzen, hauled in spanker, collapsed the jib, and ran out studding-sails. The line trailed more, and with everything she had on the two forward masts except the mainsail, her increased speed awaited only the breath of the elements. Boll, however, seemed to think otherwise. After a careful study of the wind, he made the most precise suggestions and then voiced a terse order to Lugo the steward:

"Fetch the pint of coins on my desk." I stopped short to eye him. So he was about to whistle for a wind in his own unique manner.

"A wind, Lucifer, a gale." There was a weary monotony in his tone that evening; it seemed that he stood in the shadow of his cash piece from which there was never a moment of escape.

I was sure then that Boll did not really commune with the devil for any wind one could feel. Rather, he sought some success just ahead. He, with a passion for dollars, prayed for wealth, using money as his offering to the gods of fortune. There was more proof than fancy in such reasoning: he had prayed for a record to embarrass Culver, under the guise of praying for a wind.

It was small wonder then—if I was right in assuming that his act constituted a prayer—that he failed to appreciate my chuckle that led up to the bowline-bridle incident.

"Put life in the tophamper!" Boll demanded. He was ever in favor of a downhill seat for his charge, whether for ship or self. So far, he had been blessed with success atop success, and for the calling, it seemed. But averages had leaned in his favor. When they turned, what would happen? I had heard of a drunken captain running the pass at Papeete for the fifth time, drunk and in the dead of night, when one passage strained the laws of chance. Who could tell? The luck of Captain Boll might outlive his schemes.

I was on the weather side of the poop when it happened. It was a tinkling sound, Chinese and Balinese, but arresting. I turned about quickly, as did Boll, to see a figure half clad in silk, a Moslem out of countenance, moving up to the poop. She smiled at Boll and murmured words in soft, accented Malay as she came to a stop before him.

The laughter of a woman on the deck of the Gerrymander had never been heard before; it was then as rare as a shower of pearls, and likely to break any spell. It did just that. I saw the hard look in Boll's eye grow with a steady brilliance until it threatened to consume Kim Kim. I thought of a bowline bridle and wondered at Kim Kim's punishment.

I had not long to wait. He struck her to the deck with the back of his hand, then turned away. Kim Kim, however, clung to his trousers leg, smiling up at him as she did so. He paused to look down at her, restoring a semblance of normal calm to his face as he studied her intently.

Soon he loosed himself and moved farther aft, though he continued to eye her in the manner of a man drawing fresh estimates on what he saw.

6

Since almost everything Boll did was governed by visions of a dollar mark, I was naturally curious as to how he planned to convert Kim Kim into money. Standing up in conflict to that question was Boll's declaration of the past, "I break no laws, Mr. Flint." And yet, he had violated the slavery laws of the Dutch when he bought Kim Kim. There was much I didn't understand.

All the while, I saw growing in magnitude my opportunity to serve De Loach, who had said he wanted Boll caught in his own illegality. With this in mind, I visited Boll that evening.

I was not long in reminding him of his statement about breaking no laws, adding as my excuse for broaching the subject, "You're involving me in this, you know, sir."

"What law have I violated, Mr. Flint?" Surprised at this question, I grinned and reminded him of the facts in the case. "Mr. Flint," he said slowly, "my purpose exonerates me. I did not doubt for a moment that she belonged to some Moslem prince. On her first night aboard the *Gerrymander* I examined the plain ring she wore. Engraved inside were these words: 'Sultan of Bandjermasin.' I am merely returning her to this sultan who resides in lower Borneo."

"Where's the gain?" I asked pointedly.

"Any great favor we can make with the sultans and radjas will serve us well, Mr. Flint. In this case, it will open up Borneo for the cash."

I nodded, satisfied. Boll ran true to form: he continued to take his sights over a dollar mark.

Then something happened to cause me to wonder if dollars alone governed him completely. We were talking of the islands east of Java when Chess entered, panting in his excitement.

"Mr. Reeder, sir. He—he's about to rape Kim Kim!"

Boll was up instantly. I followed him to the girl's quarters, where big Reeder, unaware of our visit, stalked Kim Kim. He bore the mark of her nails on his face and underneath the shirt almost torn off him.

With her back against the wall, her breasts and waist naked, and red in spots from rough handling, she held a dagger menacingly.

As Reeder crouched and approached her warily, Boll walked forward. He stopped in front of Reeder, facing him. The offender stared inanely at first, then glanced around at the door where I stood. Trapped, he struck at Boll. But before his blow could land, Boll downed him with a short uppercut.

Kim Kim emitted a sob and threw herself at Boll. He rewarded her with the first sign of affection I had ever seen from him: he patted her back gently.

Reeder was given a fair trial that night. He stood on the deck between Cheribon and the Doodkisten, or Coffin, Hills, between his sinful past and hereafter, a most repentant man. Before him a hard captain, known for his rigid adherence to rules, turned a deaf ear to all pleas for clemency and ordered a rope thrown over a yardarm.

Reeder was dead when the bell sounded the change of the watch.

7

We moored in Soerabaja at dusk on the following day in the midst of steamers, schooners, and sail ships of all sizes. A pilot boat had engaged us more than a hundred miles beyond the West Gat and trailed us to Soerabaja Strait with open amazement at our clip. That night in the saloons, there was talk of the big Yankee which had run past the Doodkisten Hills at sixteen knots. "Ja, and the west monsoon current threatened to ship her on past Madoera."

Soerabaja was the gateway to the Lesser Sunda Islands; Borneo was not three hundred miles to the north; the Indian Ocean was only one hundred miles to the south; and the Bali, Lombok, to Timor road lay due east. Here was the heart of the fabulous Indies; here the Dutch watchdog kept its vigil. Not far away, less than a day's cruise, the Radja of Mataram maintained his defiance to a government which had made him stadtholder. And somewhere about the Celebes, the great pirate, Pulo Besar, operated. Soerabaja seemed the last outpost of absolute Dutch sovereignty, and therefore its arsenal.

With the hot, steamy morning, I had made up my mind to use the Kim Kim incident for De Loach and myself. It seemed made to order, since Boll had actually violated Dutch law. And, by serving De Loach and Company here, I would in no way embarrass Harriet.

Boll had just left the ship, with cash pieces and a desire to enlist more schooner captains in distributing the Gerrymander Cash in remote places, when I moved to the deck, my destination the Dutch police. Before I could leave the ship, a Dutch gunboat pulled up close to the Gerrymander. Royal Marines and two customs officials came aboard and asked for Captain Boll. When I said he was in the city, the crisp leader told me they would await his return before searching the ship.

When Boll arrived later in the day, he seemed not in the least surprised or annoyed by the threatening aspect of the ship's seizure; nor was he impressed by the brusque attitude of the officials or the comedic pomp of the Royal Marines. He read the warrant, grinned, and led the way to his cabin. The first official, a tall, gaunt man with bulging eyes, a hooked nose, big lips, and a receding chin, barked out an order for the search to commence, only to be met with Boll's calm warning:

"Mijnheer, you could be in error, and that might prove very embarrassing." The Dutchman showed surprise and momentary hesitance. Said Boll, "This is an American merchantman."

"And this is der Nederlandsch Indië," the other retorted. "What have you to say before we get down to business?"

"Nothing," Boll snapped. "Go ahead and search, and regret it later."

They obliged him. I might add, however, that regret was entirely lacking in their triumphant faces when they entered Boll's cabin shortly thereafter with the item which had evoked a gunboat and a display of Dutch force all the way from Batavia—Kim Kim.

Boll was angry; he did not threaten, nor did he say anything except, "Since when is it against the law for a captain to take his woman along with him?"

"When he buys her at slave auction in Dutch territory, mijnheer," the arrogant Dutchman said before ordering the marines to take Kim Kim away.

Though the Dutch had beat me to it, the results might be the same, I reflected.

8

Boll seemed to be making quite a name for himself. All news drifted westward from our position until it reached the free port of Singapore, whence it was relayed to the world. The value of publicity was one thing, though the actual worth of notoriety was another; and there was evidence of both in Soerabaja and Batavia, each of which viewed such a crime as Boll's with the impassive eye of a routinist. But beyond, where news was slanted toward English and American drawing rooms, where echoed the pleasures of a shocked society, slavery was nothing short of the highest crime. Add to that an American captain of an American ship under the flag of a firm of probity, and the outrage smacked of a juicy morsel wrapped up in printer's ink. One could well imagine how the press might enlarge upon the Soerabaja news item, which was as follows:

Captain Boll of the American ship *Gerrymander* was charged today with violating the slavery laws of der Nederlandsch Indië. He is accused of buying a pretty French-Javanese dancer recently kidnaped from the Sultan of Bandjermasin in Borneo by a Chinese captain out of Makassar. The captain's junk was traced to Batavia, where its captain sold his cargo and disappeared. The wealthy junk owner, Hoppo Two, denied any knowledge of the kidnaping. The American captain was suspected only after it was learned that the Chinese visited the Javasche Bank of Batavia to exchange mysterious trade tokens called "Gerrymander Cash" for guilders. The Governor General has ordered a thorough investigation of this trade piece. Meanwhile a hearing has been ordered to determine whether Captain Boll should be indicted and tried by His Majesty's Court.

"Traced by his cash piece." I chuckled. There was every reason to believe the Gerrymander Cash dream had run its course. First, the Dutch had ordered an investigation, which would, I was sure, eliminate any threat to their Eastern economy in a hurry. Second, the Kim Kim episode could hardly do less than damage the good name of Culver and Adams, embarrass and infuriate Robert Culver, who would lose money in defending a despised captain whom he must aid in order to save the ship. So much for probabilities loaded with heavy odds.

Thus I reached a decision: I would begin at the beginning, honorably, which meant a showdown with Boll. When I finished talking with him, he would know about De Loach and what I wanted. I moved past the Dutch Marines to Boll's cabin. There I was met by the officer who had done all the talking the day before. Captain Boll was not there; he was either in jail or posting the required bond.

I asked questions about the law in such cases, about example cases and final decisions. They varied, as under any law, I was told, according to the seriousness of the particular crime as well as other conditions surrounding the crime; Dutch law was flexible and just. The answer, as vague as it was universal, prompted my inquiry concerning Boll's particular crime and all that might affect a decision.

"Very serious, mijnheer. Piracy and slave trading must be stamped out. Then, too, our loyal fiefs, the radjas and sultans, must be humored. *Mijn vrind*, the Sultan of Bandjermasin has put troops in the field for us in Borneo! There is your case."

"And our ship?" I asked.

"It goes with the decision of His Majesty's Court."

"And what happens to the ship if Captain Boll is convicted?"

"The Government has been known to seize ships for its own use, or auction, or to do with as it pleases."

"Uh-huh," I meditated aloud. "But how broad is your last statement? I mean by that, mijnheer, that as chief mate I am in a position to lend valuable testimony in the direction I choose." This drew all the sharp appraisal a Dutch colonial officer can muster to his face.

He eyed me at length before nodding his head and emitting an introspective *"Ja."* How auspicious the word might be I did not know until he said at last, "So you wish to enjoy an advantage in buying the ship from His Majesty's Government?" It was my time to say, *"Ja."*

"It is worth considering," he replied.

"I think so," I said. "But it must be understood that I'm to get first chance at buying the ship, and cheap."

As he studied me, a superior smile crept over his face. "You Yankees love one another so much that I can understand now the war between your states."

Angry at his smug leer more than at his words, I said, "Well, just to tumble your opinions, nothing more, let me tell you that I'm hunting Captain Boll to tell him exactly what I'm doing. And as for you, I hope he talks me out of it."

9

In the three days before the preliminary hearing, I put the Kim Kim story in a letter to De Loach, outlining my plans. I was armed and ready on the night before the hearing; I felt the stock of Tom Flint rising to the promised partnership in the solvent firm of De Loach and Company. And, I admitted with a weary sigh, I had earned whatever reward awaited me.

I had not seen Boll in the interim, though it was through no fault of mine: he had chosen the hospitality of an old Australian seaman and friend with a special Dutch guard about the house; the alternative was a tremendous cash bond or jail.

At last the day of the Dutch hearing arrived. It lasted two days; and, as I had requested, my testimony was delayed time and again: the

Dutch prosecutors hoped also to save my testimony for the trial if possible. Therefore I listened and said nothing as I weighed the balance of opinion against the necessity for any word from me. Boll's lie, which he put up in defense of self—"Since when is it against the law for a captain to take his woman along?"—annulled the fact that he intended returning Kim Kim to the Sultan of Bandjermasin. Thus the final opinion of the Dutch grand jury was as follows:

"This body, having duly examined the accusation against Captain Boll, American citizen and master of the merchant ship *Gerrymander*, and charged with deliberate intent to trade in human life by passing money or goods in return for such, in violation of Dutch anti-slavery laws, finds that the evidence warrants a bill of indictment against Captain Boll, and the shipowner, Culver and Adams."

The trial date was set for September fifteenth, seven months ahead —to allow the shipowner time to arrive and prepare a defense. But Boll, as well as Culver and Adams, was scheduled to face trial.

And all for a cash piece and Kim Kim.

BOOK FOUR ❦ 1886

12 ⪻ THE TRAIL OF THE CASH

BOLL CAME OUT OF THAT HEARING WITH A NEW AND FRESH QUALITY TO augment his love for money: it was nothing short of resentment for the Dutch.

He had sat through that hearing, his eyes calm and cold over his sharp nose; his silence had been broken only by crisp utterances, less defensive and more accusing, and always damning. When the big-lipped, smiling Dutch questioner asked, "Have you slept with the Sultan's dancing girl?" Boll replied, "Let the Sultan find out for himself." The fat Sultan of Bandjermasin, who sat nearby, scowled and placed a heavy hand over the gold dagger in his belt. Boll nullified the threat with his eyes.

The Dutchman had asked, "Have you anything to say in your behalf?"

"No. I'll defend myself in my own way when the time comes."

His departure from that hearing had been as pompous as his exit from the Javasche Bank weeks before. Though defeated, he did not so much as consider defeat. With the indictment still ringing in his ears, he had said to me:

"Mr. Flint, I have been honest with the damned Dutch up to this point. From now on they'll do well to keep an eye on me."

As I thought of my mission and placed it alongside his threat, he said, "We'll fill the islands so full of cash pieces, their trade will feel it all over. And," he chuckled, "what we learned in the Formosa experiment will help us do it."

"What's that, sir?"

"We have some twenty schooner captains working the Lesser Sundas, Moluccas, and Celebes. They're buying with the Gerrymander

Cash. We'll follow in their trail and exchange trade goods for cash pieces before dumping more. And every one we pick up along the way is one less to show up at the Javasche Bank to cost me a guilder."

"Then you're planning to put more than the fifty thousand the bank authorized into circulation?"

"Aye. A million if possible." I could see him working his way into another trap of his own setting that would serve De Loach and me. Kim Kim, a woman, a mere dancing girl, had served us well up to that point. The trial in September would tell just how well she had served us.

That evening something new was added to the threat or threats hanging over Boll's head. The Dutch had already indicted him on one charge; and by his very admission to me of fraudulent intent in the distribution of the Gerrymander Cash, he courted another indictment. As if a foregone fact and a looming probability were not enough, an opposing force lent its voice. It happened in the Big Coffin Saloon.

Boll and I were engaged in conversation with a schooner captain and a Dutch Controleur from Amboina, who had just declared himself open to reason for a sum, when Chess searched us out.

"A note, sir," he said to Boll. "From the fat old bastard who owns Kim Kim." As Boll read and smiled slowly, Chess proceeded to condemn the Sultan for a heathen, reprobate, and more, swearing to save the girl himself.

I laughed. Then Boll said:

"Listen to this. Old Bandjermasin says I am a pig and a son of a pig who is the son of a pig. I am cursed by Allah. He says he will settle matters with me at some future date."

The schooner captain lifted his brows, and the Controleur said, "That is bad, Kapitein Boll."

"Why is it bad?" Boll asked.

"Because, mijnheer, some say he is Pulo Besar."

Boll smiled and spoke to Chess: "Go tell the Sultan that the Kim Kim affair hasn't ended. Before it's over he'll look alive and anxious."

The Controleur lingered, though the schooner captain excused himself in the manner of a man who viewed a future corpse.

2

The day after, not four hours before we sailed out of Soerabaja, a British Indiaman sent a boy over with mail. My heart leaped up when I saw a letter to me from Harriet.

The boy said, "A lady on the big American merchant *Shanghai Packet* sent it aboard while our ships lay becalmed under Java Head."

I rewarded the limey with a big dollar and moved to the bows to open a letter she had written more than a month earlier. I read eagerly:

DEAR MR. FLINT:

I have thought of you quite often, and with a feeling of gratitude for having shown me Singapore, as well as for your sympathetic attitude toward my business duplicity. Blossom (the Chinese doll you gave me in Singapore) is looking on as I write this.

You'll remember I told you it was not prudent for me to go with you unchaperoned. You saw Aunt Emily at the gangway upon our return. Well, she continues to lecture me on the subjects of prudence and behavior. But I did enjoy the sights of the city.

Regarding the last question you asked that evening, which I was unable to answer—what did I tell Mr. Culver when he proposed?—I will say that I continue to put off giving him any answer. I have a number of reasons for doing so.

I shall look forward hopefully for some word from you which may release me from the odd business arrangement which you call a trap.

In the interim, may I have some report on your activities? Mail it to me in care of our friend on State Street.

Cordially,
HARRIET ADAMS

P.S. Blossom sends her fond regards.

"Cordially, she says!" I frowned. "So she's putting Culver off in one sentence, and looking forward to my aid in getting her out of the trap in the next. What's the connection? So she can say yes to Culver?"

I read the letter again. She had not called me Tom. "And Blossom sends her fond regards."

I grinned. Then I looked out over the harbor. There was barely time for me to get ashore and find some gift for Harriet and write a letter before the *Gerrymander* filled away.

A few hours later I smiled up into the tophamper, my ears closed to the creaking ship that pulled for the East Gat. All I could hear was Harriet saying:

"Blossom sends her fond regards."

3

The *Gerrymander* bypassed Bali and Lombok in her eastern run of the Lesser Sunda Islands. She raised the entrance of tortuous Bima

Bay on the northeastern end of Soembawa Island on the afternoon of our third day out of Soerabaja.

Bima was the first port of call on the appointed trail of those schooner captains who preceded us with Gerrymander Cash pieces. There the Sultan of Bima resided; there teak and dyewoods and assorted wealth cried for a buyer. The town of Bima rose up out of a swamp in the northwest monsoon, a great cluster of native huts and a few European houses under the brown-masked green of lazy coconut palms.

Bima stood up out over our bows, a promise of the magic or the error of our trade money.

Boll ordered the vessel in closer than safety allowed, since outside anchorage was unsafe during the prevailing monsoon. Ahead we saw the ancient Makassar praus propped up high on the beach; their square sterns and bluff-bows were reminiscent of the caravels of the early Portuguese.

The low coral pier inched closer, and the leadsman droned out five fathoms. Then came the order to drop anchor. The setting was stifling and somber as the purple hills seemed to close around us in a world of solitude and haunting primitiveness. The rugged mountains emptied down upon the hills and stood like cool mirages beckoning one to slake his thirst as they raced away laughing. There was missing the clamor from native boats which should have put out to meet us. All was still at the water's edge. Soon a breath of wind puffed out of that dank setting and the stench was awful.

Only one boat put out, its sole occupant laying on the oars with weary strokes as he drew nearer. A lone white man, an emaciated fellow with eyes so far back in his head that they seemed to court the hereafter, peered up at us after an age. "I'm a Dokter," he rasped. "Fever. They're dying like flies." Boll asked about the Sultan of Bima. "Fever. We need drinking water—all polluted here. Not even Pulo Besar will anchor here."

"What about trade goods?" Boll asked, only to be damned by the burning eyes of the selfless man. "I've got water to sell," Boll added.

"Water—to sell?" the man said incredulously. Then, in resigned tone, he said, "Come."

Boll and I, with old Wulsin, Chess, four volunteers, a case of gin, and six casks of water, moved ashore. A cry went up among the natives, and all who could move ran, stumbled, and crawled toward us, babbling and howling, with bamboo lengths extended for precious water. They looked up at us from sorrowful eyes; but soon with despondent and glazed eyes—Boll demanded payment for every drop of water. Some wore a remnant of clothing, others nothing but breech-clouts of bark cloth, and still others were draped with trite colorless thigh-length aprons. But all produced payment of one kind or another: spears, shells, and beads Boll rejected; priceless pearls and ivory bracelets were rewarded with water and gin. Women ran out of thatches, their veils before their faces in true Moslem manner, with their necklaces in their hands.

Aye, necklaces of shining yellow metal strung on coconut fiber; some held two coins, others more. The Gerrymander Cash! A schooner captain had been there before us.

"Only a few ounces of water for each," Boll snapped. Before one cask was drained, he refused to accept the cash as payment. His reason, in his own words, was simply this: "Let them be buried with their cash pieces. The Dutch will have to rob corpses to get them."

"How very clever," I growled. The sight before me was a picture of the horror of complete destitution. It lived, breathed, and begged in human form and voice; it sent up brown hands trembling. Behind these hands were supplicating eyes, hordes of eyes, a nightmare of brown men's eyes, all against a background of hand-hewn teak, tons of mother-of-pearl, and strings of first-grade coconut meat—riches. And they begged for the cheap water.

As Boll traded, Chess and I poured water into every cup. Boll saw us and barked forth:

"I said no water, Mr. Flint."

"They are going to get water," I said angrily, facing Boll. "Pour water, Chess." I added, "A little in each bamboo length."

As Chess hastened to obey me, Boll sent him sprawling, overturning one cask. The natives rushed forward on hands and knees and bellies to suck at the little puddles and soon the mud. I stood close to Boll and said, "I mean to see that they get water."

"Mr. Flint," he said, "I haven't time for you right now. Have your way, but remember I haven't forgotten that bowline-bridle incident."

I had already lost my victory; the fools I tried to help had conformed in the moments to Boll's way of thinking. When Boll refused to accept the cash pieces of doomed sufferers he opened up a gold mine. All but the Sultan's shares of the riches of Bima were soon ours. Then Boll chuckled and said: "We'll see what the Sultan will offer for the two remaining casks."

The Sultan of Bima, a corpulent Arab, lay in an enormous legless bed of polished brass, upon which were heaped yards of fine silver-thread batik, alive with hundreds of birds and animals of East Indian design in a dazzling wealth of rare native dyes. Boll smiled when the textile met his eye.

The old sultan sat up, glared at us, then nodded. His beard and mustache parted in his fevered face as he grinned out a yellow-toothed welcome. He lived in a semistate of oriental luxury and primordial negligence. He was at once prince and sloven; chickens ate off his colorful inlaid floor of stone, and fat dogs chewed at bones on the batik hanging from his bed. On the walls, I saw large pieces of solid ivory. To strike a comparison, the Sultan seemed one of those Moslems who had forgotten that pig meat was forbidden.

"Allah! Water! Water!" His brocaded attendants fanned him while an old wrinkled man, in turban and breechclout, squatted on a price-less rug and read from the Koran, the Mohammedan Bible.

"What is water worth, O Sultan of Bima?" Boll asked.

The mighty fief of Soembawa forgot Allah long enough to stare at a man who dared demand trade for water. He called his guard, and we were soon surrounded by ominous natives with long knives. Boll smiled. A tense moment ensued before the Sultan ordered the water seized. One of the guards placed his hands on a cask to his re-gret: Boll struck him just below the ear. As he lay sprawled on the stone floor, the others halted and looked at their master for orders.

"We'll trade," Boll said.

The pampered Sultan raked a swollen tongue across his lips.

"An ounce of water for him, Mr. Flint." I obliged, realizing that Boll's offering was nothing short of torture. That taste of clean water engendered fast trade, however, and the silver-thread batik was soon ours, as well as the ivory and a few rare pearls. The sultan owned a cask of water, and he was soon bloated with it. After that, robbing him wasn't so easy. He bargained hard and long for a price on his teak, sandalwood, and mother-of-pearl. But, oddly enough, he was pleased to accept payment for these in Gerrymander Cash pieces.

Before noon of the next day, Boll had purchased one fifth of the goods aboard the Makassar ships propped up on the long sandy beach. These goods he sold to the Sultan at a nice profit, accepting payment in the cash pieces he had purchased goods with the day before. Then, on the second day after our arrival, a few hours after a three-masted schooner from the Celebes brought St. Ebenezer to his rendezvous, a strange incident occurred:

The Sultan of Bima, jubilant and sweating profusely, came out in his gilded dory under a purple-and-yellow canopy to honor the "healer sent by Allah." He presented Boll with a piece of jade set with a large emerald. The East was baffling.

The Gerrymander moved on, down through Sape Strait into the Sawoe Sea, in search of another windfall. Boll had retrieved all but one thousand cash pieces in Bima.

4

We were two days in reaching the town of Ende on the southern coast of Flores Island. Twice the current of the strait ran against us, and then the winds, striking dry and to the west, caused us to beat for every mile east along that steep-to coast. Beneath the seamed northern horizon, purple-black valleys and caverns seemed to rise up out of the blue sea like ironbound paths fused by the god Vulcan; the ominous cast of the stern welter of rock struck the eye like some incredible burden. The mountains presented feathery thickets of bamboo which merged in shadow rather than shape with the wall of coconut palms guarding the shore. Then the town of Ende from far out at sea: it was set among stretching groves of penciled coconut palms, from which a mosque rose up in the sun like a sheet of blazing copper and ivory; directly behind the town the towering head of the great Keli Moetoe nestled in the clouds. As we glided into the placid bay, a dream setting met the eye as coconut fronds moved out of the haze, no longer tiny, brown-masked stems, but living graces waving a languorous welcome.

I thought of Harriet. If she stood at my side, the view would be lovelier, if only for the sharing. But she was not there, and I was unable to hold her in the sharp shadows of a Flores coconut palm. I turned my hungry mind back to the deck which I trod, and to the short past.

St. Ebenezer had listened to Boll's story, which began with Culver in Singapore and moved on to Batavia and the Javasche Bank; from K'ung K'ung to Kim Kim, to cash piece and back to Kim Kim.

"Kim Kim," St. Ebenezer meditated aloud, running a long-fingered hand across his brow before parting his yellow beard and mustache. His deep, intelligent eyes thinned as he said, "I read about her. Too bad you ever met her. Too bad you lost her."

Boll's reply jerked my eyes around. "I haven't lost her."

St. Ebenezer accepted the answer as a fact, so said his expression. "I have learned," he said, "that determination in some few divorces itself from fear of any failure. Such an attitude, if sustained, can topple even Dutch mountains. But how in the name of hell do you expect to retrieve her? Don't answer that—it's your own virgin thought. But answer this:

"How many cash pieces are in circulation? I've scattered twenty thousand."

"And I," said Boll, "have distributed some eighty thousand."

"Um——" St. Ebenezer lifted his brows and pursed his small red lips as he extracted a newspaper clipping from his pocket. "Listen to this: 'The Governor General has ordered a thorough investigation of this trade piece.'" He folded the bit of paper and said, "And your ten thousand American dollars made as good as gold fifty thousand cash pieces at guilder value. We've put twice the number into circulation, though we have not doubled the money in reserve."

"So the Gerrymander Cash is actually worth only half a guilder." Boll smiled.

St. Ebenezer agreed, saying, "Every bubble must expect a pin-pricking hand."

"But the Dutch will find it hard to check on our circulation," Boll said. "I'm gathering the loose ones in and letting the others stay out of circulation. There are a thousand in Bima that you, I, or the Dutch may never get."

"Captain, I'll read this sentence once more. It says, 'The Governor General has ordered a thorough investigation of this trade piece.' The word thorough in almost every tongue has the same meaning. There is only one exception—the Dutch tongue. You will be concerned when I tell you that the Dutch are as busy as bees right now. They're gathering in every cash piece they can find. By the good Lord and myself, it is so!"

Boll took it without any change of expression. Only I shrugged and broke my silence as I poured rum and raised a glass. "To Kim Kim," I said with a wry smile, "the cause of it all."

While the Gerrymander sat out the night in the Bay of Ende, we planned our strategy far into the night. It was decided that St. Ebenezer should board a passing schooner in the near future and make his way to Batavia. There he should boost the Gerrymander Cash guarantee from ten thousand dollars up to twenty thousand, or more. Then he should join us posthaste in Amboina.

But first we felt it necessary to make a test. The schooner captain, van Dee, who had preceded us at Ende, had orders to dispose of as many of the one thousand cash pieces as possible and advise us of his success through the Catholic priest there. We would see just how many of the yellow coins we could draw back into the fold in Ende.

The village came to life with the yellow east rising up in a hush of mighty incandescence above bamboo thickets and casuarina groves. By nine in the morning, St. Ebenezer had already drunk several cups of coffee with the Catholic priest, who handed him a letter from Captain van Dee. It was as follows:

KAPITEIN BOLL,
The Gerrymander:

I encountered little difficulty in disposing of the new money. At first the Dutch and Chinese traders spurned the coins, as if Pulo Besar were circulating them. But when they saw me sell for them as well as buy with them, they became interested. It was not long before the natives, particularly the Ngadas, sought them for neckpieces. They willingly allowed the shopkeepers and traders extra profit in order to obtain them. Regarding my profits at Ende, I will admit that the new money fetched me more goods than the guilder. I have entrusted the priest with my draft for another supply of your money.

KAPITEIN VAN DEE
Schooner Roode Hind

Postscript: A Kapitein Steele offered me a four-per-cent profit on my new money. I refused it.

For two days we set up shop in Ende. St. Ebenezer was our bilingual shopkeeper who bargained like a Chinaman, Scotchman, and Jew rolled into one. And the very fact that he paid less for cinnamon, coffee, sandalwood, and copra was offset by the extra value he placed on the Gerrymander Cash. By allowing the buyer more in exchange for the cash, he disrupted the trade of the Chinese and Dutch and soon had in his possession almost every cash piece that could be enticed into circulation again. On the morning of the third day we counted the cash pieces circulated in advance of our visit by Captain van Dee and drawn in by our trade goods: four hundred and nine out of one thousand had been retrieved.

Five hundred and ninety-one were still at large!

Boll was pleased. He said, "At this rate, the Dutch will find it hard to prove that we have distributed more than fifty thousand cash pieces." He turned to St. Ebenezer, then me, as he said:

"The experiment has ended. From now on we are sure." He added, "We are through retrieving our money—instead we'll spend." He got to his feet and said in the tone he used when calling upon the devil for a wind, "We'll flood the islands with the Gerrymander Cash!"

He seemed to be tying his own noose. I wondered, however, what caused the satisfied gleam in St. Ebenezer's eyes.

5

The *Gerrymander* backtracked seventy-five miles along the south Flores coast to Aimere, the gateway to the land of the Ngadas. Boll had said: "The farther inland we take the cash, the longer it will take it to reach a Dutch bank." And how the Ngada served him there is quite a story.

Far out from port, Iné Rié, a conspicuous landmark of the coast, reared its cloud-crowned head; on the other side of that volcano lay Badjawa. The coconut sentinels watched us splash our anchors far out and make ready for our first and only venture inland. Huge emerald-green fronds seemed to lift like dubious brows in the gentle breeze, and then rattle and swish with warning in a gust of wind, as if they said, "Fewer come out than go in. But enter." It was hard to look at that coast line and realize that we were anchored in the very heart of the troublesome Lesser Sunda Islands. Here was the heart of riches, piracy, slave traffic, radjas, sultans, and mystery.

The trail to Badjawa climbed up and up until the air was cool by day and cold by night. Boll, St. Ebenezer, Mr. Wulsin, and I, as well as several sail hands and natives with carts, made our way through valleys and overhanging cliffs, across ravines secluded by thickets of bamboo. At last we saw our first Ngada kampong in the distance.

The Ngada house was a high roof supported by thick strong upright beams; verandas were fashioned of split bamboo, and there women sat in the shade and worked at their looms or the dye vats. The Ngada favored blue, whether from the prevalence of the dye or from actual choice. The color was intensely blue and deep; the garb of the Ngada, a toga-like cloth in which the arms are folded inside as if to escape the chill, and falling to the ankles or to an apron effect about the knees or thighs, seemed a living blue. And the wearer:

He was a crinkly-haired, sharp-eyed, brown man, a hybrid of short stature, who reminded one of the high-caste Indian as well as the Malay and Polynesian; and again there was a faint influence of Melanesia about his linear features. He was healthy and of good posture, and the male was handsomer by far than the female.

We were met by a dozen barefoot braves who advanced menacingly with long swords that tapered from a butcher-like blade point to a round hilt adorned with plumage. They wore batik about the hairline, above which a mass of hair appeared.

"They welcome us," St. Ebenezer said. "The Radja of Badjawa sends them."

The Radja kept us waiting. He was carving a *peo* which would join the others standing in a long row before his house, the largest house of all and decorated with buffalo horns. Their *peos* stood up like shaggy umbrellas partly opened, the pole underneath carved artistically with designs which were dedicated to ancestors. Their *peos* were sacred, St. Ebenezer advised; to touch one of them was tantamount to insult, and we were warned to observe this rule above all others.

After some time the Radja, a chieftain outwardly loyal to the Dutch, made his royal appearance. His dress was a skirt in two shades of blue. He wore shell beads about the neck. The usual batik headpiece was tied around a red Makassar cap, a fez-shaped piece. He carried a silver dagger. Perhaps the brightest eyes I have ever seen shone out of his sharp face; they were as thin as his tight lips. Two of his wives appeared on the veranda, both of whom were draped in rich batik of Achinese design. Their mouths dispelled any illusions of beauty.

Boll, at St. Ebenezer's nod, advanced and bowed, then stepped closer with a necklace of glittering cash pieces. The Radja barked an order and two braves ran up to Boll and snatched the necklace. It was soon fastened about his neck, forgotten, as he glared at Boll. There were other gifts: a ring set with a huge bloodstone, a dagger of gold-colored metal from which rubies sparkled, a case of red wine, a plug hat, and squares of flower-dappled silk in many colors. When the seemingly unappreciative fellow pointed to his wives, as if he were offended, Boll handed each of them a briar pipe and tobacco. Soon four other wives made their appearance.

"He welcomes us," St. Ebenezer said, drawing from Boll. "Tell him what we're after." But St. Ebenezer reproved him with a reminder that one did not rush into trade with so mighty a potentate. We should, instead, open a bottle of gin. This we did, only to be rushed by scores of natives who appeared suddenly with bamboo lengths to be filled. One bottle after another was emptied until a full case had been consumed. Then the Radja raised a hand imperiously and the somewhat tipsy population weaved off to feel the full effect of their cozy burden in the central court. The Radja waved us inside. Chess and the sail hands waited in the courtyard.

The Radja studied Boll. He spoke, and St. Ebenezer translated his challenge: "The Radja wishes to join you in a drinking bout, Captain. If you win, you may take your choice of his wives and receive a quart of gold—interesting, the latter, isn't it? And if he wins you are to present him with many necklaces and your goods out there, and the young sailor called Chess."

Boll replied, "Tell him to trot out all his wives for my inspection." As the Radja clapped his hands, Boll clandestinely dropped a handful of cash pieces into his bamboo length. I chuckled—he was quick to correct the evenness of chance in a drinking bout.

As the wives appeared, St. Ebenezer said, "There is only one pleasure to a Ngada that exceeds drinking."

"And he has eight," Boll commented. "Find out which is his favorite." After much talk, the Radja reluctantly clapped his hands together, and another girl appeared. She was a comely creature by comparison; when she smiled she was truly beautiful. But she was no Ngada. "Balinese," said St. Ebenezer. "Her name is Tana. He bought her from a Moluccan pirate who serves the mighty Pulo Besar, the Great Bastard."

"So he trades with pirates," Boll said. "How much did he pay for her?"

"Two quarts of gold, one wife, and two buffaloes. The Radja wishes to know if you'd like to see her naked. I answered yes, of course."

"I'd rather he uncovered his gold."

The Radja growled at Boll, causing me to wonder if we needed a translator. I managed to convey my thought to St. Ebenezer, who said, "No, he simply likes the sport of winning over a white man. And he's anxious to do just that."

The Radja's eyes grew brighter and more ominous as he drank; and he drank freely until his container was turned bottom up as if to declare his superiority.

Said the Radja through our translator, "Does my favorite wife go unnoticed?"

Boll said to St. Ebenezer, "What's the proper course now?"

"Look at the favorite wife, and drink up."

Her hair was a deep brown; and her skin, as diaphanous as sheer silk, glistened as she stood naked to the waist; there was mischief and intelligence in her brown oriental eyes, and invitation in the spread of her perfectly formed lips. When her drab blue robe fell to the floor, she was an even lovelier sight—a golden-yellow sarong with red flowers in gold outline set her apart from the world of the Ngada. She was more like a tropical jasmine blossoming above a dunghill. She caught Boll's eye and held it, a Kim Kim or the kindred essence of her, first with her dimpling face, and then with her ripe cup-shaped breasts and slim waist.

"Tell the bantam prince she's not worth two quarts of gold."

"Impolicy, Captain, is like a sieve," St. Ebenezer said. "The gold slips through."

I drank slowly, as did Mr. Wulsin, and waited. Outside the sun cut shadows as sharp as a blade.

"The Radja promises us a dance we shall never forget on this night," St. Ebenezer advised. I wondered if the oddments here preceded the feast, if we were priming ourselves for a display of the primitive under the moon of Badjawa that evening; and with no apparent harmony existing between the two leaders, I feared scenes which none of us might view with cozy detachment. They drank, and like truculent beasts they eyed each other as if hostility constituted the highest social amenity. I tired of it and left St. Ebenezer to smooth their conversation with his apt translations. They were deep into their second bamboo when I strolled into the central court.

The Ngada puts his worship in reverse: the good spirits receive small attention, while the evil spirits of ancestors, jealous of the new generation always, of its gain of gewgaw and rum and untold luxury, are constantly appeased. The anthropologist is quick to label this form of worship as raw savagery, a first cousin to the religious precepts of the head-hunter. The Ngada, by and large, is less a threat to human life, though he is inconsistent. Sober and unfrenzied by dance, he is content to propitiate his peos to his ancestors with carvings and gifts. But drunk and excited by the throbbing drums, his behavior was a matter of conjecture. We could only wait for the evening.

St. Ebenezer prepared us for what the night might offer when he said: "But for the decorations, you'll think you're visiting a Taoist hell."

Neither Boll nor the Radja had tested their legs when the torches threw them in high light and shadow. They sipped at their fourth serving in a silence both lethargic and electric. I soon discovered that Boll's cunning had been duplicated—the Radja's bamboo cup was half filled with pebbles; and I learned that during my absence he had drunk several ounces of coconut oil.

From the central court came sounds of revelry, and as I peered outside moving Ngadas cast long, eerie, spasmodic shadows on the peos, huts, and dusty ground. Inside, Boll raised his bamboo and drained it; the Radja, not to be outdone, emulated him. Both awaited a refill. When the servant or prime minister, or both, had filled the cheating cups, the Radja said it was time for the dance to start.

Slowly, carefully, he got to his feet and rocked unsteadily into balance. His flashing eyes seemed to enjoy the sight of a white man about to fall in an effort to regain his feet. He saw just that when Mr. Wulsin tried to arise, and he clapped his hands resoundingly in order that his wives and guard might view the degradation of a white man. They came and babbled, and they danced from sheer joy. They were thus engaged when Boll stirred. Slowly he unfolded his legs and then got to his feet without any trouble whatever.

The Radja leered.

The clearing by torchlight presented a different Ngada from the slovenly one of the afternoon. The populace was dressed for some festival of Saturn, wherein vice to excess is condoned for an evening. The slow drums whipped up the feeling; the scant raiment of both male and female seemed to tincture the cool evening air with some indefinable savage revelry yet to be felt in its extravagant state. An impatient, nervous joy awaiting outlet.

The Radja, Boll, St. Ebenezer, and I sat on mats. The drinking duel continued, and the ground was saturated with gin as both contenders sought to prolong complete drunkenness. The torches spread into a circle, and the Radja of Badjawa spoke. The drums leaped up, and feet were set in motion. Dust obscured the movements for a time, but soon our eyes became accustomed to it.

I had expected a jerking of limbs in quick frenzy and was somewhat pleased by the utter lack of such dancing. Here was rhythm, awkward yet pleasing. The men crossed swords and leaped back as if rehearsing a battle, while the women waved their silken squares to the right and left before them, thereby lending motion to their backs, waists, hips, and limbs—all in slow rhythm to the beat of drums, clashing of swords, and rattle of shell beads. The drums held to the original tempo for an hour; then the Radja raised a hand and the beat quickened. But not the motions of the dancers, who seemed to slow as if their ears were tuned to only every other beat.

The drums possessed a far-reaching beautiful voice: they snared from the ether some spirit of revelry which transfixed the sensual ear, or else they evoked from the dormant cells of ancestral memories sadistic rites which the Ngada had lost but which continued to haunt his craving soul. Either being true, the minds of the dancers were slowly being drained of all physical awareness while being inoculated with the honey of some dream of ecstasy.

The moon rose big and round over the bamboo thicket and reared up quickly for a better view of Ngadaland. The Radja raised his hand once more, and the tempo of the drums increased. And once more the bodies slowed to the third or fourth beat. I wondered if the effect were hypnotic, or if the dancers actually defied the increasing tempo. But one fact was apparent—their magic was infectious. I writhed and strained in my sitting posture as if I felt the bodily urge to hasten the movements of those ghostly shadows. I drank deep in self-defense and turned my eyes to Boll. He gazed at another sight:

There she stood holding his eyes as if she were a snake enticing an unwilling mouse. The Radja's favorite wife, Tana the Balinese, seemed in the moonlight more a nymph dedicated to the fulfillment of love than a corporeal being sold to a Radja's bed. She glistened in the light from hairdress to the sarong about her waist, her hair flashing star points, her moist lips in smile doing the same. Her eyes, languorous and alive, accepted shadows as she lowered her long-lashed lids; and a dreamy fire leaped up and out of them when she slowly lifted them. Her body, bare to the waist, seemed woven of moonlight, quiet, still, and deep. She had surely risen up out of the drums.

Boll got to his feet slowly, his eyes chained to hers. I saw him take her in his arms and kiss her with consuming passion. Somehow I was neither surprised nor fearful; rather, I was anxious, and jealous. His act seemed justified by the moon and distant peak in the tropic sky; Boston and civilization were forgotten worlds. Therein lay my weakness, and Boll's, though it was he who manifested the white man's lack of resistance to savage magic. The Radja was too busy appeasing his ancestors to take notice of Boll and his favorite wife as they eased off into the shadows of a bamboo thicket.

The dance continued. The Radja raised his hand again, and the drums reached for a maddening throb; faster, faster they beat; and the dancers slowed and listened for the eighth or tenth beat. It was then I felt the breath of understanding. This would go on until the drums grew hot under the racing tempo, until the bodies slowed to unbelievable writhing and twisting. The art of their frenzy was an art indeed, one designed to appease the evil spirits of their ancestors. The metronome called for speed, and worship demanded disobedience, and the meeting of the two was nothing short of a mental torture inflicted by rhythm without surcease; therein the agony of restraint tore at the soul and mind until the body felt the pain in sweet, sensual courses. It was like some prolonged agony of love, the tearing out of a nightingale's tongue in search of the secret of melody—and all thrown atop a pyre to the gods.

I shook my groggy head at last and turned to eye the spot which Boll had vacated. There he sat; perhaps he had been there all the time. The moon directly overhead, the same old mountain to the south, the drums, the dancers, Boll, the Radja, and Ngadaland—nothing made sense.

The dawn was painting the east, and the moon was bleaching out in the quarter-sky, and still the dance wore on. Many lay sprawled out in the dust, their bones chilled by the cold air. Chess slept next to me on one side, Mr. Wulsin on the other. The Radja and Boll sat as before, bamboo lengths in hand, and St. Ebenezer rested on stomach and elbows. The Radja raised a hand and the drums stopped, though they continued to beat in my head. I saw the drummers fall across their long instruments as if dead; and the dancers fell in their tracks to a sleep of the dead. All was quiet.

"Now we settle business," said the Radja ominously. He made as if to rise, then sat back. He tried once more, only to fall forward. Boll got up and proceeded to lift the irate chieftain to his feet, even as St. Ebenezer shouted a warning. The Radja was quite drunk, but he held full command over his senses. And in his rage and humiliation, he uttered a cry that brought his sleeping braves to their feet.

"You have put your hands on him, Captain. He is disgraced."

The Radja reached for his dagger and struck wildly at Boll. In the next few minutes the entire kampong was up in arms. As we reached for our pistols, St. Ebenezer shouted:

"Don't shoot! Run to their *peos*! And grab a sword on the way." We raced for the shaggy umbrellas, tripping the braves and snatching up weapons on the way. Only one of our group was left behind—Mr. Wulsin. The Radja staggered about, shouting. We were told that he cried for our blood, that his ancestors demanded blood for drink. Then he espied Mr. Wulsin, who continued to enjoy the sleep of drunkenness, and stumbled to him with knife upraised.

"Wait!" St. Ebenezer cried in the Ngada tongue. "If you so much as touch him, we'll hack the totems of your ancestors."

As I have explained, the totem-pole *peos* were sacred. The ancestors, long since dead, lived beneath them, and the appeasement of ancestors constituted their religion. Thus St. Ebenezer's threat was a terrible one. It saved Mr. Wulsin's life.

The idea appealed to Boll, and he seized it for gain. He ordered St.

Ebenezer to demand full payment on the lost wager—the wife and the quart of gold. He swung a sword to show he meant business, and the Radja was quick to dispatch his men for both.

And Boll, always unsatisfied, was once more the Striker. He realized his advantage: should any of us so much as scratch the meticulously carved peos, the Ngada would feel himself doomed to a living hell by the evil spirits—and, where there was one quart of gold, surely there were two. Here was long-courted opportunity rising up out of a grave to lend him that superiority the devil had promised in return for coins tossed into the sea. He said, when the servant appeared with the gold:

"Tell the Radja we are ready to talk trade in peace."

The Radja of Badjawa felt the gain of the moment; and he was astute enough quickly to exchange chaos for harmony even as his crafty mind sought some heathen advantage. With Chess and our sail hand stationed at the peos with swords ready, St. Ebenezer and I joined the palaver. Then Boll spoke his mind:

"I will make him a present of his favorite wife." Soon the Radja smiled. "I will present him with all our trade goods." The chieftain's smile broadened. "I wish peace and trade with the great Radja, much trade, long peace. What does he say?"

"He says he is pleased," St. Ebenezer replied.

"Then tell him I wish to buy his gold." With this a great change came over the Ngada. He protested and he hedged about with offers of ivory and dyewoods, even two of his wives. "Gold," Boll replied firmly. I glanced at the coins in the measure and saw that they were British, the gold pound. I was about to ask how the Radja came by this money when Boll spoke:

"Tell him I will trade him this money for his gold—piece for piece." He tossed a Gerrymander Cash to the Radja's mat.

As St. Ebenezer suppressed a chuckle, I hid my amazement—the English pound was worth many times more than the American dollar, which stood up for five pieces of the Gerrymander Cash! But the cash piece was larger and brighter.

The Radja considered himself a trader, and he was quick to bargain. St. Ebenezer spoke: "He wants three pieces of your money for one of his."

"Tell him I am angry," Boll said. "Tell him I do not wish to be cheated. I will give two pieces for one of his, no more." There was much talk between the Radja and St. Ebenezer. The Radja haggled; he held out for a three-to-one exchange. Boll refused, saying at last:

"If he refuses to trade my way, I will destroy his peos, arrest him, and take him to Soerabaja. He has, I'll wager, violated Dutch law by trading with Pulo Besar's captains."

This surmise turned the trick. The trade was completed, and we made ready to depart.

Exit, we realized, presented a ticklish problem, since the moment their *peos* were free from the threat of the white man's hand, we would stand in jeopardy. Thus, at St. Ebenezer's suggestion, we took the Radja wives with us to guarantee our safety. I watched the kampong fade in the morning sun, and I saw the Radja and his braves standing like tiny baleful statues staring after us.

The sun was high when Boll ordered the wives to return to their kampong. All but one obeyed. The sloe-eyed Balinese beauty smiled supplicatingly and threw her arms about Boll's neck as the other wives scurried uphill, glad to be free of bad spirits in human form. Boll flung her to the ground, though she arose, smiling as before, and advanced with outstretched arms. Boll stood with arms akimbo, a speculative look on his face.

Just as Tana was about to throw her arms about him again, the silence of the wilds above Aimere was broken by a swish, a thud, and a moan. The carved tip of a Ngada arrow stuck out an inch or more from her tawny waist—the feather end quivered at her back. She slumped, smiling, and her arms, like her eyes, reached for the arms that had embraced her in yesterday's moonlight.

But the gain—Boll had traded a mere four thousand Gerrymander Cash pieces for two thousand pieces of the British pound gold.

13 ↝ ALONG THE OLD SPICE ROADS

LONG MONTHS HAD SLIPPED BEHIND US SINCE THE "GERRYMANDER" knifed through Soerabaja's East Gat for the Lesser Sundas. From Badjawa and Ngadaland we turned south across the wide Soemba Strait to Waingapore, and then moved east to Dutch Timor and on to Tanimbar. We wandered to other islands on into crystal green bays, to white beaches lined with towering coconut palms. Harriet was a distant memory. Her kiss in Singapore Road seemed as a dream. Only the longing for a flesh-and-blood recurrence persisted, that plus unanswered questions: would she, could she, marry Culver; would she return with Culver to the trial in Soerabaja?

I was sure that she had by this time received my answer to her letter, as well as the gift of fine Achinese batik; and I wondered at her expressions of delight. Or had she forgotten me and the East by this time? The laughing waves and islands seemed to mock me and my questions.

We sailed on, turning northwest to the spice islands, where the mossy nutmeg groves peered down at bays in the sunshine; where banana groves caught the sun's rays with yellow-arched leaves, in a field of emerald green; where laziness seemed justified as it moved out to a ship in the shape of friendly natives squatting on outriggers. Up the old spice trails, where Magellan's *Trinidad* and *Victoria* had sailed; where Sir Francis Drake's *Golden Hind*, alive with courtiers under sweet-smelling awnings, had paused to send her officers to the fabulous durbars of island sultans. Great explorers in the romantic annals of history at last bowed to an adventurer with a cash piece.

We had crossed the Banda Zee in the company of thousands of big brown water snakes by day and huge sea birds by night. The crew blamed these monstrosities on our departure from Tanimbar on Friday, an inauspicious day for embarking on a voyage, and on Boll's séance with the devil that evening. He kept at it for an hour, tossing, always tossing coins into the sea. But the devil served us with a sailing wind that blew lively over our starboard quarter. Boll's coin-tossing prayers seemed to draw up energy from the sea, the same as the sun drew up water.

And now the Gerrymander sat in the gardens of the sea, the Moluccas, islands of spice. She was minus several hundred thousand cash pieces, though her holds were glutted with the wealth of the islands behind and below us. And now she looked at Amboina.

Between the great Gerrymander and the green mountains lay a stretch of blue water; it ended abruptly with coconut fronds glistening wet in the morning sun. In the center lay the nondescript village where an old fort gazed at us between the coconut trees, a reminder of Dutch justice.

Boll, at the rail, said, "St. Ebenezer should be here to meet us." He had left us after the Ngada windfall to boost our cash guarantee at Batavia's Javasche Bank from ten to twenty thousand dollars. His return was anxiously awaited.

We rowed ashore through canoes and fishing boats. On land, we ducked for cover from a racing rain cloud and emerged minutes later into the steaming shadows of dripping palms. The village of Amboina seethed with all the energy of a midday yawn. Coconut meat hung for drying, and tons of huge bananas awaited schooners to Batavia or Singapore. A shriveled old Amboinese with mustache and goatee played a bamboo flute while his twin dug into a trunk of sago palm for the starchy bread of the islands. Farther up the palm-lined avenue, two Orientals singsonged over a game of Chinese dominoes while awaiting a chance customer. The attire of the females was striking: a Java sarong of hand-dyed batik, or an occasional piece of English or American printed fabric.

Under a long thatch, a sinister-faced Portuguese served the schooner captains and traders with drink. We were attracted to the place by the sound of violin music accompanied by a tinny-sounding piano. When we raised the bamboo blind and entered, we discovered that the fiddler was none other than St. Ebenezer of Singapore. He lost little time in joining us at a hand-hewn table.

"Music," he said, as if he desired to close the subject before we opened it, "is an expression related to sex; both spring from the unconscious mind as predispositions brought with us from the womb. Simply say that St. Ebenezer said it."

"I'm more interested in what happened in Java," Boll said.

"The Dutch, Captain, lift us from tendencies at birth to the enigmatical subject of human conduct. By God and St. Ebenezer, it is so!" He eyed the bottle hungrily and then poured three drinks, touched his long nimble fingers to his forehead in greeting, and said in his saintly tone:

"Aye, Captain Boll, for the Javasche Bank of Batavia refused to accept any further guarantee of the Gerrymander Cash."

Boll leaned forward, his eyes thin. "Why?"

"The Government." St. Ebenezer then began to tell of his voyage.

"Get to the point," snapped Boll.

"In my own manner and mood, sir. The last time we talked there were one hundred thousand odd cash pieces in circulation. And the count now is what?"

"A half million roughly," Boll replied.

St. Ebenezer lifted his brows and said, "Captain, if I may voice a regret, I shall say that the Kim Kim episode is most regrettable."

"Your regrets don't interest me," Boll said.

"The true value of a fact, Captain, is the manner in which it strikes one," St. Ebenezer said in soft reproving tone. "Since my regrets fail to interest you, perhaps this will. Listen." Thereupon, he drew a paper from a pocket and read:

"'Case Captain Boll; the Gerrymander Cash. The order by the Governor General is to determine if intent to defraud by the American Captain Boll is the purpose for which he passes the trade coin: every Dutch officer of der Nederlandsch Indië shall solicit this unprecedented trade piece and pay full guilder value for it; schooner captains and traders shall be urged to solicit this item diligently for His Majesty's Government; special investigators shall be sent at once to such trade centers as Makassar, Ende, Ternate, and Amboina.'" St. Ebenezer paused.

"Amboina," he said. "This is Amboina."

"So it is," Boll replied.

"And," St. Ebenezer said, "I sailed from Soerabaja with the Dutch investigator assigned to this spot."

"Continue," Boll ordered.

"Here's an item from the Dutch files. It reads: 'The latest tabulation of the Javasche Bank revealed a total of 41,000 Gerrymander

Cash pieces redeemed. When 9,001 more pieces are redeemed, Captain Boll will be prosecuted for fraud.' "

"Nine to go," I mused aloud. "And then that single cash piece over."

The close proximity of a Dutch investigator provoked thought: Boll would surely bypass Amboina with the Gerrymander Cash; he would move to remote outposts or to other fields—French, British, or Spanish—while waiting for his trial.

When I asked if it wasn't about time to start retrieving our cash pieces again, Boll replied, "No, let's get busy and beat the Dutch investigator at his own game."

We followed the Dutch special investigator, van Beel, all that day, never more than two schooners or traders behind him. Boll's genius was revealed in his first conversation with a cargo runner who captained a pretty schooner. We came up on her portside in a native canoe under a single sail, just as van Beel departed from her starboard side. We were soon aboard and sipping drinks with the cautious captain.

Boll got down to business: did Captain Ryder make this run regularly; from Soerabaja or Batavia? Both? Did he carry cargo for fun or profit? A laugh answered the question.

"Well, what was van Beel's proposition? I might have a better one."

"To trade my gewgaws and staples for the funny trade piece that's taking the islands. He'll pay a guilder for each one I bring in."

"Sure," Boll sneered. "Read this." He placed the letter from the Javasche Bank before the captain, and then the one from Captain van Dee. "Listen to what van Dee says: 'Regarding my profits at Ende, I will admit that the new money fetched me more goods than the guilder.' "

"Ja. I know van Dee. He's a shrewd one. And I know this man Steele he mentions in the postscript."

"Well, I'll ask you again if you're out for fun or profit."

"Profit," came the reply.

We sold Captain Ryder five hundred cash pieces for five hundred guilders. Before midnight we had disposed of ten thousand cash pieces to twenty more captains and traders. Van Beel had merely emphasized a fact: the Dutch would redeem each cash piece for one guilder. Boll had seized the opportunity to sell cash pieces; and, by all past experiments, no more than eight thousand pieces of the ten thousand would ever find their way to the Javasche Bank.

Whether Boll's luck would hold or not, there was every reason to admire a man who had flung ten thousand cash pieces under van Beel's nose when nine thousand and one threatened to finish his career.

2

The only destination in sight seemed a trial in Soerabaja, which raced on the track of a swift calendar toward us.

But something else had sprung up over the seas east of Java, a pirate wind. It was slow, and it always stood just beyond the lazy horizon, the one behind us or the one ahead, unseen and unfelt as it gathered. It was a wind which we might expect for several reasons: first, we carried rich cargo in our holds; next, the Dutch Controleur in the Big Coffin Saloon had said, "Some say the Sultan of Bandjermasin is Pulo Besar."

The first warning of what lay ahead came the next day in Amboina. But first:

Boll called St. Ebenezer to the quarter-deck. "Your idea of moving in on Timor interests me. I've counted six Portuguese flags here. Are you ready to look for passage?"

"Aye, Captain." St. Ebenezer grinned craftily.

"You'll take one thousand gold British pounds with you, which you will post as a guarantee for our cash piece at the value of the Portuguese escudo. You'll then put a couple of thousand cash pieces in circulation."

"I know what you mean," St. Ebenezer said.

"And you'll meet the Gerrymander at Makassar within the month," Boll said.

In the next breath, he snapped, "Mr. Flint, you'll collect the crew and make sure none of the sorry lot has jumped ship. We'll get under way for Ternate."

I could have closed my eyes and located the crew with my nose. I did, almost; they were cutting up like savages when I entered the thatch bar of the Portuguese. O'Brien was doing a Dixie jig to the tune of "Yankee Doodle" from the raucous piano, and the boys reeled about singing and making every effort to drink the bar dry. Lugo the Boot was sprawled on the ground with his back against a teakwood beam, one arm about a native girl.

I eyed all of them for a moment before crying, "All hands aboard the Gerrymander—and make lively!"

As I waited for the last one to leave, there appeared two Englishmen at the bar. One was a captain. Their conversation was very interesting; it had to do with Gerrymander Cash pieces and the Dutch, and a premium on the pieces. I listened with my back turned to the men.

I was about to depart when the Portuguese owner said he had almost forgotten that a sailor from an American steamer had brought in a letter that morning for the ship Gerrymander.

The letter was addressed to me. From Boston!

One of the Englishmen spoke to me just as I opened the letter. "You, sir, are from the Gerrymander?" I nodded. He grinned. "Care to join us in a drink—to the long life of your trade money?"

"Aye. And then we'll hoist one to a fair wind in your sails. I didn't get the name of your ship."

"The Stamford Raffles." He smiled. "She's very good at making a fair wind of it."

"So's the Gerrymander." I grinned and looked him straight in the eye. Then I left the bar.

I did not return at once to the ship; nor did I read the letter from Harriet.

A little later in the day the Gerrymander swung about lazily. Her kites, shaken out to snag a spice wind, flapped sluggishly. But with the current she came to life and literally tore through the strait for the Ceram Zee and the roadstead to Ternate.

In Boll's cabin, I said, "I overheard something at the saloon that might interest you, Captain." He lifted his eyes from the chart of the Borneo south coast and waited. "An Englishman spoke these words to another man: 'I picked up several thousand of them from the Radja of Badjawa.' What could he have been talking about?"

"Probably what both of us are thinking about," Boll replied, putting away his chart. "You're a little late with the news, aren't you, Mr. Flint?"

"No. I followed him and then made inquiries. His name is Steele and he operates three schooners. The one he's sailing is a white craft called the Stamford Raffles, and she's now on her way to Ternate."

"Steele," Boll said. "The name is familiar." He produced the letter from Captain van Dee and read the postscript aloud, "'A Kapitein Steele offered me a four-per-cent profit on my new money. I refused it.' I've been expecting some of the traders to get a little anxious." It was the way he said it that drew my sharpest eye around.

3

That night I read Harriet's letter. It opened with: "Dear Tom."
"Dear Tom," I said. "Tom," I added, reaching for the way she had said it in Singapore. Then I hastened to see what followed.

We arrived in Boston yesterday after a rough but speedy voyage. No record run, however. The April weather here seems very cold after my short stay in the tropics.
I visited our friend [she meant De Loach] this morning. Since he has not heard from you, he was an anxious listener. There was not too much to tell, though I did lessen his anxiety somewhat by voicing my faith in you. I think he feels as I do, that you will serve both of us, and without embarrassing either. It is imperative that you do this!
I am naturally concerned about our friend's ultimate aim, of which I know nothing. But I do ask that Mr. Culver be dealt with fairly—for my sake. I cannot sanction even the slightest injury to his good name, Tom.
While you work with this in mind, I shall make every effort to bring about some harmony between the two incorrigibles here. Perhaps the new freight war, which is costing both firms in coastal shipping returns, will offer some opportunity by which I can bring them together.
But they are growling at each other again! And Boston is looking on; waiting, I'm sure.
Tom, I regret that this letter is brief and hurried. Forgive me, but I just learned today that the fast steamer *John Lynn* was bound for Batavia via Suez.
Write soon.

Fondly,
Harriet

"Well, I'll be damned!" I growled. Her bid was selfish, I thought; all for herself and Culver. So she could not sanction even the slightest injury to Culver's good name.
"Why, Miss Adams of Beacon Hill? Why? Are you planning to marry the old ——?"
I was aware that my resentment grew out of jealousy; that and something else missing in her letter:
Blossom, mere doll, yet romantic bond between us, had sent no message.

4

It was a week before the majestic landfall at Ternate met our eyes. The island, no more than fifty miles above the equator, and called one of the "Fortunate Isles," had been blown into history on spice winds. Its coral beaches and jungle of green in every shade were contrasted by the constant anger of the Peak of Ternate, which stood its growling watch over the land of spice, sultan, and mosque.

Ternate Road was alive with schooners and island boats. We searched the fairway in vain for a white schooner before splashing anchor out from the reef. We waited three days. On the fourth day we learned that the *Stamford Raffles* had anchored at Tidore, a few miles away.

Boll ordered sail and away on the afternoon of the fifth day, and we moved on down to the equator before doubling back. It was a ruse to bring the cash-anxious Captain Steele out of hiding. We dropped our hooks in about the same water at midnight, and Boll and I rowed in to the village once more. On the way in, we passed a white schooner and verified her name as the *Stamford Raffles*. Boll sculled and cried, "Schooner ahoy!" only to be told her captain had gone ashore. Back in the village, we searched high and low for our man.

The next morning, the schooner had flown to Makassar by way of Manado; we heard this from a very old and wizened Chinese, who told us more as he smoked his pipe in front of his shop. "Sure. Sure. He pay me well. He bimeby take all coin you tlade me, one thousand, and pay me well—four p'cent. Four p'cent on tlade. He say he make more in M'kassar."

"You're a fool," Boll said. "You could have made from ten to twenty-five per cent by trading here." As the old Chinese grinned wisely in silence, Boll said to me:

"That white schooner won't reach Makassar, Mr. Flint."

It was Tom Flint who seemed to court the devil on the road to Makassar. I slept little and ate less; I found fault with the hands as they scrubbed the deck, slushed the masts, tidied the fife rails, and answered my calls to stations. Chess slunk away from me or turned his back when I approached, and Little Ahab, ever faithful, frowned sadly and put strained silence up between us. Old Wulsin avoided me at every turn, and Lugo, the steward, learned to step lively when I barked. The below watch dreaded my visits to the forecastle, where I often sat and glowered at nothing or at no one in particular. My mind was in Boston. There was some conflict inside me that I could not put my finger on; it ate at me, causing questions I could not answer: "What the hell is wrong with you, Tom Flint; is it Boll, Harriet, or your role in this game; what would satisfy you?"

It was Harriet.

It grew worse. The sight of water, water, somber islands, smoking volcanoes, sharks by day, phosphorescent beasts eating their brothers by night, the same small world of deck, masts, yards, and rigging, the same orders, and the same faces. I sweated and growled. I seemed to see Harriet at an altar with Culver. I lost the doldrums a day before we raised Makassar, and in a manner I shall always regret.

We were becalmed. The sea and wind were lifeless, and the sails hung damp; then a slow, leaden, hot rain again, and a steaming out over a sea without any more pulse than a surface of slow, undulant oil. The Gerrymander threw her shadow sharp on that glassy world without horizon as the sun broke through to blister backs and set the pitch to bubbling out of seams.

I came on deck on the second day of the calm to find several of the lads bunched in conversation. "Break it up!" I ordered. "You, O'Hare, forward to the bows and put a sail needle into the jib. And you'll look alive. O'Brien, I distinctly remember sending you to splice the foretrysail peak halyards. Let's try to get along with each other, O'Brien." I smiled, advancing with a working fist. Then I turned on the second mate at the break of the poop. "Mr. Blue, is this the way you handle a watch?"

There was no answer, and I turned forward lest I lose my temper. My eye fell on Chess, who was enjoying himself with a balancing act on a coil of rope. I stood with arms akimbo for some time, waiting for his eye to meet mine. "Duval, you're not much of a sailor, are you?"

"No, sir, if you say so, sir," he gulped.

"Didn't I just say so?"

"Aye, sir."

"Then you're no sailor, are you?"

"No, sir." That seemed to hurt him.

Then I thundered forth: "Why aren't you?"

"I—I'm trying to be one, sir."

"You're trying to curse and drink like one, and shun your chores."

"I'm below watch, sir. I was just practicing."

"Aren't you supposed to study your mathematics?"

"Aye—sir."

"But you're not. Very well, since you don't like your books, go fetch them!"

He was not long in returning. I opened the books one by one, scanning the markings, the pictures he had drawn, the sentences he had scrawled on the pages, one of which read, "Arithmetic is a hell of a subject." On a page in his grammar I read, "I'd sooner ring the ship's bell with my noggin than learn the difference in a adverb and a adjective." I said, "You mean an adverb and an adjective, don't you?"

"Do I?" he retorted.

For his insolence, I slapped him. He started, his big eyes widening as his hand rose to the red mark left by my palm. Then I flung the book over the side. The arithmetic, geography, and spelling book followed the grammar.

The look on the lad's face—it was that fatherless, motherless expression of a destitute youth who seemed to expect a cuffing hand at every turn; his young sorrowful eyes looked down through the scuppers at those books he despised outwardly, but loved dearly because they lent him some childish joy of possession. I felt a sharp pang of regret.

I was about to tell Chess that I would buy him more books if he ever decided to use them, when Boll's voice sounded back of me:

"You were a bit rough with the lad, weren't you, Mr. Flint?"

That from Boll, who had sent the same lad over the side in a bosun's chair to a snarling sea! It broke the cantankerous spell that the long days and nights and my dual role had brought about.

5

We approached Makassar in the south fairway and dropped anchor off Great Lae Lae Shoal to await the dawn. And up it surged over the distant mountains, fast and colorful. The southeast monsoon brought dust from far-off Australia, and it hung high to catch the morning sun's reflected rays with every shade and tint of a bleeding rainbow. When the sun shot above the horizon, the teeming city leaped into misty view on the low, swampy coast behind a hundred masts of Malay praus. We rounded the shoal and twisted through the reefs with the aid of a Malay pilot and dropped anchor in ten fathoms. We had at last reached the fabulous port of Makassar.

A sight unlike that of any previous landfall met our eyes. It lay all about us on the curving beach, leaping out of the prau harbor where the amazing balolang and soppé—the former carried two outriggers, the latter one—slim long boats with towering masts and one huge sail twice the length of the hull, lay in the water or sat on the sands. I have never seen any boat move faster than these. Merchantmen squatted nearby, their sails furled sleepily, their flags tossing up all the radiant energy of an international color chart. We sat, oddly enough, at the side of a Dutch gunboat. The famed Makassar praus, the high-pooped reminders of earlier days, sat among us and on the sands. Beyond, in and out of the water, the stilted thatches of fishermen gaped at us in the morning light. The bastioned walls of old Fort Rotterdam peered lazily, threateningly, at us, a purplish brown as it met the day roaring in from its weak side. Long stretching beaches ended abruptly with huts and encroaching jungle, with large godowns, where Chinese stored the wealth of the Celebes, Moluccas, and Borneo. Houses, replicas of the Dutch homeland, stood farther in where the teeming business district lay; and above, on the sloping hills, pepper trees met the morning in silence. Here was Makassar, a little Singapore from an outer view.

The van Kirsteen Bar, called the Pride of Makassar, was the largest of the many saloons frequented by traders, schooner captains, clerks, soldiers, plethoric Dutch exporters and shipowners. Newly decorated in mahogany, teak, and ebony, it glistened from varnished bar and huge mirror to table tops and cool stone floor. Some said it was Paris transplanted in the Celebes. "Ja, and why not?" the Dutch replied. "Isn't the wealth here?" One could order almost any drink imaginable, and van Kirsteen would wager a guilder to a stuiver that you would get it. It was only natural that many a ship's cargo was first loaded by tongues over brimming glasses here, that spices from the Moluccas, rattan from the Celebes, pearls from Borneo and the Philippines, and countless other items of assorted wealth from a thousand miles away were bought and sold and routed from van Kirsteen's Pride of Makassar. It was rumored that the richest merchant of Bonthain had launched a huge schooner in the place, being himself too drunk to attend the ceremony in person; he made his launching speech there and cracked a bottle on the bar before falling flat of face to the floor. There were other tales too numerous to mention, though one of them, fact or rumor, lent van Kirsteen and a rich Chinese a flavor which should have slowed the patronage of seamen—they financed and acted as go-between for several pirates. The name of the Chinese was Hoppo Two. And one of the pirates whom they served was said to be the scourge of the seas east and north of Soerabaja, Pulo Besar, the Great Bastard.

As Boll and I entered the Pride of Makassar on the afternoon of the day of our arrival, I felt the weight of peering eyes, the same as I had when our tall masts looked down on everything else in the harbor that morning. I could not suppress a feeling that we had been expected here for some time, that patient eyes in patient heads had studied us under telescopes for long moments before assuming bland smiles of satisfaction. I verified my intuitive perception in part as I stole covert glances at van Kirsteen. Obese as they came, and dressed like one's conception of a big-time gambler, he tugged at a handle-bar mustache and concentrated his thin-eyed, serious attention upon us.

"It seems we're objects of interest," I said.

"We are," Boll averred lazily. "But don't let the welcome mat fool you. The gunboat out there is the only honest view in Makassar."

The "welcome mat" was not too long in coming. The owner approached our table casually after pausing for routine greetings at a dozen others. He stood grinning, showing big teeth and small lips above three chins before speaking. "*Welkom, mijnheers.* American or English?"

Boll eyed him levelly. "Suppose you tell us, Mijnheer van Kirsteen."

"*Ja,*" came the ready answer, "Kapitein Boll of the *Gerrymander.*"

"That's better. Now will you join us?"

"Suppose you saunter over to that door on the right of the bar after a time. *Ja?*" Boll nodded and the corpulent proprietor smiled and moved to another table.

In due time we crossed the line separating privacy from the noise, smell, and smoke of the rabble. The fat man eyed us from a huge chair behind an ornate desk set atop an oriental rug. He poured drinks and said in English, "To our fortunes." We drank.

"Now," he said, "what brings you to Makassar?"

"An odd question," Boll replied. "However, we just drank to it."

"Of course." The host smiled unctuously. "And it's rather odd that your great and notorious ship should be anchored next to a Dutch gunboat, isn't it? Or were you there first?"

"Just say it's amusing." Boll smiled.

"Yes. Yes," van Kirsteen said slowly, laughing until he shook all over. "Very amusing. But here's one charm that won't be used against you, mijnheer." He extracted a watch, the fob of which was decorated with a Gerrymander Cash piece. "Yes, I've saved this one, the first I ever saw. It interested me immensely, I must say. It still does. But I wonder now, as I have in the past, just how long it will be worth a guilder. In fact, I weighed it on my precision scales over there, Kapitein. It is light."

"So is paper money."

"You, my dear Kapitein Boll, are a man of ready wit. It is a rare treat to meet a man of various talents: a *zeeman* who sets a record, and who launches a new money."

"A nice introduction," Boll said. "Now let's get down to business, if any."

"Oh, there's little business to talk about. I simply wished to meet a man like you, mijnheer. In fact, I'm so interested in you and your ingenious hobby that I've started collecting these yellow pieces. It's great fun."

As I frowned, Boll said, "They'll make you more money in circulation, mijnheer; they're that much like the dollar, pound, or guilder."

"*Ja.* Or the Portuguese escudo." I saw Boll's cigarette hand pause ever so briefly at this remark, though he held his superb calm. "But we—or rather I—wonder how you adjust your risk to your profit."

Boll said, "So you've started a collection of cash pieces. For pastime, mijnheer?"

"Call it that, Kapitein. But I like a profit too."

"I'm beginning to understand," Boll said. "Just how many have you collected?"

"Quite a few. I'll know the exact amount soon."

Boll replied, "As soon as Captain Steele drops the anchor of the *Stamford Raffles?*" The expression on van Kirsteen's face was proof that Boll had scored a point here. Steele was somehow in cahoots with van Kirsteen, who, it was rumored, served as a front for Pulo Besar.

"I seem to have heard of this Kapitein Steele," van Kirsteen pondered aloud. He studied us as if he wished to know what we knew of the man. Boll obliged him, saying:

"He, by the way, paid a four-per-cent premium on the Gerrymander Cash. But he ran out on us in Ternate."

"Four per cent?" van Kirsteen said. "I would not think of selling my collection for so small a profit."

"Naturally." Boll smiled. "But when Captain Steele arrives with the cash pieces he's bought up, what price will you ask for your total collection?"

"Kapitein Boll, were I a trader, I might interpret your question as the first sign of a trading proposition."

"We won't beat about the bush, mijnheer. Since this is blackmail, what is your price?"

Van Kirsteen replied with conversational ease, "Considerably more than the Dutch Government will pay. I understand they want a few thousand more, so they can prosecute you for fraud, in addition to slave trading."

"What's behind this, other than the money you want?" Boll asked.

The Dutchman replied bluntly, "We don't like your kind of competition here, Kapitein. It is a threat to certain little monopolies we've built up over the years."

"Is piracy one of them?" Boll asked.

"Back to the subject of your cash pieces, my dear Kapitein. I will soon own ten thousand of them. And you may have them for twenty-five thousand American dollars. The same rate will apply to any I get in the future."

Boll chuckled. "Armchair piracy flourishes in Makassar, doesn't it? And how much time have I to raise that sum? You see, I'm due in Darwin soon with a cargo of British—er—metal."

I wondered why Boll had sprung that lie. Then I glanced up at van Kirsteen, who had narrowed his eyes to mere slits with the mention of "metal" to Darwin.

"There's little hurry," came the slow reply, "since the firm you work for is rich enough to pay our price at the right time. And—I might add that your firm will be willing to do just that by—say, September first."

"Thanks," Boll said drolly. "You're much more lenient than I gave you credit for."

"Ja. Ja. Patience is a virtue worth developing, don't you think, Kapitein?"

Once outside, Boll said, "Van Kirsteen is the eyes as well as the front for Pulo Besar." I agreed, since what place could be better than the Pride of Makassar for learning the movements of ships, cargoes, and Dutch gunboats?

"But get set to hear something that will shock you, Mr. Flint. If we'd been boarded and plundered in the customary way, we'd be better off. Why? Because we were marked months ago by the pirate Pulo Besar, who is one of three men—van Kirsteen, the Chinese Hoppo Two, or the Sultan of Bandjermasin."

Under my breath, I said, "Shades of Kim Kim." Then I asked Boll why he lied about a shipment of British metal to Darwin.

He replied: "Unless I'm in error, that's the surest way of meeting the pirate, Pulo Besar."

"Who wants to meet him?" I asked.

"I do, Mr. Flint. Unless he can be stopped, this blackmail business will ruin us."

"That's a big undertaking, sir."

"Yes," he said lazily. "But first I must deal with this Captain Steele." It was then I remembered he had said Steele wouldn't reach Makassar.

6

Boll maintained a tight-lipped silence as we moved past oriental shops and brushed with veiled Moslem women wearing sarongs of all colors. Makassarese under palm-leaf hats, resembling the headgear of the Chinese coolie, sold fish and roasted goat, the latter a favorite with the Moslems. Near the shore, Malays loaded rice, rattan, and mother-of-pearl into flatboats from Dutch godowns. But the white schooner had not arrived. Nor had St. Ebenezer kept his appointment with us.

Our next move was to pay call on the Dutch Controleur at Fort Rotterdam. If the officer seemed surprised by a visit from the notorious Captain Boll—and he was—he was no less informative. Boll asked what the Dutch had accomplished in the Kim Kim affair in tracing the junk captained by K'ung K'ung and owned by the rich Hoppo Two. Virtually nothing, since the junk had not shown up in the Indies, and since Hoppo Two was very busy with his holdings up in the Spanish Philippine port of Davao. But he would return soon to Makassar, it was rumored.

Boll then asked a question, one which caused the Controleur's eyes to blink strangely, "Has it ever occurred to you that Hoppo Two might not be in the Philippines?" It had not, he learned, though it was not too late to entertain a possibility.

As we boarded the Gerrymander, we could not mistake the appraisal from the deck of the gunboat. Two Dutch officers, as well as the anchor watch, eyed us lazily, speculatively, like sluggish spiders spinning a web about our hull and masts. Their patient silence struck with the slow impact of a Celebes afternoon sun behind a thin cloud.

Boll's first order on deck was to cancel shore leave and station armed guards about the deck. He had already sent the boxes containing the cash pieces to the lower hold. But there, on the deck forward, under the very eyes of the Dutch, our heavy coining press sat under a black tarpaulin. The sight of it evoked a cozy feeling of defiance.

Boll seemed lost in thought as he gazed out over the water. A British merchant sent the blue peter aloft, a signal that she was about to sail. Another big ship rounded Great Lae Lae Shoal outward, and several huge sails far out announced Malay *soppés* coming in keel under horizon.

Boll startled me when he said abruptly, "Mr. Flint, at dawn you'll run up the plague flag. Keep it up until I get well. Understand?"

"Aye. And what are you laid up with?"

"Between you and me," he said, without any emphasis whatever, "let us call it white schooneritis." That night he left the ship.

For four days the watch repelled a score of enterprising captains, each of whom came to purchase a few thousand of our popular cash pieces, by pointing to the plague flag. The Dutch continued to eye us with the silence of some distant volcano awaiting eruption. But they always turned to the opposite deck when our plague flag met the eye.

Somehow I looked for St. Ebenezer with each new day, though he did not arrive. He was overdue, and I wondered what could be keeping him, thinking as I did so of van Kirsteen's remark about the Portuguese escudo, which meant that he followed our trading activities closely.

The sun dropped over Borneo on the fourth day of Boll's absence at four bells sharp. Huge flocks of sea birds moved black against the flaming sky, and tiny fishing boats tore in, each under more than a thousand feet of sail, leaning and dashing with outriggers weighted by fishermen who laughed at the close proximity of threatening reefs. Their great sails caught the shafts of sun in gold outline, and then the red shades of the evening sky, like triangular embers moving in before a wind. Then the big dome overhead cooled into a velvety blue sprinkled with low-hanging, dazzling stars. Birds perched on the abandoned praus and water snakes wriggled in the fast-darkening shallow tide rips, and night descended on ship and scene.

The sea and harbor were quiet on that fourth night. The waves pounded against the reefs in the distance, rolled in slowly, and lapped at the ship's side. All was quiet, ominously quiet, in Makassar's sprawling harbor. Even the lights blinking in the city seemed to mock us. I doubled the armed watch and waited—the pearly darkness under the Southern Cross promised more than heavenly beauty on that night.

I was lying on a cot near the wheel and dispelling the silence with slaps at mosquitoes when Mr. Blue walked up to me and whispered, "A boat with oars muffled approaching our bows." I moved forward slowly, my ears on alert. Upon reaching the cathead, I saw the boat pulling under our martingale. Not a light, not a sound from the occupant. I felt the tense hush that travels ahead of some surprise: it was as if threat, in the misty robes of a ghost, stood off our sides waiting, simply waiting.

"It is probably some drunk boatman," I replied. Then I looked over the side. The boat eased closer on velvet-padded oars, until it swung into our hull with a light thud. I was about to voice a challenge when a modulated voice gave off: "Ahoy!"

It was the Striker!

He came into view, his head over the rail, and paused. After the night aboard ship, I found it possible to excuse my mind for the hallucinating state he evoked: his face jerked rudely above the rail like a devil's head, satanic in the glint of weak light. The vision held as he said, "Hoist the cash pieces, Mr. Flint, and come to my cabin."

I was soon sitting across from him, awaiting his story. He opened slowly, saying, "Mr. Flint, we're really up against more than we bargained for. They're organized, and they're determined to stop us in one way or another. Therefore, I haven't the slightest compunction about what happened tonight."

He embarked on his story slowly. I listened intently to a new episode in the life of Boll the Striker:

7

A racing *soppé*, carrying ten Malays and Boll, bounced across the wake of the *Stamford Raffles* hauling south, and approached her starboard side. When it seemed that the keel of the *soppé* would crash into the hull of the white schooner, the sail was lowered to the boom, and Boll cried out, "Schooner ahoy!"

"Who are you?" an English voice answered from the deck.

"Mijnheer van Kirsteen sends a messenger," Boll replied. In another moment, the Jacob's ladder was loosed and the messenger, Boll, climbed aboard. The *soppé's* sail was quickly hoisted to catch a half wind that would hold her close to the *Stamford Raffles*, who hoisted her ladder and pulled on south by east.

"The captain is asleep, sir," said the officer of the deck to the visitor, "though I'll call him at once. Whom shall I say is calling?"

"The messenger," came the brusque reply.

Before long, the officer led the way to Captain Steele's luxurious cabin, where a big, ruddy-faced, sandy-haired Englishman in a robe yawned and poured a drink. He turned about lazily, an amiable grin on his face. It was short-lived when he saw his midnight caller.

"No!" he said. "It's impossible!" His drink was poised in mid-air, as if the hand that held it had forgotten its hanging presence. "But—Captain Boll, it's deucedly odd that you should be sent out to meet me." He had the presence of mind to invite Boll to drink with him before asking the important question:

"But, I say, old boy, what could you be here for?" His face seemed strained in his attempt to weigh possibilities against probabilities, though his surface veneer was admirably maintained. Only his eyes exposed his nonplused anxiety.

Boll did not answer the question directly, and for a reason: the Malays were in the process of boarding the *Stamford Raffles*, and until they succeeded in subduing the crew, he was heavily outnumbered. And, too, a pistol lay on the desk nearest Captain Steele.

He replied amiably, "How much do you want for the cash pieces you're taking to van Kirsteen?"

"So van Kirsteen didn't send you." Captain Steele laughed, as if the situation were spiced with humor.

"You're bracing up on the right tack," Boll answered. "But what's your price?"

Captain Steele studied his visitor coolly. "You know, old chap, this isn't at all according to the plan. I'm afraid I can't sell them to you." He laughed then and said, "But you'll have a chance to buy them from van Kirsteen before he offers them to the Dutch."

"His price is high," Boll said, straining his ears for some sound from the deck. In the silence that followed, he heard the signal from the Malay leader—three sharp blows against the deck planking.

Boll got to his feet and said, "I haven't got all night." His eyes fell on the pistol.

Captain Steele tensed, smiled, and said, "I'm much nearer the gun than you."

"Then I'd reach for it," Boll said.

The Englishman did just that, in a quick leap. He beat Boll by inches, and with the gun in his hand, he crouched and swung the weapon up; though not soon enough. Boll's hands closed over the captain's wrist; in the struggle that followed the hand which held the gun was slowly forced inward. Captain Steele brought his knee up to Boll's groin, though Boll held on, tightening his grip on the other's hand until the gun pointed to Steele's chest. Soon there was a spasmodic tightening of the trigger finger.

In another moment Captain Steele lay dead.

The bow of the *Stamford Raffles* quivered to port and pointed her bowsprit to a bleak cove on the Celebes coast. A schooner had been kidnaped. But Boll had recovered the cash pieces, which he had not intended buying from Captain Steele.

That was Boll's story. He had annulled van Kirsteen's threat of blackmail. The price was blood on his hands.

As I sat there looking at him, wondering at his luck, at his prodigious passion for money, and asking myself if there was anything he would not do for gold, he said:

"You can run down the plague flag, Mr. Flint. The next time we run it up, it will be for Pulo Besar."

14 ⋙ GOLD BARS FOR PULO BESAR

SEVERAL DAYS LATER THERE WAS MAIL. IT HAD BEEN PASSED FROM SHIP to ship, from steamer to fast packet, until it caught up with us. On deck I looked at my letter from Harriet with hope, fear, doubt, and wonder. I dreaded an announcement of her betrothal to Culver as much as I yearned for the word "Tom," as she had said it when I kissed her.

I opened the letter at last and read:

DEAR TOM:

Your nice letter and gift arrived on my birthday. What exquisite fabric! The threads are of pure gold. Aunt Emily says in one breath that I must return this batik, while in another she speaks of what she could do with a few yards of it. I placed Blossom alongside it, and the picture was quite oriental; and reminiscent of our wonderful evening in Singapore.

I thank you for the remembrance, Tom.

This will interest you—I have succeeded in arranging a meeting between our friend and Mr. Culver here tomorrow evening! What will come of it only the future can tell, though I'm hopeful. The coastal-shipping war gave me an excellent excuse to do this, that and Mr. Culver's talk of marriage. He proposed again not an hour ago. I am now committed to some definite answer within the week.

I seem to feel your presence in matters here quite often, Tom. How closely connected you are to all that's happening; so close, that I find myself asking your advice on matters that really don't concern you. And yet the sailor whom I couldn't bribe is always ready with some answer. Or is it Blossom, whom I suspect of being under your spell?

Our friend of State Street is quite mysterious. He warns me to brace myself for big news from the Indies. I wonder what it is, and if you have failed to tell me everything. However, I find myself more confident in you, and more dependent on you, so I shall not worry about it.

Thanks again for the gift. Write soon.

Cordially,
HARRIET

P.S. Blossom sends her love.

"By the Lord and St. Ebenezer, she said Tom like she meant it!"

I created a picture of the interior of her room. I saw Blossom perched on her writing desk. Then from somewhere in the house, I heard Aunt Emily; and there was Culver glaring at De Loach. Harriet was aiming at the impossible, I thought, thinking of her peacemaking. Then I saw her eyes as she asked questions of Tom Flint: "Is peace between them worth marrying Robert Culver, Tom?" I was quick to turn her eyes to that sampan at Singapore and say emphatically, "No! Never, Harriet!"

She smiled up at me; and I, thousands of miles away, swept her into my arms. "Harriet—Harriet, say it! Say you love me."

I was reading the letter again when Chess came up and said, "The Old Man wants you, sir—and damn quick!"

Boll sat eying me, a hard look in his eyes. Soon he handed me a letter which I read. It was short and to the point; from De Loach, though he had signed no name:

I am pleased with what you reveal. Soerabaja might be the answer. Do your best to make it so. I am sending a draft to the Dutch bank there, by fast packet, in order that you may carry on. This long faith our dear friend has in you is most interesting. I shall enjoy watching further developments between you from a sideline. I'm cheering you, of course.

I could see De Loach smiling as he lifted his brows and looked at Harriet out of a corner of his eye. Then he turned the same look my way.

I raised my eyes at last to Boll. "I opened that letter by mistake," he said. "It was in my mail."

I started, eying him sharply. His gaze did not waver as he said, "Just whose spy are you, Mr. Flint?"

I felt both a feeling of entrapment and anger as he continued to stare at me as if the situation possessed all the gravity of a rope-and-yardarm proceeding. "Spy? I'm nobody's spy, sir," I said slowly.

"You couldn't be working for Culver," he meditated aloud. "Nor Harriet Adams, since she needs no spy in order to vote stronger than Culver. Suppose you talk."

"When the time comes, I will."

"And in the meantime I'm supposed to trust you?" he asked. "Remember I said Culver's picture must come down. I let you in on the cash trade after you agreed to help me there."

"Go on," I snapped, flashing a challenging grin.

"Well, it's coming down. Any objections?"

"None," I said. "But what puzzles me is how you'll gain anything when a Dutchman's picture rests in Culver's frame."

"You seem to have made up your mind that they'll convict me and take the ship."

I shrugged. "There isn't much else to believe, is there? Or maybe the Kim Kim episode was just a dream."

"First it was St. Ebenezer who timidly reminded me of a possible mistake. And now you."

"Was I timid about it?" I asked, meeting his level gaze. "If so, I've forgotten how to be blunt. You forget that several of us are involved in this with you. In fact, you seem to forget that you don't own everything in sight, including this ship."

"I forget nothing, Mr. Flint. Nothing."

"No." I grinned wryly. "First it was slave trading and now murder to gain your ends. St. Ebenezer spoke of prosperity and skulls. He even told of a skull up on a pole with a Gerrymander Cash between its teeth. God pity you when the cash falls."

He got to his feet, lit a cigarette, and said, "Before the cash falls, I'm going to make it rise high. Do you understand?" His eyes seemed to blaze.

"That I can readily believe," I said with sardonic amusement. "And you can rely on me until it starts falling, sir."

"And then?" He sat down slowly.

"I'll talk."

"About Captain Steele's accidental death, or his murder? About my real motive in the Kim Kim affair, or about a woman I bought for my bed? Maybe you'd better talk now, Mr. Flint."

"I'll talk when it suits me," I replied, bracing myself for any show of force he might have in mind. "And when I talk, I'll talk to you."

"I'm not easily fooled, Mr. Flint. You said nothing about taking Miss Adams on a Singapore tour. But I knew about it. Now I've kept a fond eye on her for a long time."

"So have I."

"You haven't talked enough to suit me yet."

"And," I said, flexing under a forced grin, "I probably never will."

He took his time in getting up out of the chair. He was slower as he moved around the table, his shadow falling over the glossy surface from the light in the gimbals. He sauntered up to me, slowly, ominously. I was as big as he, and as eager to assert my primitive inclinations as he. If he struck, and I expected him to do just that, I knew I would not submit to it as I had done once before.

Then his hand moved forward, though not in a fist, as he said, "I'm sorry, Tom. Shake." It was the first time he had ever called me anything but Mr. Flint. "We can't fall out now. Big business lies ahead."

As I shrugged off my anger and held out my hand, he said, "Help me through this and I'll make you rich enough to marry the girl—if I decide I don't want her."

I chuckled then at a man who measured every emotion in life by a dollar mark.

2

We sat it out in Makassar for four long weeks. We were waiting to see which way the winds blew. There was little new activity with the Gerrymander Cash; it found its way into Borneo, and it was fast becoming a coin to stimulate booming trade over the long trails we had blazed; but in Makassar it was comparatively quiet. St. Ebenezer had not kept his appointment with us, nor had we heard from him. Van Kirsteen still demanded twenty-five thousand dollars from Boll for a mere ten thousand cash pieces, September first the deadline. But did he have them?

We kept our eyes and ears open, learning at last that Pulo Besar planned an annual meeting of his pirate captains somewhere north of the Strait of Salajar within a few weeks.

The Dutch gunboat no longer sat threateningly alongside the Gerrymander. She had work to do. It seemed that the ace pirate of the Indies had struck hard and fast. He had moved west with the last monsoon, which some called the "pirate season," where he cut into the Soerabaja sea lanes from Makassar and Batavia with the fury of a mad shark in a school of minnows. Pulo Besar had known that Dutch gunboats were patrolling the Lesser Sundas, Moluccas, and the Celebes at the time. And, too, it was rumored that every big Makassar prau in the harbor was busy plying strange cargoes picked up somewhere along the Strait of Salajar to scattered godowns along the south coast. Booty, which would eventually find its way to Makassar. For the fourth time the Dutch posted a higher price on Pulo Besar's head.

But what sort of person was this pirate—Malay, Buginese, Dutchman, or Englishman; was he big or small, fierce or suave? No one seemed to know, though rumor had him running to type. He was, we heard, the typical pirate of the imagination, a huge grinning brute who wore diamond earrings and a sash of red silk fastened with an emerald pin. Then we heard he was a Spaniard with a big yellow bucktooth, that he was small and handsome, that he had only one eye and a scar ran his right cheek, that he was a cripple. In summation, he was a legend, one that left wreckage and poverty in his wake.

He was also the man Boll wanted to meet. And Boll was going to a lot of trouble to arrange that meeting:

We visited an oriental shop where metalwork had become a high art. We bickered for some time with a middle-aged Chinese over the price of eight bars of lead in the shape of bullion; the lead was cheap, but we wanted the bars covered with a rough skin of pure gold and delivered to our ship within the week. The bars were intended as bait for Pulo Besar. We left the place unnoticed and proceeded to search for a schooner to take us to where we thought Pulo Besar would intercept us.

Oddly enough, there were several available; and the fact further whetted our suspicions concerning the long arm of van Kirsteen. Before the hot sun stood straight above us, we had engaged a clean two-masted craft by the name of *Api Angin,* which in Java-Malay meant Fire Wind. We refused the crew, which we were sure stood ready to cut us down the moment any pirate might challenge us. Boll selected six Malays who had worked for him in the Captain Steele affair. As I eyed them, I felt they possessed the same cutthroat tendencies we had just rejected: the disparity, Boll said, was in our favor.

Boll then visited the Dutch Controleur of Makassar with a proposition that caused me as much amazement as I saw in the face of the Dutchman.

"If I can rid the Indies of Pulo Besar, will the Dutch drop the slave-trading charge against me?" Then he said, "Put the question up to the Government in Batavia." The official replied:

"Of course, I cannot speak for the Government, though I am inclined to believe it will not entertain the proposition." He paused with finality, only to open another subject. "When you were here about a month ago you suggested that the rich Chinese merchant, Hoppo Two, might not be in the Philippine port of Davao. Well, mijnheer, we sent a capable man up there to check on him. He was there, all right. Now tell me this, do you suspect anyone else of being Pulo Besar?"

"That I'll keep to myself," Boll replied. "All I wish to say is that I think I'll meet him soon. And when I do, one of us will be the loser once and for all."

Boll and I planned our adventure to a showdown that night. We even let van Kirsteen know the date of our departure. We knew that the road to Salajar was fraught with danger for anyone marked by the keen eye of van Kirsteen. There was ample proof of this if our assumption were correct: few rich Makassar cargoes reached any destination east of the one hundred and twenty-first meridian; and few Dutch or English underwriters ever gambled that road from Makassar to Darwin.

I knew that we were up against a force stronger at the moment than Robert Culver, even the Culver of the *Barnacle Goose*. I knew also that from that moment on it was a battle to the finish between Boll and Pulo Besar.

One morning, a week later, the schooner *Fire Wind* put out into the south fairway. She was loaded with cheap goods, several cases of gin, only one thousand cash pieces, and eight "gold bars." Her destination was south and east to Cape Bula Bula. Beyond that Salajar and—what?

All that day we sailed close by the coast, in order that we might peer into the sheltered inlets where huge praus and schooners could hide by day. But the ragged edge of the Celebes held its secrets behind jutting strips of lowlands and coral spurs. Tall coconut palms swept the close horizon in a glaring color line of brown-masked green, while far inland the heads of mountains, black under the cloud shadows, rose from misty collars of lavender. Our Malays prayed on the deck, then knelt and lowered their heads to the west and Mecca until their foreheads touched the planking.

Evening advanced out of the swift east and the wind backed off and came in from the south, causing us to struggle for headway. We were almost within sight of Cape Bula Bula when a black squall rose up ahead. It rolled toward us, hissing and spouting; and then it struck. The wind tore sails loose and cried like some demoniacal soul shrieking past us. A driving wet, and it was gone. We anchored off the reef to await the dawn.

We had no more than dropped anchors when I heard a babbling among our Malays. I glanced aft and saw a figure scurrying up through the forward hatch. In another moment, I heard a familiar voice:

"By God, I couldn't stand them rats any longer, sir. They're bigger than Boston tomcats." I stood with hands on hips, studying his curly hair and brave eyes as he continued his efforts at covering a stow-away's sense of guilt under more chatter about rats. I allowed him his run of talk before saying:

"Since you don't like our rats, Mr. Chess Duval, what brought you aboard?" His head was down and his big eyes leaped up mischievously before falling. He replied, "I never did like Mr. Blue, sir. And besides that——" He paused; Boll stood close, his eyes thoughtfully sharp.

"What have we here, Mr. Flint?"

"Why, a seaman, sir, who has just decided he prefers us to the rats below."

"Maybe we can change his opinion," Boll said in his usual humor-less tone. "I never did like stowaways. But let him remain—the trip will be his punishment."

In the moonlight between midnight and daybreak, Boll, Chess, and I stood alternate watch. Far out and leaning toward us, big Makassar praus swept up the coast, sailing close-hauled. One after another, their silvered sails blew up over our starboard horizon and pressed on by us toward Makassar. Not one of them showed a light, and not one seemed to notice us rocking just outside the reefs and off the track. Toward daybreak the sea steepened somewhat, though the big praus roared on the full and by toward the strait. Then the wind died.

With the dawn we fished anchors, tacked off the reefs, and fought the southwest set of the current to await the wind coming up out of the west. The first breath struck, brushing the surface of the sea up into overfalls that resembled a surf rolling in to the shallows. The sails of the *Fire Wind* leaped out and filled, and the hull slipped for-ward as if the ship had a whip across her back. Then the howl from over our starboard quarter bore down and sent her tearing recklessly along.

We cleared Cape Bula Bula with all sails drawing hard. We blew into the Strait of Salajar on the weak tail of that wind before high noon, the only craft in sight. With our bowsprit pointing to the middle island of the strait some five miles away, Boll brought the wheel up until we aimed at the wide pass between a tiny, desolate islet and the saddle-back edge of Salajar Island. We took in sail and eased into the gap flanked by reefs and wooded strips of land.

Boll said, eying the shore of Salajar, "It's too quiet here."

"And ominous," I replied. "It doesn't seem possible that the strait should be completely deserted."

"Not when British metal moves through to Darwin." Boll chuckled.

The *Fire Wind* was in the middle of the pass, tossing in the violent current, when we sighted the big *prau*. She was coming up from the south and pointing into the pass. All advantage was hers if she were pirate; the current, wind, and narrow channel helped her along as they held us back.

At that moment, the woods off our starboard beam belched smoke. The charge was dropped neatly over our bows to send up a geyser a hundred yards away. The big bluff-bowed *prau* moved fast toward us with that, and she stood close when she ran up a dreaded flag in the East—the black flag. This was it.

Boll smiled. "Our gold bars turned the trick."

I was ready to run down all sail when the order from the *prau* sounded in English: "Proceed to Bira." We ran up a pennant, signifying obedience without resistance, and beat against the head winds coming in from around the east of Salajar until we had cleared the reefs for a change of tack. Then we ran north under the press of the southeast trade. Far behind us, the wooded screen seemed as peaceful as before, while the *prau* maneuvered for a turn in the channel. She came on fast to parallel our wake, her black flag down, the Dutch bars whipping in the breeze.

As I wondered silently what lay ahead, one of our Malays broke the silence of the deck with what seemed a most appropriate answer: "Allah! Allah has forsaken us!"

Chess said, "Amen!"

3

In Bira Bay we anchored in deep fathoms a hundred yards from the beach. A sleepy village, a mosque, a score of big Makassar *praus* under construction met the eye. Hundreds of natives under turban and tarboosh moved about in sarongs, short cotton pants, and trite Moslem gowns. A few eyed us as if they wished to come out and trade for tobacco, palm sugar, or gimcrack, though temptation was dispelled by the foreboding aspect of the big *prau* which eased up to us and tied onto our starboard side.

Soon four Malays carrying iron swords boarded us while their companions looked on. "Will see Captain, tuan," the leader said to me. I lifted a thumb to Boll standing close by. Then I heard the native say, "Cargo," to which Boll replied, "Take it." And while one of the fierce-visaged foursome stood guard on deck, the others searched the ship for almost an hour. They departed, and another group repeated the search to no avail. Boll had hidden the counterfeit bars well, and for a purpose—the harder they were to find, the more golden our lead would appear.

As the evening rolled in over the gulf, a fleet of big praus moved into the bay. They came on until the bamboo poles, always lashed to bowsprits, were used to keep the ships apart. Songs, prayers to Allah, loud conversations, and piercing cries lent the harbor and beach a piratical atmosphere absent during the day. Toward midnight an old pirate came aboard with a prize crew, unlashed our schooner, and maneuvered it into the stream. Several hours later a narrow passage up the coast opened into a hidden kidney-shaped lagoon. We were soon moored to a stout bamboo pier among a dozen praus and craft of assorted sizes. We were in the Lagoon of Lor, which opened its pass to accept more than thirty ships before the dawn.

Morning broke clear. The shadows fell long and sharp, and in no hurry to retreat from that scene of rare beauty. Limpid turquoise water rose up into an eye from a circular white beach lined with over-leaning coconut palms. Beneath the palms a forest of huge banana and taro leaves caught patches of light, sheeted flame where the sun broke solidly through, and held the colors up for notice against a dense mass of green. Across the water, the scene accepted the subtle gradations of distance as dark hills rose above the morning mists and stood up for inland horizons. Beyond the reefs, emerald dominated the shallows, while less threatening deeper hues claimed the fathoms.

The scene brought Harriet to mind. She kept me company for some time. Then I wondered, as I read her last letter again, if she had effected a reconciliation between Culver and De Loach, if she had succeeded in bringing them together. I sighed. Boston was far away.

They found our "gold" bars that morning soon after the second saying of their prayers to Allah the Protector and Bread-giver. A young *hadji*, a pilgrim who has visited Mecca, led the searching party while Chess and I watched a glaring and bearded son of Islam go through the ceremony of divorcing his wife: the husband and wife stood within arm's reach on the bamboo wharf; and he, in the presence of several witnesses, simply said to her three times, "I divorce thee." According to the Koran, they were no longer man and wife. Thereupon he turned to her and said, "Now go to the compound of the slaves. I shall sell you tonight to pay my gambling debts." She obeyed him.

A great cry went up when the *hadji* emerged with a bar of our gold held high above his head. The pirates on the beach praised Allah with the appearance of each of the eight bars. Each man anticipated his share of all booty to be divided that evening. Boll and I watched with open curiosity the direction taken by the bearers of our metal, since it was logical to assume that such a treasure would proceed directly to the pirate chief. It moved into a boat, where it was rowed diagonally across the lagoon to a huge thatch from which bright orange-and-green canopies extended.

The day climbed to its zenith. Shadows were thrown straight down. A palm looked like an umbrella upside down as the shadow of the tufted head lay dark around its base. We were left to our ship instead of being led to the wailing compound to await trial and decision. There was no guard where none was needed, so I decided to take a stroll up the beach.

I moved on past the lagoon's only promontory, keeping close to the jungle of vine and bush. The voices I had left behind reached my ears with amazing sharpness, as did the whisper of the leaves, the metallic rustle of the palms, and the lapping of the lagoon. I was in a huge sounding box, it seemed, where a jungle paused for dreamy echo.

The orange of the canopy protruding from the big thatch seemed incongruous to the color scheme. It advanced to meet me like the orange spot on a huge woolly spider. Just ahead and off the beach was the slave camp, from which I heard sounds of weeping. Beyond the shed and screened from view was the prisoners' compound.

As I drew nearer I could easily understand why there was no watch posted about that wealth of booty; the very fact that it was unguarded sent a shiver up my spine—he who ventured near broke the inviolate rule of piracy. The punishment was not a lovely death, I had heard. I pretended not to see it as I moved on past. But I had no sooner put the place behind me than I heard my name called. It came from a jungle of taro leaves. I was standing still when the huge green leaves rustled and a bull of a man stepped out to leer at me.

He was none other than the captain from whom Boll had purchased Kim Kim: K'ung K'ung!

He wore the same black sea cap and white trousers; and he was barefooted, as we had seen him in Batavia. "What's on the head, Merrycan?" he said, folding his ham-like arms. I stood with fists on hips, trying to get used to the sight of him there. "Merrycan fool," he added. "Long money, short money, no good this."

With nothing to say, I kept my mouth shut and eyed him soberly, thoughtfully. That he should suddenly appear like some jinni provoked a suspicion into an almost certain fact—Hoppo Two, his employer, was either Pulo Besar or else he was on good terms with him. But he could hardly be the pirate who had sacked ships in the sea lanes to Soerabaja if he had been in the Spanish Philippines at the time.

"Have wait you since leave ship. Wise to pass that, you," he said, jerking his massive head toward the thatch. "But come, I show Merrycan treasure to eyes pop. Then we go see him."

"Him? Who?" I asked.

"Him long wait. I wait. Both wait. Now you wait find out." He laughed, scratched his uncovered middle, and moved toward the thatch. Curiosity caused me to fall in step with him. As we walked, he laughed gutturally and asked, "Where girl you capyteen steal from K'ung K'ung?"

"We left her in Soerabaja," I replied. He laughed from deep inside him and slapped me hard on the back, as if to drive home the fact that we were brothers of a joke. I laughed, too, saying, "Did Pulo Besar enjoy the joke?"

"Pulo Besar?" he said. "Some mebby day meet Pulo Besar."

I thought it strange that he had access to the treasure if he did not know the pirate. But he entered the long thatch with all the assurance of the great pirate, himself, and led me to the center of the display before sweeping his arms in a wide circle and saying, "Long money here, Merrycan." Nor did he joke.

Surrounding me was concentrated wealth, riches that left me awestruck. Pulo Besar had put his helm aweather at the foot of a fabulous rainbow. I saw a large gold lattice with the complicated designs of Javanese art cut into its sides; a dozen like it, in gold and silver, were piled on the ground like worthless shells beside intricately fashioned gold tobacco and betel boxes; swords and spear tips of solid gold, as well as nosepieces for humans and animals, were heaped alongside silver and gold necklaces and bracelets; hundreds of precious skins of birds of paradise and bales of gold-thread batik told a dozen stories with the same ending—a valuable cargo, a black flag over the horizon, and a pirate's loot; behind me the gold and silver filigree from Makassar's silverworkers touched a cask overflowing with European jewelry, diamonds, and other precious stones; and in crate, cask, and bamboo basket, I saw British, Dutch, French, and American coins of silver and gold, as well as stacks of paper money—negotiable wealth all.

I saw only seven of our eight "gold" bars.

"We go. Him wait," K'ung K'ung said. We departed abruptly,

moving to the beach where an aged boat and a pair of oars sent us out into the lagoon and toward the only prau flying the black flag. I felt a surge of excitement at the thought of meeting Pulo Besar soon. By that time I was sure the pirate was none other than Hoppo Two, despite the Controleur's accepted proof to the contrary.

We boarded the prau. On the high poop under a white canopy sat one man. He turned to eye us as we drew near.

K'ung K'ung bowed low, saying, "This him, O my master Hoppo Two."

4

The man before me possessed a wealth of authority in his intelligent face. He sat on a short stool with his thin legs crossed in Chinese fashion, and smoked steadily, thoughtfully, from a hubble-bubble, a pipe in which the smoke passed through water; he was dressed in occidental manner, from English shoes to cravat, though a long queue and strings of a mustache, the latter falling from above the corners of his mouth to his shirt, augmented his slant eyes and saffron color to pronounce him Chinese. Hoppo Two was lean of face and body, and long-fingered; his nails were long and pointed like claws. This was the celebrated merchant prince of the Celebes.

"Be seated, Mr. Flint." His English was minus any oriental inflection. I accepted a stool and was offered bêche-de-mer from a bamboo tray, as well as gin and long cigarettes. "You are thinking," he said, "that I am Pulo Besar."

"Yes," I replied. "I've thought so for some time."

He smiled. "So do others. But let them think so."

"Well," I replied, "the only black flag in the lagoon flies above you."

He said easily, "The flag is every trusted merchant's escort once a year. I come to buy. Before evening others will come, merchants, radjas, and sultans. Since I was the first to finance the great Pulo Besar, I am favored."

"Then who is he?" I asked.

"He is Pulo Besar, the best investment of my successful career." He paused, then added, "And I am a businessman who wishes to talk business."

"There's Captain Boll over there on the schooner. He's the head of our enterprise."

"True. Now were it a month in the past, I'd send for him. But since it is today, and today rushes to meet tomorrow, say that I am a man of business who is not interested in talking to tomorrow's corpse."

I chuckled to cover my rising sense of shock. "Now, Mr. Hoppo Two, it seems you underrate Captain Boll."

"Captain Boll," he said slowly, "is a man with a prodigious imagination and great striking force; he is worthy of respect. He is also the owner of a great idea; at least Pulo Besar thinks so. But he has earned Pulo Besar's wrath. Listen:

"The schooner *Stamford Raffles* was seen two weeks ago blowing toward the reefs of Doangdoangan Ketjil. She struck the reef and filled fast. When the native chief boarded her, there was not a soul aboard her; her wheel was lashed, and there was dry blood in her cabin.

"Captain Steele was Pulo Besar's favorite," he added, stroking his thin mustache from lip to vest. I thought of Boll as he lifted his head above the *Gerrymander's* rail that night.

"You invited yourselves here through a most childish byplay in van Kirsteen's office. Since you intended to visit the great Pulo Besar, he was kind enough to intercept you in the Strait of Salajar. Did you not think it odd that you were not boarded before Bira, thereby giving you ample opportunity to heave your gold overboard? And the very fact that you did not throw your treasure over proved that you were either willing to pay a price to meet Pulo Besar, or that you actually carried no treasure."

"Now that could make sense," I said, "or——"

"But your gold, Mr. Flint, didn't make sense. It was fool's gold, which brings up a timely question—what business have I to talk over with you?" He paused to nibble a dried sea cucumber. I lifted my eyes for relief and turned them to take in a view of the lagoon under the intense sun.

The voice of Hoppo Two jerked me back to the poop of the prau. "I bought heavily of Pulo Besar's bulky goods on this trip. My praus raced under cover of darkness to my godowns on the Makassar Road. But I bought cheap, since I could dispose of the goods quickly, and at a profit. Pulo Besar claims only one tenth of his captains' take. And since ten per cent on twenty ships as active as Pulo Besar's runs into big money, he can well afford to be generous.

"Today, in appreciation of our profitable relationship, Pulo Besar sent me a gift. This will interest you, Mr. Flint. The gift was a gold bar."

It did interest me—so much so that I could not retard the slow grin that threatened my countenance. It remained Hoppo Two's pleasure and privilege to drive it back into my face.

He clapped his hand and two Chinese servants appeared. He ordered them to fetch "the crucible." As he waited, he sucked smoke through the water and long tube.

"There is nothing so foolish as an impractical joke."

The two servants appeared with a round brass container, which they placed before the master. At his order, the lid was removed. "Look, Mr. Flint." I did so; I saw molten lead.

"One does not refuse a gift from Pulo Besar. If he gives what he thinks is gold, Mr. Flint, it must forever be accepted as gold. Therefore, by all the laws of wisdom, which surely govern politic behavior, we are now looking at gold."

"White gold." I chuckled.

"But gold, nevertheless. And since we are not so foolish as to look at hot lead, we must say that our intelligence is in need of a certain adjusting agent which will reconcile the discerning eye to the eye of profound wisdom. Do you follow me, Mr. Flint?"

"I'm not sure that I do. But it will require Christ or Buddha to turn that into yellow gold."

"On the contrary, Mr. Flint, we'll say that you can do just that."

"I?"

"Yes," he said, smiling and stroking his lengthy mustache threads. "Who better than the Gerrymander's future captain can turn lead into the equivalent of a gold bar in American dollars?"

I was sure of only one fact in the moment: the grin had disappeared from my face. He seemed amused, sober, and exultant all in one expression.

"How?" I asked.

He studied me for some time. "Since Captain Boll will not survive the night, Mr. Flint, and since it is customary for the first mate of a vessel to take command with the death of the captain, you will become the master of the Gerrymander. You follow me, of course."

"Continue."

"The value of the Gerrymander and her present cargo far exceeds fifty thousand dollars, Mr. Flint. You, as captain, will naturally be interested in saving the ship from Pulo Besar, who has little compunction about burning ships. Is this correct?"

"Yes, assuming, of course——"

"We are past assumptions, Captain Flint. Mr. Culver of the firm of

Culver and Adams will naturally come to the Indies for the trial of Captain Boll. You, as captain, will present him with Pulo Besar's demand for fifty thousand dollars."

"Suppose I refuse?"

"The *Gerrymander* will never leave Makassar. And you may never leave the Lagoon of Lor."

"That," I said, covering my bewilderment with a grin, "is a pretty steep price for one lead bar."

"You forget"—he smiled—"there are eight bars. I'm afraid the sum I ask would be raised if Pulo Besar knew of this little joke."

"Yes," I said. "Yes."

"I shall expect your acceptance or refusal of this proposition before the festivities of the evening. Mr. Flint—or Captain Flint." He stood to signify that the interview had ended.

I got to my feet. "So Pulo Besar wants fifty thousand dollars."

"No—I want the fifty thousand. Pulo Besar is taking over Captain Boll's trade-money enterprise." I thought that was odd, since only a few of us knew the real secret of the Gerrymander Cash. I said nothing, so he added, "I shall prevail on Pulo Besar to work with me on the ransom of your ship."

I grinned knowingly. "You won't have far to go to prevail on him, will you?"

He replied, bowing low, "Not too far, Mr. Flint." He watched me get into the boat after K'ung K'ung. Then he said lazily, "Suppose you tell Captain Boll that we are looking forward to the evening ahead when he, if he runs true to form, will dig his own grave."

5

K'ung K'ung rowed me back to the beach in silence. I saw the *Fire Wind* to the south before the promontory screened it from view. There stood Boll just as I had left him. "So Boll is tomorrow's corpse. We'll see what the Striker thinks about digging his own grave."

I was soon aboard the schooner and leaning on the rail next to Boll. He did not glance at me as he asked about my visit under the black flag. "It was quite interesting," I said. "You'll think so too." Thereupon I told him all, slowly, carefully, in an effort to capture the every inflection of Hoppo Two's voiced threat. I concluded with, "Do you wish to be buried with hands on chest or in your pockets?"

"Mr. Flint," he said at last, "if I were you, I'd accept Mr. Hoppo Two's proposition in a hurry."

"No!"

"Yes. Let him think you're eager to get on the right side."

"Maybe I am," I said tentatively.

"Sure. Maybe you are." He turned slowly with that and faced me. "But I don't think so. However, I'd accept, and put Hoppo Two's mind to working lazily over fat profits instead of schemes. He'll tell Pulo Besar, and——"

"Pulo Besar? He is Pulo Besar!" I exclaimed.

Boll replied icily, "Mr. Flint, when you're sure he's the chief, then say that to me."

"Then who is Pulo Besar?"

"I'm not sure. But I intend to find out."

The sun slipped another notch in the hot sky, and a squall raced in from the gulf. It was over the lagoon in one moment, spouting its tons of water, and gone in the next. The sun shone again over that green dripping world. Islamite and pirate came to life after the squall, and soon the beaches were lined with them.

I took Chess with me. Soon the hull of the *prau* stood high above us, and the imperious face of Hoppo Two peered down in silence.

"I've decided to accept your proposition," I said.

"The wise live to prosper," came the reply.

Chess and I worked through the maze of *soppés* that suddenly put out from the far shore for late afternoon racing. They put us off course, and we beached the boat some distance from the schooner. I had no sooner put my feet on the sand than I saw a bearded Moslem under turban and dirty robe staring at me. Suddenly he winked an eye and lowered the robe which covered half his face.

I wanted to shout, though I merely whispered, "St. Ebenezer!" It was Chess who cried out in surprise. "Well, I'll be——" My hand was over his mouth before he could say more.

St. Ebenezer frowned, jerking his eyes toward the schooner as he did so. He stayed close behind us as we weaved through the crowd of men, women, and children. Once on deck, I told Boll what I had seen, and he led the way to the cabin. "Now perhaps we'll learn something," he said.

St. Ebenezer was not long in arriving. He entered cautiously, looked about, and threw the latch on the door. Then he tossed the robe aside and sank to a chair with a tremendous sigh. "A drink! By God and St. Ebenezer, I've been a son of Allah long enough!" He gulped two drinks before cocking his head with a question, "What in the name of international sin are you two doing here?"

"They caught us at Salajar," Boll replied. "We were carrying British gold to Darwin."

"Gold? Where's the Gerrymander? Oh, Makassar." He poured another glass half to the brim and sighed once more. "Well, the errors of mankind are confined to no individual or race. I, gentlemen, am in a hell of a situation also."

He asked if he had received any mail. I nodded and produced the letter which had caught up with the Gerrymander at Makassar. He read it, then wiped away a tear. "Yes, I told Louise—my sister—I'd return to Liverpool to stay."

"Would you go back to stay?" I asked.

"Yes," he said soberly. "And when I get free of all this, I'm going."

"So they got you," I said. "Before or after you got to Timor?"

"Before. And I have been through a rare assortment of hells. The worst came when they said that you, Captain, had disposed of Captain Steele. I felt the thong and hide, and I was put on a salt-water diet for days. But pain is as ordinary as joy—the only difference in the sensations one experiences is purely of the mind. St. Ebenezer said it."

He reached absently up for some rare philosophy, a saint's perhaps, when he said, "Beliefs are puzzling. All religions are justified, even those of savages, since all races believe in a great spirit. The Mohammedan believes in God. So does the Polynesian and Melanesian. The very fact that they don't believe in Jesus Christ does not alter their devotion. They're simply missing all the details, thereby provoking us into branding them as lost souls." He paused again.

"By God and St. Ebenezer, it is so!"

He eyed Boll slowly, then me, and Boll again. "Yes, I suffered because this Captain Steele was eliminated.

"But I learned much. I lay in the hot, stinking hold of a ship in chains while the Great Bastard chopped up the Soerabaja sea lanes. I almost escaped at Tomea, and—listen to this—with full knowledge that the Lagoon of Lor was the rendezvous! If we could have gone to the Dutch with that, Captain, I'm sure they would have closed their sleepy eyes on the Kim Kim mistake."

"You'll be more careful with your wording," Boll said. "A mistake in my opinion is a mistake only after all cards are down."

St. Ebenezer winked an eye at me, touched his fingers to forehead, and bowed. "My mistake," he said. "But what's your fate?"

"We don't know," Boll snapped, "except that Hoppo Two told Flint I was doomed to die tonight."

St. Ebenezer chuckled, separated his beard at the chin, and peered at Boll. "And just what are you going to do about it—die?"

"I haven't made up my mind yet," Boll said drolly. "But answer me this: who is Pulo Besar?"

St. Ebenezer's great eyes glanced off into space and his hands, the same long, classical hands, unlike any I had ever before seen, lifted until all ten finger tips touched. "I tried to answer that in Makassar," he said. "First I suspected van Kirsteen. But he did not possess the brains. Then I turned a curious eye on Hoppo Two, who has brains. The two combined form a seeing eye and a brain. Therefore, since brains and vision rule the world, it is only natural to assume that they together constitute the legend of Pulo Besar." He lowered his hands and stroked his beard. "Have you a better explanation?"

"You do pretty well with your theories," Boll said. "But I was told by an old Moslem that only one man sits up on a great improvised throne and hands down decisions."

"I have heard that also," St. Ebenezer said thoughtfully. "I have heard, too, that the Sultan of Bandjermasin might be the Great Bastard. But my choice of all, if Pulo Besar is one man, is Hoppo Two. He has been openly accused, and never has he denied the charge."

"I'll join you there," I said. "But who are his twenty captains?"

St. Ebenezer shrugged and said, "Talk does not lessen my predicament. I'm a fugitive, gentlemen, from the prisoners' compound. I escaped by stealing the robe of a Moslem who slept on the ground just outside the bamboo pen." When asked where the predicament lay, he replied, "They'll miss me the same as the old man will miss his robe. The guard will count thirty-nine prisoners soon. The fortieth is here."

"And if you're caught?" Boll said.

"I know too much to go free," the venerable old adventurer said. "And unless someone confesses to the murder of Captain Steele, they'll continue to think I know too much to live." Boll's sharp eyes pierced him in the instant; and St. Ebenezer's big eyes hardened and held with a look I had never seen before. Then he raised his glass and said, "Since none of us, except perhaps Mr. Flint, stands much chance of seeing another sunrise, suppose we drink to the other side of the sky or ground."

"I'm not ready for that," Boll said, arising. "I'm going for a walk. Suppose you come along, Mr. Flint." At the door he said to St. Ebenezer, "You'll be safe here while I follow a hunch that might save all of us."

Once on deck, he said, "We're going to the prisoners' compound."
When I asked why, he replied, "To enlist thirty-nine other prisoners,
maybe. Tell Chess to keep a sharp eye out. You'll keep your distance
behind me, and wait on the dog-leg spur."

I waited for some time before he returned. He moved on past me
without any sign of recognition in the swift tropic twilight, weaving
his way through the horde of human beings bowing to the west. On
deck he said nothing, though I felt the presence of the Striker rather
than Boll. He moved carelessly toward the cabin, emitting a single
lone chuckle as he rapped on the door.

"What I learned will interest St. Ebenezer," he said, rapping
again. Then he tried the door and it yielded. We had expected to find
St. Ebenezer behind a locked door with a glass of gin in his hand and
big-worded philosophy on his brilliant, anxious tongue. But we were
due for a surprise:

Instead of our self-styled saint we found Chess unconscious, but
otherwise unhurt. There was a little pool of blood on the floor. That
was all. When Chess came around, he remembered nothing except a
sharp blow on the head. The blood was not his.

Outside the last chant of Moslem prayers droned, "Allah! Allah!"
They faded out against a background of a million night insects that
chorused the advancing evening over the Lagoon of Lor.

15 &ℰ BOLL VERSUS THE GREAT BASTARD

THE ARABS FELT THE COMING EXCITEMENT OF EVENING AS THE SETTING sun rolled on toward Borneo.

The dais for Pulo Besar was rising up on the sand with its back to the jungle wall. Huge pillars of wood were propped up and fastened at the top with curved beams, like the torii before a Shinto shrine. Then a huge platform for the throne was put in place under these, and a series of steps fell into place to form a stairway thirty feet or more in length. Torches, as yet unlighted, were spaced some twenty feet apart, circling from Pulo Besar's throne to the water, a good two hundred feet away. The throne faced Mecca and the dying sun.

I saw turbaned men draping batik from the torii-like structure while others spread oriental rugs over the platform floor and down the steps. Gilded buffalo horns and painted hides lent a touch of the Hindu from distant Bali. Soon the throne sat atop the platform; the seat from which the great pirate would hand down decisions was a box upon which was printed, KRUPP ESSEN. It was covered with batik in another moment.

Night fell fast over the lagoon, and under torchlight Moslem and pirate, hot-blooded and alert, milled by the hundreds. The stage leaped into view in the light of a score of torches. We had been favored with an excellent view. From our schooner's port bow, the dais and central stage of white sand lay just over the rail. Our prize seats were not ours alone; a dozen visitors, sultans and radjas who had come to buy, were escorted to the rail alongside us. They were seated on silk-covered crates and improvised benches.

Soon we saw men pulling ropes hard by the lagoon. Out in the dancing water the torches outlined the prau of Mr. Hoppo Two maneuvering for a straight view over the central clearing. Then another great prau drew abreast of Hoppo Two's, wedged into position up over our starboard bow, and squatted there with merchants from Makassar, Ternate, and Amboina.

As I searched the decks of both praus for a glimpse of a familiar face—Hoppo Two's or van Kirsteen's—a grinning Malay bowed low and showed a paper, upon which he said was inscribed the names of our prominent visitors. He had been sent to translate the ceremonies and auctions. How very thoughtful of Pulo Besar, I thought. The Malay turned about in the moment and read from his sheet in the torchlight:

"The Sultan of Sandakan." The Sultan nodded and we bowed. "The Sultan of Batakan." The same procedure followed until all of the Borneo visitors except one were introduced. Then came the great surprise:

"The Sultan of Bandjermasin."

Boll and I peered at the huge bearded face we had seen at the hearing in Soerabaja. It was framed by a white Kashmir shawl embroidered in purple and gold; the rich piece flowed out of a white turban. The costume of the fief was fringed with gold threads. He wore a large ruby pin on a band at his forehead. But he scarcely moved a muscle as he pierced us with sharp eyes.

The translator said to Boll, "They are interested in your yellow money." Boll was soon passing cash pieces among them and talking up trade. I frowned, comparing him as I did so to an insatiable octopus who will try to eat a little of the enemy that is killing him. I kept a sharp eye out in search of a clue to puzzles—the strange disappearance of St. Ebenezer, the blood on the cabin floor; I searched for the face of van Kirsteen or Hoppo Two.

Chess kept close to me, his mouth agape as he drank in the strangest scene his young eyes had ever beheld. "What's going on here?" he asked. I shrugged, and he said, "By the Lord and St. Ebenezer, something tells me we made a bad tack in coming here, sir!"

Below, there was the first sign of activity. An escort of men armed with spears made an opening in the crowd, through which a dozen others made their way with heaping trays of mutton, dried fish, cakes, and fruit. On one tray, a yard in diameter, was some kind of huge omelet. Coconut mush, shrimp, djamboe ayer—a pink, pulpy, watery fruit—mangosteen, and durian were followed by large round loaves of sago bread, jerk meat of the buffalo, and whole sides of the beast fresh from a spit. I was suddenly very hungry.

On the heels of the food bearers came the officials of the mosque of Bira. Some wore the orthodox tarboosh, others the white turban, and all were clad in white jackets, batik aprons, and sandals. They marched to the sides of the carpeted steps and raised their hands. Then, without a break in the ebb and flow of preparations, two Malays brought up a long beam, thin, and curved like a buffalo horn, decorated with intricate carving, and embellished with scrolls and flowers standing above it. This piece was supported by two poles planted at the side of the dais, and it served as the pulpit from which the Koranic texts would soon be read. Two long ropes were strung on each side of the dais, and a score of men and women entered and hung their gifts on it: tiny houses, and strings of beads, bamboo ornaments, and more houses. The translator said the houses were intended as homes for the spirits. In this respect, the ancient animistic rites of the native blended with the religion of Mohammed.

The Caliph stepped forward and spoke. A hush descended over the scene and, in the pause for complete silence, the voices of night insects and the whirring of moths about the torches rose up in a heavy drone. He spoke once more, and I saw the women remove their veils. Then a dozen young girls in Hindu dress moved to the scene and flanked the Caliph. They wore gilded and white headdresses of buffalo hide, gold necklaces and bracelets. They seemed to pop up out of one's imagination from distant Bali, causing me to realize once again that this religion was boiled in a pot and flavored with Hinduism and animism—the latter a belief that all objects, such as trees, flowers, and rocks, are endowed with souls.

The Caliph read from the Koran and then chanted: Mohammed had seen the great tablet in heaven, upon which was written the creed of Islam; the angel Gabriel had revealed it. Allah was God, and Jesus Christ had a place near Allah, along with Adam, Noah, Abraham, and Mohammed. But only Mohammed had been conducted into heaven by the great white horse named Alborak. Mohammed saw an angel with seventy thousand heads, and in each head were seventy thousand tongues, and each tongue spoke with seventy thousand voices at once. Heaven was made up of many heavens, one of solid silver, one of solid gold, another of precious stones, and so on, but in each the faithful enjoyed music, wine, and maidens, as well as the face of Allah. . . .

"There is no God but Allah, and Mohammed is his prophet." The vast audience, with few exceptions, cried, "Allah! Allah! Allah!"

With a final shout to Allah, the festivity ended, and food was passed to all. I tore into a whole loaf of bread and a huge piece of buffalo meat with great enjoyment, still looking for van Kirsteen and Hoppo Two as I did so.

Then I saw the former on the merchant's *prau*, and I turned to Boll, who had refused to eat. But Boll was busy, very busy—he was tossing coins atop the heads of the surprised Moslems and doing a bit of low chanting himself: "A wind, Lucifer, a wind!" Nor did he pause when a great shout split the air over the Lagoon of Lor and a score of armed Malays escorted one man to the carpeted steps of the dais. "A wind, Lucifer, a gale!" he said, as Pulo Besar, the Great Bastard, moved to his throne.

Van Kirsteen's face glowed in the torchlight from the craft next to us, and I knew he was not the notorious pirate. Neither was the Sultan of Bandjermasin. So Hoppo Two, by virtue of his absence, was Pulo Besar! Or was he?

Further conjecture was futile in the tense hush following that outcry; silence seemed awake and active and watching, as if the jungle with its millions of threatening voices stared at us with hungry eyes before a bloodcurdling yell and a butcher's charge. Every eye dug into the half-concealed face of the brown man who occupied the box throne, who sat perfectly still as he slowly scanned the audience from left to right; and who, I am sure, felt greater tribute paid him under that pall of silence than in the rousing cheer.

I glanced at Boll. He stared also, though in his thin, sharp eyes I saw more than ordinary interest: a glowing calm and fierceness.

I could not hear the great pirate's voice as he spoke. But the speech in Malay was relayed by bull-throated men, and on to us by way of our translator: he called his governing board of captains, we were told; and when the six appeared, he extolled them, saying in conclusion, "I shall reward all twenty of my captains through you later. And now, fetch the prisoners before me."

The first prisoner to stand in the center of the clearing was a tall Malay with a proud head and erect shoulders. He heard the charge from one of the pirate captains: "He, of Bula Bula, it was said, reported the presence of my ship in a cove to a Dutch officer. A *hadji* says it is so. The curse of Allah upon him, O Master."

Pulo Besar asked the prisoner if this were so. "No, Great Karaeng Pulo Besar, upon the Koran, no. Allah knows me the innocent victim of the captain's anger. I fought him when he tried to sleep with my wife."

"Did he sleep with her?"

"He did. He is not a son of Mohammed. He is a pig! May he be doomed to live on the thorn of the rattan for seven eternities. I spit in his face." Thereupon the *Hadji* witness was called, as well as the wife of the accused. Then the decision from Pulo Besar:

"This man is not guilty. Pay him twenty pieces of gold from the accusing captain's shares and set him free tomorrow at Bula Bula." Then he allowed the accused the privilege of divorcing his wife, and a great cheer went up.

The next prisoner was a huge fierce-visaged man who wore gold earrings, turban, and breechclout. His crime was piracy! He had plundered a Dutch schooner with the help of the five men who stood at a distance behind him. Was this so? It was, the man shouted defiantly. Said Pulo Besar: "Piracy is the highest crime." When our translator acquainted me with the pirate's words, I chuckled appreciatively. But I had not heard all, and I was amazed at the genius of the Great Bastard when I heard what he said next:

"Independent acts of piracy do not go unpunished by Pulo Besar. They are dangerous because they are always laid to me. Nor do I get my share of the loot. Piracy in Indonesia must come under my jurisdiction. Now why did you not join the great federation?" The man said he did not know how to find Pulo Besar.

"But you have found me," came the mocking reply. "And too late for your own good. You will hang." In another moment the offender and his five men marched between two guards to the prisoners' compound and a waiting hangman.

"Justice!" The cry rose up. "Pulo Besar is just!" There was no mistaking the man's strong hold over his followers; he served the masses as well as the merchant princes, and in doing so he served himself. Pulo Besar, I realized, was indeed a great man, for only true genius could organize and sustain an economy, however illicit, that would serve also to discipline the spawn of the east.

One by one the prisoners appeared. I was beginning to wonder if Boll had bypassed an opportunity in which the prisoners might serve us. He had spoken of such when he visited the compound. But as the prisoners slowly met with deserved or perverted justice, I realized he would get no aid from that source. Theft was punished with forty lashes, murder with death by fire, and rape by the severing of a man's virile organ.

I said to Boll: "I haven't seen Hoppo Two this evening. But if I had a telescope, I could soon tell if he is Pulo Besar." Boll asked how, and I replied, "By his long fingernails." He was not long in borrowing one from a sultan; Pulo Besar, however, had drawn his hands inside his robe by that time.

At that moment I heard the crier's call for the last prisoner: "St. Ebenezer of Singapore!"

2

The crier sounded that magic name again. There was a strained silence, and then a babble of voices from near the throne. As sultan and radja leaned forward in rapt attention, Boll chuckled. I glanced sharply at him, though the raised voice of Pulo Besar caused me to turn an alert ear in the moment. His voice was familiar and then it wasn't. And the telltale fingers, if the pirate were Hoppo Two, remained hidden by the robe.

Boll turned to study Chess speculatively for a time; he said at last: "Boy, you could earn my good will if you tried." Chess was no more surprised than I when Boll said, "The back of that throne is against the jungle. It's unguarded. If you could slip through the crowd and climb that palm back of where Pulo Besar sits."

He held a pistol between his waist and the rail. He held Chess with his eyes.

I saw resentment leap up in Chess's face; and I wanted to pin a medal on him when he replied bravely, "I'm not mad at Pulo Besar, sir. He never made me ride a bosun's chair."

Boll merely studied the lad. He did not so much as glance at me when I laughed.

As a cradle-shaped moon lifted through the latticed palms, the crier announced the slave sale.

A grinning auctioneer claimed all attention; he was a two-hundred-and-fifty-pound Turk who wore a red tarboosh and red balloon pants tied with a sash of golden silk. Never have I seen a man of his size move with such verve and grace. He swung a long sword and a short tasseled whip. "I, by Allah"—he laughed—"shall grow rich tonight or else I shall be hanged poor. The captains' slaves, all fresh and in good health, all firm and fleshy, will soon parade before you. Bid, tuans, bid high. Then after all the captains receive their shares, the prizes of the Indies will appear before your eyes. Concubines and dancers for radja and sultan, and any man who can pay the price."

The male slaves entered and stood up for appraisal. A savage from Formosa with tattooed mustache stood more than six feet in height.

He was quickly purchased by a merchant of Ternate, who doubled the bid voiced by a sultan. The auctioneer kicked him on the buttocks and a guard led him to a spot near the water. Next a Polynesian girl: "Bought and sold three times since she left the island of Samoa. Firm flesh, beauty; see her brown skin and white teeth, O buyers, and her round teats—she can suckle many offspring." The jolly auctioneer jerked the robe from her breasts and ordered her to dance; her antics, more ludicrous than provocative, drew a titter from the audience.

"Thirty guilders!" The auctioneer scoffed and put her aside, which pleased the crowd. Then a voice spoke up, "One hundred." She brought three times the amount a quarter hour later.

The sale continued, increasing in fury as the moon climbed higher. The tempo quickened. Groups of five were sold on the second bid or trotted back for a return later. The sale ended with a Sumatran mother's awful scream: her male baby, after bringing twenty guilders at auction, was rudely jerked from the milk of her breast.

Chess, at my side, growled, "That's a damn dirty trick!"

Pulo Besar sat like a statue as the revenue from each sale was heaped at his feet. Twice I had studied him under the telescope, and soon a third opportunity came. His hands snaked out of his robe for a moment, though they were lost to me almost instantly.

And now the last course, out of which I felt that climaxes long overdue must surely spring, or else the threat hanging over Boll was but an idle bluff. Then I remembered Hoppo Two's quiet assertion: "If he [Boll] runs true to form, he will dig his own grave."

Soon twenty pirate captains stood before Pulo Besar and bowed. Fourteen squatted on the sand while six, which made up the governing board, moved halfway up the steps. At the same time a score of dugouts moved in and out of the lagoon on the far side of Hoppo Two's prau with the treasure of the thatch. Before long it lined the steps from the sand up to Pulo Besar's seat. The sight was more than impressive: all that wealth of gold, silver, and jewels piled high on rich oriental carpets against a background of silver-thread batik, and gleaming like some dazzling dream out of the *Arabian Nights*, seemed to capture the very soul and essence of the tropical East; it swelled with the beauty of raw adventure, of thrilling argosies under black flags beating around reefs to fabulous horizons, of cruel justice and spice-flavored legends. I had never expected to view such a display of riches and colorful splendor.

The sight was but a symbol of the Great Bastard's power, of the man who ironically sat on a cheap crate labeled: KRUPP ESSEN. But then, I realized, no throne could be better suited for its metaphor, the powder keg of the Greater and Lesser Sundas.

Fortunes were quickly divided: six parts for division among twenty captains and their crews, and the seventh—the autocrat's tenth—for Pulo Besar. Then the crews raced forward to transport their wealth to twenty ships; a mad scramble ensued which seemed to be enjoyed by every captain as well as lowly pirate. The stage was soon free of loot; only Pulo Besar's share remained. The captains advanced once more and bowed. Pulo Besar spoke, and six captains stepped forward to receive the "gold" bars we had brought from Makassar.

Boll chuckled.

In that moment Pulo Besar lifted his hands and held them suspended as if he blessed his satellites. I brought the telescope to my eye in a hurry, hoping to verify or annul an opinion that had grown to almost positive belief. If I saw long clawlike fingernails, my surmise would prove correct. The long-awaited opportunity came; it fairly leaped the distance separating us and drove hard into my eye with the answer. I looked again, as if my mind doubted what I had seen. I clutched at Boll's arm and said, "Well, I know now that Hoppo Two is not Pulo Besar."

And Boll, with culpable indifference, replied, "I've known that for some time, Mr. Flint."

I scarcely heard Boll's reply as I studied the hands that rose up from Pulo Besar's lap once more. Ten finger tips touched, moved apart and together again in meditative gesture. In the moment I knew the true identity of the great pirate.

The shock had been partially cushioned by the knowledge that he was not Hoppo Two. But even then I could not believe what I knew to be a fact. I could understand why Pulo Besar wanted to take over our cash trade then. And I suspected that the Kim Kim mistake had been planned ahead by the pirate and the Sultan of Bandjermasin.

I said to Boll, "It's small wonder St. Ebenezer didn't answer. He's up there on Pulo Besar's throne!"

Boll said, "I've had my suspicions since I visited the prisoners' compound. There wasn't any fortieth or escaped prisoner."

I wasn't ready for the next surprise. But it came when the Turk in balloon pants raced into the arena ahead of a dancing girl. The surprise appeared to be a dainty entremets to appease the eye, though the Turk's presence told of Pulo Besar's urge to mulct friendly sultan, radja, or merchant prince of idle wealth. In this instance the pirate chief had reached deep into his bag of secret treasure for a gem most likely to fascinate every eye as well as to provoke Boll into "digging his own grave," as Hoppo Two had put it. She was beauty itself, tropical and sultry, clad in a brilliant sarong of red silk dappled with large white flowers. The piece of cloth was familiar.

Then Chess cried out his surprise: "By God, that's Kim Kim!"

She was Kim Kim.

3

Boll's reaction was reminiscent of rolling thunder over a horizon; he churned fury inside him with almost his usual economy of motion. There was every reason for his hate to nurse desire for murder, since Kim Kim's presence and probable sale once more could only reveal an astounding plot in action—a perpetual swindle by the Sultan of Bandjermasin under the protecting wing of Pulo Besar. Kim Kim's buyer, if the plot retained its acrid flavor, would feel the Dutch pincers in due time. And Boll, who had felt just that, whose trial loomed over the edge of a short calendar, felt the pressure of the moment, which was made worse by a fact:

St. Ebenezer, our partner in the cash trade—who knew that this captious move must surely incite action from an American captain whom he had neither molested nor threatened in the presence of an audience which might talk—peered at Boll through a telescope.

There was no mistaking a fact: the crux had arrived. It involved Tom Flint, since a far-reaching decision was due from him. I had to decide which would serve me better, St. Ebenezer or Boll. Hoppo Two's proposition had in effect meant that St. Ebenezer had suggested my role in milking Culver and Adams of ransom money; and that role would serve De Loach and me in more ways than one. Perhaps it was just the opportunity I had waited for. But once again I seemed a man who dallied with indecision, a man too small for the job assigned him.

In my debate, I saw St. Ebenezer's soft eyes grow cold.

I seemed to hear him again as he spoke of skulls and prosperity with a devilish glee—a skull up on a pole with a Gerrymander Cash in its teeth! He, allied with the lawlessness and evil of the Indies, its far-reaching brains and force, was not a partner who would serve me for long. I made my decision quickly: I chose Boll.

With that decision, I said to Boll, "I'd go slow here, since I think this is what Hoppo Two meant about your digging your own grave."

He did not surprise me in the least when he replied, "To hell with the Chink."

Kim Kim went into her dance. The long drums felt the beat of Malay fingers, and after testing the jerky cadence of a strange rhythm, she stood with naked feet planted in the sand and swayed back and forth in writhing motions. More like a professional Siamese dancer who has conquered the most difficult undulations and postures, she danced with her hands, arms, and waist. There was a tenuous beauty in her oriental face, where the ecstasy of a spell cast by some pagan muse enhanced the sleepy, natural melody of line and color. Her eyes were made up with kohl, which enlivened her expression. Her body was bare but for the sarong about her hips, which, with arms lifted above her head, she sent into maddening circles and ellipses. Her haunches seemed to claim her beauty in the moment, and it served to stir the savage in her hypnotized audience.

Boll's hands gripped the rail as if he felt a spell that subordinated his coin-tossing séances with a devil. Chess leaned over the rail, his eyes glued to her. "Damn, but she's beautiful!" he said over and over, drawing Boll's eye at last.

"You know what will happen to her, don't you, boy?" Boll said. Chess looked up, curious. Boll showed the pistol again as he said, "They'll sell her to some Arab, that's what."

Chess eyed the pistol, hypnotized. He was torn between fear, doubt, and a desire to save her. He turned to me at last. "Shall I, sir?"

I studied him. Then I eyed the throne against the jungle, the single palm lifting behind the great pirate, wondering if he could make his way there without forfeiting his life. "You're a good lad, Chess," I said.

"If you say so, sir, I'll do it. There's damn little I wouldn't do for you."

"It's up to you," I replied. Then I faced Boll. "What will we gain if Pulo Besar dies?"

"Nothing, Mr. Flint. But if he should feel a pistol at his back at just the right moment we might gain a lot." He faced Chess, who stared at the black jungle behind the throne, and said, "The right moment will be when I mention the name of St. Ebenezer."

"St. Ebenezer?" Chess repeated in a daze. Then slowly he took Boll's pistol and placed it in his blouse. As he turned fearful eyes all about him, I pulled him close, patted his back, and murmured, "Good luck, Chess." He was soon lost in the crowd.

As Boll and I faced the show once more, Kim Kim folded her body until her head touched the sand. Her feet remained in fixed position, the same as before and during her performance. The dance was over, though the spell lingered. It was broken by the ugly intrusion of a voice, the auctioneer's:

"She is for sale. Do I hear a voice? Do I hear, by Allah, a thousand guilders?"

"A thousand guilders!" The sound leaped from the deck of the *prau* next to us, where van Kirsteen sat. I saw the owner of that voice arise; he wore a flaming vermilion turban alive with pearls and topped with a frontlet of white gold and diamonds; his costume was of the same color as the turban, though its gold threads seemed to set it on fire. His collar was jeweled, as were his breast and sword. Directly behind him, two attendants stood with gold fly whisks in motion.

"The Radja of Mataram," said the translator. I looked again at the Balinese overlord and stadtholder, a man important enough to wage war with the Dutch. His handsome, beardless face was sharp with an authority that goes with absolute kingship. Further appraisal was cut short when I heard Boll's voice:

"Eleven hundred guilders."

"Twelve!" the Radja of Mataram cried out; and Boll said easily, "Thirteen." In short moments the bidding reached two thousand guilders.

"Twenty-one," Boll said in dead level tone of voice.

"Twenty-five!" shouted the Radja, hoping to silence Boll.

"Twenty-six."

Mataram's ruler, used to having his way, studied Boll with fierce, imperious eyes, before leaping over the stern of the *prau* to the beach. On the sand, he cried, "Three thousand."

In another moment, Boll leaped to the sand and stood in the central arena. "Thirty-one hundred," he said.

Kim Kim started when she saw him. Seated on the sand, she made as if to rise before sitting back and toying with the sarong fashioned from the very bolt of silk Boll had given her. Mataram jumped the figure up to thirty-five hundred, and Boll dogged him with that same one hundred guilders more. Soon the figure climbed dizzily upward from four to five thousand, and then six. The Radja paced the beach like a Bengal tiger and sent the bid soaring to seven thousand guilders. It was a tense moment. Out of the hush, Boll's voice gave off with:

"Seventy-one hundred."

"Seventy-five!"

"Seventy-six."

"Eight thousand!" The Radja was more than angry.

"Eighty-one hundred."

"Nine thousand!" the Radja said. He paced the ground near the steps of Pulo Besar's throne, and Boll moved closer. "Who is this man?" the Radja asked in simple exasperation. Pulo Besar answered him:

"Captain Boll of the American merchant ship *Gerrymander*."

"The Radja sneered: "Boll? Is this the man who trades with strange money? So. And does he propose to pay for her in worthless money?"

For reply, Pulo Besar said, "Let us hope so."

"Yes." The Radja smiled thoughtfully for some time. "Then I shall make a final bid of ten thousand guilders."

Boll paused to eye Kim Kim, the Radja, the auctioneer, and Pulo Besar, all in sober meditation. He seemed to consider the situation from every angle before speaking with inspired ease: "Ten thousand and one guilders."

He had bought Kim Kim again, if only for short minutes; and she, anxious and woman, rushed up to him. I saw her arms creep sinuously about his shoulders and neck. Then Boll did something which seemed to dwarf the many surprises he had dealt me—he ran his hands over her back tenderly before crushing her to him and pressing his lips against hers.

4

When the Turk extended his hands, palms up, for the sum of ten thousand and one guilders, Boll said, "Draw up a note for the money, payable in Makassar within three days."

The Turk, nonplused, turned to Pulo Besar, who said, "I am very patient, Captain Boll, but I have never been called a fool."

"My note is good for ten times the sum," Boll argued. I realized that he knew the utter futility of words at this time, that he was slowly working into his own game.

"But your note is no good here. Pulo Besar does not rob ships of notes. You have five minutes, Captain, or the girl goes over to the Radja of Mataram."

Boll's answer was a sharp command. "Mr. Flint," he said in the manner of the Striker ordering the afteryards squared, "you'll explain a swindle to the Radja of Mataram." Then he spoke to the Great Bastard, saying, "Since you trusted me to pay twenty-five thousand American dollars for ten thousand cash pieces, why do you balk at this small sum?"

"Because, Captain, I no longer trust you for the first sum mentioned. The memory of Captain Steele is too fresh for that. And now that you have forced yourself among us, guilty of murdering one of us, you possess the temerity to challenge the inviolate rule of auction."

"So you do not trust me." Boll chuckled. "I brought along enough gold to pay your every demand twice, did I not?" Here was a ticklish question: unless Hoppo Two played his own game single-handed, St. Ebenezer would know that the bars of gold were lead; there was a chance that he did not know the truth about the bars. The answer seemed to press against Boll's brain like the cold snout of a pistol, since the reply that came was the one we did not want.

"It seems that you have made a great mistake," Pulo Besar said. "But it is not your first, is it, Captain? Let us say that it is your last."

"I seldom make mistakes," Boll replied, eying the robed man on the throne.

"No?" came the slow reply. "Then I will send for Mr. Flint."

I was soon standing beside Boll on a lower step. "Now," Pulo Besar said, "I want you to meet your successor, Captain Flint of the *Gerrymander*, whom I may appoint as manager of my newest enterprise, the cash-piece trade." He paused for effect. "I cannot only make money out of your cash piece, I can milk the shipowner of thousands more than the petty sum you agreed to pay for the cash pieces in Makassar. Now, Captain Boll, can you say you have made no mistake?"

"Yes," Boll said, playing for his moment. "I've long known Mr. Flint for the damned traitor he is."

Pulo Besar was at that moment exulting over his victim: "Your knowledge of Mr. Flint's prudent duplicity, Captain, does not alter the situation in the least. The murderer of Captain Steele will soon rot in his grave while the man whom you call a traitor will prosper."

Boll spoke to me out of a corner of his mouth: "He can't afford to be unmasked, and he doesn't know that we know him. Work up as close as possible to him." This meant that we should maneuver so as not to be too heavily outnumbered when Boll called his name.

"Come, Captain, and learn your fate. I am trying to think of a death worse than that of lying over a bed of voracious ants, or swinging from a deck to the sharks, where you're snatched back after losing a foot. I have heard that crabs pinch live meat slowly from a man staked in the sand, that they work inside you through the tenderest parts of the anatomy."

Boll passed the six captains and their "gold" bars and walked up to the throne.

I saw the two giant Malays who hovered close to Pulo Besar lean forward with their spears as Boll drew near; they held their rigid pose. All the while, I was counting the steps above me and measuring distances from every side, wondering if Chess had reached his position as planned. I lit a cigarette and moved casually past the six captains and on up the steps. And there I stood not ten feet away from Pulo Besar.

"Allah is just," Pulo Besar cried out in Malay. "There is no God but Allah and Mohammed is his prophet!" The crowd echoed his words in a great rumbling sound.

Then Boll raised a hand. "May I have a word with your captains before you sentence me?"

Pulo Besar replied, in the true voice of St. Ebenezer, it seemed, "A man about to die should be humored." I stood by, ready—for exactly what I did not know. But the very air hung heavy with quiet foreboding, like unseen malevolent eyes in a jungle, waiting, just waiting. Boll turned around and faced the captains, who squatted with their "gold" bars.

"Tuan," he said, pointing to the largest of the captains, "is your chief here a believer?"

"He is a true son of Allah."

"No, he is not. He would be killed if caught in Mecca." There was mocking laughter among the captains. Then he said, "Is that gold you have there, or is it lead?" They laughed louder, and I heard Pulo Besar join them. The great chief's laughter lent me fresh hope, since here was proof of a house divided—Hoppo Two was playing a singlehanded game. Boll said: "If you will scrape the surface of your bars, you will find lead." Boll was checking his seas and winds, it seemed.

They shrugged, grinned, and decided to humor a fool about to die. One forced a knife point into a bar and leaped back with an exclamation. Suddenly all were hacking at the metal. Then they looked up at the throne, their sober faces alive with foolish expressions.

"Pulo Besar cheated you," Boll said slowly, as if every word he spoke must count. "He will cheat you again, for he is not one of you. Do you want to know who he actually is?" Out of the tense silence, Boll said:

"Now he could be Allah, or even St. Ebenezer of Singapore."

That did it. Curiosity is universal, and Pulo Besar knew it. I expected the order that came, and I wondered if Chess had managed to reach the position behind the throne. I was watching St. Ebenezer closely when he sounded the order.

"Seize him!"

I saw him stiffen and turn his head slowly, a sure sign that Chess was there.

The order of the Great Bastard went unheeded: the crowd remained silent and motionless as it awaited some explanation from the six paralyzed captains. Boll's words—"He would be killed if caught in Mecca. He will cheat you again, for he is not one of you"—were forcibly augmented by bars of lead where gold should be—and gold, or its sudden disappearance, speaks in a strong voice among all men.

As the largest of the captains broke the hush of silence and asked the great chief for some explanation concerning the bars, Boll said to me, "Get Kim Kim. Up the steps with her, quick!"

Then he turned to Pulo Besar and said, "Tell your captains that you did not know you were cheating them, St. Ebenezer."

There he sat—St. Ebenezer in the role of the greatest pirate of the Indies—trembling and afraid. He feared the mob with any admission of error on the part of a man who had never condoned error; and he feared the gun at his back. He played for time, for some miracle to save the situation confronting him. All the while the crowd seethed. A murmur grew into a roar.

I brought Kim Kim up the steps almost unnoticed. We were close to the throne when St. Ebenezer raised the hands of Pulo Besar. When a hush fell over the crowd, he cried:

"Captains!" Then he fell forward with all the speed of a mongoose, crying out at the top of his voice, "Seize them!" Chess fired, but too late.

Somehow I managed to dive between the two Malay spearmen who charged Boll. I struck Pulo Besar's arm just as he fired. The bullet, aimed at Boll's heart, struck his shoulder, spinning him around. Then the gun was aimed at me before I had an opportunity to tear it from the enraged pirate. "For your treachery, Mr. Flint!" he growled, and fired just as I fell to the steps.

Boll had rushed the two guards. As I glanced up, a spear in his hand was driven through the body of one of them. The Malay stared wildly, shook all over, and collapsed for his last spasmodic jerks. The other lost his balance and was impaled by his own spear when he fell to the sand. The gun still smoked in Pulo Besar's hand from the shot fired at me, when I heard Boll's cry: "Grab Pulo Besar! To the jungle!"

The great throng was in wild uproar: pirate and Moslem sent up deafening cries as they charged in a body. They raced for the throne, trampling torches underfoot and throwing the whole scene into sudden darkness. Whether their spears were meant for us or for Pulo Besar, I did not know. The effect was all the same as I leaped with St. Ebenezer from the top of the steps to the jungle floor amid the hissing of spears on all sides. Boll had gone ahead of me; he was lifting Kim Kim from the ground when I stumbled upon him.

Chess spoke for all when he cried, "Let's get the hell away from here!" St. Ebenezer, unable to fathom the temper of the mob, ran with us.

We stumbled through vines and bushes in the darkness of a steaming jungle. Trees seemed to reach out and strike us down; we fell into ravines and raced up out of them into tangled vines which slashed our clothing and cut our arms, legs, and faces. The noise of the arena faded behind us; but as we stopped to see if we were pursued, a great cry went up:

The dais had collapsed.

16   PIRATE CANNON AND GAIN

WE HALTED IN A CLEARING WHERE HUGE BANANA LEAVES STOOD IN silhouette against the serene tropical sky. The night was racing away before the new day that would rise up out over the Boni Gulf within the hour.

We sat in silence for some time—Boll, Kim Kim, Chess, and I; and our prisoner, who had until minutes before been the greatest pirate of the Indies, brooded over his loss. We listened intently for any pursuit from the beach, though there was little sound above the brush of the wind and the metallic rustle of the fronds surrounding our little ceiling.

Chess broke the spell of night over a close-pressing jungle with, "By God and St. Ebenezer, I've lived on this day!"

"You did right well by yourself, boy," Boll said. "You came through at the right time."

"Aye, sir," Chess replied. "If I do say so myself."

Boll's shoulder was bleeding profusely, and it was Kim Kim who busied herself with the wound. She stuffed a part of Boll's shirt into the hole and bound it fast around the shoulder and underarm.

Boll faced each of us in the pale starlight: first me, then Chess, Kim Kim, and at last St. Ebenezer. He chuckled and said, "Pulo Besar." There was no answer, and after a time he got to his feet.

"You'll come with me. We've got to work fast." When I asked what he meant, he replied, "If we wait until daybreak, we'll never get Pulo Besar's share of the treasure."

"No!" I said, amazed. "Haven't you had enough?"

"Mr. Flint," he barked, "I've been a captain a long time. And never have I failed to complete a voyage."

I, however, wasn't so anxious. I argued that we had our lives, which was more than I had expected to save when spears flew all about us. Boll was adamant: "There's wealth back there, Mr. Flint. We're going after it."

We approached the beach warily and looked at the torches that gleamed anew. Through the screen of bush and tree separating us from the wreck of the dais, we took in the scene at a glance:

Near us a dozen prostrate figures lay, some with spears in their backs and bellies, others under the planking that went with the surge of the crowd. They were still in their last pose, all grotesque reminders of St. Ebenezer's words about skulls and the cash piece; the scene was literally a harvest of the Gerrymander Cash.

Beyond the deserted wreckage, small groups argued. Amid shouts and brandished weapons, one Moslem or pirate would dart away from one group to join another. The majority had moved down the beach halfway to the dog-leg spur, while others had put across the lagoon to the canopied storehouse, where each captain conducted a division of the loot. The prau from which van Kirsteen and his merchant guests had watched the show was moving out into the lagoon. Our schooner, the *Fire Wind*, sat quiet and deserted. Our Malay crew had either turned pirate or made their escape.

Only Hoppo Two's prau seemed alive. It had not moved. We saw K'ung K'ung and the crew; and Hoppo Two sat there smoking his hubble-bubble pipe as if nothing had happened. His eyes dwelled on the wreck of the dais, as did Boll's: Pulo Besar's share of the wealth lay among the twisted planks and dead bodies.

We waited. Soon a score of pirates approached the tangled ruins and pointed. They talked among themselves for some time before departing. Boll said, "They won't touch it until they decide on a leader." He added, "We will."

K'ung K'ung left Hoppo Two and moved from one group to another. Before long, a sizable crowd had gathered on the beach at the stern of Hoppo Two's prau. Then, as the minutes passed, many of the pirates from the boats, as well as those who had gone to the canopied thatch, joined the throng at Hoppo Two's craft. The Radja of Bandjermasin appeared on the deck. Then van Kirsteen took his place next to the Chinese.

"A new Pulo Besar will emerge," Boll said. I thought of Hoppo Two's threat to Boll, of the hot lead in the pot, of his threat to the Gerrymander. I had wondered why he had not told Pulo Besar of the value of our bars, though I was beginning to understand his reasons for silence: he had known, perhaps, of our gold-covered lead before it left Makassar; and had Boll not advised the captains of their loss, Hoppo Two would have done so in his own devious manner later. It all boiled down to this: he coveted the profits of Pulo Besar; he wanted to head the vast piratical organization which St. Ebenezer had created.

Boll said to St. Ebenezer, "Hoppo Two must have known I would not go down without a fight. We served him well, didn't we—Pulo Besar?" He seemed to enjoy St. Ebenezer's curses as the palaver at the prau drew closer to the inevitable conclusion, a Chinese victory.

St. Ebenezer's tone was almost pleading as he said, "Captain Boll, if you'll allow me to walk out there, I'll promise you'll never regret it."

"You forget you're no longer in charge of your heathen," Boll taunted. "Hoppo Two is making a bid for your office. He knew about the lead bars, mighty Pulo Besar." He laughed, adding, "Just St. Ebenezer, a mere man, aren't you?"

"Gloat, damn you!" came the reply.

"You're nothing to gloat over." Boll's baiting tone persevered. "With fortune and power gone, you're an ape for a damned Chink who's watching your share of the loot like a buzzard."

"God damn you, Captain!" St. Ebenezer's voice lifted incautiously.

"You were going to kill me slowly, weren't you?"

"Aye! By the good Lord and——"

"But you abdicated in a hurry, Saint."

"By God and myself, I am not dead yet!"

Boll smiled. "So you want to walk out there. For what? To turn about and run—or die? Surely, your lordship over cutthroats should present some better plan for, say, at least retrieving your fortune."

"For you?" St. Ebenezer growled.

"Why not? You were ready to take mine. But perhaps you'd rather see your successor take your share. At any rate, you expressed a desire to walk out there."

"What's on your mind?" St. Ebenezer snapped.

"Simply this," Boll answered readily, "if you dare to step out on the beach, let's make it pay. Now, listen—your captains didn't take ships with toy guns, did they?"

I saw St. Ebenezer's eyes narrow craftily. His small red lips spread into a thin smile as he eyed the largest prau at the pass on our left.

He bargained: "For my freedom and half the loot."

Boll looked down his sharp nose and said, "I'll make no promises." He seemed to know that St. Ebenezer would hardly refuse any action which might present an opportunity for him to restore his vast power and wealth. Pulo Besar would gamble to even the score with Boll and Hoppo Two. St. Ebenezer's nod of acceptance verified this.

Boll glanced at Chess and Kim Kim before saying, "There are five of us, St. Ebenezer. We'll need four Moslem robes and turbans." He pointed to the dead just outside the protecting screen of bushes.

"The dead serve the living," St. Ebenezer said, moving out into the open. Since every Moslem faced Hoppo Two's prau, the "saint" was not detected until the last moment. There was a shout from the deck of the prau. St. Ebenezer quickly prostrated himself in Moslem manner, bowing to the west and crying out, "Allah! Allahu! Ah! Hu!" He went unrecognized, and they paid him no attention after that.

2

We were soon covered with our robes and moving out of the jungle one after the other from different positions. We passed the throng slowly, so very close that we could have touched any of the backs at the edge of the crowd. Hoppo Two was talking. As we moved on, van Kirsteen's voice sounded.

The new day was just under the faint horizon when we boarded the deserted prau that blocked the pass. The ship was not two hundred yards from where the crowd stood at rapt attention; it sat starboard beam to Hoppo Two's port beam. Beyond us two pirate craft were propped up on the beach without any life showing on their decks.

The two old guns on deck were at last hauled by rope tackles and pointed toward Hoppo Two's prau. This type of gun, a carronade, minus trunnions, was a close-quarter cannon, a muzzle-loader requiring from five to ten minutes between shots. Boll said we could lose a battle in the time we might lose in handling the clumsy armament. St. Ebenezer checked their loads, adding several lengths of chain to heighten their lethal effect. He chuckled in a cruel, vicious way as he worked. Boll, under tarboosh, and I, under turban, watched the ex-pirate, while Chess, with robe dragging comically, held a pistol on the helpful prisoner. Kim Kim sat unconcerned, her back to a mast.

A lonely lookout from a ship nearby shouted a warning. Hoppo Two got to his feet and called for silence. The lookout cried out again, causing van Kirsteen to point our way.

"They've seen us," St. Ebenezer said slowly. "Now let them feel us." A dozen men from Hoppo Two's group leaped for the cannon facing us broadside.

"Stand ready to load," St. Ebenezer barked. He held a match at the fuse to set off the charge. Boll ordered the Dutch flag run up, and then he gave the order to fire.

Seconds later, the calm over the Lagoon of Lor was broken by the thunder from our first cannon. A darting tongue of fire and a quick curtain of acrid smoke, and the sounding box of the lagoon reverberated with echoes. As I ran forward to check our score, a cry, a blend of screams and anger, rose up from the throng up the beach. I saw Hoppo Two's prau rocking, a mast down, and her deck just abaft of midships raked clean by our shot. Men hung over the rail, dead, and others leaped about grotesquely. A few were running up to the carronade forward, though the greatest threat milled on the beach.

The throng, in wild disorder, was collecting itself for a charge. Just then Boll's cry, "Fire two!" sounded; and out of moments of throbbing suspense, a lick of yellow flame exploded deafeningly. I ran to help St. Ebenezer, not waiting to view the carnage wrought by that last shot. The howls of agony and pitiful moans rose up in a volume of sound to equal the booming of our cannon, to tell a story my eyes did not in the least wish to view.

"That one was dedicated to my faithful followers," St. Ebenezer cried. He was wrestling with the heavy gun in an effort to point its nose into the crowd.

"Hell, that's not necessary!" I cried in protest. I pointed. "They're running now!"

"Proceed," Boll ordered. "This is no time for pity. Mr. Flint, you'll look alive on the rope tackles here and help bring this rifle into position. Then you'll see if you can raise some sail and stand ready to work her for a run if necessary." Kim Kim, afraid, and clinging to him, was brushed aside and ordered to help with the sails.

Then an answering charge sounded. It struck our prau at the poop with a thud. And from up the beach, a drone of angered voices preceded an ominous wave of humanity moving slowly in our direction. I was quick to agree with Boll then, and I applauded his decision when, moments later, the bark of small arms from the Moslems sent bullets singing too close to us for comfort.

Our cannon spoke again: the heavy load of scrap metal and chain tore into the crowd. It stopped them momentarily as the advance ranks were leveled.

The morning seemed jarred up out of the east by pirate guns. The east was quickly lighting up to expose us, a mere few against a horde. As if to augment a heavenly light, Hoppo Two's deck seemed to explode in a shower of sparks. In the space of seconds, the deck glared redly, then the ship lay hidden behind sheets of flame.

"By God and St. Ebenezer, what beauty!" It was the old "saint" reveling in his destructiveness. Boll, with three pirate rifles at his side, was picking off stragglers who tried to reach the cannon of other ships. Chess, no longer in his robe, was swabbing the hot cannon. He sweated and grinned.

"They're coming again!" I cried. I hauled sail in an endeavor to bring the ship around for cannon aim. Just then a loud explosion sounded from our portside. A mast went with it, and a load of grapeshot swept by us, taking everything in its path.

I saw St. Ebenezer pause and study the new threat. He reached slowly for a gun at Boll's side and raised it. A second later, the single Malay emerging from the pall of clearing smoke leaped high into the air.

"They're still coming!" I yelled. Then, from across the lagoon, a cannon spat viciously. The crude bow of our ship felt the impact. The whole ship shuddered as the port hull forward caved above the water line. Boll glanced from the distant prau to the surging crowd and took a chance.

"She's got our range. Fire when you're ready! You, Mr. Flint, trim your sail and stand ready to slack away aft when we fire."

That was quite an order, but with the help of Chess, Kim Kim, and the seaward set of the current, we fulfilled it, one eye for the ship and the other for the pirates on the beach. They were drawing close, too close. The explosion came, and the distant prau, struck at the water, listed quickly.

Our prau came around, swinging by her anchor until she crunched land. One carronade, now on the crowd, belched, and that Moslem charge was broken. Those who could run disappeared into the jungle. The smoke of black powder smelled of death. The beach was clear; not a man showed himself in the morning light. But St. Ebenezer fired into the jungle, then at distant praus, as if his lust for battle remained unsatisfied.

He was mopping his face and smiling—a hard, cruel smile—when the jungle wall at our starboard quarter came suddenly alive. There was no time in which to tack around to the opposite shore or to turn our cannon on the mob; we were caught by the rush of some hundred yelling robed men who fired as they raced down to us. Boll's order, "Fall flat!" was unnecessary. I was crawling aft for a gun when I saw St. Ebenezer's shocked eyes turn slowly to a red hole in his upper arm.

He cursed, then stood to shout defiance. Boll fired, as did Chess. Kim Kim, her face alive with fear, lay near Boll.

"Boarders!" St. Ebenezer cried. "Hold them off!"

The pirates reached our *prau*. A few clambered aboard, only to be repelled with shot and spikes. We used gun stocks for clubs, and we saw always two where one had gone down. A bullet nicked my ear and another cut the flesh of my little finger. Then the swinging tip of a cutlass grazed my thigh. Chess, aft, was lying low until a head rose up above the deck. He was quick to his task then. One by one they fell into the water. But more arrived—those driven off farther up the beach by our raking shot were racing toward us. We could only retreat to the far side of the deck and hope for luck in repelling them.

The battle seemed all but lost as Boll and I fought hand to hand with the boarders. Chess fired carefully, his back against the far rail, and St. Ebenezer swung his gun with excellent effect, shouting to the top of his voice as he worked. "God save the Christians!" he cried. "God damn the heathen!" Boll, cornered, fought with pistol, fist, and foot.

"To the cannon!" Boll cried. While Chess and St. Ebenezer loaded the muzzle, Boll and I fought from behind wreckage and the ship's dugout. Then, with St. Ebenezer's words, "Ready! Ready, fire!" we fell back. So did the boarders. They raced for the opposite deck and the safety of the beach.

The loaded cannon from our point of vantage was of greater aid in saving the situation than any fired shot. Had Boll not held St. Ebenezer's fire, the heathen might have finished us between shots. We used the time in hauling up anchor and steering the clumsy craft, with one small sail now, into the current. We made quick sternway and came up on the opposite shore of the pass some distance downstream, our guns still pointing at the beach.

The next bark of the old gun sent all survivors scurrying. They did not rally to their boats for a water attack, nor did they show any activity on the nearby *praus*.

We lay on deck, grimy, hungry, and bleeding, until noon. We split hour watches, waiting for the attack from the remaining *praus* sure to finish all of us. Not one of us had the strength left to haul a sail; and so great was the damage to the gear, we could not have made any headway. But not a ship fired a gun that morning. We did not learn until later that Hoppo Two had been killed on his *prau*, or that van Kirsteen had fled. The great organization that had terrorized the sea lanes was without a leader.

Our wounds ached and threatened us with fever and blood poisoning, though fatigue seemed our worst enemy. St. Ebenezer slept, rousing from time to time with cries for water. Boll remained calm and watchful.

Toward noon, he said, "The *Fire Wind* seems safe." He got to his feet with difficulty and staggered from the poop. Shirtless, his trousers torn and bloodstained, his tarboosh on the back of his head, and his face smeared and blood-streaked, he looked less the victor and more the vanquished. He roused St. Ebenezer and Chess and said to me:

"Cover me. I'm going after the treasure."

"You're too weak to swim the pass," I said.

He pointed to a dugout with outrigger. "Mr. Flint, if I were dead, I'd raise up for that much wealth."

I saw him weaving toward the wreck of the dais, a man ready to fall at his every step. I watched him as he crawled along in the ruins, lifting planks and stiff bodies in his search for treasure. He kept at it for hours, falling, getting up, and carrying on.

When the *Fire Wind* sailed out of the Lagoon of Lor late that afternoon, Boll collapsed on deck beside Pulo Besar's treasure.

3

Chess and I set sail and pulled fast for the open sea. The Lagoon of Lor, with all its lush and gross beauty, ran out behind us as the shoaling waters of the pass raced under our keel. Soon the easy swells of the sleeping gulf rose up to embrace the schooner's hull. We crowded sail on her and beat out into the gulf. By moonrise, running with a brisk following wind, I paused to survey the deck for the first time since braving the gantlet of projecting reefs without a pilot.

Boll was lying as still as death on the portside. I eyed him for some time, at last meeting the frightened eyes of the girl who loved him for no more reason that I could imagine than his gift of red silk. Perhaps she was bound up with some austere shadow of his memory as the physical embodiment of his winds and passions. I heaved a sigh and turned to face the sea about to blossom under a Celebes moon.

I was suddenly very lonely. I would have traded places with Boll then, if the girl watching over him were Harriet.

But everything held to a pattern, the same as I had often repeated—the cash, Kim Kim, and the smell of gain.

BOOK FIVE ❧ 1886

WITHOUT THE AID OF CHESS, I MIGHT NEVER HAVE SUCCEEDED IN bringing the *Fire Wind* up alongside the *Gerrymander* in the still harbor of Makassar. He was faithful and cheerful at a time when fatigue threatened all of us. He pointed to our luck at being aboard a light schooner; had we been on the heavy *Gerrymander*, we could not have survived the long hard tacks to Makassar, considering even the impossibility of two hands managing the heavy yards necessary to every tack.

I'm sure his songs and constant chatter played a part in keeping me on my feet. Down the Gulf of Boni and up the Strait of Makassar he sang a chantey:

> "She was a funny ole guy;
> She had a double-barrel squint in her eye;
> Her pretty little feet would cover up a street;
> She had a mouth like a crack in a pie.
> She had a head like a Mexican calf;
> A pretty little cemetery laugh;
> She was an ironclad clipper
> With a gunboat brig,
> And a feather in her main-top gaff."

He paused at intervals on deck to look out over the sea, shake his head, frown, and sing: "The mightee Captain Boll." A chuckle, and:

> "He blew out her sticks for gold,
> If she was an ironclad clipper,
> He's the guy who'd rip her
> O' the cargo in her after hold."

He added verse after verse, always turning to me with, "You love a good sailor, don't you, sir?" With no answer forthcoming, he would add, "Damn right you do."

We cheered when the *Gerrymander's* tall masts came into view. Then, amid the hustle of getting Boll and St. Ebenezer aboard the ship, we learned that the news of Pulo Besar's fall had preceded us. Makassar had celebrated the news two nights before; or, rather, one element celebrated while the other mourned. As Dutch officers, honest merchants, and sailors came to congratulate us, silent Moslems gathered on the beach to eye us and our ship with patient malevolence.

Mr. Blue had doubled the guard.

Boll's fever raged for a week. It slowly abated under Kim Kim's care. I was unable to persuade her to rest. Nor were threats of any avail. Her murmurings, her caressing hands and lips, her odd prayers and strange songs, maternal at times, passionate at intervals, seemed to be the medicine Boll needed.

St. Ebenezer was up two days before Boll. He roamed the deck, a prisoner, though none of the crew knew why. Chess, the hero by his own tongue, savored the secret of St. Ebenezer's dual role. It lent him a cozy importance.

Boll was walking the deck on the middle of July, his hollow eyes looking at the stretch of Makassar and far ahead.

Van Kirsteen had survived the battle in the Lagoon of Lor, though he did not return to Makassar until the evening of July twentieth. He hailed us from a *soppé* that came up to our stern just after dusk and asked for an interview with Boll. It was short and to the point, with Boll holding a figurative dagger at his fat throat until he signed a confession as to his part in sustaining Pulo Besar's piratical rule of the Indies. The confession served to guarantee his behavior in the future: he agreed to appear in court with testimony against Pulo Besar and the Sultan of Bandjermasin; he agreed also to use his freedom in serving Boll and the Gerrymander Cash as he had served Pulo Besar.

2

Van Kirsteen's confession threatened to annul any advantage De Loach and I had gained. As I asked questions that only the future could answer, a letter from Harriet arrived by Chinese junk.

"Ten to one the news of Boll's indictment reached Boston," I said, opening the letter. Nor was I wrong:

Dear Tom:

Our friend warned me to brace myself for the news. Despite that, I wasn't prepared when the papers carried the story of Boll's indictment. His buying a girl! How horrible! Mr. Culver is furious. I am at my wit's end, since the news, which has shocked Boston and caused our friend a chuckle, has upset my plans for ending the long feud between them. And just when I was making great progress.

I did manage to bring them together for one evening. I'll tell you about this later.

My full concern has shifted once again to the Indies, to the outcome of the trial there. It is hard to adjust Captain Boll's behavior, since he has no cause to lure Mr. Culver to the Indies again.

Or does this baffling man brew fresh schemes?

What are your plans there? What does all this mean? Is the ship as involved as Mr. Culver thinks? I feel more and more dependent on you, Tom, and more in sympathy with your unenviable position. Is it cruel of me to interfere again with a request that you look about you for some way to serve all three of us: Mr. Culver, our friend, and me? This sounds impossible, I know, but I have such confidence in you that I dare ask it.

(Next day)

I have just returned from a conference with our friend. We are at odds, since he does not wish to give an inch of ground, now that he sees a chance to settle the score with Mr. Culver. If I had some lever, I might force him to make peace. But my threat to withdraw financial aid is of no avail. He reminds me of what he said when I came to his rescue.

And now Mr. Culver tells me that any talk of peace between them must wait until he deals with Captain Boll.

Tom, the trap, as you call it, is closing in fast. News writers are clamoring for passage to the Indies to cover the trial. They're a merciless lot, and I shudder to think of what they would do to me if they uncovered my duplicity. The whole Figurehead Affair from Mr. Teale on would be plastered over every paper as "The Harriet Adams Affair."

The *Aladdin* arrived today. Mr. Culver plans a fast easting down, with Mr. Cott as captain. She'll sail in ballast, as Mr. Boston's request for time to get her cargo has been refused. This suits me. I am as anxious as Mr. Culver to reach the Indies.

I am anxious to see you, Tom. Perhaps you'll show me Soerabaja or Batavia. Aunt Emily warns that she will keep a sharper eye on us this time. And our stubborn friend on State Street grins wisely as he dares me to sway you from the fulfillment of your duty there.

Blossom sends her love.

Fondly yours,
Harriet

"Bless you, Harriet!" I said. "That's the sweetest letter yet. Blossom sends her love, and Harriet says, 'Fondly yours.' So she is more and more dependent on me, and she has such confidence in me that she asks the impossible of me.

"I'm beginning to believe Blossom was a good investment."

I forgot Culver and our friend De Loach, and even Boll and the Kim Kim trial ahead. I grabbed Chess and proceeded to cut a caper about the deck.

Soon the whole crew was dancing the hornpipe to a tune from the sailmaker's fiddle.

Harriet was on her way to me!

3

One week later we slipped the cable and sent the patient *Gerrymander* toward Batavia, where Boll planned to bargain with the Dutch over a most valuable item: Pulo Besar.

It was on the first night out that Boll called us in to "splice the main braces," which meant a social chat was in order.

The hard eyes of Robert Culver looked out of the portrait and saw Boll, St. Ebenezer, Mr. Wulsin, and Tom Flint seated around the gleaming table. And had Culver's ears been real, he would have heard Boll say, "We'll see what the late Pulo Besar has to say before we talk to the Dutch."

He began with Mr. Wulsin; he called his name and waited until the old bosun was hopped up with suspense before saying:

"St. Ebenezer was Pulo Besar."

Wulsin eyed the self-styled saint with eyes that reached up for the very pinnacle of shock before taking a dive to the depths. All he said was, "The Lord and St. Ebenezer!" It was the way he said it.

St. Ebenezer's chuckle was every bit as eloquent as Mr. Wulsin's voice of surprise and despair.

Boll said, "Mr. Flint, have you noticed how our partners in the cash dwindle?" He eyed St. Ebenezer at length. "So you were the Great Bastard," he said, his voice like drumbeats in a strained silence. "You're a man to be admired. Or rather you were. But Napoleon wasn't a great man on St. Helena. He committed the great mistake when he didn't go with his Waterloo. Now let's hear you talk."

As St. Ebenezer helped himself to whisky, his eyes twinkled merrily. "Talk is a prosaic mannerism which can be an effective tool for artisan or conjurer," he replied with his former ease. "There was a time when I was a master at it. But alas, circumstances rob my tongue of statecraft, Captain. The old master bows to the greater rogue."

"It's too bad," said Boll. "Yes, too bad, since I need you." He desired the rise of hope in his victim, and he saw the eyes of St.

Ebenezer light up with it. "But answer a few questions for me. First, whose blood was that on the cabin floor when we found you'd disappeared from the schooner?"

"It belonged to a goat." St. Ebenezer laughed.

"A goat?" Boll said, smiling. "And what caused you to think that I wouldn't go forthwith and count the prisoners in the compound?"

"Frankly, Captain, I thought Hoppo Two and I had given you enough to think about. But I might have known better."

"Yes," Boll replied. "I checked on the escaped Moslem. There wasn't any. That was the second time I suspected you. The first was when van Kirsteen spoke of the Portuguese escudo. But what was the secret of your dual role?"

"I was St. Ebenezer in beard, and Pulo Besar without it. I learned to wear a false one on the stage in Liverpool years ago. It served me well. My voice was no problem to the actor. Only my hands gave me away."

He glanced at his beautiful hands. "I'd never thought of them as Judases."

I wedged in a question: "How could you govern piracy and travel with us at the same time?"

"That was simple. I had twenty loyal captains; and a dozen spies, like van Kirsteen. I stepped into the role of Pulo Besar even when I was in Ende and other ports with you. I was quite a genius. St. Ebenezer says it."

"So does Tom Flint say it," I replied.

"Now here's a nice question," Boll said. "Why were you so anxious to draw my blood slowly?"

"There were two reasons for that, Captain Boll. In the first place, you were in my way. I wanted the cash-piece trade for myself; and since you were the type of man who seemed unmanageable while alive, I wanted you dead. At first, I waited for the Dutch to put you out of the way. They may yet. However, I worked to keep them from pouncing upon you, in order to keep the cash trade alive. I served you well there.

"The second and big reason, you killed Captain Steele."

"So what?" Boll snapped.

St. Ebenezer's great eyes hardened, then softened as he said, "My name is Steele, Captain. He was my son."

The statement fell upon my ears like some slow shock to already numbed senses. Boll's eyes narrowed for a moment before his face assumed an expression that said he stared at unalterable destinies as if they were but fruits in season for his plucking.

As the ex-lord of the pirates glowered from his chair, Boll drew a sharp conclusion: "Since you've lost nearly everything, you might as well lose the rest. Where's your fortune hidden?"

"I'm an unusual pirate. It isn't hidden. Most of it is in a London bank."

"A little out of reach," Boll said thoughtfully.

The pirate in St. Ebenezer wasn't quite dead, however. He reminded Boll of an item which was worthy of consideration—he knew the secret of the Gerrymander Cash, and he knew that there were too many in circulation. He said, "So I'll trade out with you."

Boll was ready with an answer: "You haven't much to trade."

"You amuse me, Captain. Suppose we get down to cases. You've had your fun, and I know you're not about to miss the glory, and the effect of such glory on the Dutch, of bringing in Pulo Besar. So I'll help you out of the Kim Kim mistake and say nothing of your cashpiece trade if you'll keep the secret of my true identity. That's all I ask."

Boll said, surprised, "How can you help?"

"Very easily. Captain, I am a student of human nature. Man is both a lucrative and disappointing subject. He is seldom baffling, and after a time he is therefore uninteresting. But not you, Captain Boll."

"Get to the point," Boll snapped.

"In my own manner and mood—Your Lordship. As I was saying, you baffled me. How? Now while in Singapore, I went to all sorts of trouble to interest you in what is generally a man's downfall. A woman. But I was unable to find a living creature made of solid gold —literally, sir. Flesh was not your weakness, it seemed. And yet, you had to have a weakness other than greed for money. But you did not drink to excess, and you were not half as cruel as you pretended. Your every act was calculated; you lived for one purpose. If you ever kissed a woman, I'm sure you felt of her purse instead of her lips.

"But a woman was the logical answer. She is the bait that eventually lures. So I conceived the idea of dressing up the lure with profit. I gambled that, if you were presented with the problem of purchasing a woman, the woman would somehow strike a harmony with your sense of profit. It was not a fantastic idea, as the case proved.

"The Sultan of Bandjermasin and Hoppo Two were willing tools. I sent K'ung K'ung to you with order to sell Kim Kim to one man— you, Captain Boll."

Boll glared; St. Ebenezer chuckled as he raised his glass and said, "To the mighty Captain Boll."

4

In Batavia, on the fifth of August, Boll reached up for dizzy heights. He went all the way to the Governor General of the Dutch East Indies, and in the manner of a king, rather than a mere mortal. Before a dozen high officials, he was the Striker again, and a ruling disparity which caused the iron-faced Governor General to grimace often that morning. He opened his case with such impolicy that I was sure he was his own worst enemy.

"I'm not here to ask for any favor, mijnheers, so you can erase the lordly expressions from your faces. I'm here to trade." And he paused, forcing the inevitable question, before voicing an answer which caused them to stare at him incredulously: "I have captured Pulo Besar."

The ruler of the Dutch East Indies blinked his eyelids in fatuous manner and joined his skeptical countrymen in an exclamation, "Neen!"

Boll replied, "It is true. Now what's he worth to you?" After shock subsided, a spokesman reminded Boll of laws which must be observed in any case. "Damn your laws!" Boll said easily. "If you don't want him, say so, and I'll trade with him. He'll pay dearly for his freedom and another chance to sail your seas."

A dozen voices sounded in the exchange of conversations and died away to one with the question Boll played for: "What do you want?"

"You might think I'd ask you to dismiss the slave-trading charge in Soerabaja. But I won't, and here's why." He told of the planned swindle conducted by Pulo Besar and the Sultan of Bandjermasin, at last chuckling and saying, "I can prove it, which will force the hasty Dutch Government of these parts into the embarrassing position of punishing a pet sultan and precipitating a war."

The host of officials were due for sharp surprise here. They listened to the annoying American captain as he voiced the name of van Kirsteen of Makassar, and even Pulo Besar, both of whom would appear in his behalf, he said, to swear that the wily old Arab of Bandjermasin had sold Kim Kim to him in Batavia; that the Sultan had put her up for sale again in the Lagoon of Lor.

"Who bought her this time?" the Governor General asked.

"I did," Boll replied.

They had never seen such a man. He seemed to court the ill will of men in general with singular advertence while reaching coincidentally for their unwilling respect. And his temerity, occasional frankness, and bellicose airs earned him both in heaping measure.

"If you are not asking us to dismiss the case against you, what do you want?"

"Freedom to trade with my Gerrymander Cash pieces in the Dutch East Indies."

The Governor General asked us to retire to an anteroom while they considered his demands. We obliged and waited out a long hour, only to be advised upon our return that we would be notified of their decision within a fortnight.

Boll eyed them cynically. "I'm afraid, mijnheers, you don't want Pulo Besar as much as I thought you did. My ship sails tomorrow for Soerabaja."

Outside Boll grinned lazily and said, "Ten to one they don't want a war in Borneo, Mr. Flint." I had no answer; I was waiting impatiently, aware that the Striker had played hard and fast against any government's double weakness: first, the business-minded Dutch in Holland might recall a governor general who could not politically subdue the sultans and radjas; second, the capture of a pirate of Pulo Besar's fame was in itself tantamount to a great political and military achievement on the part of the Colonial Government.

I was naturally worried, since I had bypassed opportunity time and again in order to win over Boll and Culver with the decision of a Dutch court in the Kim Kim case of September. If there were no trial, then I'd not likely serve De Loach; and I might never sit in that partner's chair on Boston's State Street.

At nine that evening four Dutch soldiers escorted a Government messenger aboard the *Gerrymander*. In the captain's cabin, he presented a letter from the Governor General. It was as follows:

KAPITEIN BOLL,
Geachte Herr:

The Government of der Nederlandsch Oost Indië has, after due consideration of every aspect of the case, reached a decision in your favor. The charge against you, resulting from the Soerabaja examination of February last, and set for trial in September, will be quietly dismissed, provided, of course, you deliver the pirate Pulo Besar to Dutch authorities at once.

Regarding the cash-piece trade, which our Government feels to be incongruous with Dutch economy, a further though limited concession will be made in your behalf. You may double the sum of your guarantee at the Javasche Bank, realizing that the Government will prosecute relentlessly when and if one item of your trade money above the posted guarantee is redeemed at the Javasche Bank.

Boll grinned as I heaved a mighty sigh of resignation. My partnership in De Loach and Company seemed to disappear with the flourishing signature of the big man of the Indies.

5

With the delivery of Pulo Besar to the Governor General himself, Boll seemed to reach up with prodigious ease and snag his dazzling star. Fame was his, and he strutted into and out of the bars of Batavia and Soerabaja, the intrepid captain and adventurer who set sailing records first and conquered pirates later. He looked down his long nose in supercilious manner at the host of great, near great, and the rabble who sought him out to shake his hand; he peered down from his star, it seemed, an imperturbable god whose rhythm was a force greater than that of mere mortals. Force was his passion, fame its echo, and he was nothing short of a symbolist, a master of power by his very bearing.

Bankers, Government officials, and the society of Soerabaja courted his favor, as did the myriad shippers and captains who felt the freedom of those seas east of Soerabaja for the first time. He had succeeded where the Dutch had failed; he had dispelled the legend of Pulo Besar, and in doing so, he had destroyed organized piracy. Underwriters emerged out of their shells and insured cargoes between Soerabaja and Darwin, Australia. The Lesser Sunda Islands joined at once, in the minds of all, the civilization of Java. All because of one American, the indomitable Captain Boll, the Striker. "The mighty Captain Boll!"

He had made a fair wind to Java.

And he, out for gain, shed a part of his glory and let it fall on the Gerrymander Cash. St. Ebenezer had made the cash piece a charm endowed with good luck—and the luck of Captain Boll stood up for irrefutable proof. Sailors and apprentices and captains of schooners felt safer with the coin on a string about the neck. To a seaman, luck was the number-one entity, and he overlooked no opportunity to honor the goddess of luck. But Boll did not let enthusiasm die there. Pressed for the talisman, he picked his captains with shrewd discernment and spoke of luck in terms of trade with the cash, thereby dispensing several hundred thousand cash pieces at one guilder each. These were destined for remote places.

The cash piece was king; it was twin of Boll and spawn of the devil. Boll, surprisingly, rode his star nicely in one sense of the word. The dessert, a constant diet of praise, was enough to throw any man out of his orbit. But Boll remained himself, a man anchored to his own inflexible ideals and passions, to his greed for gain; and the anchor by which he kept his head in sane currents was a vision of other horizons, cash-strewn and Culver-free. The cash trade was free of a bit in its teeth, and he planned to scud before the winds of a gale to reap new fortunes. He was even then talking of Bali and Lombok. The Radja of Mataram had sent him an invitation to visit his palace in Lombok.

And he said once again, on the night before we sailed for Lombok, "Culver is next. His picture will come down."

As I listened to his threat, I was aware that his luck, combined with his precision timing and striking power, made of him a force to be reckoned with in any case. There was every possibility that he might succeed in unseating Culver from the *Gerrymander*. And after Culver, the partners in the cash-piece trade would be reduced to two, Boll and Tom Flint. After Culver, supposing he went down before Boll, who, other than Tom Flint, could be next? I studied his arrogant face and smiled.

"Somehow, I expect Culver," I said. "He would naturally make every effort to save the *Gerrymander*."

"He'll be here." Boll smiled. "But we won't."

As it happened, we hoisted the dripping anchor early on a morning in late August and pulled under easy sail through the East Gat for Madoera Strait and the Bali Zee.

6

The east monsoon still blew steadily. It came in with force over our starboard bow from east-southeast. As we passed the tip of Java and steered more to the south, the wind met us almost dead ahead. The *Gerrymander* was good at pointing up into a wind, and she met the trade as close by the wind as any heavy vessel of her time. We took her on under all plain sail as the order held for "full and by."

With Java under our stern, the north coast of Bali rose up steeply from the sea with great depths of sea close to and slanting, generally, toward Mataram across Lombok Strait. The road to paradise, littoral Bali and Lombok, charmed the eye with form and color in exquisite etchings; already the Peak of Bali rose tenuous against the sky line. It was a beautiful world to which Harriet would come.

The *Gerrymander* beat on to the strait dividing the islands and stood off for the run across to Mataram. The wind was drawing hard through the strait, stronger in the narrows, and the highest peak in the Indies, Mount Rindjani, stared dubiously at us from far inside the island of Lombok, as if daring us to cross over. The races, whirling eddies, and overfalls ahead as far as the eye could penetrate advised a seaman's eye that the currents ran contrary to the weak wind on that day. The seas broke dangerously in the strong ebb which, it was rumored, might last for eight hours, and the tide rips spoke in a strong voice to a sailing master: "Wait for slack water." It spoke wisely, since the strait was flanked with spur reefs and rocky islets. However, His Lord and Majesty Boll was no ordinary master; he would go through. The *Gerrymander* would obey him.

She tried. Boll pointed her south of the wind, tacking more like our approach than I thought wise. The current was in our favor, however, as the ebb had a southward set; but as the day wore on, the wind hauled and blew contrary to current, and strong. He carried her some five miles off the Bali shore with his tacks, but the main battle of stream and wind lay ahead. He tried hard, and the *Gerrymander* strained herself to make headway for him, but the unsteady sea beat us back.

The next day the current ran with the wind in the afternoon, though both were too strong against us. We were doomed to spend another night at anchor with our objective a mere twenty miles away; or so I thought, until I heard Boll say, "The quickest way to Mataram is around the island of Lombok by way of the Alas Strait. I'll chance it." And that's the way we reached Mataram. We entered Alas Strait at sunrise, and we were through it to the Indian Ocean before the noon breeze blew in. And that breeze swept us under the rugged coast in high water, full and change, at a fast clip which we held almost to Mataram.

So much for the stubborn sea. The reefs were threaded on the Ampenan Road and we entered the mouth of the Jangkok River for safe anchorage. The palace of the Radja of Mataram was less than a mile upstream.

But Boll was in no hurry. "We'll sit it out," he said, "and wait for Culver, and a welcome from over there." His thumb pointed in the direction of Mataram.

The welcome came early on the following morning. A pompous Balinese overlord in a European carriage arrived with a guard carrying guns that had seen service in the German invasion of France in 'seventy. He presented himself as Prime Minister of Bali and Lombok, and said our arrival was not only a pleasant surprise, but that it was timely also. He presented Boll with a sealed letter and departed after a long speech of welcome which he concluded with:

"We shall send for you tomorrow when the sun sinks over the enchanted island of Bali."

With the sunset of the next day a sixty-foot schooner with a gilded hull under hard varnish, and sails of silk in red and yellow patchwork, moved toward the Gerrymander. Uniformed sailors, in identical waistsarongs of many-hued batik, stood the deck like marionettes and sat at the oars on each side of the craft. The oars were for working the craft upstream. The same official returned for Captain Boll, and with a second display of the Radja's pomp.

As Boll and I sat alone near the stern of the craft, Boll surprised me with a statement: "Mr. Flint, Culver's picture is coming down —and fast."

"Now that's interesting," I said. "But I've often wondered what you hold against Culver."

"I hold nothing against Culver. He merely owns the Gerrymander, which I want, and which I'll get. But we'll have to sail mighty close to the wind."

"What do you mean?" I asked.

He faced me squarely in the tropic twilight and said, "It's time you put your cards down alongside mine. Who's paying you, and for what?"

I hedged, asking why that information was so important to events ahead. "Because Culver is on his way here for a showdown. And the Radja of Mataram sent another letter yesterday. He has a proposition up for my consideration."

"What sort of a proposition?"

"That I don't know, though I'm sure it's one he'll try to twist around to his advantage. But that is only natural in this world."

"Or any other," I added, grinning. "Now take me for example. I'm tempted to disclose my motive—purely for what it is worth to me."

"Perhaps I can help you," Boll suggested.

"That's what I'm talking about. But I'll wait."

"Have it your way," Boll replied, walking forward of the deck.

The schooner was soon around the bend of the Jangkok and sliding along to the dock. It was dark by that time, and I saw the palace, a huge mass of stone, in silhouette against the evening sky. But another sight lay still and threatening just ahead of the Radja's luxurious craft:

A heavily armed Dutch schooner.

Her lights blinked off and on as uniformed men moved about her on deck; and she flew a flag of truce under the official Government ensign. I said to Boll, "Odd, isn't it?"

He shrugged and led the way on up the dim terraces to the palace.

We reached the grand terrace, and the palace stood a big and amazing work of art before us. The guard, numbering about a score of richly dressed Balinese in uniforms similar to our recent oarsmen, smiled at attention as we followed the Prime Minister up a short flight of marble steps to the massive entrance. The doors were of solid polished mahogany some twenty feet high and half a foot thick; they opened into a long marble corridor where chairs and benches of marble and gilt lined the walls, which lifted gracefully in the pattern of the outer Tudor arches. At intervals of twenty feet colorful statues lent relief to a world of marble: Vishnu, the "Preserver," stood with four arms and four heads; Siva, the "Destroyer," sat cross-legged with four arms in various pose; Agni, the god of fire, sat atop a gilt pedestal with two heads, three legs, and seven arms. The characters repeated themselves, though in different poses.

Boll was quickly received, though I was asked to sit in a small room to await presentation to the Radja. After an hour, the overlord returned for me and led the way to a room lined with twelve guards. From this room, which was hung with tapestries in gold, silver, and crimson, I entered the Radja's office.

The Radja, a man no older than Boll, sat on a great throne, a dozen feet in length, with pillows at his back, flanked by mace-bearers and officers of his guard. He wore gold-thread batik, a red turban with a diamond sunburst in the center. His official ribbon, the Dutch colors, ran from right shoulder to left hip. The man's gleaming, fierce eyes, together with his costume and the richly engraved throne of brown wood, which was studded with gold and precious gems, stood out against the indigo and brown velvet background like a blaze in the night.

He eyed me in silence as I advanced, his one hand at his chin, the other composed over a round drum pillow. As I stood at a respectful distance, he flicked the wrist at his face and said, "Advance."

I stepped forward, bowed stiffly, and said, "I am Tom Flint, Your Highness. We met at the Lagoon of Lor."

"Yes," he replied absently.

The Prime Minister advanced and bowed. He announced the presence of His Dutch Majesty's Minister, van Kleegermarq. "Let him wait," the Radja answered. "I cannot work myself into a warlike mood for peacemaking when I am busy with more profitable business." As the official bowed and departed, he turned to me again.

"You and your small band handle pirate carronade well." I grinned, drawing from him, "I wonder if you could distinguish yourselves as well for profit as for your lives."

"We left with profit, Your Highness," I replied.

From the corner behind us a familiar chuckle sounded. I turned to see Boll with feet propped on a priceless gold-and-ivory table, his cap on his head at a rakish angle, as if he were the Dutch stadtholder in Mataram.

The Radja rubbed a lip with a forefinger, glancing from me to Boll and back again. "Profit, indeed," he said without any semblance of a smile, "and a lovely dancing girl."

Boll studied the prince for some time before surprising me with, "Radja, Mr. Flint will be glad to hear your proposition, so come on over here and let's discuss it."

My surprise was even greater when the pompous Radja obeyed in the manner of a vassal. It seemed to prove that the art of trading was less a respecter of robe and office and more inclined to favor the trader of greater resource, who in this case seemed to be the Striker. Boll held to his disrespectful pose until a table was drawn up for us, and servants brought sweetmeats, Dutch gin, and fruits. The mace-bearers and guard remained out of earshot, and the powwow opened.

Boll said, "The situation is simply this: Culver will be here soon, hoping to relieve me of command because I have inadvertently embarrassed the firm." I saw the Radja's eyes widen and thin with interest at this remark. Boll talked on:

"The Radja here has as his guests a number of radjas, sultans, and rich merchants, who do not want to see piracy abolished for several reasons: first, because the Dutch need their law-enforcement eyes diverted from their fiefs—in the Radja's case, unless the gunboats are hunting pirates, they're apt to sail to Mataram; second, the radjas, sultans, and merchants can buy better from a pirate; third, a pirate is a balance wheel between the hotheaded element and the rulers—he can insure peace when and where the radjas and sultans want peace, without any Government red tape.

"That brings us up to the present. The guests voted eleven to one for a new Pulo Besar. The dissenting vote was cast by the Sultan of Bandjermasin. They will finance the venture with boats, men, and money; they agree to advance the man of their choice one hundred thousand dollars." He paused to sip at his drink before literally overwhelming me with his next words.

"But I want a better role, Mr. Flint."

"You!" I exclaimed.

"I," Boll replied calmly.

Boll's part in this new development had a spurious ring. In the first place, piracy offered less gain and more risk than his present venture. Atop that, knowing Boll as I did, I realized that I would be the last man he would tell of this owing to my undisclosed mission. Therefore, he was playing some game with the wily Radja of Mataram.

The Prime Minister entered once more and bowed before us, remarking on the impatience of the Dutch Minister, van Kleegermarq. The Radja said again he could wait. The court official departed reluctantly and Mataram turned his attention to Boll and the tray of sweetmeats.

"The better role is just this, Mr. Flint. But first I'll say the Radja and I don't see eye to eye in this case."

"Captain Boll wants all," the Radja interpolated, smiling wickedly across the small table at Boll, then at me.

"Including your palace, I imagine," I added with a laugh.

Boll ignored us, saying, "I can handle the pirate end of the deal, as I'll explain later. However, in order to maintain my strong position with the Dutch—which I may need to protect the Gerrymander Cash trade should more pieces roll in at the Javasche Bank than I anticipate —I must represent a power greater than that of a mere captain of a merchant ship.

"The Radja here happens to be that power, Mr. Flint."

I made a grimace and leaned forward, elbows on table. "I don't understand all I've heard."

"It's as simple as this," Boll said tersely. "He's at odds with the Dutch, which is one of his reasons for inviting me here, and which is why I came here."

The Radja's habitual glare lost its impression of hostility again for an imperious smile. "And," Boll continued, "since he's playing at war to gain a few points from the Dutch, with no real desire for a war he would surely lose right now, I've put in my bid to serve as the Radja of Mataram's peace negotiator."

I saw it all then, and I sat back to eye him. He was pretending acceptance of an offer for piracy in order to humor the Radja. He was nothing short of a genius at uncovering Dutch weaknesses and follies, and he was shrewd enough to worm his hedging self into a position from which he could profit on these weaknesses. I realized then that the Dutch did not want war any more than the Radja of Mataram; that war and peace, harangue and treaties, would be juggled back and forth for some time before any stern reprisals were felt.

"If I could produce peace out of chaos at the right time, I could flood the Indies with cash pieces and receive the Dutch blessing as I did it."

"True enough," I said, "until the Dutch got enough."

The Radja, by nature as impatient and nervous as any young ruler, paced the floor, then sat down. "When shall we expect your decision, Captain Boll?" he asked.

"As soon as I get through with Mr. Culver."

"And your trade-money business?"

"Yes," Boll replied.

The Radja, too, played deep in his own game. He raised his brows and said with an imperious gesture, "Of course, Captain Boll, we shall employ patience in awaiting your decision to head our pirates. But— it seems you need my immediate aid in another matter. Should I appoint you Mataram's official peace emissary, your position with the Dutch would be greatly improved."

Boll said, "Immensely."

"Then perhaps I should demand your quick acceptance of the role of Pulo Besar."

"I'm not ready for that," Boll said flatly.

"Then I find it necessary to demand some guarantee of your future acceptance, Captain." Boll said nothing; he was in no position to argue in the moment. The Radja seemed his match and more as he said:

"The guarantee I demand is the dancing girl, Kim Kim."

7

The Prime Minister entered again, bowed lower than before, as if trying to efface himself as much as possible. He advised that van Kleegermarq threatened to depart and return with force. The Radja smirked, thinned his eyes, and nodded. In short time, the guard escorted a huge, big-boned, angry Dutchman to the throne. He clicked his heels and bowed with a jerk and stood still, awaiting the Radja's order to proceed. The stadtholder, however, humored his propensity for galling the Dutch as far as possible in even such trivial matters as court manners. Instead of allowing van Kleegermarq the courtesy of stating his mission, he launched forth into a lengthy recitation of matters of state:

"The Dutch Government is fully aware of the demands I make. Whenever the Governor General can bring himself to his senses and send a diplomat here to make minor concessions, instead of gruff men with no power to carry on amiable negotiations——" He talked on, arising from his throne, and pacing back and forth. He raved, circling the fuming Minister, who, in obedience to tradition, was forced to turn his face to fief and bow. This van Kleegermarq did until he performed like a mechanical tin soldier. "—I do not ask for the state of Badoeng for the power nor riches involved, but for the right to enforce Dutch laws which prohibit its princes from looting wrecked ships. Badoeng shall be mine or else the Dutch will be forced to subdue the state at great expense. Yet——" He kept His Majesty's emissary standing there for some twenty long minutes before asking: "What is your business?"

"This," snapped the Dutchman, extending a document. "It is from the Governor General."

"You will read it, mijnheer," the Radja riposted.

"Ja!" He unrolled the paper and began with: " 'The Radja of Mataram is in a position to render a great service to the whole of the Indië by surrendering to the bearer of this message an alien who——' "

As he read on, I sat up, alerted. The substance of the message was nothing short of a bid for Boll, whose "fabulous scheme" had been uncovered not two days after the Governor General exonerated him by letter in Batavia, in which the Dutch had annulled the charges in the Kim Kim affair and granted Boll permission to double his deposit guaranteeing the cash piece in the Javasche Bank of Batavia. The exposé had come about through the diligence of Dutch special agents, who had counted in the Moluccas, in the Celebes, and aboard more than thirty trading schooners enough Gerrymander Cash pieces, which, if and when they found their way to the banks for guilder redemption, would almost double the number guaranteed by Boll's deposit in the bank.

"Thus," van Kleegermarq announced as he scanned the paper, "the Dutch Colonial Government of the Indië is convinced that fraud, premeditated and willful, was and is the motive behind the mysterious trade coin sponsored by Kapitein Boll. Therefore, the full force of the law will be trained on the perpetrators of this fraud, namely: Kapitein Boll and the owners of the vessel, Culver and Adams of Boston, U.S.A.

"Attached is a warrant for seizure of any trade coins the vessel might now be carrying as well as a warrant for the arrest of Kapitein Boll."

The Dutchman presented the papers to the Radja and clicked his heels once more as I turned a probing eye slowly toward Boll.

He simply sat there, smiling and calm.

The Radja said, "So you did not come to talk peace." He seemed disappointed after his uninvited opening diatribe.

"Neen." Van Kleegermarq smiled hatefully.

"You Dutch are most arrogant," the Radja hissed, his fingers stroking the ribbon on his golden blouse in fastidious manner.

"*Ja!*" came the reply. "Diplomacy seems a useless art in these parts, Your Highness."

"I shall make a note of your worthy observation, mijnheer. But you desire this Captain Boll. How very odd, mijnheer, that we should be of the same mind."

He arose from his cushions and walked the floor, pausing occasionally to glance at Boll. He moved to a tray of sweetmeats near the throne and ate slowly, his thin lips working in perfect harmony with his eyes. In time, he smiled, eyed Boll shrewdly, and called for his Prime Minister. With the arrival of the official, he proceeded to dictate:

He regretted his stand against the Dutch in this matter, and his reluctance in sending such reply to the worthy Governor General was matched by the genuine grief he experienced in a further indulgence of incompatibilities. However, he had only that day appointed the conquerer of the notorious Pulo Besar to the high office of Foreign Minister; he had done this in salute to the Dutch Government, which had shown not only its own appreciation and gratitude, but that of the victimized sultans and radjas of the Lesser Sunda Islands as well, when it honored Captain Boll. He was at a loss to understand the sudden about-face attitude, the malice accorded the intrepid captain on the very heels of open esteem. Since the appointment of Captain Boll to such office had been considered by all a stroke of diplomatic genius, which could only convince the venerable Dutch Government of his desire for a lasting peace and prosperity, he begged the just rulers to lend the matter further thought and advise him posthaste of a final decision.

He said at last, "List my titles, and the word *friend*. Write it up and return it here for my signature."

Boll grinned.

The Radja of Mataram merely studied Boll with a cryptic smile on his face.

In the interim of waiting, van Kleegermarq was invited to relax and join us at the table. He complied in hostile manner. Boll asked questions, at last drawing the Dutchman out.

"Ja, Kapitein Boll," he exulted, "regardless of this uncertain last-minute luck of yours, you are faced with ruin in the Indië. Ja. I shall gladly tell you of incidents which prove my words."

"Last-minute luck, you say?" Boll said easily. "I'm tempted to let you arrest me and prove the Dutch fools again." Thereupon he produced the letter signed by the Governor General and read a part of the last sentence: " '—the Government will prosecute relentlessly when and if one item of your trade money above the posted guarantee is redeemed at the Javasche Bank.' I can circulate millions of them without violating that, mijnheer." He did not add that this was the very secret of the cash.

The Radja frowned, and the Dutchman glowered as Boll said, "But I'm looking ahead. Don't forget that."

"Ja," van Kleegermarq said acidulously. "You should, since the cash pieces are threatening that last line of our great Governor General's letter."

The Radja brightened, and Boll asked, "How so?"

The Government's man savored his reply; he leered as he said, "In Batavia, four schooner *kapiteins* whom we questioned about your cash-piece trade were told that they, too, might be indicted for fraud if it was discovered that they had helped circulate a fraudulent coin in Dutch territory. Would you be interested in knowing what they did?

"They rushed to the Javasche Bank and traded your worthless pieces for guilders. Nor is that all. The bank in Soerabaja predicts a run from the Celebes and Moluccas to exchange the coins for guilders. There is more.

"The rumor along the water front in Soerabaja is that your cash piece is doomed—not because of the arm of the law. Neen. But because you, Kapitein Boll, who have caused them to stand up in the eastern and northern islands as a symbol of trade over the guilder, cannot sustain their value, because you have no more on hand!"

Boll chuckled. "Now that's odd. I've got plenty of them."

"And if you haven't, there will surely be a cash-piece panic in such places as Amboina and Makassar. If you have plenty, our bank will be waiting patiently."

Boll considered the logic of the Dutchman's words, admitting with

lifted brows the profound truth and threat which stared him in the
face. It was true that our supply of cash pieces was running low. He
realized the value of cash piece to save cash piece in the remote trade
centers; he heard almost the sighs of relief and renewed confidence
which one simple sight might invoke in Makassar, in Amboina, in
many parts; and that sight was the Gerrymander working in for
anchorage.

The Prime Minister entered and bowed. The Radja accepted the
written reply to the Governor General, read it, and examined the seal.
Then, after asking the Dutch Minister to wait outside for a moment,
he reached for the quill and inscribed his signature with a flourish
typical of the man.

With that he got to his feet, smiled craftily, and said: "Captain
Boll, I have shown my willingness to meet your every demand. You
remember your words of the afternoon, 'If I could produce peace
out of chaos at the right time, I could flood the Indies with cash
pieces and receive the Dutch blessing as I did it'? Under the threatening circumstances, I hold here more than you asked for. Much more,
Captain."

He then held the instrument up with thumb and forefinger of each
hand and very gently tore its edge. There was serious threat in the
act, and it shone in his astute Hindu face as he said, "Now, Captain
Boll, about the guarantee of your future decision."

My eyes leaped at Boll and back at the foxy genius of Mataram,
who played a great game of politics. Boll sat back and locked his eyes
with those of the unyielding Radja before asking:

"Suppose my decision should be against playing the part of Pulo
Besar?"

"Then you lose the dancing girl."

Boll considered this for long moments before reluctantly saying,
"Very well."

His decision added to his string of titles and appellations a most
exalted rank: Foreign Minister of Mataram. And he had traded Kim
Kim for that.

I said aloud: "The mighty Captain Boll!"

18 &3 THE FALL OF THE CASH

THE DYING TROPIC SUN OVER LOMBOK PAINTED THE CASTLE AND FORMAL gardens spilling down the slope in a riot of red and gold. Shadows reached like cool fingers for the still, glazed waters of the Jangkok River. The burnt-out odors of the day seemed wafted seaward, and the steamy aroma of the valley and mountains closed slowly over the scene of shore, river, and ship.

I stood alone at the pier watching Boll step up the gangway of the golden schooner. He had just delivered Kim Kim to the Radja.

"You stay here and wait for Culver. And keep your eyes on the Radja," he said to me.

He seemed lost within himself, and minus the propulsion of the Striker. I detected, I thought, a sign of fatigue and the faintest stoop about his shoulders. Soon the schooner's sails hauled aloft to snag a breeze and the craft inched lazily out into the stream. Boll leaned against the after-rail, his face painted with the bronze and red of the sunset.

The schooner crept softly down the river, as a dozen Balinese dugouts and canoes with outriggers moved in pursuit of ship or sunset. The soft, happy cries of the fishermen racing out to sea for flying fish in the moonlight rose up as lively, soft music puncturing the gloom Boll left in his wake. I followed the moving craft until the bend of the river swallowed them up. A faint wake, and the river glazed over to reflect images of the clouds. Beyond, a grizzled old mountain, seeming very much like a Hindu god lifting a wary head up over the horizon, brightened toward the sun and darkened to the east.

Harriet claimed me. The longing for her was fierce.

I made my slow way up the terraced steps and sat beside a fountain gushing up for the blind eyes of a white image of Brahma, and there I sat to watch the sun and land slug out the day. Harriet would be here soon. My mind went back to van Kleegermarq's threats of the night before and to the daring fulfillment of one of them. I saw Culver coming up with a club on one side, the Dutch with another, and the Radja with still another, and all moving down on Boll. But the Dutch had struck one blow:

The Dutch schooner had pulled from the palace wharf ahead of us; and when Boll and I reached the *Gerrymander* at dawn, we found the crew in a state of anger and excitement. The trouble? The men pointed to the Dutch schooner running fast into the strait beyond the reefs and cried, "The damned Dutchman! He did it!"

"What?" Boll asked.

The answer—it was tantamount to a mortal blow, and its effect staggered Boll somewhat—"The Dutchmen, sir, swarmed aboard. They surrounded Mr. Blue; and the leader showed Mr. Blue a warrant. They searched the ship, and—sir, they left with the coining press!" They had taken our coining press!

Boll asked, "And the box of cash pieces?"

"No, sir. Chess outsmarted them. He stuffed the top of the box with sailcloth. It wasn't half filled with cash pieces."

I thought of the Dutchman's words: "The rumor along the water fronts is that your cash piece is doomed—because you, Kapitein Boll, have no more on hand."

He had spoken of a cash-piece panic. That I could readily understand: with more than a million cash pieces in circulation, and each standing up for a guilder in trade, the sudden worthlessness of the coin symbolizing a fresh prosperity in the eyes of native and trader could only engender panic.

Boll, and only Boll, could avert panic. And he, as if in answer to the cries from distant trade centers, eyed the remaining cash pieces in the box and gave the order: "Make ready to sail."

On the bank of the Jangkok, I watched the gilded schooner round the bend. The day turned from setting sun to twilight as I climbed the steps of the terraced gardens to the palace. I wondered what lay ahead, though not for long—there I came face to face with another act rising fast out of the curtain of the last one:

Kim Kim.

2

She raced headlong toward me. Her flowered red silk covering stood out in the breeze behind her to expose her shapely limbs and breasts. She sobbed as if her very life ebbed from a wound, as if she raced in pursuit of its cause. I realized this was true. I could not imagine her a contented bird in the Radja's rookery, nor could she. She threw herself at me, her eyes pleading. I held her close to me and stroked her hair as I frowned up at the palace. I wondered what I could do or say to mitigate her suffering. Nothing? Nothing. The answer beat against my brain like the hammering of her physical heart against my body.

There had been reluctance on Boll's part in surrendering her, though she would not understand that, not Kim Kim, whose mind went only where her heart directed. All I could say was, "He'll be back, Kim Kim. He'll be back."

As I continued to hold her and look at the palace, something diverted my attention. There stood the Radja, his face livid in anger and showing the red marks of her nails. I must have started, for she lifted her head and glanced behind her. In the next moment, she broke away from me and ran down the steps, taking them three or four at a time until she fell. Then she rolled and scrambled to her feet. At the river, she paused for a look behind her before glancing in both directions. I watched her until she rounded the bend toward the Gerrymander and Boll.

I walked up the steps, passing the Radja, who continued to stand in statuesque silence, peering at the bend of the river, and moved on indoors where I could grin out my pleasure.

Why I was singled out to dine with the Radja that evening I did not know; and he, with a further display of captiousness, took his time in hurdling all matters at hand with the thoroughness I had learned to respect.

I entered his apartment to find him clad in white silk embroidered in a maze of tiny wreaths of gold thread. His collar was of gold cloth and tight about the neck, his turban of white and green-gray silk. The streaks on his face made by Kim Kim's nails showed plainly, and the memory of them flashed from his eyes. As we ate spicy peppered foods and fruit, he asked a number of questions in perfunctory manner: what had Captain Boll done to gain the ill will of Mr. Culver; and how did Captain Boll manage to hold his seemingly servile position under the American shipowner? I answered his questions as briefly as possible, causing him a pretense of satisfaction at what surely whetted his appetite. He contrived to smile disarmingly at me with thoughtful lips and eyes, though I knew he was playing with words in an effort properly to reconcile my position to all events of the past, present, and future before putting his gain to some use.

I lit a cigarette, sipped at a tasty alcoholic cordial, unlike anything I had tasted before, and eyed his elegant surroundings. Wealth could be monotonous, I reflected, though I realized that this crafty man had insulated himself to the anonymity of his setting by turning his abundant energy to the science of statecraft.

"Since there is little harmony between shipowner and captain," he said, "I am wondering if the captain has betrayed a trust there, if he would not use me to my disadvantage also." He paused, then said:

"Captain Boll arrived here basking in the sun of his own strong position. By a quick twist of fortune, he now rests in the palm of my hand." He lifted an upturned palm and stabbed it with a forefinger. "I can crush him by closing my hand, like this, or I can leave it open. If I follow the latter course, how long would my elusive friend the captain remain in my palm?"

"Are you talking about the future Pulo Besar?" I asked.

"Yes," he replied slowly. He smiled, then leaned forward. "Mr. Flint, I am more than anxious that he accept our proposition. If he refuses, I shall naturally make every effort to force his change of mind."

"Why are you so anxious for Boll to head the pirates?"

"Because he is a pirate by nature. He can serve us well." He smiled craftily. "But would he?"

I realized that Boll was all that stood between me and Culver, that only through a strong Boll had I the slightest chance at detecting Culver's vulnerable spot. I said, "Boll would be of little use to you if he were crushed."

"Quite true." He weighed the subject for effect before appealing to me again. "What is your opinion? Can I trust Captain Boll, or is he the type of man who will repeat today's performance?"

So that was it, I mused before replying, "Boll made a great sacrifice today. I am sure he will return Kim Kim."

He smiled, his thin, energetic mouth and clever eyes accepting a hawklike expression as he said, "You will, of course, advise him to do just that, and soon. Otherwise——" He lifted his palm again and, under the threat of his smile, he closed it slowly.

I was the Radja's guest in the weeks that followed. I met visiting sultans and radjas, all bent on pleasure and further accession of wealth. Moslem and Hindu sat on the terraces and watched the Radja's dancing girls perform; they nibbled at sweetmeats and eyed the bare-breasted girls with sensual eyes for long hours. I played checkers with the Radja: it was his favorite game, and one in which he excelled.

Before the *Gerrymander* returned, he said to me, "Someday, Mr. Flint, I shall present for your eyes a game of Mogul checkers. I seldom play checkers in such style without big stakes." I was unaware that a scheme was working in his head as he spoke.

The days passed slowly. I wandered to the town where the sea met the river. Coconut palms towered above a typical Balinese village. Below the fronded ceiling there stood the usual wharves and warehouses, the maze of houses, unusual in design, some open, some closed, but all exuding a gracefulness that is uniquely Balinese. Marketing was done in the open air during the southeast monsoon from huge baskets and trays placed above large stone platforms. There was the ivory carver, the silk merchant, the silversmith, the lacquer maker, the old man who fashioned gilded headgear from the hide of the buffalo, and the carver of huge monuments for cremating the dead.

Almond-eyed women with lovely rose-and-copper skins and classical faces went about unashamed of their uncovered breasts; their modesty forbade, however, the showing of any part of their legs. In colorful turbans, sarongs of priceless batik, and always some decorative piece—a red or yellow hibiscus, or an intricately fashioned bracelet or necklace—the women moved about gracefully, lazily, and happily.

I thought of Harriet with every show of beauty. I longed for her. I eyed the strait out over the reefs for some sign of a big ship.

The first ship to enter the mouth of the river was not the one carrying Culver. I was roaming the palace grounds late one afternoon when I heard someone call my name. I looked toward the river and saw Chess. The *Gerrymander* had returned ahead of Culver. What, I wondered, was slowing the *Aladdin?*

Chess grinned, shook his curly head, and raced to where I stood. "Lord-a-mercy, am I glad to be back among civilized people!"

"What are you doing here?" I asked, scolding under my smile.

"Mr. Blue sent me to fetch you, sir. Captain Boll and Kim Kim left us. He's going on to Batavia."

I led him to a seat on the shady side of the palace, listening to his words of awe-stricken wonder as he sought to reconcile the palace to the "edge of hell." He was soon seated and answering the maze of questions I shot in rapid succession. At last he made a grimace and exclaimed:

"Belay, sir, and I'll tell the whole damn story."

His aim for a maturity beyond his years was refreshing as he launched into the account of the *Gerrymander's* recent voyage:

"Now I see we are in for it, and I says to Little Ahab, 'The devil's got the conn o' the ship and he's crowding for Fiddler's Green.' The Striker and Mr. Blue have us hanging by the gills, and the first thing I see is Lugo the Boot logged for refusing old man Wulsin his whisky. There's grumbling and orders to lay aloft, and then sea after sea, and us running by the wind. Sopping squalls, and us up in the stirrups."

"Wait. I don't want an account of sails and weather," I barked. "What about the cash trade and Boll?"

"Oh," he said. "In Soerabaja, Captain Boll ordered Lugo and me to follow him with satchels full of the coins. We did. He went to the Big Coffin Saloon."

I listened, tincturing a boy's observations with an adult eye as he told me all that happened. . . .

3

Soerabaja . . . Boll's entry into the packed saloon was tantamount to a sensation. Every eye followed him to the bar in a hush as silent as a wake. He broke the silence with, "Drinks for the house." The owner came up, shook hands reluctantly with, it seemed, a dead man vacationing from the monotony of a grave; he said he'd heard the *Gerrymander* was at anchor, but that he'd scoffed at the idea until every captain in the place swore that the hideous figurehead was out there laughing at a Dutch gunboat. There was an ominous quiet in the saloon after that; it hung in tight layers, like the smoke; and Boll, feeling it, grinned, faced the crowd, and said:

"I hear I'm licked." Silence, and he went on: "Well, there's later news. I'm not. I hear also that I have no more trade money." He then called up Chess and Lugo, saying, "Spill your satchels on the floor."

The cash pieces shone under the lights like the gold they had once represented, and the calm eye of the Striker over the room seemed to insure their color even then. Necks craned, and inane faces turned slowly to face inane faces. Not a sound was heard in the Big Coffin.

"The Dutch have spread the word that they have my coining press. So they have. But I've got cash pieces, and I'll not encounter much trouble in getting some Chinese metalworker to strike more." He lifted a drink without taking his eyes off the crowd.

"The Dutch say they can prosecute me for passing more of these cash pieces. But they can't. Why? Because the Dutch letter here, signed by the Governor General, himself, states plainly that fraud exists when more than the guaranteed amount shows up at the banks for redemption.

"They won't show up." He chuckled.

"Who wants them at a guilder each?" Boll asked. There was no response, and his cynical smile stood up to mock the crowd. "Then who wants to redeem any at a guilder and ten each?"

The vacillating audience found its speech, though in a low buzzing exchange of opinions. Soon one grizzled Dutch captain stepped forward with a hundred or two cash pieces, and Boll peeled off guilders from an impressive roll, saying so all could hear:

"I'm paying a ten-per-cent premium from now on. If any of you have rushed to the bank for even money, you're the loser—unless you get them back here by tomorrow noon."

With that he paid for all drinks, ordered the cash pieces on the floor retrieved, and stalked out of the place as if he were the soul and body of the Javasche Bank.

The next day he paid the premium on four thousand pieces; but before nightfall, he had sold nearly ten thousand pieces to the doubters of the night before. Confidence had been restored.

Makassar . . . The *Gerrymander* ran northeast from Paternoster Eilenden under quartering and beam winds up to four degrees south; and from there up to the south fairway, she met nearly everything the sea had to offer, bows-on and bows-under. Then the elements grew sane and the monsoon eddied up the strait between Borneo and the Celebes. Makassar's harbor felt the *Gerrymander's* hook in the early afternoon, and the town itself responded to the ship's presence before nightfall.

The situation in Makassar seemed to warrant the turning of the grim old muzzles of Fort Rotterdam's guns on the ship:

In the first place, the harbor was crowded with native craft from Borneo, the spreading Celebes, and distant Moluccas; and the loaded boats had vomited forth thousands who had come to witness a public hanging where the Dutch thought it would do the most good. The doomed man was none other than Pulo Besar. His name was still magic; it carried the romantic ring of exploit under a whipping black flag. The Dutch were wary and touchy that day, since they expected an uprising. And the appearance of the notorious *Gerrymander* on that very day did nothing to dampen the fuse under a powder keg.

The marines rowed out and ordered no one to leave the ship, since the presence of Boll or any of his crew might infuriate the mob and thereby set off the spark. But Boll, haughty as ever, said he had business ashore, and that they had better dig deep into their lawbooks for some fine toothy edict if they hoped to keep him on deck; they could fish or cut bait, and lively. They rowed off leaving a lone marine on the after-deck.

Boll waited an hour. By that time a crowd had gathered on the low beach a hundred yards away. It was Moslem, silent, and threatening; it was patient as it eyed the ship of the man who had conquered the redoubtable Pulo Besar. A few Dutch soldiers marched back and forth on the strip of foreshore between ship and milling throng, and a Dutch gunboat worked up and turned broadside to the beach, its guns ready for any emergency.

Boll chuckled, ordered Chess and Lugo to fill their satchels with cash pieces before lowering away a boat. He was soon approaching the shore, grinning out his silent opinion of Dutch and Moslem. The boat beached, drawing the guard, which Boll, with Kim Kim at his side, ignored as he advanced on the quiet crowd. He walked, as Chess put it, "like Moses through the Red Sea," his eyes cutting a path through the mass of people. They arrived at the Pride of Makassar without hearing a single threat from the myriad bearded faces under tarboosh and turban.

Once inside the place, van Kirsteen advanced, tugging at his handlebar mustache, seemingly very much perturbed at Boll's untimely visit.

Boll asked if there was a plan afoot to rescue Pulo Besar, only to be advised that the Great Bastard was no longer useful to the merchants and princes; that he, van Kirsteen, had heard of other plans. Had Boll? Boll had, though he had heard also that an American shipowner must be dealt with first. Then the proprietor said:

"You picked a bad time to come here. There's a cash-piece panic here, and all that's holding it off is the excitement of a hanging." Boll asked for the facts. The situation, van Kirsteen said, simply held to the pattern of the economic tide of any firm's stock, in that its flood and ebb were regulated by its real or fictitious worth, which time alone could uncover. Makassar, the core of trade in the northern Indies, had drawn Boll's cash pieces like a patient magnet until the Chinese and Arab merchants, repeatedly warned by the Javasche Bank, owned more than they wanted. They were afraid to accept more, and afraid not to, since the former procedure threatened them with slow bankruptcy and the latter with loss of business and perhaps quicker ruin. A few, however, refused to honor the Gerrymander Cash, causing natives to view the accepted twin of the Dutch guilder with trepidation. Since nothing is more likely to engender fear and panic as the sudden crumbling of monetary values, there is no urge more natural than the hope of saving quickly all that's left to save. The native Makassarese and schooner captain were no different from anyone else, and they urged the merchants to accept their cash pieces at any price. Thus, when the run started, the cash piece dropped from guilder to stuiver value.

Van Kirsteen said there were more than fifty thousand cash pieces in the hands of the merchants who sat back, fat and chuckling over their gain, and laughing at their recent fears. Aye, for the Dutch would redeem the cash pieces at a guilder each, but only if they were shipped to Batavia.

Boll asked if the cash pieces were on their way to Java, and van Kirsteen said they were due to leave that morning, but the Chinese captain's love for a hanging scene kept the loaded schooner in port.

"What schooner?" Boll asked.

"The *Blue Dragon*." Boll repeated the name twice, slowly.

After more talk, Boll followed van Kirsteen to the crowded bar, where the owner asked for silence. Then Boll repeated the act he'd put on in the Big Coffin Saloon of Soerabaja, bursting forth with an idea as fresh as profitable discovery, and one to further perplex the Dutch; to his audience, he said:

"I'm raising the value of the Gerrymander Cash to a guilder ten. It's worth more than the guilder by ten per cent—and to prove it, I'm depositing twenty thousand American dollars, *not with the stubborn Javasche Bank, but with Mijnheer van Kirsteen*, who will redeem every piece you bring him."

"When does this go into effect?" a captain asked.

"Tomorrow," Boll replied after a moment of thoughtful silence.

That night, while Makassar waited for the hanging of Pulo Besar, the schooner *Blue Dragon* mysteriously sucked her hull of the harbor waters and sank in eleven fathoms. Fifty thousand cash pieces went down with her.

On the following morning, Boll searched out an old Chinese metalworker. He showed the Gerrymander Cash and asked, "Can you duplicate this piece?" He could. "But no gotee light metal." Boll said he had a few hundred sheets of the light yellow alloy. The Chinese and Boll bargained for a long hour over the price. The Chinese singsonged, cursed, spat, and pulled his queue and stringy beard, at last accepting Boll's first offer.

"How long before they will be ready?" Boll asked. The reply, "Thlee weeks," evoked another argument. It ended with a promise on the part of the Chinese to deliver thirty thousand cash pieces—all that could be produced from the supply of metal—to van Kirsteen within two weeks.

Boll had no sooner boarded the Gerrymander that day than the Dutch officers of the gunboat came aboard with a search warrant.

They were hunting for Pulo Besar—they had hanged the wrong man on the night before!

Amboina . . . The Gerrymander tore into Ambon Bay under all plain sail, standing dangerously close to the steep lee shore. The Dutch pilot stared at a madman's ship, light in the water, and faster on the wing than anything that had ever before split the entrance to the bay. But Boll was in a hurry, since Mr. Wulsin's joints predicted wind out of the west, which would slow the run back to Makassar; and, too, Boll was fighting off ruin where it counted, where the Gerrymander Cash should reign proudly.

The ship had not ridden her anchor a full hour before the palm-lined beach was crowded with natives dancing up and down like a populace utterly berserk. Dugouts with outriggers raced the hundred yards to the ship, and the deck was soon alive with cash pieces begging to be spent. Boll learned that the Chinese and Arabs had emulated the Dutch merchants by refusing to accept a single coin in trade. He forthwith ordered rum, silks, and gimcracks put ashore, and there, under the eyes of the merchants, he sold a big guilder's worth for every cash piece.

His genius in that case was deserving of praise: he looked ahead as he traded for every cash piece he could get into his hands. His next move was to advise the crowd that from that day on the Gerrymander Cash was worth a guilder and ten—but only at the stores of the merchants. The protest of the merchants was cut short when he posted American currency to guarantee their behavior in this direction.

The Amboinese were without any voice but that of happiness,

though out of the crowd one old confirmed Chinese trader-merchant mocked Boll with words of wisdom:

"This unlearned student of economics looks to the source of this prosperity which honorable captain revives with his coming, wondering how mortal can be at right place at right time allee same time."

Boll's reply was emblematic of the Striker: "Since a mortal can't, wise friend, what can serve him better in his absence than the god men serve, money?"

The old saffron-colored man bowed low and replied, "It has been said that money which changes value is a curse of the gods and doomed to a short life in the span of the universe. With its death, false prosperity is drowned in tears of anguish. The death of cash-piece prosperity is rumored. It is said that honorable captain has little trade money left."

"I have enough," Boll snapped, "and I can get more."

"Honorable captain is resourceful. But still say, how can mortal be at right place at right time allee same time?" He grinned, stroking his yellow goatee, as Boll scoffed and said:

"Down to cases. It seems I have bought up all my trade money here. Now if you are to stay in business, you'll do well to buy it back." That was his reason for drawing in every cash piece possible.

The Chinese and other merchants recognized Boll's excellent position in that moment: he actually had the power to regulate their flow of business and profits, since none could deny that the cash piece bought more goods from the native than the guilder, any more than they could dispute the fact that the cash piece in circulation made business more brisk than before its coming. Thus even the old Chinese who had spoken with venerable sagaciousness was forced to eat his words.

"You'll pay a guilder ten for each one," Boll told them. "Which will make you think twice before letting the Dutch own them at a guilder each. And you'll take enough to scatter in remote spots, where they won't show up soon to start off another panic."

The ten big merchants came out of their huddle with a decision: they agreed to take five thousand each. Boll chuckled and sent Mr. Blue and Chess to the *Gerrymander* for the fifty thousand cash pieces. And in doing so, Boll committed the greatest error of his career, one which not only put him on the defensive, but which, by revealing a true condition, struck at the very heart of the fabulous cash-piece bubble; it was a small error, though it is ever the slightest mistake that uncovers a scheme:

Boll, his prodigious mind dazzled by greed and power, had forgotten that the last box of cash pieces was almost empty. Chess and Mr. Blue returned with less than half the amount the merchants desired.

There was unmistakable triumph in the odious leer in the old Chinaman's face when Boll said he'd return in one month with the remainder; his old eyes seemed to say: "So there is truth in the rumor that the honorable captain has little trade money left." They glittered on with, "False prosperity is drowned in tears of anguish."

Boll stared for hours at a time during the hard, fast run back to Makassar at the big empty cash-piece box, upon which was printed in big black letters an apt word: EXPLOSIVES.

4

Chess hadn't quite finished his story. He said, chuckling: "And that wasn't all, sir. The captain made a record run back to Makassar. Aye, by God and St. Ebenezer, he made watch and watch of it. He ordered more sail than she could carry, sir, and when he went below he locked the halyards so Mr. Blue couldn't take in any sail.

"He kept eying the empty box. And he said to Lugo, when he fetched him whisky one afternoon, 'Steward, we'll return to Amboina and make the damned Chinese look alive.'"

Chess laughed again. "But we didn't."

"Why?" I asked.

"Well, sir, we got to Makassar in the night. We didn't wait for morning to run the shoals and reefs—we threaded them like a needle. Lugo, Mr. Wulsin, and I rowed the captain ashore; and we went with him to the Chinese metalworker's place. The old Chinaman appeared and said he had already delivered the cash pieces to van Kirsteen. Then we went to the Pride of Makassar.

"There we learned something that will make your eyes pop out of your head, sir. Aye, sir. By God and St. Ebenezer, it will!

"Van Kirsteen had boarded a Dutch gunboat only the day before—cash pieces and all—for Batavia!"

Thirty thousand cash pieces in the hands of the Dutch were nearly enough to ruin Boll. But not quite. However, he was approaching the end of his venture.

Before I could say anything, Chess laughed and said, "And guess what we heard in Soerabaja on the return trip. The *Aladdin* had been there. Mr. Cott is her captain! Imagine that old bastard! Miss Adams and Mr. Culver are aboard, sir."

The presence of the *Aladdin* in East Indian waters evoked into mind a wealth of thought. A fight to the finish between Boll and Culver invited De Loach's man Flint to a weighing of schemes out of which he might pluck a decisive victory. If Boll won, then Culver must lose; if Culver won, then Boll must go down in defeat. And with Boll's loss, I should be forced into a new and quick defense in order to so much as hold my own against the victor. Another aspect reared its head: if Boll won, his tight rein on the future would surely preclude any worth-while victory on my part. I was forced by such reasoning into an acknowledgment of my true position in the outcome:

Should either Boll or Culver win over the other, I would be the loser! Therefore, the task ahead sounded a challenge: Tom Flint, in order to forestall a victory by either, must seize the initiative at just the precise moment. But how?

The answer was so close and yet so far away; it begged in the shadows of my mind for the light; it sent me in search of past events which should, in some manner, join the present in a Gordian knot. If I could untie the knot, then I should be master of the situation. But how?

I am not sure what it was that caused the idea to leap into my mind. At any rate, my eye reached back to that night when the *Gerrymander* eased in to anchorage off Little Fortune Island. I heard the splash of an iron box! Then the full significance of the past drove in hard to connect with another fact:

Boll needed those cash pieces which rested in seven fathoms. With them he could sustain their false value for a time. Culver, too, needed them: with that iron box in his possession Culver could, by threatening to give them to the Dutch, dictate Boll's future in his own uncompromising style. And, for that matter, so could the Radja of Mataram use those cash pieces in the same manner.

"Then why couldn't I?" My question was quickly answered: "Because they would not, could not, lend me any power over Culver." Only Boll could hope to win with them; or lose with them if his enemies obtained them first. But here was something to think about, at least; a nucleus that continued to invite my fancy.

I thought of Boll's threat: "Culver's picture must come down." If it did, if Boll emerged the victor over Culver, then—— "Aye! By

God and St. Ebenezer," I said, "that's the time those cash pieces would serve you, Tom Flint!"

So I found myself allied in purpose with Boll once again. However, my anxious eye hovered over a box of cash pieces just off the northeast anchorage at Little Fortune Island. Somehow, I could not dispel a hunch that the Gerrymander Cash in the care of Davy Jones would rise up importantly with the fall of the cash.

19 &ᶜᵍ THE RADJA'S CHALLENGE

THE "ALADDIN'S" ANCHORS SPLASHED NOT ONE HUNDRED YARDS DOWN-stream from us before sundown of the next day. She loomed as a vengeance ship—so quiet and patient she seemed after stalking us over half the stretch of the Indies. None the worse for wear on the voyage, her hull glistened black, and her yards gleamed like polished brass in the last sunlight of the day. I was less interested in the ship, how-ever, and more curious about the life on her long deck, particularly that aft. Harriet. With the aid of the glass, I studied her intently.

The first familiar face I saw belonged to Mr. Cott, or Captain Cott. He eyed the *Gerrymander* from under drooping eyelids; and the stretch of his lips, hinting of a smile long anticipated, was every bit as patient as it was mocking. He had a right to hate, I admitted, though complete justification did little to correct my dislike of the small man inside him. But he was once again a threat of uncertain importance.

Closer to the break in the poop, Mr. Culver stood with arms on the rail; he seemed relaxed and calm under hasty appraisal, though some-thing about his iron-jawed face belied his pose. The longer I studied him, the more his face revealed. His eyes were sharp and hard and burning, and his mouth assumed a stretched and taut vigor, more like a mouthing of a vow often repeated. I saw him scan the ship from trucks to water line, from counter to bow; and there his eye held to the monstrosity carved by a drunk-crazed artist. The figurehead ac-cepted the red glint of the sun like every other surface facing the west; it was then a red devil-bird that Culver saw. He hated the ship for what it was, for what it had done to him, and he was perversely pleased with himself for doing just this, no matter how silly his lengthened grudge might appear to others. He was Robert Culver, and that definition sufficed.

But Boll had done little to Culver, except to glorify the object of his hate, that and flick at the sores of the man's vanity. Little? That was hardly the word, since in doing these things Boll had stabbed at the heart of Robert Culver with greater effect than he could have realized had he scuttled both the *Aladdin* and the *Shanghai Packet*. Thus cause preceded effect, and effect stood in the form of a man who could hardly be expected to humor the Striker a second time.

A boat put out from Culver's ship and pulled toward us. Mr. Culver wanted me aboard the *Aladdin*, and I was soon standing in his august presence. As he glowered at me, showing his poor opinion of a man of Boll's choice, I thought, "Mister, you couldn't have timed your arrival better." The fall of the cash seemed made to order for what he surely had in mind.

He said at last, "I suppose you know why I am here."

"No, sir," I said.

"The news of Captain Boll's disgraceful conduct has been plastered across every newspaper in Boston."

"What disgraceful conduct, sir?" I asked.

"Do you stand there and pretend no knowledge of his dealing with slaves?"

"Oh, that." I smiled. "Why, he had no intention of violating slavery laws. Instead, he planned to return the girl to the Sultan in a bid for his favor. It was a good idea, a means of opening the cash trade in Borneo."

"Cash! Cash!" he growled. "I'm sick of hearing the word."

"So are the Dutch," I said.

"Which pleases me immensely," he returned. "I hear they have almost enough of the damned pieces now to finish him."

"Let us hope not, sir—for your sake."

"My sake! You are impudent, young man."

"I'm sorry, sir," I said with marked politeness.

"Fighting pirates!" he said as if to himself. "Is there no end to his damnable escapades?"

I maintained a sober face as I studied him. He was too stubborn to discard his Boston dress of heavy coat, vest, and stiff collar; he refused to submit to a change in scene and clime, to an infraction of a rule which would serve him with more gold and power; he placed his ego up for dictatorship over his conduct, choosing to keep alive in childish manner the sores of a wounded vanity instead of searching for a balm. But, I asked myself, how could he be the man he was and still be a man whom Harriet would consider marrying?

I savored my reply. "Perhaps, sir, you need more officers like Mr. Cott." I saw his jaw harden. "But you," I added before he could voice his dominant self, "forget that expediency governs the Gerrymander Cash trade, of which you are a partner."

"I forget nothing, Mr. Flint!" he snapped.

"No," a voice behind me said with friendly sarcasm, "Mr. Culver forgets nothing."

I spun about-face and saw Harriet.

She wore a white dress with a low, circular neck outlined in tiny ruffles. The heart-shaped, ruby-set pin I had given her in Singapore was fastened at the divide of her breasts. Her eyes leaped into mine, as did her smile of genuine welcome. A surge of pride, joy, and admiration assailed me as she advanced with extended hand. I wanted to shout, "Harriet!" to sweep her into my arms, though I let my eyes say all. She did not remove her hand at once; she looked deep inside me in one serious moment before saying:

"It is nice to see you." She hesitated before flashing a smile and a word: "Tom."

I could not manage an answer; I was that shaken. My eyes left her face, after what seemed an eternity, in search of a wedding ring on her left finger. It was not there. She smiled, followed my eyes to her finger, and said, "Not yet."

"Or never!" I added stanchly. Then I asked, "Where's Blossom?"

"Below."

"Mr. Flint," Culver's voice intruded, "what's this I hear about Captain Boll and this Radja of Mataram?" As I turned to face him with a frown, he said, "I hear Boll is his official Foreign Minister." I nodded, and he went on: "It is said also that this office and some twenty thousand more cash pieces are all that stand between him and a Dutch jail."

I was watching Harriet.

He smiled savagely, adding, "I must meet this Radja of Mataram, Mr. Flint. I think I can relieve Captain Boll of that foolish, last-hope title and thereby complete my work here.

"The sooner the better," he snapped.

2

That night I doubled the guard. The ship, loaded with treasure, was, after all, Culver's, and I was afraid that he might decide to claim it. I hugged the poop on the weather side and looked upstream for some time. From my point of vantage I commanded a view of the village, the *Aladdin* under her dim flickering lights, and a portion of the deck. I watched the stars pop out of the gauzelike mist blowing in from the southeast and hang dry for moments before winking out again. The moon stood a few points to the east of the zenith and painted every surface in soft phosphorescence and sharp shadow. The halcyon night lulled one; and then it ran on fiercely as Harriet joined it in my mind.

I sent a note to Harriet by Chess and then paced the quarter-deck impatiently. He returned soon and said with a knowing grin on his face, "She wants you to sit with her on the *Aladdin*'s deck, sir. She said Mr. Culver and Aunt Emmy—I think that's the name—were playing cards in the saloon. I saw old evil eye on deck, sir. He was——"

"Damn Mr. Cott!" I said, moving off.

Chess called after me, "Good luck, sir. She's worth seven ships of gold, I'd say." He grinned, adding, "Tack right in, sir—but watch out you don't miss stays."

The *Aladdin*'s gangway was down, and there on deck, smiling down at me, was Harriet. The moon looked larger then, and the tinkling sounds from the Balinese orchestra in the village rang sweeter in my ears. I was soon standing beside her.

We moved aft, to chairs under a sailmaker's awning. We had exchanged a few words on the way to the poop, though I remembered only her presence at my side. I drew a chair close to her, where I could look to my heart's content.

I spoke out of a trance, "Harriet, you've come back at last."

"Yes." She smiled as her eyes examined my unruly hair, my face, and shoulders.

"And I'm trying to pin a star down for another view," I said. "I was a fool for not kidnaping you when I had the chance."

"I'd make a poor captive," she said. "I'm not a slave girl, like—what is her name, the girl whom Captain Boll bought?"

"Kim Kim."

"A fascinating name—Kim Kim. Tell me about her." I told her sketchily all there was to tell, concluding with, "I imagine she's with Boll in Java." She seemed unsatisfied.

"But I didn't come here to talk about Boll and Kim Kim, Harriet. I want to take you to the Balinese village. I'd rather hear you, and about you."

"There's so little to tell," she said, lifting her eyes to the starry sky. "Our friend sends you his best."

"And how is he?" I asked absently.

She eyed me directly. "Worried." She added, "It's quite a story—if you're interested."

"Should I be more eager to hear that than——"

"You should," she reproved me with a little laugh. "The saloon may empty any moment."

"All the more reason for visiting the village. Listen to their music, Harriet."

"Amos has been losing money," she replied firmly. "But I said that in a letter."

She was never more inviting; never lovelier. A big moon was wasting away over a palm-studded lagoon. I reached out and took her hand in mine and drew her forward. "So Amos has been losing money," I said seriously.

"So Amos has lost money," I said again. "But kidnaping you seems more urgent—or will you come willingly?" I was up and drawing her toward me.

"Mr. Flint!" Her eyes belied her tone of voice; they twinkled, pleased, though they wanted total acquiescence from the male.

"Tom," I suggested. "You're going to a lot of trouble not to say it. Why?"

Her answer was, "Tom"; that and a challenging smile which did nothing to mask her interest. I asked if she was ready to go. "Suppose you get Aunt Emily's permission," she countered.

"I'd sooner face a Dutch court. However, I think I can do it."

"You wouldn't dare." She laughed. "Not after——" She hushed suddenly.

"Not after that night in Singapore?" I said. "Why not? I'm still in love with you, Harriet. She can't change that."

Her eyes evaded mine when she said, "Perhaps not, Tom, but she can make you very uncomfortable while she recites the many reasons why you should look elsewhere."

"That I doubt," I said. "I can't imagine any feeling but a nice one in loving you." There was no answer as her eyes singled out a star winking on and off just above a distant palm. "So I'll go ask Aunt Emily, if that's necessary."

I did not have far to go: Aunt Emily was at that moment near enough to hear my words. She said, "Ask me what, sir, and who is it?"

"Tom Flint, chief mate aboard the G-53; or may I say *Gerrymander* in your presence, madam?"

"*Gerrymander*," she snapped. "So you're the young man who

flitted about our ship on another moonlight night. Well, what do you want?"

"The pleasure of escorting your niece to the Balinese village. You see, a sailor doesn't like to spend a night off aboard a ship."

"True." Her eyes probed me from over her glasses. Her lips were drawn into a stern little pucker that seemed to lend her small figure an authority often assumed by persons of diminutive stature. "True," she repeated. "And once a sailor, always a sailor. Mr. Flint, Harriet and I shall accept your invitation."

I made the best of a situation. I felt the sharp eyes of both women asking with subdued amusement how the "sailor" would react to third-party interference. However, with resentment not only concealed but cast out of me, the course invited my coming around on the other tack: under my breath I said, "Even a cake of Boston ice can thaw." As long as vanity exists in a woman, there is a means of approach; and since few women outlive that venial sin, vulnerability exists. "Ease the helm, Mr. Flint. Bring her by the wind," I said in salute to that fact.

A native orchestra sat on the beach. One man played the finger drum, another hovered over a brass gong, and still another played the bell jar. We watched and listened, and soon a Balinese girl of perhaps twelve emerged from the crowd to perform the finger dance. The evening wore on, and when we returned to the *Aladdin*, Harriet's aunt said she had seldom enjoyed an evening more. I had used caution in voicing compliments, aware that her sharp discernment searched for unction or barbarisms in a sailor's speech and tone.

On deck, I held the little lady's hand and said with simple directness, "You're good company, Aunt Emily."

She put up gruffness for defense as she replied, "Why don't you admit that I was unwanted, Mr. Flint?"

"Why, I thought you knew that." I grinned.

That did it: she thawed. "I like an honest man, even if he is a rebel." She studied me seriously for a moment before saying, "You remind me of my Jim in many ways. Perhaps the only thing that's wrong with you is the company you keep."

I said, "Why, I thought you liked Captain Boll, ma'am."

"And I'm not so sure that I don't, Tom Flint," she said.

She left us alone on a deck flooded with moonlight. Harriet smiled at the moon, the village, and then at me. I could not read her eyes, though I was content to sit close and admire her. She broke the silence mischievously with:

"As I was saying, Amos has been losing money." I started, though I sat back, resigned to the story: I'd let her get everything off her mind on this night in order to claim the tropical evenings ahead. She jarred me into a listening mood when she said:

"You played quite a part in the Boston side of the story."

3

She embarked on her story then. "It began in Portland, Maine. Amos did not wish a schooner to sail in ballast to Boston, so he contracted for a cargo of lumber to Baltimore at a very low price. However, a few days before that, the *Cape Race*, now a Culver-Adams coastwise schooner, contracted to make several trips to Baltimore with lumber. Before long, all coastal freight rates were down. Then one day——

"Four of the biggest shipowners on the Atlantic coast paid Mr. Culver a visit. Here's what happened. The millionaire spokesman said, 'We're in business for money, not for fun. We have ships tied to wharves because we can't put them in the stream with freight rates being what they are. Unless you raise your rates we're prepared to end this dogfight in our own way.'

"Mr. Culver reminded them of a parasite firm, De Loach and Company, saying, 'You men are lacking in resource. Now had you come here to offer some aid instead of a threat, I'd have listened to you. But as it stands, I'll see you in hell first.'

"The foursome stood bewildered until Mr. Culver shouted, 'Sit down!' They sat, and they listened. 'If you're so all-fired hot to make money, then help me get rid of the parasites. How? Why, gentlemen, you sound like a bunch of lame-brained schoolboys who don't know a belayin' pin from a capstan. Here's what I propose:

"'We'll beat the parasites and steam too. We'll each get a steam freighter and barges. We'll put them into the coastwise trade and tow from Maine to Charleston. We'll lose money, but by God and a purple dolphin, we'll soon own the trade for our own rates! Now if this appeals to you, I'll raise ocean rates tomorrow.' They agreed to accept his proposition.

"Amos was marked for ruin, Tom. I got word of the news through Mr. Boston, who sat in the meeting. You can imagine my sense of entrapment, can't you?"

"Aye." I saw her, the biggest stockholder in both firms, between the hammer and anvil of warring factions.

She said, "I was forced to act quickly in order to salvage what I could. But what I should do posed a pretty problem." She paused, as if debating on her course.

"You'll remember I said something in one of my letters about postponing my answer to Mr. Culver's proposal. I thought of my reasons for doing just that and decided on a plan. I invited Amos to be our guest at dinner several days later. In the interim, I was—well, exceptionally nice to Mr. Culver."

"Why?" I asked, leaning forward.

"When one is caught in a trap," she replied, "one is likely to use the weapons at hand."

"Did your aunt know about Culver's proposal?"

"No. Mr. Culver had exacted a promise from me: I should make up my own mind before mentioning the matter to Aunt Emily. He was afraid of her opposition, and I was equally afraid that she might side with him.

"But the night before Amos came, he proposed again. I listened attentively, maintaining my silence until he had declared himself very much in love with me. He had not said that before. When I said, 'I doubt your love, sir,' he countered with, 'There's nothing I would not do to prove my love for you, Harriet.'

" 'That is a broad statement,' I replied, 'which I am sure you voiced in a moment of zeal.'

" 'If that is true,' he said flatly, 'I shall, nevertheless, be bound by it.'

" 'Very well, sir. I shall give you an answer within the week.'

"Amos came the next evening. Mr. Culver was not pleased. But he was courteous. They talked about things in general. I decided to sit by and listen for a while.

"At dinner, Amos turned the subject to steam versus sail. He wanted to draw Mr. Culver out. While I, desiring agreement between them for once, spoke up quickly: 'Steam will win. It's more economical.' To my amusement both men took sides against me. They were in accord for the first time in years, and they beat down my arguments one by one. The dinner ended there, and we retired to the parlor.

"Brandy was served the men, and I said, 'Why don't you two drink to higher freight rates?'

"Mr. Culver spoke: 'Deep-stream rates went up today.'

"I pretended surprise, and I asked who raised them. 'I did,' he said. When I asked if coastal rates had risen also, he replied, 'How can they, when there are bloodsuckers in the business?' I asked if he had for-gotten that our guest operated a coastal fleet, drawing from him a laugh and, 'No.'

"Well, Amos laughed and said business wars were costly; and Mr. Culver remarked, 'Yes, as devastating as armies in the field.'

"I said, 'Indeed they are. So I've decided to put an end to this one.'

"'You?' Mr. Culver asked. Amos looked surprised. 'And how, may I ask?' Mr. Culver added.

"'I'm beginning here,' I said. 'For two men of long experience to be caught in the trap of profitless enterprise, when a word or two of sincere discussion might have averted such, is utterly ridiculous. What would my father say to both of you? He'd say:

"'"You boys will either bury the hatchet or suffer the conse-quences." He would say, "Robert, was Amos really to blame in the Figurehead Affair, or was the occasion merely an excuse for turning your resentment at life on your best friend?" He would do exactly what I'm about to do, and that is ask a question:

"'Amos, were you responsible for that figurehead?'

"'I was not!' Amos replied vehemently.

"'But you allowed it to be placed without first examining it, didn't you?' I asked.

"'Yes. That was my error. But the carver, a reputable man, asked that an artist's whim be humored, that nobody see the work until the unveiling.'

"'And you told Mr. Culver this?'

"'I have never had the chance,' Amos replied.

"Mr. Culver was on his feet. He was angry. And, for that matter, so was Amos. Mr. Culver asked why I had arranged this meeting and what I expected to gain from it. I replied, 'Harmony, sir. And since you have convinced me that you are seeking some harmony with life, I am sure that this meeting will determine your sincerity on that score.'

"He looked sharply at me. My words had jarred his memory into a recognition of his proposal of the evening before. He sat down, and I went on:

"'Harmony,' I said. 'I mean by that a healing of old sores. Silly, childish sores. There's nothing more foolish than this figurehead grudge. I mean a public healing over.'

"Mr. Culver said, 'What are you driving at?' to which I replied, 'A working arrangement wherein Culver and Adams absorbs a worthy and annoying rival.'

"Tom, both men leaped to their feet, and their faces seemed to ask if I had lost my mind." She laughed. "And from your expression you seem to be asking the same question."

"Yes," I said. "But what happened then?"

"Mr. Culver said a schooner on the rocks was a bad buy. Amos seemed the calmer as he smiled at me and said, 'I'll have to refuse—that is, until I talk to my silent partner.' Mr. Culver turned to him and said, 'Whoever the fool is.'

"Amos faced him and replied, 'That remains to be seen, sir.' To me he said, 'I'm afraid my backer would not care to be revealed, even if that person decided to sell *all* of the firm, down to its very heart.' He meant his ultimate purpose as well as you, Tom.

"I said, 'I had in mind the name of Culver, Adams, and De Loach, Amos.' Mr. Culver gripped the chair until his hands were bloodless; he glared at me, then Amos. He felt the supreme test, as he surely remembered his words, 'There's nothing I would not do to prove my love for you, Harriet,' as well as his vow to be bound by those words. But he felt defeat, and he saw in the future the amused eyes of Boston as the town lifted its brows at the firm's new name—Culver, Adams, and De Loach. It was too much for him. He stalked out of the room after saying the matter was one for the directorate to decide, and one which he would vigorously oppose.

"But it never quite reached the directorate. Amos said he could pretend he had forgiven Mr. Culver and let it go at that, for my sake. But here was another obligation that outweighed that point.

"That obligation, he said, was a partnership he had promised you, Tom."

"Go on," I insisted. "Did the freight war continue? Did you give Culver his answer that week?"

"I forced Mr. Culver into a conference with the shipowners; and out of it, they met with Amos. The rates did not go up until a month later. Everyone lost money before that war ended."

"And your answer to Culver?"

"Well, the Boston papers carried big headlines before the week ended: 'BOSTON CAPTAIN INDICTED FOR SLAVE TRADING IN JAVA!' Mr. Culver found it necessary to extricate firm and ship from the cash-piece boomerang. He seemed not in the least annoyed when I suggested that we shelve the subject of marriage until our return from the Indies."

"But had he insisted on your answer, Harriet—what would you have said?"

"Tom, I have never had the slightest intention of marrying Mr. Culver."

4

The sun heaved its mighty head over the mountains next morning, cutting through the mists over bamboo thicket and casuarina grove to etch the palm lashes on the close shore. The side of the *Aladdin* seemed sprayed with some fresh lemon-yellow varnish after a lack-luster dawn.

I whistled as the hands holystoned the main deck. I felt as fresh as the morning. Harriet's assertion of last evening was responsible for my high spirits, and as I heard her say again, "I have never had the slightest intention of marrying Mr. Culver," I admitted only one regret: the ship had eyes when she said it, thereby preventing my taking her in my arms then and there.

The Radja sent his Prime Minister down-river that morning to invite Culver and his party to the palace. He promised to return for them at three. The golden schooner was punctual, and I left the *Gerrymander* in charge of Mr. Blue, who said:

"The Balinese girls, sir. What about shore leave? Whisky and bare teats don't mix, sir."

"Well, we can hide the whisky, Mr. Blue. And all hands aboard by the third watch, or I'll log any offender."

Chess had heard. He grinned, turned away from me, chanting: "I thought I heard our chief mate say, 'Give one more pull haul, then belay.'"

As I boarded the Radja's schooner, I saw Harriet, her aunt, and Culver on deck. The same patchwork sails of brilliant reds and yellows, and the batik-clad oarsmen, as well as the court official and pundit, lent the Radja's schooner royal splendor. Their striped turbans glinting in the sun, their golden earrings dangling to the collar brocade of thigh-length coats, the oarsmen pulled hard at long red oars for an upriver landfall.

The land on the north of the river grew more beautiful as we approached Mataram. I have seen land- and seascapes which dazzled an eye with grandeur and fresh originality, though there were some added color and majesty in those far-reaching pleasure gardens of the Radja of Mataram. Perhaps it was the company I kept, who marveled also at the beauty of the terraced hillsides. They seemed to slope up in gentle stairways, in shaded lavender framed in brownstone, past green lawns to other steps shadowed in indigo and purple. Beyond, temples stood carved in white against the mountains; and the sky overhead, so quiet and still, seemed to pause in tribute to a tapestry done on hillsides.

Placid pools for Balinese girls lay ahead, these and further surprises of Hindu beauty which seemed to say the reason for the terraced gardens was simply to lessen the shock in an eye to the palace grounds. As we crept along, a Sassak, the subjected Moslem race of Lombok, moved along with a woman wearing a veil; not a dozen feet away, under the shade of coconut palms, bare-breasted Balinese girls sat.

The schooner pointed more to northward, and soon her silken sails bellied; the oars relaxed and the ship gathered headway. Then Harriet cried out, "Look, Tom!" She had said "Tom" in a manner that caused Culver to jerk his fiercest eye around, that caused me an upsurge of joy.

She was looking at the Radja's red sandstone and white marble palace. It sat atop a hundred long sandstone steps stretching in a quarter circle and broken by a dozen fountains and pools, each of which lay in a frame of flowering plants beneath a Hindu statue. The edifice itself was of Hindu-Mogul style: it sat in the center of a huge terrace some three hundred feet in length, a square building with a dome at each corner, a larger one in the center, each topped with gold balls of three sizes ending in a spearhead. The dome of white marble, dazzling in the sunlight, was streaked with sheets of gold and set with agates, jaspers, and bloodstones.

We had already passed a half mile of formal gardens, in which tree, vine, and shrub had been placed in precise patterns; where the mountain streams had been captured and diverted to send fountains of water high into the air.

Harriet, impressed, said, "It's unbelievable!" Culver, unable to contain his shock, glared and said something about the insane East and its prodigality.

"The palaces in England and France are more acceptable," Harriet said. "They don't jump at you. But this!"

As we walked up the steps to the palace, a cool breeze eddied down, perfume-laden as it swept past a flowering jasmine. I turned to Harriet and smiled, realizing that only Culver was unreal in such a paradise. She answered me with a smile and some quizzical awareness of me; it flashed from her eyes, adding to my humor a renascent bliss akin to that evening in Singapore.

I knew, however, I could not stand still in a dream, for Robert

Culver was real, as I would soon learn, as real as Boll and the stadt-holder whose schemes stood up in refutation to his romantic abode. I was able to reach out almost and touch five diverse powers: Boll, Culver, the Radja, and the Dutch Government; the other was Harriet. Each claimed my attention and some measure of service, since this core of the capital of the regency was surely a mill which would grind out the fate of all of us.

"Who is this Radja of Mataram?" Harriet asked.

"The big gun of Lombok and Bali," I replied before reaching into my mind for the little I knew of the recent political history of the regency. Culver listened as I recited the facts in brief: The Balinese princes recognized Dutch authority but retained their autonomy, even as they gave up their right to refrain from claiming cargoes of wrecked ships. They agreed to suppress slavery and piracy. Native misrule had caused the Dutch to set up direct government four years earlier, in 'eighty-two. But the Radja, the most powerful prince, who dabbled in slavery, who desired another Pulo Besar, was in himself all that the Dutch sought to eliminate. He fanned wars between the princes of Bali in order to strengthen his own rule; he suppressed the Moslem Sassaks, and flaunted his disrespect of the Dutch.

I had not completed my account of the Radja's doing when Culver fell behind to assist Aunt Emily up the steps.

"Harriet," I said quickly, "the terraced gardens are beautiful in the moonlight. May I show them to you this evening—minus Aunt Emily?"

She looked at me and wrinkled up her nose in a mischievous smile. "Yes, Tom."

5

The Radja awaited us in the same room where Boll and I were received. He studied Culver closely, though when introductions were done with he said:

"You may sit with me, Miss Adams. You are most welcome." He did not take his eyes off her, nor did his hand atop the pillow move one iota; that hand was to me more indicative of his bearing than his voice.

Harriet moved to the throne with a marked assurance to paragon Boston's high caste, and she reached for its distant applause even as Culver stood glaring at her. She further irked Culver when she allowed the Radja to hold her hands and search her face with his fierce eyes.

"You are not married? Excellent. Most excellent. You are not in love?"

"Perhaps." Harriet laughed.

He scoffed, "Love, my beautiful one, is not a subject for doubt. You are in love or you are not. If your heart is open to conquest, I shall win it."

"But, Your Highness, aren't you married?"

"I have many wives, but not one of them is as lovely as you. Speak your heart, or I shall make love to you. At once!" he snapped.

"I think I am in love, Your Highness." She smiled.

"With which one of them?" he asked, pointing to Culver and me.

"Your Highness!" She laughed. "They are both listening."

His face thinned perceptibly. "Light of the stars, my palace is yours. There shall be entertainment of an unusual sort in your honor tomorrow evening."

With that he dismissed her and bowed low until she and Aunt Emily had passed through the big doorway. Then he raised his head and faced Culver. His crafty glance moved on to me.

"Be seated," he ordered, rising from the throne. "Mr. Culver of Culver and Adams," he said pensively, glancing at neither of us. "A shipowner who, I imagine, is here to punish an obstinate captain."

"Correct," Culver said.

"You will speak only when addressed," the Radja said sharply. He paced back and forth in meditative silence. "I, too, have a score to settle with your illustrious captain, Mr. Culver. But I am more interested in the future than in the past." He stopped at the far end of the huge room and faced us.

"As you know, I not only honored Captain Boll with high office; I made it possible for him to continue his trading scheme when the Dutch threatened to stop him. Why? Because I plan to use your captain. But he is slow in accepting my proposition. Very slow."

He moved closer, his energetic eyes flashing. "It would be worth much to you, Mr. Culver, if I were to relieve him of his high office, wouldn't it?"

"Yes, Your Highness," Culver replied.

"I have been thinking," the Radja said, stepping closer to us. "Now if I removed him from office, thereby letting the Dutch and you cast lots for him, he would be quick to accept my proposition."

Culver's face assumed a curious expression, though he did not ask why the prince wanted Boll.

"However," the Radja said, resuming his ambulant conversation,

"Captain Boll is a man to be admired. To toss him to you without any more reason than to speed him to a decision in my favor would be most unfair. Such behavior on my part would not be in keeping with the code of sportsmanship expected of a great radja."

I sat tense, expecting some decision already fashioned in his scheming head, one which he would unfold only after he had exonerated himself in his own mind, and ours, from any burden of blame. He faced us, his hands behind his back, and asked a simple question:

"Mr. Culver, do you possess any skill at the universal game of checkers?"

"A little," Culver replied, surprised.

"Excellent. It is only fair to tell you that I am a skillful player. I have no intention of letting you win from me." Culver seemed as perplexed as I, though he said nothing.

"However, I have lost upon occasion," the Radja said slowly. "Mr. Culver, I challenge you to a game of outdoor checkers tomorrow evening. In order to make the game interesting to the spectators as well as ourselves, we shall play for a prize—Captain Boll.

"If you win, Mr. Culver, I shall relieve Captain Boll of his office."

20 &s MOGUL CHECKERS

THE MOON STOOD STRONG IN THE EAST AT EIGHT THAT EVENING; IT flooded the peaks and valleys in a silver path to the romantic gardens of the Radja. The palace was bathed in moonlight and sharp shadows, and the gardens and statues, the fountains and terraces joined the Mogul edifice to complete a picture as unsubstantial as a dream. Soon all that was missing arrived. With Harriet, the night was indeed a dream.

As she walked toward me, her thin white dress, plain and unadorned except for a gardenia corsage, whipped about her limbs to outline her supple figure. Her hair, up on her head, let fly wisps which animated her smiling face. I held out both hands, and she came to a halt with hers extended. The night was promising.

"Beautiful, isn't it, Tom?" she sighed. "It's one of those nights that Boston couldn't believe."

I looked about in that wilderness of cultivated beauty for a spot where we could talk without any ear or eye to hear and see us, where only the ripening moon might search us out. The bend of the river beckoned, since there a mountain stream, hemmed up in a score of stair-step pools, seemed to climb the gentle hillside. We walked in silence to the still river before Harriet broke the spell.

"What sort of a person is this Kim Kim?" she asked.

"A gorgeous woman," I replied, "with the mind of a child and the heart of a tigress. She loves Boll."

"And he?"

"I don't know," I replied. "However, he did take her in his arms at the Lagoon of Lor. And that is a lot from Boll."

"Is that where you met the pirates?" I nodded. "Why not tell me all that has happened since I saw you last?"

"You mean I haven't?" I grinned.

"Only Kim Kim," she said. "And that story was too brief."

"Very well"—I grinned—"here goes. In Batavia, Boll and I went to the Javasche Bank——" I talked on, past K'ung K'ung and the purchase of Kim Kim, to Soerabaja and Boll's arrest, to Bima, Ende, the Ngada kampong, and the death of the lovely wife of the Radja of Badjawa.

As I talked, we reached the climbing pools, each of which dripped to the one below to the sounds of tinkling music. The sandstone steps took us up and up, in the shadows of flowering vine and shrub on one side, past glistening pools on the other, where blooming aquatic plants floated lazily.

I paused there, forgetting all else but her. She, too, seemed aware of the magic of gardens under a perfect evening sky. She peered into a cool, sluggish pool in the same manner she looked up to search beyond the surface of my eyes. I held her hand without showing any threat of doing more, and she merely sighed when I brushed it with my lips. She studied me for some time after that and then said, "We were in Badjawa, weren't we?"

"Were we?" Then I said, "Her name was Tana, Harriet. She died with an arrow through her." She shuddered, and I moved hurriedly into another subject. "The Gerrymander Cash was fast gaining a place in the East. We traded fast and well. Then came Amboina."

She seemed enraptured, and I clung to her cool bare arm as I helped her up each step, paying more attention to the beauty of her face and neck than to the recount of adventures incident to the cash piece. I paused and plucked a huge red hibiscus. This I placed at her ear as she looked up at me with curious interest.

I said, "You and your beauty present a problem."

"You left the Gerrymander in Ternate, Tom." She smiled.

"Let's leave it there." I sighed before picking up the story thread once more. From Ternate to Makassar, from van Kirsteen's Pride of Makassar and blackmail to the death of Captain Steele of the Stamford Raffles; from there I took her down to the Strait of Salajar on the Fire Wind to our capture by the pirates and our stay in the Lagoon of Lor.

She followed my every word with eager ears and eyes as I described the lagoon, the ceremonies, the sudden appearance of Kim Kim, the racy bidding for her between Boll and the Radja in whose gardens

we walked. The beauty of stage and the horror of the play held her
suspended between fascination and revulsion to such strong adventure; she seemed to feel the presence of something intrinsically
permanent and intractable in the unfolding scenes. With the fall of
Pulo Besar and the battle with the pirates, I raced into the wake of
the great adventure, into Boll's fame, ending my story with:

"Boll was at the height of his glory. He made a few mistakes." I
told her of his last run of the islands, of the fall of the cash, and about
the Radja's cunning.

We reached a simple little bower beside the top pool. Rustic seats
of bamboo, enclosed in a thin wall of blossoming vine, were shut out
from everything but the moon's eye, the sigh of the evening breeze,
and the murmur of falling drops of water. I sat beside her and watched
her pensive eyes as they lingered in review of my story, as they brightened under the Balinese moon over Mataram.

"So Captain Boll is hemmed in from all sides."

"He is. And now the trap is ready to close on him. Listen to this,
Harriet. Today the Radja challenged Mr. Culver to a game of Mogul
checkers." I told her all.

"It is just as well," she said. "This cash trade must end before it
causes more trouble."

"Boll won't agree, Harriet."

"No," she replied. "He won't agree. So he must go."

"Nor do I think he'll do that," I said, surprising her.

"Then Mr. Culver will force him out."

"Scandal will attend legal proceedings. Don't forget that. Culver
won't enjoy that, nor will the firm."

"Oh, he has in mind something else. He intends to beat Boll at
his own game if he meets with opposition from him."

"Hm-m," I reflected. "I would ask what, but I imagine you know
I'd go straight to Boll with it."

"Why should you?" she asked.

"Because I'm on a mission for Amos De Loach. Had you forgotten
that? And a strong Boll is all that can help me complete that mission.
Boll must win over Culver. Then, when and if that takes place, I'll
play my own little game with Boll."

She turned her face from the moon-splashed blossoms in the water
and studied me. "Would you side with Boll, Tom, if I asked you not
to?"

The perfume of her, the sight of her sitting so close to me and
wearing a tropical red flower in a moonlit garden, all were cogent

reasons why I should say, "No, if you ask it." But I did not speak those words; instead I sent a cantankerous voice to her ears loaded with the opposite:

"Why should I throw everything overboard when I'm pledged to help De Loach mend a wrong?"

"Tom, did I tell you that I've tried to convince Amos that he can gain little even if he succeeds with whatever he has in mind?"

"No, you didn't tell me that. Even if he does reverse himself there, which I doubt, it doesn't alter the situation from another angle. As you know, Culver has little use for me. And I'm not too fond of him. There's also another reason. Do you care to hear it?"

She studied me from a restful position in the reclining bamboo settee, her eyes dancing with amusement or applause as she smiled into my close face over her shoulder.

"Yes, stubborn Tom Flint."

"Then open your pretty ears. I'm not about to help Lord Culver get his selfish business done with so he can break records in getting you back to Boston and out of my life. Not I, when I'm so much in love with you it hurts!"

Her eyes widened with that, though they remained locked with mine; her lips lost their smile. "Tom," she said, "why did you have to fall in love with me?"

I glanced at the star points in her hair, dancing like the images of the moon in the deep pools of her eyes. "I didn't," I replied. "It was this heart of mine that fell in love with your picture aboard the Gerrymander."

"There's a picture of me there? I had forgotten."

I told her of my talks with the girl in the gilded frame. As I spoke, the moonbeams lent a gleam to her velvet cheek and neck that was magical. She was all that was beautiful. I lowered my eyes, afraid of the passion they released, afraid that she could not see in them a clean love for the inner woman that stepped congruously with those violent emotions evoked by her eyes and lips.

She tried to smile, though she failed. Her hand reached for mine as she frowned and lowered her eyes. I saw them raise and look at me. Her hand squeezed mine, and then she was on her feet.

"This setting!" she whispered, breathing hard. "One can almost lose all sanity here!"

I was standing also. "Or come to one's senses," I put quickly. "Harriet, even Kim Kim knows her heart. She doesn't fight it as you do. She's the smarter."

I was holding her close; my fingers at her chin tilted her face up to mine for the truth. Her eyes showed fright, fascination, and debate as they roamed my face in an effort to avoid my eyes. Her lips were loose and trembling, as if waiting for the press of mine which would scatter all debate and fear.

"Kim Kim. Is she happy?" she asked softly. Her fingers twisted a button at my collar which caught and held her eyes for a moment, and only a moment.

My arms closed tightly about her as I reached for her lips. They were as willing as mine, and I forgot scene and setting, Boll and Culver, radjas, ships, and men as her arms crept sinuously about my shoulders and neck.

There were moments of heaven, and then the dizziness of a partial descent to no less a glory as I released her lips for a meeting with her eyes. A smile, a flash from her eyes, and she lowered her head to my shoulders, as if she sought to find refuge inside me rather than reveal all of herself to my probing stare.

"You asked if Kim Kim is happy, Harriet. She follows her heart. You're learning a little about that happiness which comes with complete surrender."

"I was taught differently," she said softly. "But I like it this way."

I kissed her again.

"It's tropical," she said in a voice that seemed to encompass a mystery without trying to fathom it. "Something steals over one here."

"Is that why you kissed me, Harriet? Are you trying to say you don't love me?"

Her answer was not quick in coming, though I knew it must emerge sooner or later. I stroked her hair and cheeks for some time before tilting her chin once more. She smiled up at me with questioning eyes and asked:

"Kim Kim won't be happy if Boll returns her to the Radja, will she?"

"No."

Her voice hushed me as she said pensively: "The Radja and Boll, and Kim Kim."

Then I said, "Tom Flint and Harriet." She smiled up at me quickly, as if she were thinking the same thing. "Does that sound as good?" She nodded slowly.

"Then you do love me, don't you, Harriet?"

"Yes, Tom—since that morning in Mr. Ruscomb's office. Remember?"

I remembered, though her admission fogged off everything else in the moment. I could hardly believe that she had said, "Yes, Tom." But there she stood with the echo of those words in her eyes. I said under my breath over and over, "Lucky Tom Flint." All I could say aloud was, "Harriet."

"I tried to tell myself I didn't love you, Tom, since it wasn't and isn't the practical thing for me to do—under the circumstances. No, Tom"—she smiled—"I shouldn't have let myself fall in love with you. If it hadn't been for this night and setting, you might never have known. At least, not so soon."

"Not so soon! It's been a long time since that night in Singapore. But why shouldn't you fall in love with me? Is it the difference in your world and mine?"

"Tom Flint," she said with a little show of defiance, "you'd do justice to any Beacon Hill drawing room."

I smiled and said I wasn't so sure about that. Then I asked if she was thinking about Aunt Emily's opposition.

"No, Tom, it's nothing like that. Besides, Aunt Emily likes you."

"That's fine," I said. "But since it's customary for a man to propose to the girl he loves, I'd like to know if there is any reason why I should be an exception to the rule."

"Tom," she said, moving slowly back to her seat, "I might as well tell you. Mr. Culver and I are in accord in so far as Captain Boll is concerned. You are on the other side. I am not in favor of Amos's attempt at some hidden vengeance through you. You know this, and yet you are opposing me there too. I told Amos just what I'm about to tell you—my second trip to the East was to end all this."

"Wait! Hold on there, Harriet. What about those letters? The last one, for example. You asked me to look about for some way to serve all of us, Culver, Amos, you, and me. You said: 'I have such confidence in you that I dare ask it.' Remember?"

"Yes."

"Did you mean that?"

"Yes."

"Then why tack away from sandalwood and spice to storm?"

"Because Mr. Culver is what he is, and there is no hope of changing him. You and Amos are younger.

"You are both working against me when you persist with foolish aims. If you win, supposing you do, I will feel it more than anyone, won't I? What, Tom, does Amos really want?"

"The *Gerrymander*."

"The—*Gerrymander!* Why?"

"To paint her figurehead a bright red, he said, Harriet—and to rename her the *Robert Culver*. It's all for the last laugh in Boston."

"No!" She seemed never more surprised. "What an odd sense of revenge! But if he gets the ship, I stand to lose, Tom."

"And gain," I said quickly. "Remember, you're a big part of De Loach and Company."

"I didn't mean materially. But I don't like it, Tom Flint." She got up and faced me with unmistakable agitation in her eyes and voice. "And I won't tolerate it!"

"Why?" I put antagonistically. "Afraid you'll be exposed and embarrassed?"

"I no longer fear that," she replied militantly.

"You needn't, as long as I'm around."

"I didn't mean it that way. I meant that if exposure comes I won't care."

I sighed, "We sure got off the subject in a hurry. If I remember, I was about to propose to a lady who had just said she loved me. I wish Blossom were here."

She was quick with her reply: "Tom Flint, if you love me enough to propose to me, then you'll put aside Amos's vindictive aims and help me straighten out everything in a hurry. Amos will listen to you."

I grinned at her. "You forget I'm working for a partnership in De Loach and Company."

She said in mollifying tone, "You can turn your efforts for another man's vengeance into some aim for harmony."

Her hand reached for mine, and she smiled as before. "Tom, help me with Amos. Write to him. Tell him the attainment of his ultimate goal cannot leave you with any feeling of accomplishment. Do that and I shall see that you get your partnership."

I thought: "So it is that easy; all I've worked to bring about can be snuffed out like the flame of a candle." As I looked at her, I realized that she was worth the lost effort, and more. And yet, there was something too easy about it to engender any lasting self-satisfaction with my acceptance. I remembered Boll's words before we boarded a pirate craft to do battle at the Lagoon of Lor: "Never have I failed to complete a voyage." I felt the strength he must have known with each completed voyage.

But there was now more at stake than mere resolves and fanciful voyages.

I wanted to tell her that, if Culver lost, then I might use those cash pieces at Little Fortune Island as a lever over Boll to get the Gerrymander; I could then force Boll and Culver to cease hostilities. But I could not reveal that much.

"Harriet," I said, "I'm sorry. I can't turn back now."

There was neither shock nor resentment in her face as she studied me; a faint trace of hurt or disappointment, perhaps, but that was all. "Suppose I ordered you to do it, would you?" she asked.

"I can't, Harriet. If I did, I wouldn't be Tom Flint." I omitted purposely what I could have easily said just then: "I wouldn't be working to your advantage if I agreed with you now. Nor to anybody's advantage in the end." But I did not say that; I would gain nothing just yet by revealing my plan. I could only wait until the showdown.

I caught her hand and closed the distance between us, and when she turned away from me, I drew her close.

"No. Not now." She smiled at me and shrugged slightly. Then she turned to go. "Thanks for a wonderful evening, Tom." She moved slowly down the steps.

I watched her until she disappeared into the shadows of the palace. Then I stalked the quiet river downstream, with no objective in mind. The moon bore down with mocking rays on the glazed river and terraces at my right; the wind moved through the coconut palms in a metallic rustle that seemed more like lengthened chuckles from the mobilized elements. The tropical East, noted for turning sane and sober men into fools, rejoiced in its lazy manner over another convert.

2

The morning broke with strong winds out of the west, the first harbinger of the overdue northwest monsoon. Clouds scudded in from over the strait in huge overlapping layers, and one squall followed another. The river backed up as the seas crashed over the reefs and drove choppily in for Mataram. Coconuts and driftage bobbed up in the swirl before the palace by noon. I thought of the *Aladdin* and *Gerrymander* at the mouth of the Jangkok, realizing they were in no great danger. My sympathies went out instead to any craft caught in the strait that day, particularly in the northern approach.

The day wore on, dull and uninteresting. Harriet kept to her apartment, while Culver paced the main hall without any word to anyone.

The Radja was not seen that day, though he sent word that the checker game had been postponed until the weather cleared.

It was almost noon of the next day when the river stilled somewhat and the clouds hung motionless and undecided above us. Early in the afternoon the east winds came in gently, and the river fell back to the sea. The day steamed out for the promising night.

As the first stars popped out, three long, lonely blasts from a conch shell sounded from the village.

The Radja, sitting on the grand terrace surrounded by his guests, hurriedly got to his feet and moved off. Soon three blasts of a conch were returned from the palace roof. There is something weird and lugubrious about a conch note; it sounds coeval with the ageless islands, reminding one of the lassitude of a dispirited race long dead. There is a sharpness in the sound also, a quavering echo that seems to strike the ear when the actual sound is gone. It is native and devoid of meaning, and yet it is at the same time vibrantly alive with message. The Radja rejoined his party soon after.

I did not learn the significance of this signal until later in the evening—it was an order to loot a vessel stranded on the reef.

Harriet, her aunt, and Culver arrived, and the great outdoor dinner moved into its stride. The setting faced the moon. Sultans, radjas, and merchants sat apart from the Radja's dancing girls, the sky a roof, with colorful frescoes on the plaster walls gleaming in the lantern light on one side, the moonlit river and valley on the other. Barefoot servants served everyone where they sat. Harriet avoided me. She spoke, but to "Mr. Flint," and turned her attention to Culver.

As the dinner wore on, the Radja moved slowly, purposely, into a most interesting story. A master of suspense, he described Captain Boll as a man of much force and reserve. He told the story of Pulo Besar's downfall once again. Culver tossed cigar after cigar into a large porphyry basin, where bones and odd bits of food were thrown in hit-and-miss fashion. The Radja did not end his tale there; rather, he built interest for his most entertaining climax. He told of Boll's visit, of Culver's trip, supposedly to rid his company of an ungovernable captain, of van Kleegermarq's mission.

The Radja smiled. "Now there is the dancing girl, Kim Kim." He retraced the story, telling of his desire for her at the Lagoon of Lor. He told that story through and then connected it with events of the evening: "When Captain Boll returns he will be either my political agent or the pawn of another man. Indeed." He faced us, his energetic, clever eyes laughing.

"Since I've challenged Mr. Culver to a game of outdoor checkers, it will afford me great sport to play for the captain."

I had heard of checkers played in the Mogul manner, though I had never expected to witness the sight. A conventional checkerboard was set up between the Radja and Culver, while on a terrace some six feet below them, a huge checkerboard of black and white marble squares, each a yard wide, was lighted with torches at each corner. Soon the Radja's dancing girls were placed on this amazing duplicate board as pawns, twelve on each end, one team representing Culver's checkermen, the other team the Radja's.

The girls were dressed for the occasion. Culver's pawns wore soft, fragile white waist sarongs of silk, upon which mythical fishes were outlined in gold. Hand-tooled leather headdresses, sitting high on their heads, were splashed with lustrous seed pearls. Their necklaces and bracelets were white, and their breasts were uncovered in Balinese manner. Their shapely, tawny bodies gleamed in dancing light and shadow, as if out of some magnificent sixteenth-century dream. The Radja's twelve girls were similarly dressed, though their silk sarongs were of red and gold woven into a fiery brilliance, and their headpieces were gilded. Never had I witnessed a more colorful sight. The prosaic game of checkers had reached up under the aesthetic eye of the Radja of Mataram for a dramatization that would have excited even America's Phineas T. Barnum. And, as if to remind one that incredulities were bound up in sensation from which there was no release, the faces of the opponents were tense over the item at stake—Boll.

If Culver won, the Radja would strip Boll of title and office and throw him to the Dutch and Culver.

The Radja ordered his noblemen to see that the girls were moved from square to square in response to the play on the small board. With that, he, representing the black, moved first as the game demanded. But his finger was not lifted from the ebony disk as he turned to Harriet and said:

"You, of course, will champion one of us. Which?"

Culver, glaring at the Radja for delaying the game at the start, glanced sharply up at Harriet, who studied the board, the faces of the players, and, at last, the twenty-four girls on the marble board. Every eye and ear strained for her decision, which was not long in coming:

"Since I rebel at the thought of a human being's fate resulting from such sport, I shall champion neither of you." She did not smile as she looked squarely into the eyes of both players and then into mine.

"But," she added, "I hope you lose, Your Highness."

She had spoken for my ears, said her face: since I had refused to help her unseat Boll, then she would proceed without me.

I grinned—to show her I stood firm.

The Radja smiled as he lifted his finger. The game was in progress. A nobleman moved a red-clad girl to the corresponding position on the marble board. Culver quickly moved up a man to defending position and the Radja slid his first active man up for Culver's jump. It was taken, and the girl on the big board was led from the game. Culver's position on the board ran obliquely from the double corner on his right, leaving the Radja free to move a man down for the gain of a jump into free ground. Culver moved up for the same take, though the Radja brought up a man to save his forward position. Then Culver moved up for another jump, and in doing so he traded even with the Radja.

Each had lost two men, and the duplicate board on the terrace a corresponding number. Culver's left forward man was shoved up to the left, drawing the Radja's threat to the side of the board, which forced Culver up and behind the other's forward man. Both men played with more boldness than foresight, each reaching for the subtle variations in which the game abounds, wherein keen resource is demanded both in attack and defense.

As the game progressed, Culver, vulnerable above his double corner, aimed at the left and lost two men in rapid succession. He was forced to evacuate a position which the Radja, with the loss of two men also, opened up for his future kings. They were soon down to five men each. The terrace board emulated the smaller one.

Seated at the edge of upper terrace, sultans and radjas, the merchant princes of the Celebes and Moluccas, followed the game with enthusiasm heightened by the betting. Since all were sure the Radja would win, they wagered heavily on which of the girls representing him would stand when the game ended. There was whispered conversation among them as they exchanged remarks that had to do with the anatomy of the beauties on the big board. The Sultan of Bima liked them fat, while a prince of Flores liked them tall and thin.

A glance at the terrace below showed Culver's girls concentrated more to the left of his board, while the Radja held to his last line of defense and moved down the side with more caution than aggressiveness. Culver, while strong in a spot, stood to lose or win much when he deployed his forces, as he surely must.

In two moves the game changed—Culver earned a king to harass the rear of the Radja's attack; but the Radja leaped into the opening and raced to kingdom one jump ahead of the pursuing king. He moved out fast under a crown and eliminated Culver's helpless man in another move. Each had one king, though the Radja owned one more aspirant than Culver.

With kingship on the big board, a girl's headdress was replaced with a golden pagoda-like crown. The "kings" towered above the remaining beauties.

Soon Culver struck up his left side and hemmed three of the Radja's men while racing to kingship up the right center. The game wore on slowly; the moon climbed up in the sky one length, then two; the remaining Balinese girls stood like statues minus any sense of fatigue, like gorgeous flowers plucked and potted to squares of marble. One by one they departed from the extravagant checkerboard until only four remained, two in white, and two in red. On the smaller board they were kings, on the big one they were merely marionettes fighting for Boll's ruin and good fortune.

With Culver's move, Harriet tensed. I saw her hand move instinctively to her face and away as the threat diminished somewhat. The Radja, almost hemmed in, raced for the center of the board toward his second king. For long minutes the kings moved in and out, threatening and defending as they did so. Long intervals of thoughtful silence ensued in which neither player glanced up from the board as he sent his mind ahead of moves never made and into some perilous move, safe at the time, though costly later.

I was not at all surprised when Culver managed, more by anticipating five moves ahead than by any stroke of luck, to maneuver himself into a spot between the Radja's two kings. It was a brilliant play since only one of the Radja's men could run for a double corner.

Harriet's eyes locked with mine for an instant. They were less challenging.

Skill asserted itself, and the game was reduced to two kings for Culver against a single defender for the Radja. But here the game slowed, since it is difficult for two kings to bottle up one in the double corner. Back and forth the kings slid, and back and forth the three girls moved on the polished marble.

I felt Harriet's eyes on me again. I turned to look at her. She smiled.

Harriet startled players and guests when she interrupted the tense play. I was the most surprised of the lot when she said, "Your Highness, may I represent you on the terrace board?"

He brought a silk handkerchief to his face as he studied her. "For luck?" he asked.

"For luck," she said, flashing a smile.

As her aunt ordered her to sit, remarking, "Such scandalous conduct!" I stepped forward and escorted her to the lower terrace, asking her on the way, "Whose luck? I thought you wanted Culver to win."

She stopped and faced me. "Tom, the Miss Adams of the shipping firm does favor Mr. Culver. But she is not here tonight."

"I don't understand," I said. "Who stands in her place?"

There was no answer other than a mysterious smile as she moved to the big marble checkerboard.

She made a lovely addition to the picturesque scene, her eyes and smile dancing with a spontaneity as rare as checkers in Mogul style. She swished gracefully back and forth in the corner, as the noblemen commanded, a slave herself to the pursued Radja's racing brain. She seemed more glamorous under the tall golden headdress than her Balinese sisters of the game.

As Culver deviated from the trying routine in an effort to lure the Radja's king into the open, Harriet laughed lightly. "Careful, Your Highness."

In grim silence I echoed her words, reminding myself that she stood up, a pawn for my close future. How very important she was out there in the moon and torchlight. Aye, as important as Boll in my plans, whom she actually represented.

Two kings on the small board chased one from one double corner to the other, causing two beautiful Balinese girls to smile and leap at squares evacuated by Harriet, who returned their smiles with vigor. I saw the end, almost. Harriet seemed about to run for a middle corner off the double. I sighed heavily when I saw it was Culver's move; he had to move, and he had to release her. He did.

Then the Radja moved between Culver's kings, and one Balinese girl walked from the big board.

Harriet looked up at me and laughed. I wondered if her mind, like mine, was at the bower by the top pool. I had no time for further pensiveness, however, for checkers had reached the killing stage, wherein skill and only skill counts, with perhaps an advantage gained by some error in foresight only a moment before. I felt that Boll, wherever he was, must surely feel the tenseness of the moment.

The game could not go on forever, I realized. Nor did it. The Radja's jump had sent him in retreat toward his single corner, where four moves later Harriet stood facing the triumphant Balinese girl representing Culver who had hemmed her to end the game.

Harriet simply stood there before saying, "Tom! We've lost!" I leaped to the big checkerboard where, under the eyes of all, I took her in my arms.

"Yes, we've lost," I replied. "But why do you say we? Isn't this what you wanted?"

"It was. But one of us had to give in, Tom. And—well, you were too stubborn."

My lips were pressed to hers in another moment. I was unaware of the Radja's smile, of Aunt Emily's cry of "Harriet!" or of Culver's angry glare. It required another presence there to bring me back to the world of realities. I looked up quickly as I heard:

"Nice work, Mr. Flint."

3

Boll had returned, and in time to witness his own fresh loss. He knew nothing of the item at stake in the game, though he soon learned of it. He said to the Radja, "I'll make my report in private and get back to my ship."

"Captain Boll"—the Radja smiled—"matters of state can rest until tomorrow afternoon, at which time you will tender your formal resignation."

Boll said nothing as he eyed the Radja calmly.

"It so happens, Captain Boll, that Mr. Culver and I have just completed a most interesting game of Mogul checkers. There was an item which we played for. Seldom do I lose. It is most regrettable that I lost this evening."

"And that item?" Boll said.

"You, Captain," the Radja said easily.

Boll glanced from the Radja to Culver, then to me and Harriet. As his eyes fell on the Radja again, he said, "Go on."

The Radja got to his feet. "Perhaps at the time you hand me your resignation, you will find it most advantageous to accept another proposition which urgently awaits your decision." He smiled, bowing low.

Boll, too, smiled: he felt the pincers which the Radja used in forcing him into a game of piracy that he had not so much as considered seriously. He sharpened his expression then, a sure sign that he was aware of the increased pressure against him from every side. Culver's strength, which Boll had never discounted, had reached up for new and respected estimates with his victory at checkers. Boll could only weigh a falling cash piece against a heavy Culver; and while doing this, he could not deny the wily Radja of Mataram a timely victory also. So much for what lay uncovered. What else Boll had in mind surmounted conjecture. He said:

"So you have thrown me to the Dutch and Mr. Culver. Now your proposition offers me escape from both, doesn't it?"

Said the Radja, "You possess a sharp mind."

"I have to keep it sharp," Boll said, smiling, "since I'm forced to deal with Dutchmen, pirates, shipowners—and radjas." There was unmistakable sarcasm in his tone. "Now this idea of yours to speed my acceptance of your offer was very clever. But was it clever enough, Radja?"

A superior smile on the Radja's face was his answer. The words that followed seemed unnecessary: "So clever, Captain Boll, that the ruin of your cash-piece trade and my removing you from office could reach Dutch ears at the same time. What then?"

"Should that take place, and should Mr. Culver find it in his heart to no longer need me"—he glanced at Culver as he said it—"I would be a very slow fool if I failed to join you. But none of these things has taken place."

"They are as inevitable as the sunrise, Captain Boll. You left here to breathe life into your dying enterprise. Did you? And while you were gone, serving me less than yourself, who should appear but your shipowner? And is it not customary for a captain to bow to the will of the owner?" He smiled at all of us, very sure of himself.

Boll seemed to tire of talk. As if he had toyed with a game of sport for the sheer joy of tumbling an opponent at will, he said, "You ask a lot of questions, but only I have the answers to them. Now I'll ask a question. Do you think I trusted you any more than you did me? No. Now you want my resignation. It's too bad, since you went to a lot of trouble to make that one mistake."

"Mistake?" The Radja stiffened somewhat.

"Yes. You're as changeable as the value of the Gerrymander Cash. I've known this for some time. And since I seldom deal with whimsical men without tightening all the braces, Radja, I wrote a letter to the Governor General—not as Captain Boll, but as the respected emissary of the Radja of Mataram. I have here a copy."

The Radja, nonplused, accepted the paper and read. Boll held his quarter-deck smile and waited as the Radja hurriedly devoured its contents with frowns and a general tightening of his facial expression. "Captain Boll," he snapped, "you resort to pretense. But it will avail you——"

"Do I?" Boll put convincingly. "I posted the original letter with the owner of the Big Coffin Saloon in Soerabaja with orders for him to deliver it to the Dutch if I failed to pick it up within two weeks. The Dutch, Radja, don't like pirates."

I knew then that the letter contained the Radja's scheme to put a new Pulo Besar in the waters of the Indies.

Boll said, "Nor do the sultans and radjas sitting over there like blunderers."

The Radja's laugh was lacking in mirth or complete self-assurance. He rallied with a natural reply: "You lack proof, Captain Boll, and my word of denial would outweigh your charge with the Dutch."

Boll shrugged. "Perhaps you're right. I'm not interested in the results—any more than I'm interested in the detailed entries in my ship's deck log, which were made on this very night—following an exchange of conch blasts. A vessel on the reefs was, in violation of Dutch law, looted."

The Radja started. His eyes narrowed quickly and sent flashes surely engendered by ideas of murder running free in his crafty mind as he said, "You are beginning to annoy me, Captain."

"The schooner put up a fight," Boll said. "It was great sport to watch your men fall into the current. I wouldn't have missed it for even a game of living checkers."

"Captain Boll," the Radja voiced thoughtfully, "perhaps we should discuss the matters you have brought to my attention with some hope of settling any trivial differences."

"One thing at a time," said Boll. "I would not think of spoiling the result of your game of checkers."

"Enough!" the stadtholder of Mataram snapped. "What is your price?"

"Now that is different, Radja. But as I said, one thing at a time. I'll send Mr. Flint to see you soon with the copy of this letter, which will secure for you the original. He'll name the price." He swept Harriet and me with his eyes and let them rest on Culver.

He added with a chuckle, "He'll name a fine price, since it will be my wedding gift to him."

As the Radja bowed, Boll said to Culver, "There's nothing like a little game of checkers to sharpen a man's wits for a bigger game."

With that he turned to me and asked, before moving off, "Coming along, Mr. Flint?"

21 &ε THE SHOWDOWN

On the way to the "gerrymander," boll said to me, "mr. flint, there isn't a cheap metal in the Indies. I found an expensive alloy in Batavia, and I ordered a few hundred thousand cash pieces struck. But the old metalworker went straight to the Dutch with it. We're out of cash pieces, and we can't get any more in time to save the trade."

"Have the Dutch redeemed that one cash piece over?" I asked.

"Not yet. But when I don't appear with more of them in trade centers, they will flood the banks."

"Soon?"

"Soon." He chuckled and said, "I didn't expect this to happen, but I'd just as soon deal with Culver now as later."

"You expected it then?" I asked. "Eventually?"

He dealt me a great surprise when he replied, "I did not, though I prepared myself for it."

"How?" I was very curious then.

"You'll learn that when Lord Culver sends for me." He added, "And when he does that, Mr. Flint, you'll take Culver's picture down and wrap it nicely. On second thought, I'll reserve that pleasure for myself." He laughed as the glistening yards of the *Gerrymander* drew closer under the big moon over the Jangkok River.

"Just you and I and Mr. Wulsin will go to see Mr. Culver." When I asked why he included the old bosun, he advised that Mr. Wulsin was a partner in the cash trade also. "We're moving into a showdown, Mr. Flint."

"So I gather," I said.

"And while we're talking of a showdown, where do you stand in all this?" he asked.

"Same stand," I replied.

"So you're not ready to name your employer or purpose?" I answered negatively, causing him to ask if I favored him over Culver.

"That I do, sir," I said emphatically.

"And after that, Mr. Flint?"

"Same stand."

"You know I might be making a mistake in carrying you along in my plans after tonight."

"You might," I agreed.

"But I make few mistakes. All you could want, as I see it, is money in your own right before you marry the Adams fortune. And when the shares are divided, and when you milk the Radja, you'll have money."

I was pleased. He continued to place money above everything else. His own shortsightedness there helped cover in his mind any other motive I nursed. If he had known just what I planned to ask of the Radja, he would not have sat so securely behind his dollar-mark judgment. Nor would he have revealed his plans for the future.

"Mr. Flint, you'll get the ship ready for a voyage tomorrow. We're going to drive hell out of her soon." I turned a sharp eye on him. "To Soenda Strait," he said, "and Little Fortune Island."

I managed to cover my surprise and disappointment. I thought he had forgotten those cash pieces there, though I might have known better. I managed to ask him in calm voice:

"Why do you want to go there?"

"Cash pieces. Remember?" I remembered, and I asked what he had in mind. "A little more money, Mr. Flint, and a chance to prolong the Dutch charge of fraud. We're going to make another run of the islands. We can restore confidence with cash pieces and trade for the loose cash pieces as we do it."

I was thinking fast, hoping to outwit Boll. I said, "So we're leaving soon for Little Fortune Island—that is, if you win over Culver."

"His picture is coming down, Mr. Flint."

"You're almighty sure of yourself, aren't you? Well," I said, "I'm for you. And I'm out to get all I can, including what the Radja has to offer." I faced him then and said, "Let me have that letter, sir. Something tells me I'd better deal with that fox, the Radja, in a hurry."

The Radja granted me an audience without any waste of time. He dismissed a bevy of island girls in a huge harem and asked me to name my price. I did, causing him to stare at me with unbelief. He could not understand that any man with so wieldy an ax should want less than gold or jewels. But my request more than appealed to him, since he was convinced that through me he could strike harder at Boll, whom he now despised with a vengeance. And my request, in the form of a demand, was simply this:

He should send a swift schooner ahead of us to Little Fortune Island and raise the box of cash pieces in seven fathoms off the northeast anchorage. A light schooner could beat and fly wing and wing where a big square-rigger would be handicapped by weight. And barring reverses, the schooner, with a day's start on us, should reach that spot off the Sumatra coast ahead of our ship. There the schooner would wait with the cash pieces—if she succeeded in finding them—with a white pennant under the Dutch bars.

The Radja approved my plan. He had a schooner. The *Nautch Girl*. At anchor in the harbor of Benoa, Bali, not far away.

The day was breaking when I boarded the *Gerrymander* with a chest of treasure which the Radja had presented to me as a wedding present with a double purpose—it should serve to satisfy Boll that I had demanded money. I smiled as I gazed at the morning driving in. I could hardly wait to give the chest to Harriet and to tell her of my success of the wee hours.

Instead, I decided to visit Boll and let him see with his own eyes the price I had exacted from the wily Mataram. I did not pause to rap at the door to his quarters since the door stood ajar, and since my mind was on the *Nautch Girl*. I stopped suddenly, however.

Boll was standing beside a bed upon which Kim Kim lay. Her arms reached up to him. Boll's hair was tousled as he stood close, looking down at her. Her hand found his and drew him to her again. Then her arms were about his neck. She kissed his eyes, lips, and face with all the stored energy of a voluptuous savage. I heard her cry, her murmuring, her words of broken English, Dutch, and Malay.

As Boll's arms encircled her, I turned away unnoticed, saying to myself, "So Boll has learned that honey has the color of gold."

I moved to the deck and gazed upriver. All was still and quiet. The placid river in the make of the dawn had the appearance of sluggish wine; the valley was draped in a thin curtain of mist, and the bluing sky overhead, bleeding out of purple and orange in the east, seemed to hang in the hush of expectancy. It seemed justified.

The beauty and fierceness of a tropical morning promised a long-awaited showdown.

2

Culver sent for Boll late in the afternoon.

We boarded the gleaming sister ship at dusk. Boll carried the log and all papers pertaining to the cash-trade enterprise, as well as Culver's picture wrapped in sailcloth, while Mr. Wulsin, fortified with whisky, followed us with a piece of soft wood in hand and a whittler's disposition in mind. Mr. Cott welcomed us aboard with a leering grin.

Robert Culver met us at the cabin door. His bushy brows and sideburns bristled above a stiff collar. And, as if he were attending a board meeting in Boston, he hid his stocky frame behind a conventional frock coat. He eyed Boll and me slowly, though he was unable to reconcile Mr. Wulsin's presence to what the evening offered.

Boll erased his dubious stare with, "Mr. Wulsin is a partner in the cash trade."

The four of us were hardly seated at the captain's table when Harriet entered. "We will get down to business," Culver said when she had taken her place.

"Yes," Boll replied. "I have the full report of our venture." He followed the figures in a big ledger, recounting expenses and profits in chronological order. The ledger told the story of the adventure from the first events in Batavia: the banking of the cash-piece guarantee, the first transaction with Charlie Blink, the next with K'ung K'ung, the leasing of a warehouse, and furious buying to start the cash piece rolling. Then Cheribon and Soerabaja and the purchases of the new money by captain after captain. Figures whirled, and we felt the cash gathering headway.

Mr. Wulsin paid no heed as he sat back and whittled away. Boll went on, to Bima, Ende, and far into the Lesser Sunda Islands, trading past Ngada gold at Badjawa, moving on up across the Banda Zee to the spice islands, from Amboina to Ternate, and thence to Makassar.

"We traded and sold cash pieces, sir," Boll said. He named the total expenses from Singapore, including the striking of the coins, the ship's expenses, and the moneys posted to back the cash.

"More than one and a half million cash pieces have been put into circulation. The profit is well over three quarters of a million dollars, counting Pulo Besar's treasure."

The impressive financial report drew a flash of admiration out of

Culver's eye, though he, as the rest of us, did not lose sight of a fact: many of the cash pieces would slowly work themselves to a Dutchman's bank. But Boll had been honest to the last penny, and Culver knew this. He had included such windfalls as the Ngada gold, the treasure of Pulo Besar, both of which he could have claimed as personal shares, free from division with even the crew.

"So," Boll said, "your share is half. The remainder is mine to divide with Flint, Wulsin, and the crew."

Culver wedged in captiously, "And how many cash pieces have you on hand?"

"None," Boll replied.

"Good," Culver said. "We'll settle up and close the venture."

"But you agreed to a year," Boll reminded him, "which leaves us three months to go."

"I've made enough, Captain Boll. I'm getting out before the firm is further disgraced and the ship is confiscated. There's nothing else I can do and still save face."

"So you're breaking your part of the bargain," Boll said, simulating dejection. "I didn't think you'd do it." He turned to Harriet. "You heard him say a year, didn't you?"

"Yes," she admitted reluctantly. "But I'm afraid Mr. Culver has no choice in the matter, since the firm stands to lose what's left of its reputation."

"So," Boll said, coming back into his natural role, "I'll admit defeat on that score, since I thought you, Miss Adams, would force him to keep his part of the bargain."

He turned to Culver and snapped, "What happens to the Gerrymander?"

Culver contained his triumph under a thoughtful mask as he said, "Under the circumstances, Captain, I'm afraid I'll have to get along without your services."

Boll was patient and captious; he was forcing the play of Culver's hand down to the last card. He threw up another man for view again when he said quite sorrowfully, "This is all rather sudden, sir, considering the way I've made her pay. Now I had hopes of a better reward for my efforts in your behalf."

"I regret that your conduct won't allow it."

"No? I'm afraid I don't agree with you," Boll answered quickly. "Whatever I've done, you've sanctioned, to all appearances. Can you deny that?"

Culver replied with finality, "You're through, Captain Boll, you and your entire crew of freebooters. Mr. Cott takes over."

Boll smiled, leaned on elbows, and locked eyes with the unyielding Culver across the table. "You're a bit hasty, aren't you? You forget that two can play the game. I mean the profits haven't been divided."

"I'm not that blind or stupid, Captain," Culver said with marked asperity. "The Dutch know where you've staked out your wealth, to even the warehouse in Soerabaja, where you hid the pirate's treasure. You'll divide to the penny, all right, or you'll face more than a Dutch court." He paused for effect and went on:

"No, Captain Boll, you haven't a spar to cling to, unless it's a yard-arm to hang from. You've run out of cash pieces at a time when they alone can save you from being eaten alive by cash pieces that won't stand up to the brewing panic for another month. And the Dutch told me something——

"They won't prosecute you yet. Not until that single one over comes into the Javasche Bank to be redeemed for a guilder. And those cash pieces are trickling in, Captain Boll, trickling in, slowly but surely, from the Lesser Sundas, Ternate, Amboina, and Makassar. There's a fat Dutchman who sits there in the Batavia bank and chuckles every time another one comes in. He has the expression of a hangman."

Harriet frowned slowly as she studied Culver and his rising passion for Boll's end. Her eyes traveled mine and then lingered momentarily on Boll's face. She seemed surprised that it was that easy to rid the firm of Boll; and I joined her with rising trepidation as I heard Culver reading the riot act in no uncertain terms.

Culver exulted, "Captain, I went to Batavia to get my ship and firm out of the Dutch claws your scheming brain got us into. I succeeded up to a point." Culver got to his feet, poured whisky without offering his guests any, and walked back to the table and stood. "And that point was simply this: if I could show evidence of faith beyond lip service—by aiding the Dutch Government of the Indies in apprehending a slaveholder and swindler—you—I would be free to leave these waters with the Gerrymander, provided I agreed to keep her out of Dutch ports.

"I think I know just how I can aid the Dutch."

Boll chuckled, stretched himself, and poured drinks for Mr. Wulsin, himself, and me before saying, "Now that you've said your piece, I'll say mine."

"I'm not interested," Culver snapped.

"Oh yes, you are," Boll said, slumping lazily into place at the table. "You're very interested, you just don't know it." He laughed, eying Mr. Wulsin surreptitiously.

"Or else you're too arrogant to admit it. You're a typical shipowner, tight-fisted, complaining, willing for a crew to maim itself or die in getting your ship through with a cargo. When it's done, you stiffly acknowledge the fact, afraid you'll bend your face or lose your pocket-book if you put any warmth into your smile. You're typical, Robert Culver, except for one very fine defect in your make-up. That I put to good use.

"I owned one fourth of the *Lydia Case* when you offered me the *Robert Culver*. I sold out and took the job because I had already decided to get rich. I knew your pet hates would help me. They did, and just as I thought they would. So far I haven't missed a stay in my run for riches." He paused to chuckle before adding, "I wonder what happened to that old carver, Mr. Teale. Without his work of art, I might never have looked you up."

Culver still felt the strength of his position; he said Boll's opinion of him didn't bother him in the least, nor did Boll's ambitions interest him. He stroked a sideburn and glared. Old Wulsin looked up with his red-rimmed eyes, glanced at all of us sorrowfully, and continued to whittle away, his knife and wood hidden by the table. Harriet studied my face, and Boll smiled calmly.

"I'll tell you a little secret," Boll said. "I knew the Gerrymander Cash trade would fall sooner or later. I didn't expect it this soon. I talked to bankers and financiers, all of whom agreed that it could not live with government opposition. It would have eventually ruined the Dutch money standard. The Dutch found that out a little late for their own good.

"Only you and I and company stand to profit, Mr. Culver." He paused. Next he said, "And if we can accomplish in nine months what I thought would require a year, so much the better.

"Aye. So much the better for me."

"I don't follow you," Culver snapped.

"It's very simple." Boll smiled. "You had something I wanted, something you hated. And I heard you curse the *Gerrymander*. You said you'd make her pay, and pay. Well, I was the man to make her pay. You were greedy, and I knew it. Now your own hate and greed have caught up with you. I played for that when I started the cash. Now it's here."

"What are you talking about?" Culver asked.

"Listen. You're involved, Robert Culver. The moment I get a receipt for your share of the profits, you're involved with the Dutch. No matter what sort of deal you made with them, they can't take me and let you go. You've got something there to think about.

"You can't take half the profits without taking half the results."

There was meat on that bone, and Culver gnawed at it; his face showed as much. Boll allowed him a moment of cogitation before saying mildly, "Now if I were in your position, I'd think that over in a hurry—I'd even consider selling the *Gerrymander*."

I leaned forward with that, my expression of slow, deep surprise the same as Culver's, Harriet's, and old man Wulsin's. Boll held our eyes. He was tossing his coins, calling for his winds, and I felt the weight of what he suggested, as did Culver. That question I had pondered over for long months—how did Boll hope to take Culver's picture down?—seemed to rush forward to its answer.

Culver asked, "What are you driving at?"

"Just an idea," Boll remarked. "Just an idea. You might escape any part of the cash-piece explosion when it comes, should you, instead of handing me a receipt for several hundred thousand dollars, hand me a clean bill of sale to the *Gerrymander*."

3

Culver recovered at last and got to his feet. "What is this?" he boomed forth. He was angry now, very angry. Harriet was up on her feet also. Only old Wulsin, shaking his head dolefully as he whittled on, seemed unperturbed.

Said Boll, in answer to Culver's question, "Merely an honest captain trying to buy a ship when he could just as easily get it for nothing."

"I won't be forced into a sale," Culver retorted.

Harriet was angry. She turned to Boll and said, "You can't get away with it, not if I have to——"

"Harriet!" I said, moving to her side. As she faced me, I said in low tone, "Let them alone. If Boll wins, I think I can win over him." She studied me for some time before squeezing my hand and resuming her seat in silence.

When I turned away from her, Culver was looking at me. "Mr. Flint," he said in no uncertain terms, "you're as guilty as Captain Boll. And I won't forget that."

"Guilty?" I smiled. "Of what—except winning Harriet?"

Boll sat smiling at Culver. "It's nothing, Lord Culver," he replied, "to what you're going to hear. But where's that pat hand you dealt a moment ago? I'll remind you again that two can play this game, particularly when the dealer of the so perfect hand overlooks the value of a receipt in the other's. ·

"God protect poor shipowners," he said deprecatingly. He grew suddenly serious. "That, Mr. Culver, is what I want. The Gerry-mander in exchange for my share of earnings in the cash trade."

"And I, Captain Boll, will see you in hell first!"

"Very well," said Boll, arising. "We'll divide the gain tonight. It so happens Pulo Besar's treasure is aboard the Gerrymander instead of in the warehouse in Soerabaja. So we'll divide evenly, and you'll sign the receipt I write out. The facts in the case will make you as guilty as I." Boll smiled.

"I refuse to sign such," Culver snapped.

"Oh, you'll sign, all right," Boll replied, "or else you'll forfeit your share of the wealth, as well as find yourself the laughingstock of Boston. It will be quieter my way."

Culver knew what Boll meant. So did Harriet and I. Boll placed gain above shallow enjoyment, however, as he saw Culver losing his ship either way he turned: to the Dutch or to him. He was taking no chances in this game.

Boll got up as if to pour himself another drink. Instead, he feigned interest in Mr. Wulsin, saying, "What's that you've whittled out, bosun?"

Mr. Wulsin started. "Oh! Just a little model of an object I've sailed with for several years." He held it up for all eyes to see, smiling proudly through his yellow beard as he eyed his handiwork.

Harriet gasped, "The figurehead!" Culver leaned forward slowly and stared as if he were void of any expression for the eternity of packed seconds; only then did the full significance of Mr. Wulsin's words join with that hellish image of the Gerrymander's figurehead to flood his face with murderous intent. He arose slowly, gripping the arms of his chair with his hands, and leaned over the table.

"You! Who are you?" he asked, as if he feared the answer.

Boll answered, smiling, "Why, he's just the old bosun who's worked aboard Culver's Gerrymander for three years." He turned to the old man. "Aren't you, Mr. Wulsin?"

"Aye, sir," came the droll reply.

"And he's been a good one," Boll lied glibly, facing the irate ship-owner. "He played his part in our cash trade also. He, sir, was our mintman—he struck the Gerrymander Cash." He turned another question to our bosun. "What was your name before you picked up the odd name of Wulsin?"

"Teale, sir—Augustus Teale."

I opened my mouth to voice my amazement, though I simply sat there as dumfounded as Robert Culver. I had not been prepared for that revelation, and I stared at the useless old bosun with unbelieving eyes, even as I realized that Boll seldom joked. Then I peered at Boll the genius, Boll the Striker, who, with rapid-timed punches, had scored again. I turned my eyes on Culver. He sank slowly to his chair, not once taking his eyes off the man who had long ago caused Boston a titter at his expense, and who, through the machinations of a scheming captain, threatened to do so again. If he had possessed a gun, I'm sure he would have used it first on Boll and then on the apparition who was Mr. Teale; but he had no gun and his eyes failed to kill.

Only Boll seemed pleased. The rest of us, including the old figurehead carver, were hanging onto the tail end of a threatening drama.

Harriet seemed horrified. The longer she eyed the old bosun and his replica of the piece which had caused hate, strife, laughter, and ridicule, the more she seemed to shrink from him.

Boll spoke: "Mr. Flint, you've often asked why I carried an old sot along as bosun all these years. Well, the reason is simply this. Mr. Wulsin, or Mr. Teale, is here to tell Mr. Culver why the figurehead turned out like it did."

"Another drink, sir. Aye," said the bosun. "I'm a wee bit nervous." He was soon talking. He told of De Loach commissioning him to do Mr. Culver's likeness, of the argument with his wife over the advance payment, and of his inability to execute the piece after she had struck him with a mallet. He talked on, saying at last, "Mr. De Loach was innocent." Tears streamed down his face—a drunkard's tears. "Aye, he was innocent. By God and St. Ebenezer, he was!"

Boll smiled. He had come well prepared to deal with Culver. He had overlooked little. The last revelation served him as well as the first, in that he was able to deal out truth to destroy the cancerous germ that sustained Culver's hate of ship and De Loach.

As Culver said, "I don't believe it"—and it was apparent that he did not wish to believe it—I wondered why Boll had saved this trick.

"So you don't believe it," Boll said. "Boston will, Mr. Culver." Then he asked, "Now do we trade my way?"

Culver brought himself up sharply, by his eyes, I thought, to send concurrent flashes of malice and challenge at Boll. Then he seemed to stare at or through the *Aladdin's* bulkheads at future headlines of Boston newspapers. He said at last:

"It seems I'm licked. I'll give you my decision in the morning." When Boll said there was little use in prolonging the agony, Culver replied, "Perhaps I'm not licked yet."

Boll got to his feet lazily, grinned, and proceeded to study all of us before ripping the covering of sailcloth from Culver's portrait. Then, at a time when surprise seemed to stand up for nothing short of sluggish repetition, he restored its energy with word and deed: he took the old carver's knife and cut Culver's picture neatly out of its frame, swung the empty square over his shoulder, and said to the astonished man who had sat for the portrait:

"Now there's a promise fulfilled."

It was indeed, I realized, as he strode arrogantly to the door. The show was rushing toward its last curtain—for Culver's picture seemed down to stay.

I was up with the spectacular dawn. The indigo mantle still lay over the river, Balinese village, and palms. The southerly wind would die with the sunrise, as usual, and the calm would last until noon, but before that the surge of color in the east would sear an eye with fondu purples, reds, and flame. The lagoon seemed to yawn out of peace, a picture of lovely beauty unsullied by commerce.

The hands were busy with the morning washdown of decks. They sang, groused, and pouted, though Chess and several of the younger ones struck up laughter as they invented fresh lyrics to an old chantey:

> "O, a ship's deck is a place to dwell,
> 'Til the soojie-moojie makes it hell.
> O, a bucket o' slush on——"

Said a sailor, "A boat from the *Aladdin*, sir." I turned to see Harriet and two oarsmen.

She waved as she drew near. Closer, she said, "Since I've never been asked aboard the *Gerrymander*, Tom, I'm inviting myself." After ordering the watch to make the ship fit for a lady's presence aboard, I got into the boat with her and returned her escort. Then I pulled for the lagoon.

"Any news?" I asked casually.

"Yes. But first, let me hear that plan you have in mind." I only half heard her, I was so busy admiring her in the early morning light. She sat with her hands folded in her lap, smiling a wan little smile. It was a tired smile that suggested in its own way a long discussion after Boll and I left the *Aladdin* the night before.

The indirect rays of the sun, not yet over the distant mountains, painted her cheeks and lips in soft shades. Plans, schemes, conflict! She annulled them; or, rather, she inspired me to fight harder to put an end to them.

"Harriet, I'm not so sure my plan will work. It depends on the fox of Mataram."

"The Radja?" Her brows knit beautifully.

I told her all, slowly, from the birth of the idea of putting the cash pieces in Davy Jones's locker up for a balance of power to my recent conversation with the Radja. "The *Nautch Girl* should now be on her way to Little Fortune Island."

"So Captain Boll has his eye on Little Fortune Island also. It won't be easy for you to control that balance of power. And how are you going to use it, Tom, if you do succeed?"

"Well—nobody will get hurt too much."

"I'm glad, Tom. It's a wonderful idea."

"It's all that's left. I hope it doesn't backfire."

"And you want an unsuspecting Captain Boll at Little Fortune Island?" I nodded. She very abruptly changed the subject with, "I wonder what you'll be like when all this is behind us."

"I haven't planned that far ahead." I grinned.

"That is a poor answer to a woman in love. I expect you to rub out that set quizzical frown and devote a little time to me with nothing else in mind."

"Now that should be easy, and I'll admit looking that far into the future."

She teased: "Now had you? Are you sure your eye wasn't on a State Street office, measuring a desk, or the color of the walls?"

"Well, I might be a little guilty of such, Harriet. You wouldn't mind, would you?"

"Yes." She smiled, drew a breath of the flower-scented land air, and looked deep inside me.

My eyes were jerked pleasantly into a new emotion in the face of a fact: she admitted a small surge of jealousy where none was actually due, and the sensation of it flowed sweetly through me. The oars in that moment were hindering tools which I hauled in and let drip before I slipped into the seat beside her. Her face was soft and obedient as I drew her close and kissed her.

"Tom," she murmured. "Tom." The long lashes fell over her eyes slowly and opened slower, telling a story of sweet contentment. I could have floated on with her up to the moon and stars and remained there with never a thought of Boll or Culver.

"We're drifting," she said at last, causing me to ask how she meant it. The laugh released us from the clouds. "Tom, I've something to tell you. It's about Mr. Culver and Captain Boll.

"You asked if there was any news."

"Harriet," I scolded mildly, "you have one habit I'm going to change. The next time I hold you in my arms, I don't want any sudden talk of business."

"Tom"—she smiled—"tell that to Aunt Emily. She's looking at us —and over her glasses."

"Dear Aunt Emily," I sighed, reaching for the oars in a tardy face-saving endeavor. "Now about the business at hand." Harriet laughed, and I was soon seated where an oarsman should be. A short silence ensued, in which pleasantries were suddenly evanescent as our minds faced realities.

"There's activity on the *Gerrymander's* deck," she said. "It so happens that Mr. Culver called Captain Cott into the conference last night after you departed. Does that suggest anything to you?"

"No——"

"You remember Mr. Culver said, 'Perhaps I'm not licked yet.' Well, Tom, has it ever occurred to you that Mr. Culver, if he had those cash pieces at Little Fortune, could improve his position with the Dutch Government so much that he might save the ship and the firm and thereby score a victory over Captain Boll?"

I forgot the oars as I leaned forward in amazement. "So the old boy doesn't know when he's licked! Or maybe he isn't," I added.

"That depends on the trustworthiness of our friend the Radja," she said. "But, Tom, suppose you look at the *Aladdin* and tell me what's going on."

I did, saying at last, "She's getting ready to put out also."

"Yes, Tom, for Little Fortune Island. Mr. Culver is waiting for the noon wind."

As I rowed slowly toward the *Gerrymander*, Harriet said, "It's hard to imagine that a worthless coin holds the power of victory and defeat over the heads of its creator and sponsor."

I did not answer her, as I thought of a skull upon a pole with a Gerrymander Cash between its teeth. I soon shook off the dread feeling that stole over me and turned the subject to buoyant, living things. I said:

"It promises to be a good race. I only wish you could go with us."

She smiled out over the lagoon before flashing me a look of interest and fond anticipation. "The Gerrymander," she said, looking at her big, long hull, graceful bowsprit, and tall masts. She gleamed in the morning sun, a great thing of beauty and speed. I felt her rolling under me again, her yellow bottom showing above the foam, her bow dipping to bury her figurehead to the gammoning. Such a three-sticker under Boll's urge of sails should win easily over the quiet unassuming *Aladdin*.

And then I saw her for what she was. A feeling of resentment ran through me as I saw a cash-piece carrier, an ocean runner prostituted to island trade. She must have felt her shame as the C-A pennant at the main truck seemed obscured by a yellow cash piece. I thought of Culver's threat, "I'll carry her down as a scoundrel degrades a virtuous woman," and I saw a threat fulfilled. Perhaps that was why Culver had left her to the cash-piece trade.

Harriet said, showing that she saw the brighter side of the famous runner, "My father would have loved the Gerrymander." She flashed an admiring eye up to the big yards and added, "Our ship. Let us hope we can say that after the race." Then she said it:

"I'm going with you, Tom."

2

Later in the morning, I said to Boll, "The *Aladdin* is going to Little Fortune Island also, sir."

"I'm not too surprised, Mr. Flint. Mr. Cott has a long memory." He sent his eyes up into the rigging, grinned, and eyed the ship downstream. "We'll go see Culver. Perhaps we can learn the course he has in mind."

We came up aft of the *Aladdin*. Culver leaned on the rail, awaiting us. From the boat, Boll looked up and said, "I hear you're shaking out her canvas, sir." Culver nodded. "It's too bad you don't know when you're licked."

"Captain Boll, I'll show you who's licked. By God and a purple dolphin, I'll teach you a thing or two about putting a ship through!"

"You, or Mr. Cott?" Boll scoffed. "I'll leave you so far behind in the stream, you'll think you're becalmed. Aye, I'll feel shame at having raced a barnacle bed with a hull atop it."

"Captain Boll, you've got a long-sparred tongue. But we'll see who carries a broom at the masthead when we get there. You'll look like a

Liverpool button on the horizon, you'll be so far behind. Aye, I'll leave you hanging in the wind—for keeps!" Mr. Cott walked to Culver's side.

Boll chuckled. "I just came out to tell you about *Captain* Cott. He's damned timid with sail. He'll cut sheets while you sleep—he's a nine-knot sailor."

"Grind your own bait," Culver retorted. "You're a flash-packet Tom Pepper. But I'll make you look alive before we touch at the island."

"When you go under Java, reach deep," Boll advised.

"Aye, when I do," Culver snapped. He wasn't about to reveal his course. He came back nicely with, "And when you pass Java Bulge, Captain, stand off. Maybe I'll leave a mess boy there to wait for you with a signal—if I take the Java Sea."

"You'll be rowing this tide-walker pretty fast, won't you?" Boll asked.

Both men seemed to have forgotten the main feud; it was a seaman's duel of words then, as each expatiated upon the joys of a great race ahead. With the major premise dwarfed, the pair seemed to emerge from their ugly aims to bask in the sun like rational beings. The wholesomeness of their act seemed to prove there was some hope for them.

Culver grinned as he said, "I'll wait around a day or two for you—record-runner." He laughed with enjoyment as he added, "Captain Boll, before the wind makes in, come aboard and we'll splice the main brace and bet the proverbial hat."

I don't think I ever saw Boll show surprise more than in that moment. Culver had invited him aboard to a sociable drink before wagering the customary hat in a race between ships.

"And after that," Culver said, "I'll have something to regret—the fact that I raised a glass with a damned rogue who was once a good sailor."

"Aye." Boll smiled. "And I'll no doubt regret drinking with an old shiver-the-mizzen who never was a sailor."

A refreshing atmosphere hovered over the cabin in that short period of truce; it reminded me of yuletide conviviality as each man sheathed his claws and kept alive sailing threats as salty as the sea. Then the holiday ended, and they eyed one another as before.

3

Harriet and Aunt Emily came aboard before noon with their baggage. Aunt Emily frowned at me over her glasses as I helped her up the gangway. "Mr. Flint, you're causing all sorts of trouble," she scolded. "I doubt if Robert will associate with us after we travel on this ship. But—youth must be served."

Neither she nor Harriet had ever been aboard the *Gerrymander* since she had been fitted out. I took them on a tour of the ship, saving to the last the rich appointments of the after-quarters. Aunt Emily warmed when we moved aft; she remarked, "Everything for a lady's comfort is here. Too bad the figurehead wasn't placed on the *Aladdin*."

Harriet was soon standing before her portrait in Boll's cabin. I walked to her side and said, "That girl kept me company on our easting down. I fell in love with her then." Harriet glanced from the portrait to me, her smiling eyes questioning my sincerity. "It's the truth," I said.

Aunt Emily frowned at the picture. She was about to say something when I heard the cry from deck: "All hands on deck." It was followed by the entry of Chess.

"The *Aladdin* is making for the sea, sir!" he said.

"Good luck, Tom," Harriet whispered. There was confidence and long faith, like Kim Kim's, in her serious face when she put a hand in mine and said, "From now on, I'm leaving everything to you."

On deck, I saw the *Aladdin* shaking out her sails, her hook dripping as she eased away in a southerly wind that wasn't running true to form. Ahead of us, and blocking our run for the sea, she had to get under way first. The wind which favored her was also our wind.

I was soon aft, glancing up at the running gear. Said Boll, grinning, "Get ready to drive hell out of ship and crew, Mr. Flint. There's more than Mr. Cott aboard the *Aladdin*."

Soon I heard Boll calling for sail in lively manner. He ordered men to the rigging and to the halyard winches, barking orders right and left. The wind blew in aft and then from the port-quarter. It would hold there, it seemed, and we tacked accordingly, quivering gently forward under topgallants and royals set for the wind. The *Gerrymander* tugged forward, straining at her fetter to the tune of a creaking tophamper.

Boll leaned on the starboard rail, lost in study of the *Aladdin*, while I put a Balinese pilot at the helm and called for the lookout's alert eye. It was ticklish sailing past the reefs.

I wondered if the *Aladdin* would weigh southward on the ebb current for the Indian Ocean and a westerly run under Java, or pull north with a breeze to carry her into the Bali Zee. But the *Aladdin* had to run out past the coral heads before she could declare her hand.

The wind pennant stood out stiffly, pointing to the starboard bow, a good omen for a run up to the steady easterlies, or the hellish west monsoon already overdue. The watch, up to its ears in work, and listening for eight bells and noon, was surprised when Boll ordered the below watch out to unlimber our suit of roaring-forties canvas.

The lookout advised a spur reef ahead, and good fathoms. Port the helm it was, and easy as you go for the shoal; and then lively, lively, with sheets for a twist in the slow wake of the *Aladdin*.

The royals slatted and hung limp. A calm settled down over us; it lasted four hours. While Mr. Cott, ahead, had slipped the *Aladdin* into the three-to-four-knot current which set the ship in the south-ward drift with her rags hanging limp. Boll laughed.

We sat at the edge of the bay awaiting a wind. It seemed an eternity before the mizzen royal quivered. Soon after, the breeze eddied down out of the east-southeast and the vast ceiling of canvas came to life. But before that, the *Aladdin*, a mile out, caught the land breeze and slipped forward with a beam wind, her light sails set and pulling for the northern edge of Bali.

We were off on what promised to be a great race. A race inspired by a box of once-worthless cash pieces which stood up as virgin gold for the winner. Culver sent his great *Aladdin* reeling ahead of us in an effort to serve the Dutch and himself. It was a race to one man's victory and another's defeat, with sails ablow to Little Fortune Island.

The flood current set northward that evening, and with a lusty following wind we tore by the northern Bali coast at a good clip. The log line trailed in the spume and the *Gerrymander* rocked on for Sapoedi Strait and the Java Zee. The *Aladdin* stood ahead of us, lost in the dry winds of a black night. Not even a light showed ahead. The moon appeared late, warped, and misty, revealing low scudding clouds in a race with two American ships.

Boll did not leave the deck that night; he stood in silence, fore-casting the voyage, the thousand-mile race, taking into consideration the sails and running gear, the lines, ages, and health of both ships, the weather, and the all-important daring of the two masters. The Striker drove a ship. Whether or not the old captain of the *Barnacle*

Goose would emerge on the *Aladdin's* deck was no longer a matter of conjecture.

The crew was excited over the prospect of a race. The forecastle was awake later than usual; a fiddle sawed away discordantly inside as a few lads sang, and others played poker for small squares of tobacco. The lookout whistled softly. Kim Kim, with Harriet on the poop, laughed gaily as she repeated words both alien and fascinating to her: "Man. Man. Me. You. Him. Pretty." The over-all picture seemed to predict a sane voyage. I wondered—until I saw Boll tossing coins into the sea as he invoked the devil up out of it in a dead level tone of voice. He was praying for a real wind.

The night wore itself out.

Sapoedi Strait moved weakly toward us with the change of the daylight watch. The lookout announced land on the port bow at two bells, and the elements sighed, panted a last breath, and left us hanging in the calm. We had not sighted the *Aladdin* that morning. She was far ahead, or behind. I doubted that she had dared the dangerous short cut through Gili Jang Strait.

A fickle land breeze blew in, laughed at us, and departed, causing old Teale, alias Wulsin, to say, "One more drink and I'll get behind her and blow."

A couple of hours later the trade blew in, weak; we put every stitch of canvas on her and moved sluggishly ahead, only to meet with backing winds and gusts out of the west and northwest. But we heard the lookout's cheer: "Sail ho! Square-rigger ahead!" We had maneuvered up to within a mile of her when the wind came in from the northwest straight over the bowsprit. We could do nothing but tack, and the *Aladdin*, over our weather bow, was beating into the head wind with less success than we.

Boll was in his element; his eyes, calm and steady as his voice, could not wholly mask a sailing master's love of a race. His nimble genius seemed jerked back from schemes and cash pieces to his first love as he sounded the orders necessary to tack a square-rigged ship:

"Ready about—stations for stays." Then: "Ready. Ready. Man the weather fore and main, lee cro'jack braces." The men worked, fast. The race was then in their blood. Order after order fell from his lips. Then:

"Sheet home the fore- and mains'ls." He ordered the headsails hauled aft and then cried out in a drone, "Steady out the bowlines." She was pointing close to the wind. Too close. I saw the weather clew —the mizzen royal—shaking; and the helmsman eased her off.

We split tacks, slowly gaining on Culver's ship, as Mr. Cott pinched her, or sailed too close to the wind. She had her royals furled and her courses fast; she labored without any staysails flying. Boll carried all plain sails on the *Gerrymander*, and with the mathematical precision of a wizard, he fought to beat through the strait. We were almost caught aback in a gust, but we were ready to turn about. We did, though the *Aladdin* lost her head and missed stays, and she put us forward of her when Mr. Cott was forced to wear his ship around far behind us. We had made a fair wind of it.

Had Boll lost a life in putting the *Gerrymander* about, he would still have courted the admiration of every hard-pressed man among us. Within fifteen minutes from the "All hands!" order, she was around, her yards trimmed, her ropes coiled, bowlines hauled, and with only one watch before the mast.

Through the glass I saw Culver pacing the deck. He took over then, and the *Aladdin* let fly her kites and loosed her royals to the wind. It was now a duel between Boll and Culver, between the Striker and the legend of the *Barnacle Goose*. The first brush of it lasted all day, with both ships trying to get through the strait to the Java Zee. Culver was drawing up on us slowly at nightfall, and with the wind drawing back and freshening out of the east, both ships ran the strait under a crowd of sail.

I saw several schooners that day, and I searched for their names. Not one of them was the Radja's *Nautch Girl*.

With the sickly moon later that night, we made out the foreyard of the *Aladdin* behind us. With the first morning watch, she still sat hull under horizon, her sails misty in the weak moonlight. The wind was good that night, and with morning and squally clouds astern, we held our distance. Madoera Island was running out behind us, and the north shores of Java lay still and quiet over the port bow.

We had covered almost one third of the distance of the race, and still neither ship had gained an advantage. But the real race lay ahead, as I would soon learn.

4

Harriet invited me to breakfast with her that morning. She wore a simple dress of white. A wisp of hair curled at her forehead, and I toyed with it, laughing as it sprang back into place.

"Has our chief mate nothing more to do than play with a ship's kitten?" she asked, pouring coffee.

I grinned, sipped the brew, and exclaimed, "Little Ahab didn't make this coffee!"

"No, sailor. And you might as well develop a liking for it." Before I could reply, she asked, "Have you seen the Radja's schooner yet?"

"Harriet, you know, a woman as pretty as you should never bother with problems. However, I hope you fried my egg. Good. Now to your question, I haven't seen the *Nautch Girl*. And I hope I don't, until she stands off Little Fortune flying a white pennant under the Dutch flag—the signal that the cash pieces are ours."

Kim Kim entered. She wore her favorite cloth fashioned into a brief sarong. Aunt Emily would have called it scandalous. I was beginning to wonder if her daring exposure of waist, limbs, and bosom was due entirely to artlessness and setting. By all standards, she was the naïve island girl. And yet she was woman. As I glanced at a gold pin at the divide of her breast, I realized that she had purposely used it to hold the silk as low as possible.

Harriet studied her also, even as I glanced her way, as I placed her in Kim Kim's dress in my mind's eye. The picture I saw was pleasing.

Kim Kim admired the pearl buttons and the lace trim of Harriet's dress. "Pret-ty," she said. Then she pointed to me. "Him? Him." Excited, she added, "Him—you—man?"

Harriet laughed and humored her. "Yes. Him mine."

As she took her place at the table, Boll entered. He eyed us, removing his cap and oilskins, and took a seat next to Harriet.

"Culver's driving hard," he said, looking at Harriet. Then he yelled, "Cookie! Skoff it up and make lively!" He turned to Harriet again. "It would be poor sport to run away from Mr. Cott."

"Are you sure of running away from Mr. Culver?" she asked, pouring his coffee.

He leaned toward her, frowning. "I've been wondering just which side you're on."

Harriet glanced up at him. "Can there be any doubt?"

"To me, yes. You stand to lose a ship. This ship. That makes sense, doesn't it?"

"In a way—yes."

"Maybe Mr. Flint has won you over to our side."

"Here I am, Captain Boll." She smiled from him to me.

"I don't understand it. Now you could be the one he's working for. No—no, that doesn't add up." He shrugged it off, grinned, and said, "Mr. Flint, you're getting a prize here."

Harriet said, "I'm not so sure. He hasn't complimented my coffee yet."

As Boll said, "Yes, a prize, Mr. Flint," Kim Kim's eyes leaped curiously from Boll to Harriet, and back again helplessly. The conversation was but a jumble of words to her.

"And ask her someday, Mr. Flint, how we met." He took Harriet's hand in his. "And you didn't forget me, did you, Miss Adams? It was really you who placed me in command of this ship, wasn't it?"

"Perhaps. I merely repeated what you said—the ship was built for speed and slowed with wood spars and hemp."

Kim Kim saw only Boll holding Harriet's hand. Her spontaneity gone; she seemed both childishly sullen and jealously alert. Her hand at the divide of her breast was nervous. Used to Boll's ways, I thought nothing of his play; but Kim Kim, whom I had seen pull Boll down to her lips in passion, viewed a threat.

Boll said, "That's right, Miss Adams. Now let me tell you something: if it hadn't been for you, I wouldn't have offered Lord Culver any part of my shares for this ship. I'd have taken her."

"Thanks, Captain Boll." She flashed a smile my way.

"You're welcome. You're worth it." He took her hand in both of his then and said, "Now I'm driving this ship to save everything I've gained."

"Yes?"

He leaned closer to her. "Will you wish me luck?"

Before Harriet could answer, Kim Kim was up. She put herself between Boll and Harriet and said fiercely, "Him—my man!"

Harriet looked up at her, smiling. Her hand caught Kim Kim's as she said, "Yes, Kim Kim. Him your man."

Boll merely looked on. I was glad when he took Kim Kim's other hand. Confused, she glanced from Boll to Harriet, her fear abating somewhat. "Him my man," she repeated. Then her face gradually assumed a smile.

"Him—Tom—you man."

"Yes, Kim Kim. Me—Tom. You—him."

"Yes. We have man. You pret-ty man. Me pret-ty man." She seemed satisfied, and suddenly pleased that she possessed something in common with her occidental sister: love placed them on equal footing.

5

On deck later, I saw the clouds astern had thickened; and the *Aladdin*'s sails, now creeping up on us, were silhouetted in gray against the advancing storm.

The glass was falling. It had dropped from 30 to 29.40.

Our royals were set and pulling. Behind, I saw the *Aladdin's* royals come in. Soon her trim down to topsails advised that she expected big weather. I decided to hold to topgallants. The royals were in, and we were battened down when the first gust hit hard, backed, and left us in a becalmed suspense. Beyond the *Aladdin*, I saw the horizon closing in in a wall of slanting gray, dipping out of the black cloud like the fin of some monster. I counted off the seconds, waiting for the *Aladdin's* shudder, noticing the waves chop up with white crests behind her. The sea was all confused.

The wind bore down on us just as the cloud dumped its ballast atop the *Aladdin*. She paused, then staggered, leaned forward and to the sides, spinning her mastheads about in vicious arcs. Then the sea leaped up at her from behind. Moments later the same weather paid call on the waiting *Gerrymander*.

Harriet, in oilskins, stood with me when it struck. The leaping seas and the scream of the wind in the rigging evoked excited pleasure in her face. She was then a true daughter of Dean Adams, Master Mariner.

There was wind for all, enough to warrant the mizzen relieved of all sail. It blew out of a moderate gale into fresh gale in a matter of minutes. The ship went through her antics, rocking and straining forward like a thoroughbred, her yards squared to catch power; all kites were in. But there was too much canvas aloft for the foresail to hold her up; she plowed under a sea and came up with a green sea rolling a yard high down the deck. Before the tophamper could be relieved, the main topgallant blew; it thundered above us like a Gatling gun. Ahead and alee, the horizon ended at the bows; and astern, there was no ship in sight, nothing but a gray wet world that hid even our wake.

We clipped off fifteen knots all that day, our world a mass of spray, rain aslant, and seas on deck. The sea growled up behind us, ran the length of the ship, and tossed at us from port and starboard.

That evening Boll called for sail that was better left furled. All that night we sailed down longitude, from one hundred ten degrees, driving hard for one hundred six and Soenda Strait. Boll's mariner's mind effected a balance of push and the *Gerrymander* rode higher, skimming off the top of the waves. He ordered the course altered a point to the south, hoping to trick Culver, who, when we had last seen his ship, was holding up for a safe free run around the Java Bulge. The wind held aft, and we scudded on.

Before morning the wind blew into a whole gale, and the life lines were up on deck. But Boll, dripping like the sails, stood grinning. "We'll take in no sail, Mr. Flint."

It remained for the gale to trim sail for us—it obliged by carrying away a main-topsail. To counteract this loss, we were forced to slow her. The great foresail was reefed and she was reined down at last. We would drive on, Boll said, with a new sail where any blew "damn quick on the yard."

Morning and daylight, weary bones, wet skins, and stubble on faces under red eyes. But no one complained. The sky was mast high and hanging less than the ship's length in any direction.

At seven o'clock the helmsman was about to sound six bells. Then all of a sudden the bell clanged like a demon gone out of its head; a cry went up, and all eyes followed a pointing finger. I shall never forget that sight:

The *Aladdin* had emerged from that pall of mist, half her length behind it, her bowsprit raking unbelievably at our stern. She was driving head on, advancing inch by inch until her jib boom seemed sure to tangle with our spanker, or crack over our stern rail with the next trough. And what held that boom off, scant inches away from severe tophamper loss to the following ship, I shall never know.

She was saved by our bell and not by her drowsy lookout. She cried and moaned as her helmsman jerked her off. But on she came, obliquely off our starboard, gaining an inch a minute, and holding close to us, too close, not fifty feet away, and tearing through at a clip that caused even Boll to voice surprise.

Boll ordered sail crowded on the *Gerrymander*, one after another, and still the *Aladdin* rocked, tossed, and split the sea with her bobbing cutwater until she sailed even with us. We could scan her deck by that time, and we felt the spirit of the old school of mariners when we saw Culver, water running down his face and sopping Boston business suit, standing the poop and shouting orders at the top of his voice. Mr. Cott ran about like the second aboard, while the roaring voice of the captain of the old *Barnacle Goose* reached our ears with:

"Set t'gallants'ls, and look alive! Lively there!"

Then he walked to the rail, faced Boll and me, his wet fingers raking the water off his uncovered head before separating wet collar from wet neck. Cupping his hands, he cried out:

"Where's your sails, Captain Boll?" He laughed. "By God and a purple dolphin, I'll send you oars when I reach the strait!"

She seared close to us, her colors snapping forward. She dipped her ensign and we returned the courtesy. The *Aladdin* moved obliquely off from us, though still ahead, with Culver far aft and laughing at us.

6

Sail after sail was run up. We tried for the Striker's maximum speed. We hit squall after squall, or rather they bounced up behind us, dumping ballast aboard for a blend with the gnashing gray waves which found a great joy in leaping aboard. In some seas the wheel was too heavy for one man, and in others the poop seemed level with the streaked seas about us. The glass reading was 29. The wind tore through the rigging and the *Gerrymander* drove on, but never ahead of Culver's *Aladdin*. The elements wept about us all day, clearing for intervals in which we saw the ghost of a *Barnacle Goose* we could not leave behind us. Perhaps we would never get ahead of her—it was said the *Gerrymander* carried the wheel and bell of the *Goose*; if so, our ship would not betray the Culver of old.

It was neck and neck all that day, with backing winds, with Culver pulling away from us a point to the north as we approached the northward thrust of the Java shore. Boll chuckled, holding down in that wet close horizon to west-north, bringing up a threat of the northernmost projection of Java ahead. Late in the afternoon, when the storm showed signs of blowing itself out, the *Aladdin* lay over our starboard quarter, head over horizon.

Then I saw it, another set of sails ahead of us. Before darkness fell over ships and sea I made her out through the glass. My hopes sank as I sounded her name:

"The *Nautch Girl*."

7

I told Harriet what I had seen. She held my eyes for some time before asking if I knew of some way to slow Boll.

"Aye!" I exclaimed. "But who will hold Culver?" There was no answer. "By the Lord, he's a better seaman than I thought, Harriet! Even Boll is surprised."

We consulted the chart and read: *Sedulang Reefs, 6° 07′ S., 107° 35′ E., outermost reef four miles from coast; dangerous, covered by two fathoms of water. At nine fathoms vessels will then be two miles off the reefs.*

I called the leadsman, and Boll smiled. "The southern danger is worth the few miles we'll gain on Culver." He took it, and we held to it until the leadsman chanted out ten fathoms; only then did Boll order the ship a point to the north. Even then we scraped at midnight, causing a round of shudders and stomachs leaping up for throats. But the two and a half miles saved at the risk of ship and lives put us into Soenda Strait ahead of Culver, who had circled far to the north.

Boll was Boll, and there was no end to his luck.

The *Gerrymander*, leading at sunrise of the next day by virtue of temerity versus rules of safety in the stream, slipped into the southwest set of the current of Soenda Strait for a morning of calms and variable winds at the edge of the Indian Ocean. It was only then that Culver gained back all but a mile of his loss.

The outcome of the race seemed to rest in the hands of the elements. The blustering winds of the Indian Ocean struck at about sunset. We were forced to beat against head winds and a northeast set of the current. We made little or no progress until midnight. Then we saw Culver slipping up on us, close-hauled and pulling southward. We stood about even once again, though a land wind out of the northeast would have favored us.

Boll held to his position, letting Culver drift out of sight; then he stood the poop with coins in hand and talked the devil up out of the sea: "A wind, Lucifer! A wind from Java!" For nearly an hour he kept at it, with Kim Kim asleep at his feet.

On deck for the first time in days, Aunt Emily pointed to Boll. "What on earth is that madcap doing now?"

I had no answer that she could understand.

Boll had slept little since Mataram, and he had departed from the deck only after freezing the halyards. He had almost worn out the crew and himself, though he stood fresh in strong contrast to the weary hands on the main deck. Several lads, washed into the scuppers, squatted like bedraggled pups, and Little Ahab allowed his chin to hang limp; Mr. Blue, a lesser Boll, was merely his calm, enigmatic self; and Mr. Wulsin, who was more the worthless bosun than Mr. Teale the carver, did little more than drink and whittle. Boll continued to feed the devil coins and words; and everyone waited, tense and expectant, afraid of the wind he might get, and still afraid he wouldn't get it.

All that night I watched in every direction, hoping to see the *Nautch Girl* slipping by west of us. But I did not see the schooner.

The east wind did not come, though the westerly backed down as if the devil stroked its mane. The current obeyed the breath of the monsoon and we beat slowly westward, while Culver, miles south of us, began working to the southwest. With daylight, the *Aladdin* was all but royals under in her reach for southing.

There we were, off Java Head, not more than seventy-five miles from Little Fortune, and yet long hours away from our goal. Here was one of the disadvantages of sail: sometimes you sail due north for southing and touch port coming in from the west or east.

To Boll—he had an anxious look on his face—I said, "If we don't make southing, Culver will sweep into the bay from the west by midnight."

"I am thinking of southing and more," he replied, ordering me to put her starboard tacks aboard and reach for southing.

We chased Culver all that day, gaining slowly. The *Gerrymander* worked very close to the eye of the wind, a trait which not all ships possess. Boll took the wheel, eying the weather clew up in the mizzen. Our wind pennant had blown. When it shook, he did not ease her off in a hurry; he played with the wheel. He had that fine sense of balance, so sensitive and keen that few seamen can ever attain it without spending a lifetime aboard a given vessel; and he used it, edging in closer and closer to the teeth of the wind. His maneuver forced Culver to do likewise or else reach for such southing that he could never hope to win when he attained his westing.

We sailed in sight of each other all that day, the *Gerrymander* pulling ahead and more to westward, while Culver was forced farther south to attain less westing. By nightfall Culver was out of sight.

The wind, however, backed down and hauled in from the southwest. Then it puffed out, leaving us in a calm. The wind did not die to the south of us, since only a good wind could have brought the *Aladdin* roaring up close to us.

Boll cursed.

With the make of the wind out of the west-southwest, Culver sat trimmed for it. Forced to haul the yards ourselves, we saw him take that quartering wind, his port tacks set, and leap toward us.

We put the ship on the port tack in record time. Boll amazed me with his order then: "Close in ahead of Culver on the leeward side."

"Helm up!" The *Gerrymander* and the *Aladdin* converged slightly, gradually closing in. It is difficult to imagine two captains allowing such risk of collision, though the bows were drawing in to where they would soon meet. They were no more than fifty yards apart when Boll cried, "Weather ship keep out!"

Boll voiced a rule of the stream applying to two ships close-hauled on the same tack. There was confusion aboard the *Aladdin*, and yet there was no action which should set her off her course. Soon, from the sister ship, Culver's voice rang out:

"Ahoy! We're holding our course and speed!"

"So are we!" Boll cried. He turned to me and said, "I never thought I'd have to win a race this way."

"What are you up to, sir?" I asked.

"Watch me." To the helmsman, he said, "Put her head across the *Aladdin*'s course. Easy. Easy as you go."

In the black of night our red running light was drawing ahead of Culver's green. We were within fifty feet of the *Aladdin*, and still closing in. If confusion reigned aboard the *Aladdin*, so did our disciplined crew gape and utter protests. Our poop was even with the other's bow, and still no more than fifty feet held us apart. The *Aladdin*'s jib boom was pointing then straight at our foremast, and with the distance closing in fast. I saw Boll's strategy:

He was forcing Culver into one of two measures to protect his ship: too close to heave to with sails set, he could only cut all sheets and let fly the driving sails or come on and risk his bowsprit, and the tophamper with it. There was no chance to run her off then, as Culver hurried his decision. But before he ordered the sheets cut, Mr. Cott had started cutting away.

Boll chuckled. "I knew Mr. Cott would beat him to a decision there."

The ship behind us ran off in a hurry and lay helpless. She could not repair her sheets soon enough to take her place as a contender. As we moved away, Boll drew the first round of applause from the crew.

Though he had resorted to extreme measures in winning the race, not one of the crew could deny him the true appellation he had earned over the years—the Striker.

We left the *Aladdin* there as we straightened her and hauled on north by west, rocking under the press of canvas like an express to the Bay of Balimbing. Far behind us, the *Aladdin*'s red light winked off and on with the motion of the wave tops.

We anchored off Little Fortune in the night. As the island danced into my eyes at dawn, I searched for a sign of the Radja's *Nautch Girl*. It was not there.

23 ❧ A PROMISE FULFILLED

LITTLE FORTUNE ISLAND WAS LOW, WOODED, AND LESS THAN A MILE long; it burned green and palm-fringed in the sun. A few miles north of the island, the wall of jungle on the Sumatra mainland rose slowly up out of deserted sea and thin line of beach and rolled away to the distant mountains.

As we worked up to the northeast anchorage, our leadsman droned out the fathoms, "Ten, nine and a half!"

Boll looked pleased. "In seven fathoms at anchorage. So who wins, Mr. Flint?" He laughed.

I said nothing as I screwed my face into a thin, tight mask and waited, wishing for long eyes to search the waters on the island's other side for the Radja's schooner.

Boll moved forward, yelling, "Careful where the hook falls!"

I remembered, as if it had been only yesterday, our first and only visit here. We had slipped into the Bay of Balimbing with the night wind abeam, Boll at the wheel, a frustrated group of mutineers on the main deck. I heard Boll talking his wind down to our sails as we sat for favorable weather to a run up through Soenda Strait. He called the wind down to the royals. I remembered looking at an unlit corner of a forgotten world, where the anchor had no sooner dropped than the crew, seeking some subtle vengeance, dumped the box of cash pieces overboard. And now—that same box in Boll's possession meant that he would own the *Gerrymander* at his own terms; that Culver would be the final loser in his battle with Boll; that Boll could stretch the yellow pieces over the Indies and thereby stave off ruin for a time. The same box, in Culver's hands, meant that Culver could dump that extra, all-important cash piece over Boll's guarantee into the hands of the Dutch, thereby finishing Boll once and for all.

And did that box lay close to the Gerrymander's keel? The balance of power I needed might still be there. I looked up again; the Nautch Girl was not in sight.

Then I looked at Boll, scarcely able to believe that he had blown the Gerrymander Cash into a monster bubble that controlled even his own fortune or doom. In all brevity, Boll was great; in reflection one could only ask, how great? The answer seemed to haunt me, since only I might hope to stand in his way now.

The Gerrymander eased to a gentle stop, and the anchor slipped with a rattle of chain and a splash.

The Gerrymander squatted, panting almost after her great run. She responded to a strong hand, did that lady. She was all a mariner could ask for, an obedient slave prostituted for gain by an owner who hated her every beam, spar, and plank. But Boll knew her moods, and he knew Kim Kim's. She seemed a twin to Kim Kim.

Boll searched the horizon for the Aladdin, grinned at the empty line where earth was sewn to sky. The wind, from the southeast, was holding Culver back. Boll ordered a glass-bottom boat over the side, and cables, hooks, and a windlass made ready. He was sure of finding that box of cash pieces, while I stood there, afraid that he might do just that. I debated upon the advisability of letting Boll go down and find out if the box lay there.

I had little time in which to arrive at a very important decision, I realized. He continued to check the gear, with always one eye out on the restless Indian Ocean. As I watched him closely, I kept saying to myself, "The Nautch Girl has had ample time to retrieve the box." The thought persisted, though it was freighted with contrary questions: had the Radja's divers, if they had beat us to the spot, been able to find the box; had they been able to hoist it?

Harriet stood by, silent, watchful, and waiting. Aunt Emily moved close and asked if this was some wake. Kim Kim paraded the deck in one of Harriet's dresses. Then Harriet said, "If the Radja failed you, Tom, what are you going to do?"

"Take matters in my own hands," I replied firmly. "Boll must not get possession of that box."

"I'm so anxious for all this to end," she said in a tired voice.

"It won't be long now," I answered. "This has to be the end."

I checked the weather again. The wind drove choppy surfaces across the bay. A schooner might seek the leeward side of the island. I glanced slowly at the dancing coconut fronds and drew a picture of the island. And unless the schooner lay just around the promontory ahead of us, she was nowhere near the island.

"Sir," I said to Boll, "hadn't you better check the other shore—for a Dutch gunboat?" His reply was a laugh followed by, "Mr. Flint, you remind me of Mr. Cott. This is no time to cut sheets."

"No," I reflected as he stood ready to go over the side. "This is no time to cut sheets." My time was up, and I resorted to bluff as I said:

"There's nothing down there, sir."

He straightened up and eyed me. "No?"

"No."

"You're tardy with your information, Mr. Flint." He stood with hands on hips as he studied me intently. "Why, if this is not some foolish joke?"

"Go on," I bluffed, "and learn whether or not I joke." He advanced slowly, trying to put the finger of his mind on what was happening here. He reminded me that he had not forgotten the bowline-bridle incident, to which I replied, "Nor have I forgotten that crack on the chin, sir. But that's a small matter."

The crew to a man, except the lookout, stared inanely; and the man at the masthead cried out: "Schooner coming in from around the island!"

"Name her colors," I ordered, hope leaping up inside me.

"Dutch, sir. She's flying a white pennant under the flag."

I faced Boll. "I repeat, there's nothing down there. That schooner carries the cash pieces, sir—for Tom Flint."

Boll faced me, his face as calm as before. He said at last, "I'll look first. Then, if you're right, maybe we'd better go below and talk this over, Mr. Flint."

2

I went to Boll's cabin after making sure the Radja's schooner would stand by, well armed. Boll awaited me, anxious, though he masked his alert mind with the usual calm so typical of the Striker.

I took my place at the table and accepted the drink he proffered. "We've spliced the main braces many a time, Mr. Flint," he said affably. "We'll do it again." We drank together before he asked, "What's this all about?"

"Let's start at the beginning," I said. Thereupon I told him of my desire to own the *Gerrymander*, of my plans during the Kim Kim hearing, of my failure there to my deal with the Radja. He listened without any change of expression other than that of a rapid absorption. I omitted De Loach's part in the affair as well as Harriet's position in De Loach and Company.

My story came to an abrupt end with, "That's why I wanted you to beat Culver."

Boll smiled. He had not once removed his slitted eyes from my face. "So you want the ship. Somebody else is in this, Mr. Flint. Who?"

"I said I wanted the Gerrymander, didn't I?"

"Now that," he said slowly, "is all very interesting. But it doesn't all fit together, Mr. Flint. You are about to marry the biggest stockholder in the firm of Culver and Adams. And yet," he said slowly, "you're trying to steal her best-paying ship. It doesn't make sense."

"Maybe I'm trying to save it for her."

"And Culver?" he drove back at me.

"No," I answered stoutly.

"Then you had better talk," he said.

"I'm sorry I can't reveal more just now. Only Harriet can do that."

"Mr. Flint, you'd better send for her. I'm sure you realize that I am in an excellent position to destroy all you've done. I can trade with Culver where you can't; and if I so desire, I can let him keep the Gerrymander."

"In that case," I said, "I might be forced to work with Culver and the Dutch. As you know, a box of cash pieces could hardly fail to whet a Dutch mind into a trading proposition."

Boll was quick with a truth: "But you, tied to somebody else, could hardly work with Culver. No, Mr. Flint, you could not. So one fact remains: Captain John Boll isn't licked."

"I came here, sir, aware that you could reverse your position with Culver if you so desired. And I would not have declared myself had I been minus the lever with which to guarantee your actions."

"It seems you don't know me, Mr. Flint."

I studied him closely. I had every reason to respect his agility of mind. I weighed carefully every aspect of the case, sending my mind out in search of any and every possible advantage which he could put to good use, and fetching my mind back with a feeling of complete security in my position. And, I may add, I did this with all the caution of reasoning that any man, knowing the Striker as I did, would surely employ in dealing with undisclosed possibilities in this very urgent game. There was to my advantage the element of surprise, wherein

Boll, who had not so much as suspected me of crossing him in the final play, was sorely put to deal with me. He would try, however.

"Sir," I said, "I may not know you, but I know this case. I'll give you this much to think about—you can't work with Culver and find yourself any better off than before you took his picture out of the frame. While I can take a lot of cash pieces to the Dutch, or dump them one by one into the sea."

Boll was up on his feet. "Now perhaps we'd better come to some terms, Mr. Flint. Sit down, and let us——"

Just then we heard a cry from the deck: "*Aladdin!* Coming in fast!"

3

I raced to the deck, Boll staring after me. The *Aladdin* was drawing close. She leaned to the wind a mile out, taking in her canvas as she came. Soon she sat close by, her anchor cable playing out. Mr. Cott stood at Culver's side at the rail, his face set in a leer. It was Culver who drew my attention, however. He was not the picture of the Culver I had seen last. He stood bare to the waist, his hard, ruddy face fierce under a battered sea cap. Harriet and Aunt Emily could hardly believe their eyes. He tossed a cigar over the rail and barked:

"Where's Captain Boll?"

"Below, sir—waiting for you."

"Where are the cash pieces?" he demanded gruffly.

"That, sir, is a foolish question, since we arrived here first." He nodded then and asked about the schooner standing off a little distance from us. "She's got something to do with all this," I replied. "She flies a Dutch flag."

"Too bad she's not a gunboat," he wished aloud.

A tense, awkward silence hung over both ships as every eye and ear aboard them studied both Culver and me with expectancy. Harriet and Aunt Emily were not exceptions. I broke the quiet over Balimbing Bay, jerking all eyes my way again, as I said:

"We'll be waiting for you in Captain Boll's cabin, sir."

"I'll never set foot on that—that ship!" His voice was stripped of all expression; rather, it seemed the very quintessence of malice.

"Suit yourself." I spread my hands wide. I felt his eyes darting tongues of fire from a crusty face. Then I sounded the order to stand by and raise the anchor.

"Wait!" Culver said equivocally. I did. He was soon crossing over, glaring at the ship he hated; and his hate was a hot and driving thing, a part of him he would never lose; a scar on his soul, if he had a soul left. Harriet, at my side, studied the paradox, a bare-breasted Culver, a stranger—the physical embodiment of the captain of the *Barnacle Goose*. She frowned and looked to me for some assurance that everything would be all right in this wayward, inconstant world of events.

We moved directly to Boll's quarters. He sat there, the same lord and master, who, by his expression, seemed to say he could rise up and brush aside all obstacles before him at will. And I wasn't so sure that he would not do just that. He grinned enigmatically at me, then at Culver, who, against his will, studied the finished quarters of the ship for the first time, hating himself, Boll, and me, I am sure, for bearing witness to his appraisal. I took a chair next to Harriet and waited for the crux.

Culver turned on Boll suddenly. He proceeded to voice his opinion in no uncertain terms of the other's racing tactics. Boll reminded him that the race had ended yesterday, that today was a new day, one he would long remember.

Boll was assuming the initiative, which suited me perfectly. It was necessary that Boll should uncover whatever he had in mind. He was not long in doing just that in his own inimitable style.

He said to Culver, "Sir, I was a bit rough with you in the race. My humble apologies. Now I have been thinking also, sir, that perhaps I was a bit hasty in my efforts to force you to turn the *Gerrymander* over to me. You've been a good partner. You took chances along with me."

I was not alone in assuming a tense expression. Harriet's face was sharpened with suspense, as was Aunt Emily's, Culver's, and mine.

Boll moved on, slowly, carefully: "Of course, there are risks ahead, sir. I refer to our joint guilt of a Dutch-trumped charge of fraud ahead of us. But we can weather that, I am sure."

He grinned at Culver, whose expression was slowly undergoing a change. Hope and doubt, another surge of both, showed in Culver's face. These were joined by open suspicion.

"How can we weather that charge?" Culver asked.

Boll smiled. "We'll make them cut sheets, sir." His temerity here, a reminder of how he had won the race, provoked Culver into a sort of growling respect for the Striker's lack of unction.

He snapped, "Yes," in a semisatisfied manner before asking, "How?"

Boll replied, "A good sailor doesn't tack ahead of the weather." He left it there to stand in his favor as he went on: "We can make the

Gerrymander pay. Under me, we can drive her from Boston to the Orient and back faster and with more cargo than any three-sticker afloat. Can you deny that, sir?"

"No," Culver admitted grudgingly. "But what are you driving at?"

"Just this," Boll said. "Instead of taking the ship, as I can do, I'll be satisfied to own her jointly with you—half and half, sir."

Harriet spoke up: "I'm not interested." I nudged her, frowning. I wanted Boll's hand to unfold completely before I had my say.

Culver weighed Boll's proposition as he asked, "What about the cash-trade profits—do you wish to buy a half interest in the ship with your share?"

"No," Boll replied. "We'll split the profits."

Culver reddened perceptibly. "Why, this is not as good a proposition as your last one, in which you offered to relinquish your share for the ship!"

"No"—Boll smiled—"not for the present, perhaps. But in time, yes." He paused, then said, "And in another view, Mr. Culver, it's a much better proposition than before."

"How?" He eyed Boll sharply, as if he doubted the Striker's sanity. "In what way?"

"Don't forget, sir, that we must face the Dutch in this together, no matter the outcome. First, you must make up your mind to do this. You are no coward. Not the captain of the *Barnacle Goose*; not the man who drove the *Aladdin*."

It was only then that I saw Boll's hole card: he was feeding Culver with rich servings of their collective invincibility in a bid for Culver's agreement on that one score. And with Culver's nod, those cash pieces I held as a threat over both Boll and Culver might become instantly worthless to De Loach and me. I started. Boll smiled my way, and then he drove hard at me as he said easily:

"Mr. Culver, on second thought, I'll even up the proposition— I'll turn over half of my net share of the cash-piece profits to you for a half interest in the ship."

I grinned angrily as I realized that Boll had shortened his offer at first in order to lengthen it at just the right moment.

Culver was weakening. It was time for me to step in.

"Mr. Culver," I said, "why don't you ask Captain Boll why he is less hoggish with you than at your last meeting? You must know by now that the Striker never makes concessions without good reasons."

"I've been weighing that point," he replied. Then he faced me, somewhat surprised. "Are you and Captain Boll at odds?"

"Slightly," I replied, ahead of Boll, who said:

"Mr. Flint is working against both of us. And, sir, so will everyone until we unite and crush all opposition."

Said Culver, "And just what is your position, Mr. Flint?" He spoke to a lowly second mate, though I opened his eyes when I said:

"I own the box of cash pieces, sir."

"You!" He was on his feet, staring from me to Boll.

Soon his face showed a little smile of satisfaction. He added malice to it when he faced Boll. "Captain Boll, I think I shall do business with Mr. Flint." He sat down and smiled; he was quite pleased with the turn of events.

"Mr. Flint," he said slowly, confident of his success then, "allow me to compliment you. It was nice of you to think of Harriet in this case—and you may be sure I won't forget it."

"I don't think you will ever forget it," I said in a tone of voice that brought his eyes up sharply.

Boll smiled. "Mr. Flint wants the ship also. I'll remind you again of the value of our uniting ourselves, sir."

"Flint—he wants the ship!" Culver voiced surprise in low tone. With that he chuckled. "Mr. Flint, aren't you going to a lot of trouble to make a monkey of yourself?" He faced Harriet for support, and, not finding it, he said, "What goes on here?"

I said, "Mr. Culver, Harriet and I want a little harmony to come out of this meeting. If either you or Boll owned that box of cash pieces, you know what the result would be. But it so happens I own them, and I want both of you to make a few concessions here.

"I am prepared to take the case, cash pieces and all, to the Dutch, in whose waters we are anchored. They will, I am sure, be pleased to deal with the situation."

Culver scoffed, "You can't take the ship to the Dutch without Captain Boll's consent."

I saw him moving to Boll's reasoning then. "No?" I replied. "I think I can. You see, the members of the crew could be brought face to face with the facts in a hurry. Under Boll, they face delay when they'd like to go home. Under you, they would be blackballed. They could not find berths on any ship. So I can take over here when I please.

"I could also get the crew to enter a petition for Boll's removal."

"That would suit me," Culver said quickly.

"Now would it?" I smiled. "Let's consider the circumstances. There's the cash-piece trade, a pirate's treasure aboard, and the possible fate of the ship herself in Dutch hands. If Boll is removed, then you alone are responsible when the Dutch get that one cash piece they want.

"I can almost guarantee any move I choose to make, since I, you must remember, control the box of cash pieces that brought us here."

I paused when Culver's frown deepened. He knew enough of the Dutch to realize the power of my threat. I added the final thrust in lazy manner: "Now if I were Captain Boll, I'd say, 'I can just see all this in the Boston papers.'"

Culver glared at me. Boll rubbed the point of his nose as he considered the strength of my position.

"But I don't want to do any of those things."

"What do you want then?" said Culver.

"I want to see the shares divided. I want your promise to give Boll a clean start with another concern after all of us untangle him—and you—from the Dutch web."

Culver's bulging eyes possessed a naïve sort of shock that provoked laughter: he could not understand the meaning of selflessness any more than he could see himself submitting to any such reasoning.

To Boll I said, "You'll close out the Gerrymander Cash as best you can to the advantage of all, and swear never to cross Mr. Culver's path again."

Culver leaned forward. "But Captain Boll said you wanted the ship."

"Yes," I replied, "I was coming to that. There's an old feud that Mr. Teale caused. And since you know now that you've done Amos De Loach a great wrong, it is time for you to make amends."

"De Loach!" Culver shouted. "Are you talking for De Loach?"

Boll said, "So you're working for De Loach? I might have known it." He faced Culver. "We'd better stick together."

"Can you? And can you win over me, Captain Boll?" I asked. "If so, how?" There was no answer. "I'm offering both of you the easy way out. And if you don't want it, remember I still own that box of cash pieces." I added firmly, "Which I'll use."

Culver paced back and forth. I heard his mutterings: "De Loach!" He faced me, moved on. "De Loach! And a damned second mate." He added, "Holding the edge." Then he paused. "It's unthinkable." He spoke out then: "What do you mean by making amends?"

"I think De Loach and Company is prepared to take this ship off your hands—for the same price which Culver and Adams paid the bank for the note on the *Cape Race*. Then we'll make a lady of her."

Culver was fast turning from red to purple in his anger. I brought him up for fresh estimates when I asked a question of Harriet: "Does De Loach and Company back that offer?"

"Harriet!" Culver boomed forth. "Are you—are you in any way hooked up with De Loach?"

"I am," she replied.

"Harriet!" Aunt Emily cried, wringing her hands. "Of all the scandalous things I've heard! If this ever leaks out in Boston! Oh no!"

"It won't, Aunt Emily," I said, causing her to brace up and speak with a force lacking to her a moment before: "Perhaps I can trust you, Tom Flint. The Lord knows I can't place much trust in anyone else around here."

No word was spoken in that room for long, long minutes. Every exchange of glances was sober and tense as we awaited the only decision Robert Culver could voice. It came at last:

"You win, Mr. Flint."

4

By sunset the wealth we carried was divided. Culver's share was taken to the *Aladdin* under cover of canvas, while Boll ordered his share left in the forward hold. The crew of the *Gerrymander*, suddenly rich, fell to gambling. Chess, in the middle of it, caught my eye.

"That lad, Chester Duval. I've been thinking, Harriet. Could we use a boy of his age—as a sort of son?" Before she could answer, I walked down to the main deck and jerked him up roughly.

"Come with me, Chess." He gathered his share and followed. When I had him before Harriet, I said, "Chess, if you leave her side until I order it, I'll toss you to the sharks."

"Aye, sir." He grinned up at Harriet as I signaled the *Nautch Girl* to move up with the box of cash pieces.

The rusty box was no sooner deposited on the deck than the Radja himself, dressed in white satin, came aboard. "One last drink with the mighty Captain Boll, Mr. Flint," he said. We went to the captain's cabin, where Boll sat in deep study of a map.

He looked up, eying us in the same lordly manner of old before saying, "Sit down."

The Radja of Mataram smiled craftily and said, pointing to the map, "Are you planning a voyage, Captain?"

"Aye. They say the pearl take in the French South Seas is enormous."

The Radja's brows lifted. He glanced at Kim Kim, who sat on the floor fashioning a silken square into a headpiece, and remarked casually, "So you'll be leaving the Indies? It is just as well, since Pulo Besar himself awaits me at my palace."

Boll's chuckle possessed a triumphant ring. The Radja ignored this, however, and said, "Pulo Besar arrived at the palace before you sailed. He sends this message to you, Captain, a very odd one: 'I'm glad you realized the Kim Kim mistake.' He said to tell you that some saint called Eben-a-eezer said it."

"Tell him I said it wasn't a mistake," Boll said tetchily.

The Radja bowed, a mocking smile playing on his face. "I shall deliver your reply," he said. Then his eyes fell on Kim Kim hungrily as he said, "Captain, my visit here is prompted by my continued interest in an item which has brought us together twice before. I am prepared to make a final bid for your dancing girl—twenty thousand guilders!"

Boll did not hesitate as he replied, "Kim Kim is not for sale at any price, Your Highness."

5

The Radja had no sooner bowed at the door than a cry sounded from the deck. I heard the word, "Fire!" and raced out of the cabin, not knowing whether we had been attacked or set afire. When I reached the open, I saw smoke pouring out of the sail locker just under the poop. I leaped toward the spot, but before I could reach it, dry sailcloth seemed to explode. A tongue of flame leaped out on deck.

The crew came to life in a hurry. Cries and running feet, orders from all directions, and buckets over the sides told a story of a sailor's nightmare—a burning ship. I looked up and saw Harriet, her mouth open. Moving toward her was Culver, while running up from the other side were Boll and the Radja.

How had the fire started? No one seemed to know. I studied Culver for a fleeting second and then shelved the puzzle.

The flames were fast making headway. The after end of a sailing ship carries her poop, officers' quarters, chartroom, and more—her very brains, heart, and pulse—and that part of her was burning viciously. Within short minutes the fire was eating into the superstructure and licking at the holds with maniacal fury. The lamps' glow, as darkness settled over the lonely world of Indian Ocean and bleak coastland, seemed feeble against the glare from the break of the poop.

The fire seemed to laugh at mere mortals with buckets. It darted out at the chain of water carriers, licking up the outer stanchions like a devil on the loose. I thought of Boll's talks with the devil, wondering as I did so if the devil was jealous of the end I had hoped and labored to bring about. The steel masts glowed in red and orange, and the shadows of halyards danced an evil saraband against them. The quarter-deck was soon untenable, and the men of both ships were driven from between decks, first by smoke, and later by the crashing floor. There was no chance of getting the few drums of oil nestled there, unless we chopped through. This we effected, reaching all but one.

I managed to work my way into the captain's quarters for a valuable object. I groped through the smoke, crawling along the hot carpet for parched air safe to breathe. As I took Harriet's picture down, the flames broke through and the skylight above caved, showering me with glass and live coals. I thought of the thousands of dollars in the old safe in the corner as I crawled reluctantly to the opening. The safe was open: Boll had not forgotten his money! As I looked back inside for the last time, the whole place burst into flames. The ornate cabin sizzled in its rush for ruin and ashes.

The red-and-yellow glow of the *Gerrymander* broke the smother of the dark tomb of night over ship and scene, lighting up the smoke that rolled up from her bosom. Boll ordered Mr. Cott to pull his ship some distance away, to take Harriet, Aunt Emily, and Kim Kim with him. Above the clamor of voices, the cracking of flame, minor explosions, and all, I heard Kim Kim's scream of terror. I had no time to assist the men who kept her from rushing after Boll.

The Striker! It was an apt name for Boll once again. He was everywhere, clipping off orders and tearing in where others held back. He ordered forward sail set for a run into shallow water, for an opening of her valves and a rest awash. But his orders fell on deaf ears. He struck terrorized men to the deck, and when not a sail met the wind, he turned his eyes aft, then below.

"Tom," he said, working at my side, "if Culver did this, I hope he roasts in hell." Then I heard him say, "She's the greatest ship that ever sat in the water."

In another moment he moved down through a hatch.

"If Culver did this." I could not shake those words as Culver's promise leaped into mind: "She's going to pay, and pay, until I bleed her of every cent she'll earn—until I rob her of self-respect. Then I'll carry her down as a scoundrel degrades a virtuous woman. And only I know her fate in the end!" Was this the fate he had planned? As I thought of the insurance and all, I saw Culver in the role of an evil perfectionist.

I wondered even as I fought the sweeping blaze. I soon forgot Culver, however: our ship was on fire! The ship for which I had labored with everything in me!

Fight seemed futile: charred beams and planks fell below, causing other fires, and water could not be dipped fast enough to control them. The flames licked hungrily up the mizzenmast, curling the steel of our rigging and eating wires in two; blocks fell unheard, and only the big crossjack yard received any notice as it struck the poop with its furled sail a gleaming torch. The spanker boom caved and then the mizzen ratlines turned into a fiery ladder. The blaze devoured the poop where Boll and I had stood a thousand times; it spoke a voice without termination, a howl of authority, hellish and crackling, its satiety by no means attained.

Suddenly I remembered Boll's share of the treasure: bales of gold-threaded batik, the cargoes of unique diversity, all wealth, and all down in that threatening crucible. Then I remembered that Boll was down there. A dozen men were sent after him, and all were driven out. Some stood looking foolishly at a square of silk, others at gold betel jars too hot to hold for long. From the holds, the scorched air lifted smoke, and the water we poured down those belching maws hissed and dried, precluding even a vapor.

At last, as if he were the devil himself, the same man who had lifted his head above the deck in Makassar after Captain Steele's death appeared—Boll. "The ship's doomed, Mr. Flint," he said sorrowfully. Then the devil's face gave way to a mortal's.

There was something in his arms, and as the smoke parted I saw a limp form. It was Chess! Above the crackle of the flames, Boll said, meeting my eyes, "He almost sat in Lucifer's bosun chair."

But Chess was alive and soon on his way to Harriet. It was then I turned with sagging shoulders and lifted my hands in a hopeless gesture.

"All right, men," I bellowed, "belay all!" It was no use to fight on. The Gerrymander was doomed, a funeral pyre to accident, or to one man's hate. Culver! Where was he?

"Every man off!" I cried. "You too, sir," I said to Boll. I had no sooner spoken than the deck amidships shuddered, rippled, and lifted, bursting open in places, accompanied with an awful roar, and another. Flames shot up from over the sides and through the deck. It was then every man for himself. I had forgotten the case oil below, and I remembered it too late. Trapped on all sides, I could only make a run for the rail, hoping to avoid a hole in the deck.

I saw the old bosun and I heard his scream as the deck caved under the carver of the fiddlehead on the ship. The avenging ship claimed Mr. Teale, alias Wulsin, for all time.

And if there was poetic justice there, it reached up for its pinnacle in the next moment: Culver raced past me, his face frantic. His trousers were on fire. Just as he moved blindly to the rail, the big mainsail yard crashed down on him. I saw it strike him a killing blow just before I made the leap. I thought of De Loach, wondering how he would view this end, realizing as I did so that he, great man that he was, had never wished for anything like this. Then I dived, and the waters of Balimbing Bay closed over me, cold and burning. It was the Radja of Mataram who helped me into a boat.

6

I stood on the beach where everyone was gathered in silence. My arm was about Harriet, whose face showed pain in the baleful orange light. I wondered about Boll as I gazed at the burning ship. Surely he had jumped with the rest of the crew.

The Gerrymander evoked long memories: she sat out there burning, she who had run to a record she still owned; I heard her canvas bellying in the winds of the roaring forties; I saw her great foresail, and I heard the wind humming in her rigging. The troughs opened up for her, and green seas, long squalls, and sunny skies lapped, struck, and beamed down upon her. "We can travel in this weather, Mr. Flint." It was Boll's voice in retrospect. "Bend a fresh tops'l, Mr. Flint." "Bring the wind out on her port quarter." "Take a drink Flint, a deep one. You'll need it." "Topgallants should not be furled in such a small blow, Mr. Flint." The Gerrymander sailed on, cleaving heavy seas and clement seas, and I was speaking, "You're reaching your eighteen to twenty knots with blood, bone, and agony." Still she roared on.

She was every inch a thoroughbred, her every plank, spar, rope, and block a champion. With a soul to inspire winds up in her trembling white towers, and musical notes as the breezes strummed her rigging, she was too young to die. But she had lived, if the fact offered consolation; and she would continue to live in the graveyard of ships, a gallant, obedient lady, one to whom the respectful heads of all seamen must bow. I wondered how Boll, her master and driving twin, must feel. He had said, "She's the greatest ship that ever sat in the water." His feet seemed to root in her planking; and how, I asked, could he tear them loose?

"The Gerrymander," I murmured.

She lit up the sky of the sequestered bay, her fires dancing up into the sky, reflecting against the close peak of Langar, her burning hulk mirrored in the sea, lively and bright. I said huskily, drawing Harriet's understanding eye: "She's a victory won only to be lost to us. But she is a lady, no matter what they say."

A voice beside me answered, "You're damn right she is, sir." It was Chess. I put my arm about him and drew him close. We would clean his vocabulary later.

The fire had gutted her aft; the stern post fell sizzling, and the hull burned forward of the ship to the foremast. The big steel mizzenmast leaned like a giant of the forest into the red water, the furled sail on its crosstrees burning like grotesque signals to another world. Then Chess cried out:

"Look! Someone is moving at the bows!"

I looked just as Chess shouted, "It's Captain Boll!"

I started. It was Boll, but why was he there? Then I said I was going after him.

"No, Tom. No," Harriet said. "He will surely jump." I sensed more than logic in her words; there was pain, and quick, anxious fear in her tone, eyes, and clutching hands. "Stay with me, Tom."

Boll was busy. I saw him scooping up cash pieces out of the box and dumping them in a boat just under the bow. He kept at it until he seemed spent. Then he faced the fire creeping up to the proud bows of the Gerrymander as if he had ample time to take stock of the situation, as if he wished to indulge in some reckless ceremony of farewell. He faced us, his hands on hips, and God knows what in mind. Perhaps he was saying to himself: "The smell of gain is good from any source."

Then his voice lifted above the fire with one word: "Kim Kim!"

She was soon swimming to him.

The stern was under then, sizzling and hissing, and the ship sank slowly, her mid-deck slipping under, her great bows tilting upward. The deck forward stood at an angle of forty degrees. The "image of

Culver," the hideous figurehead, looked farther out over the bay, silent and unconcerned with all the past, the present, or the future.

Then Boll jumped. He was soon in the boat, where I saw him help Kim Kim over the gunwale. Together they stood for a moment locked in each other's arms. And then Boll fell to the oars with slow, timed strokes.

The *Gerrymander* slid slowly under with a hiss and a watery sob. Floating planks, still afire, lit the great bows in her last moments, sending a flickering light to the dragon-bird figurehead; Mr. Teale's carving seemed to come to life. Its wings beat, I thought—as shadows and weak dancing flames created an illusion of animation—in an effort to soar away from the ignominy of a watery grave. Then it was gone; it was under; and the fire on the floating timbers sizzled out, drawing the black curtain of night over the tragedy of Little Fortune Island.

The *Gerrymander* settled down to the bottom of the sea, to her last, and eternal, anchorage. Her end sounded finis to a legend and a bubble.

The Gerrymander Cash struck a memory like the cash piece in the mouth of a skull upon a pole—it had-taken its namesake.

7

The sea healed over that night after the fire. Harriet held up bravely until I told her about Culver's death. And it was Aunt Emily who responded to Mr. Cott's unctuous request for orders with: "Ask Mr. Flint. He'll be taking over from now on."

And this I did with Amos De Loach's help, and with memories of regret for a tragedy which I had done my utmost to forestall. I built a monument in my mind to even the crafty Radja, whom the Dutch finally deposed in 1894; and to Robert Culver, or the captain of the *Barnacle Goose*. I never learned how the fire started, and I never voiced my suspicions. And so it was that time healed all wounds, and Harriet and I, with our adolescent problem, Chess, and later with another of our very own, found in Boston, instead of the tropics, our garden of happiness.

There was another memory, another monument in my mind. It was for the living—Boll and Kim Kim:

It was dedicated less to the dominant Boll, Boll the Striker, who worked his way to Batavia and strode boldly into the Dutch Javasche Bank with his cash pieces and redeemed, himself, that one cash piece over. Nor was that memory in salute to a rumor of later years—after he had been banished from the Indies—woven about a seaman and his lovely lady who were reported to be working a trade coin into riches in the South Seas abounding the French island of Tahiti; the memory of which I speak grew out of Boll's departure that night after his ship had gone down:

I saw him again as he pulled at the oars. He seemed undecided on his course as he looked at the *Aladdin*, the beach, and the mainland. Then he turned about, and, without a word of farewell, he, Kim Kim, and a boat loaded with treasure and cash pieces disappeared in the dark night toward the somber coast of Sumatra and new adventures.

I'll always love a good sailor.